I0631948

GEORGE ANTON SCHAEFFER:
Shipping Germans to Brazil

BY:

LEE B. CROFT

SPHYNX PUBLICATIONS

Phoenix, Arizona, USA

MMXII

This is the "Market Edition" with ISBN 978-0-9858908-2-7. There is a variantly titled "Presentation Edition" (GEORGE ANTON SCHAEFFER: Shipping Germans for Brazil) without an ISBN. Both versions are available at www.lulu.com/LeeCroft

Sphynx Publications is located at 11622 S. Tusayan Ct., Phoenix, Arizona, 85044, USA. Telephone is 480-496-0229 (agent's cell is 480-567-4501). E-mail at Lbcroft@cox.net.

The author of this book, Lee B. Croft (1946--), is a teacher, scholar, and Professor Emeritus of the Russian Language and Culture at Arizona State University, where he taught and administered language programs for thirty-eight years. He is the author of thirteen books and over 200 scholarly articles, translations, and reviews. Many of these can be accessed, directly or indirectly, through www.lulu.com/LeeCroft.

Part of the front-cover background of the "riohills" is from http://www.rioholidays.com. A differently proportioned version of the back cover's sailing ship is to be found unattributed on http://www.bcmj.org, cf. article by Gerry Greenstone, MD, in Vol. 52, No.10, December 2010, p. 534.

Introduction

The reader should know that this is a work of "faction," in the sense that every fact now known about a real individual, George Anton Schaeffer (1779-1836), is related in its chronological order. And George Anton Schaeffer's personal context—its geography, its politics, and its progression of a fascinating abundance of actual historical characters—is related as accurately as I could write it, so that well recorded history is not intentionally violated. But I have filled in the gaps between the known facts of George Anton Schaeffer's life with conjecture plausibly based upon the known facts and on Schaeffer's character as I've come to understand it. Since you, the reader, cannot be sure what of this "faction" is actual fact and what is plausible conjecture (fiction), you must presume this historical narrative in its totality to be a work of fiction, the creation of me, the author. I do hope that I've brought Schaeffer and his times back to life for you. Certainly I know him well by now.

This book, GEORGE ANTON SCHAEFFER: Shipping Germans to Brazil, is the third and last book of a trilogy—THREE books depicting Dr. Schaeffer's life and times. The first book, GEORGE ANTON SCHAEFFER: Killing Napoleon From the Air, takes him from his birth in Germany in 1779 to his involvement in Napoleon Bonaparte's invasion of Russia and a bit beyond to 1813. I am very pleased to have published this first book in the year 2012, the bicentennial of the historic 1812 Battle of Borodino for Moscow. The second and preceding book, GEORGE ANTON SCHAEFFER: Arm Wrestling Kamehameha, treats Dr. Schaeffer's circumnavigation of the globe, giving primary focus to his adventurous year and a half (November 1815 to July 1817) in the Hawai'ian islands. This third and final book of the trilogy, GEORGE ANTON SCHAEFFER: Shipping Germans to Brazil, views Dr. Schaeffer's return to Europe and to Brazil, from where he engaged in transporting thousands of German colonists and mercenary soldiers to Brazil for the benefit of Dom Pedro I. It includes a colorful chapter on his wife Barbara's activities in St. Petersburg during the five years she lived there waiting for her husband to return. Dr. Schaeffer died at Frankenthal, the colony he founded in the Bahia State of Brazil, in 1836.

I first decided to research the facts of George Anton Schaeffer's life when I realized for the first time, sometime in the early 1980s, that the man who was involved in a Russian plot to build a balloon to kill Napoleon in 1812, the man who was co-regent of the Hawai'ian island of Kaua'i for more than a year and built forts there that remain to this day, and the man called the "creator" of the German emigration to Brazil *was the same man*. Each of these THREE chapters of Schaeffer's astonishingly peripatetic life had individual scholars presenting it to our historical understanding. But each of these scholars, mainly because of language limitations, were limited in their knowledge of the other chapters. My advantage over even the most competent of these scholars—I'm thinking here primarily of Richard A. Pierce and Carlos Oberacker—is that I was for thirty-eight years a Professor of Foreign Languages in the academic department that is now Arizona State University's School of International Letters and Cultures. Russian is my language of specialty, but finding help in the translation of sources and correspondence in German and Portuguese is less problematical for me. So I have been "working on" George Anton Schaeffer for more than twenty-five years...giving talks, writing papers, engaging others in correspondence and interviewing them.

Over the years I have tried to travel to every place George Anton Schaeffer traveled: Germany, Russia, Turkey, Australia, Alaska, Hawai'i, China, Brazil... I've tried to stand where he stood, touch what he touched, see what he saw. Following him around the world almost two hundred years after him has changed my life. My wife and I have now spent two decades of our summers in Hawai'i in places connected to George Schaeffer's activities there. Hawai'i's "mana" has captured me as it did him, and I actually wrote most of this text during my periods of residence in Hawai'i.

Lee B. Croft

Waikiki, July 18, 2009

5

ACKNOWLEDGMENTS

I have many, many people to thank for their contributions to this work. First among these is my wife, Dr. Lesley Hoyt Croft, who listened to me read every word of it to her many times, giving me her wisdom as a published scholar and a voracious reader in editing, suggesting changes...and for her emotional support. Others who have heard me read parts of it and gave me their thoughts include my son Hayden L. Croft, who is establishing himself as a film critic and writer, my brothers Jerry and Wayne Croft, my sister Nancy Jacobson, my now deceased father William S. "Bill" Croft, my wonderful mother Norma Croft, and Lesley's mother, Kathryn Hoyt. Then there are so many other friends and relatives: Wolfgang and Claudia Kasmayr of Dachau, Germany, who aided in finding German documents and Dr. Schaeffer's birth records and gave us their hospitality, Richard and Billie Hyde Watson, who have even stored written chapters in their house for reasons of security, George and Debby Morgan, who have shared our time in Hawai'i, Paul and Sara Muriello, and Eugene and Peggy Wedoff. All of these people have been encouraging to me.

The list of the scholarly "giants" on whose shoulders this work rests is also long. Please go through the bibliography that I provide and read my annotations. All these hundreds of people contributed something, sometimes substantial somethings. But I feel that I have to give first and special named mention to the late Richard A. Pierce (1918-2004), the leading previous scholar on Schaeffer and Russian America, for his large corpus of work and his helpful and encouraging personal correspondence and communication. Other personally contacted contributors include Stephen K. Batalden, Walter D. Wetzels, Patricia Polansky, Peter Horwath, John Alexander, Jane Mund, Clarice Deal, Charles Oelfke, Peter Littke, Delbert D. Phillips, Dwight Brown, Timur Guseynov, Tanya Domenico, Tatyana Dhaliwal, Don Livingston, Saule Moldabekova Robb, David Mashuri, Charles Winkler, Agnes Kefeli-Clay, William H. "Mick" Hawley, Mark Curran, Kenneth N. Owens, William Brumfield, Christopher W. Croft, and Sarah Gould. Also, I have been inspired by the marine art and early contact history of Raymond Massey and the Hawai'ian cultural and historical art of Herb Kawainui Kane and Brook Kapūkuniahi Parker. They have carried on well the tradition of Hawaiian historic art exemplified by John Webber, Louis Choris, Jacques Arago, J. Alphonse Pellion, and others.

Lee B. Croft

6

A NOTE ON THE NAMES

I refer to my main character here as "George Anton Aloysius Schaeffer." Other spellings of his name abound in the research on him. Most problematical is his last name, which may have been spelled either "Schäfer" or "Schäffer" in his original time and place. There is evidence for both the single "f" spelling, and for the double "f" spelling. In present day Münnerstadt, Germany— George's birthplace-- there is a street named "Schäfergässchen" and there are people there to this day who spell their name "Schäfer" with only one "f." There were no people listed in the 2002 phone directory there who spelled their name with two "f's" as "Schäffer." On the hand-written German birth record, one simply cannot be sure…it might be either way. Militating for the double "f" is the spelling in Russian, which we have in George's own hand wherein he clearly transliterates his own name, signing letters and documents as "Шефферъ," that is, allowing for modernization (omission of terminal "yer"), "Sheffer" with *two* "f's," even though Russian generally has no geminate consonants in its native words or names. In Russian he is uniformly "Egor (translation of "George," pronounced "Ye-GOR") Nikolaevich (patronymic for "son of Nikolai (translation of Nicholas)) Sheffer." Also, in the 1960s, a Brazilian professor, Enrico Schaeffer, wrote genealogical works on his "collateral ancestor" and spelled the name with two "f's." And, most definitive, is the fact that J. F. Hammerich Publishers of Altona (Hamburg) spelled his name "Ritter von Schäffer Dr." on the title page of the book Schaeffer wrote about Brazil in 1824. For all these reasons I spell his name with two "f's," but, of course, this does not mean that any number of "Schäfers" in the world are not possibly related to him.

Then there is the matter of the German umlaut…the "two dots." I am generally changing the name to "Schaeffer" instead of writing "Schäffer" because I desire to facilitate ease of English-language search-engine access to research concerning him, given that the majority of works on him to date use the English (also Portuguese) "Schaeffer." I do use the umlaut on other words, though perhaps not entirely uniformly. For example, I am writing "Münnerstadt" and "Nürnburg." But, because the English reader knows it better that way, I write the city name as a translated "Munich" instead of writing "München." My aim, of course, is to indulge the English reader's expectation while retaining a certain foreign flair.

So, my main subject character is either George or Georg or Egor or Yegor or Jorge. He is either Anton or Antonio. He is Aloysius or Alois. He is Schäfer or Schäffer or Sheffer or, as here, Schaeffer. It all depends on the source— German, English, French, Russian, or Portuguese—and the translation or transliteration therefrom. In Hawai'ian, he was "Kepa," but this was never written. Dr. Schaeffer was indeed an amazing polyglot with an oft-mentioned-by-others extraordinary ability to "pick up" and use even exotic languages. The list of languages he used in his life is long, including: German, French, Latin, Yiddish, Dutch, Czech, Slovak, Hungarian, Roma, Ukrainian/Galician, Russian, English, Brazilian Portuguese, Tlingit (Kolosh), Aleut, Hawai'ian, and Pataxo. He had passing contact also with Spanish, Chinese, and Latvian.

For Hawai'ian names and place names, mainly in the second book of the trilogy, GEORGE ANTON SCHAEFFER: Arm Wrestling Kamehameha, I try to be linguistically accurate, including the "'" ("okina" symbolized by the apostrophe in my work instead of the vertical hash for reasons of processing convenience) as a sign for the Hawai'ian consonantal glottal stop, writing, for example, "Hawai'i," "Kaua'i," "Ka'ahumanu" and "Kaumuali'i." Also, I try to render the Hawai'ian plural accurately...as in "kahuna=kāhuna" or "mu=mū." Citations of the sources are not, however, uniform in this and not all authorities agree on certain of the spellings. Schaeffer and other European contemporaries from the time of Captain James Cook's first contact with the Hawai'ians spelled the Hawai'ian places and names diversely as the words sounded to them. Schaeffer, who was reputed to speak and understand Hawai'ian better than other Europeans who had been there longer, apparently (evidenced from a transliteration of Schaeffer's written Russian equivalents) perceived and spoke Hawai'ian with more than *half* of Hawai'ian's stock of eight consonants replaced by his own native German or acquired Russian consonants. He, like many others, replaced Hawai'ian "p" with "b," "h" with "g," "k" with "t," "l" with "r," and "w" with "v."   Thus, an English transliteration of Schaeffer's Russian word for "Kamehameha" is "Tomi-omi," for "Honolulu" is "Gonerua," for "Oahu" is "Ovagu," for "Hanalei" is "Gonnarej," for "Kaumuali'i" is "Tomari," for "Lana'i" is "Rany," for "Ka'ahumanu" is "Kagumanu," for "Kaua'i" is sometimes "Atuvaj" and sometimes "Gauaj," for "Moloka'i" is "Maranaj," and for "Hawai'i" itself is "Ovagi." One might think that so many replacements of native sounds with foreign sounds would result in unintelligibility. But it did not, because the replacements, using only consonants that *Hawa'iian did not have* (such as Schaeffer's "g," "b," "t," "l," and "v"), caused there to be NO NEW PHONEMIC CONTRASTS in the speech perceived by the Hawai'ians, who understood Schaeffer easily and often praised his "mastery" of their language. Linguists know this phenomenon well. In his Things Hawaiian: A Pocket Guide to the Hawaiian Language (Island Heritage Publications, Aiea, Hawaii, 1998, pp. 10-11...notice here the lack of the okina) Albert J. Schultz writes: "At first, all these letters were used (to represent the Hawaiian sounds). But it really made no difference which sound or letter you used. For instance, whether you said 'tai' or 'kai,' the word still meant 'sea.' In the same way, you could use either 'lani' or 'rani' for 'heaven,' 'vai' or 'wai' for 'water.' And this held for any words containing these sounds." For the purposes of this book, however, I write the Hawai'ian names, places, and words in conformance to their modern usage (e.g. not referring to them in text as being in the "Sandwich Islands") and spellings as explained above, the picturesque variants of Schaeffer and his contemporaries notwithstanding. I do this for the modern reader's ease of reference to people and things currently Hawai'ian.

For Russian names and place names I follow the US Library of Congress system without diacritics (e.g. "Kondratii Ryleev," and "Sysoi Slobodchikov"), but the citations preserve the transliterations of others, often reflecting popular English spellings (e.g. "Tolstoy" instead of my transliterated "Tolstoi"). Occasionally I stray from my own convention in the interests of reducing English-language confusion (e.g. using "Semyon" instead of "Semen" to transliterate the common Russian name). Again, the criterion here is to aid others in English search-engine access. I have tried to be accurate in textual inclusions of the Portuguese names and places, writing with the diacritics "Antônio" and "São Paulo" and so on. The search engines generally will access these topics, however, with the diacritics omitted.

Russians frequently address each other by first name and patronymic. The patronymic, the apparent "middle name," is formed for males from the first name of their father plus the suffix –ovich or –evich; and for females from the first name of their father plus –ovna or –evna. Thus George Anton Schaeffer is called "Yegor Nikolaevich" (George, son of Nicholas) and Barbara Hindernacht Schaeffer is called "Varvara Vul'fgangovna" (Barbara, daughter of Wolfgang).

A NOTE ON RUSSIAN DATES

The Russians used the Julian Calendar in the eighteenth, nineteenth, and twentieth century until March of 1918, long after the countries of western Europe and most of the rest of the world had changed to the Gregorian Calendar. This means that the dates for events that transpired in Russia and the Russian Empire were basically eleven days behind the date commonly used elsewhere in the eighteenth century, twelve days behind in the nineteenth century, and thirteen days behind in the first eighteen years of the twentieth century. I give the "old style" date first, then the "new style" date when known and applicable when citing dates relevant to the Russian imperial period of history, which includes much of this trilogy. Thus, the date of the Battle of Borodino for Moscow is given as 26 August (Russian Calendar)/7 September (French Calendar), 1812, because of the twelve-day difference of dates in the nineteenth century. Russian birth and death dates are given in citation as those of "Mikhail Illarionovich Golenishchev-Kutuzov (5/16 September, 1745—16/28 April, 1813)," showing the eleven-day difference in the eighteenth century and the twelve-day difference in the nineteenth. Russian dates in the empire's North American territories (e.g. Alaska) were an additional day behind the Gregorian Calendar date because of the lack of an international global dateline convention. At www.calendarhome.com you can see that although the dates were different, the days of the week were the same.

TABLE OF CONTENTS

CHAPTER EIGHT: Returning to Europe

CHAPTER NINE: Barbara in St. Petersburg

CHAPTER TEN: Brazil

10

Chapter Eight-- Returning to Europe

Macau:

The trip from Kauai to China on the *Panther* was pleasant for George. The late summer weather of that 1817 year was nice and the wind was firm and steady. He spent most of his time talking with Captain Isaiah Lewis and John Marshall. These men agreed with his point of view that the American captains were generally unscrupulous, cruel and exploitive to both the natives they encountered and their own crews. George gave his opinion that the economics of the Pacific trading business was now such that the captains could not make a profit for themselves and their owners without cheating both the natives and their own men.

A likeness of George Anton Schaeffer at age 45 in 1824.

"It costs too much now to outfit a ship and pay good men what they deserve," said George. "So the captains take on native crew members and work them to death without paying them. They pillage native villages, giving nothing in exchange. They flog and kill their own, shoot and kill the others. It's become a terrible business."

"The only way to make a justifiable profit," commiserated John Marshall, "Is to trade in slaves, sandalwood, or opium."

"I think that whaling may wind up being a profitable business," said Captain Lewis. "People are burning more and more whale oil to light their homes, and the whalebone and the spermaceti are growing in demand as well."

"You may be right about that," said George. "I talked to an American whaler, a Captain Josiah Barnes, whose ship was anchored in Sydney Cove during the war between the United States and Great Britain. He said he had taken seventeen sperm whales off the coast of New Zealand, and that they would bring him a fortune back in New England."

George then asked John Marshall, "Do you think your Uncle, John Jacob Astor, will enter the whaling business?"

John Marshall replied, "He's into any business he thinks will be profitable. He's not only in the fur business. He buys and rents property, founds and runs banks, buys and sells opium. I wouldn't be surprised to see him go into the whaling business as well."

"From what I've seen in the oceans of the world," commented George, "There is certainly an endless supply of the whales."

When they were well into the China Sea, Captain Lewis sent up extra lookouts, fearing pirates.

"They come at you in fleets of junks," he explained. "The only way to stay out of their clutches is to see them before they see you."

"Are there many pirates in these waters?" asked George.

"Yes, many," said Captain Lewis. "There is one pirate commander, a man called 'Admiral Apo-tsy,' who controls this area with a very large fleet of ships. You might know that back in 1809 he and his men captured the *Bering* when it was still the American ship *Atahualpa*. James Bennett was the captain."

"I know James Bennett," said George, "But I didn't know that he had been captured by pirates. What happened to him?"

"Admiral Apo-tsy removed the *Atahualpa*'s cargo, then held the ship and crew for ransom," explained Lewis. "The American Consul in Canton, a Mr. Benjamin Chew Wilcocks, paid dearly to rescue Bennett and his ship."

"I met Consul Wilcocks' brother James at Waimea," said George. "He and I got along very well. It's a good thing the Americans have a Consul in Canton. The Russians don't. Are there any other pirates in this area?"

"I think Admiral Apo-tsy is pretty much in control of this area now," related Captain Lewis. "But a few years ago there was a woman pirate commander who was in control."

"A woman pirate?" asked George.

"Yes, a woman pirate," said Lewis. "Her name was Ching Shih. She started out a prosititute in Canton, but married a pirate commander named Cheng Yi. She and Cheng Yi adopted a son they called Chang Pao. The family of them then increased their pirate fleet until it included 400 ships and over 17,000 men. When Cheng Yi died at sea during a gale in 1807, Ching Shih married her stepson and took command of her husband's pirate empire. She robbed and captured many, many ships and pillaged villages on the rivers that run into the sea. She was so powerful that she even threatened the government."

"I have heard of her," said John Marshall. "She had very strict rules about the treatment of captives. She particularly forbade the raping of female captives. If a sailor raped a female captive, he was beheaded. If a female captive consented to fornication with a sailor, he was beheaded and she was thrown overboard with weights tied to her legs. Sailors had their ears cut off for even the smallest infraction of her rules."

"What happened to her?" asked George.

"She and her main rival, a pirate commander called 'Admiral Opo-tae,' purchased pardons from the government in exchange for their ships and releasing their men. Her stepson Chang Pao became a government customs inspector whom we may well meet in Macau. And I've heard that Ching Shih now runs the brothel in Canton where she once worked."

On August 26th, 1817, the lookouts of the *Panther* spotted the islands proximate to the Chinese coast where the Pearl River enters the sea. A junk sailed out to meet them and they took aboard a Chinese pilot, but just then they were becalmed and could not move. Not a breath of wind was felt for nine days.

On Sept. 4th, the *Panther* was at last able to anchor at Macau. This was where they would remain, since Canton was not accessible to them. The Chinese government very strictly regulated foreign trading ships and the foreigners they brought with them. The rich trading city of Canton was 100 miles up the Pearl River from the sea. To get there foreigners had to engage a Chinese pilot and sail upriver past Macau and anchor at Whampoa, still 40 miles away from Canton. Foreigners in Canton were not allowed to ride in sedan chairs or to learn Chinese. The goods from Canton had to be transported to the foreign ships at Whampoa by the Chinese. But this trade was only allowed to take place in the official "trading season" from October to January. At other times foreigners were not allowed in Canton at all and had to reside in Macau.

When George and his companions, Filip Osipov and Grigorii Iskakov, first looked around Macau, they were repulsed by the city and its people. The city was a trading base in China of the Portuguese, and it was aswarm with a diverse humanity. George had never seen such a densely populated place. People

14

cooked and ate in the streets where sewerage trickled past. The buildings looked rickety and decrepit, their bamboo frames bent and splitting, threatening to topple them into the streets. Beggars were rife and aggressive, so that Filip and Grigorii quickly developed a threatening gesture to shoo them away anticipatorily. George quickly found opportunity to use his ability to speak Portuguese, making friends with port officials Jos dos Sindos and Antonio de Silva Joachima, and even a city councilman named Manuel Pereira.

Captain Lewis and John Marshall had tried to find George and his companions accommodations at the Macau house of the American Consul, but servants there told the Captain that the Russians would be taken in at the residence of the Swedish Consul, a Mr. Anders Ljungstedt. Ljungstedt personally welcomed George and his men into his Macau home, a two-storey quadrangle of buildings around a well-tended garden courtyard. George was given a room in one wing, and Filip Osipov and Grigorii Iskakov shared a room in another. Every afternoon they shared a splendid banquet with Consul Ljungstedt, which was prepared by his Chinese cooks. They drank rice wine and proposed numerous toasts to "friendship and international understanding."

Unattributed portrait of Sir Anders Ljungstedt (23 March, 1759-10 November, 1835) from the Chinese-language website at http://www.hudong.com/wiki/1759.

George and Anders Ljungstedt got along famously. Ljungstedt was a big man, a Swede from Linköping, who was twenty years older than George. He spoke fairly well in German, but he had worked as a teacher in Russia for ten years, from 1784 to 1794, and then he served the Swedish government as a Russian translator and interpreter, so his Russian was as good as George's. He had come to China in 1797 with the Swedish East India Company, working as supercargo in Canton. When the Swedish East India Company ceased its Chinese operations in 1813, Ljungstedt stayed on in Macau as Swedish Consul to that city and made a personal fortune. In 1815 the Swedish Government named him a Knight of their Royal Order of Vasa.

Several evenings, Anders Ljungstedt translated to George portions of the memoirs he was writing in Swedish about his long residence in China, and George was most effusive in complementing these memoirs, urging Ljungstedt to find a publisher in Europe who would see to their translation into English, French, German, and Russian. In this work, Ljungstedt maintained, without offense to his many Portuguese friends, that the Portuguese had no exclusive rights to sovereignty in Macau. The Chinese clearly respected him greatly. They had given him the name "Long Si Tai,"meaning "Peaceful Thinking Dragon."

George and Filip Osipov and Grigorii Iskakov stayed with Anders Ljungstedt in Macau for almost three months. George told Ljungstedt all about his adventures in Hawai'i trying to provide the Russian-American Company with a base for provisioning and trade. George said he was returning to St. Petersburg to ask Tsar Aleksandr to consider annexing the Hawai'ian islands, since no other nation had yet claimed them.

"I know another man who has thought of that," said Ljungstedt. "His name is Peter Dobell...a very interesting fellow, a real swash-buckler. He's about your age or maybe a few years older. He's from a wealthy Philadelphia family and was even in an American dragoons regiment in his youth, but has now disavowed America, claiming to be an 'Irishman.' He came to Canton on a ship named the *Sylph* he acquired somehow from the fabulously wealthy one-eyed Philadelphia banker, Stephen Girard, who bankrolled the United States government during the war with Great Britain."

"I've heard of Girard," said George. "He helped Dr. Benjamin Rush with the Philadelphia yellow fever epidemic in 1793 and afterwards built a great hospital there. He's said to be the only American richer than John Jacob Astor."

"That's what they say," agreed Ljungstedt. "And Peter worked for him for several years, even serving as United States Consul to Bourdeaux, France. He was appointed upon Stephen Girard's recommendation in 1800 by Former U.S. President James Madison when he was earlier the Secretary of State. But he left that position and he left Girard somehow, keeping the *Sylph* in the bargain. It was he who brought the first shipment of opium here directly from Turkey on the *Sylph* in July of 1811, then was stranded here by the British embargo during the war. He ran a tavern in Canton not far from my house there and I would see him often."

"Has he been to Hawai'i?" asked George.

"I don't know for sure," answered Anders Ljungstedt. "He once told me that the *Sylph* had sailed along with Captain William Heath Davis' *Isabella* from

Petropavlovsk to the Island of O'ahu, but he may have given command to someone else and stayed in Petropavlovsk."

"I first sailed to Hawai'i on the *Isabella,*" said George, "But Davis was no longer the captain. It was Charles Tyler."

"Well, my American 'Irishman' friend had met Russian Navy Captain Ivan Kruzenshtern here sometime before and discussed the Hawai'ian Islands with him," continued Ljungstedt. "Later, after the War of 1812, he began working for the Russian-American Company out of Petropavlovsk. I'm told he's become a Commissioner with them like you are. In 1813, he set out for St. Petersburg by land across Siberia to propose that the Tsar acquire Pacific trading bases in either the Philippines or the Hawai'ian Islands. I've since heard that he made it there and is advocating this."

"If he did, he may have already helped my cause, then," said George. "What was his name again? I want to remember it for certain."

"His name is Peter Dobell," answered Ljungstedt. "He's the uncle of Captain James Bennett who used to ply these waters in the *Atahualpa* which the Russian-American Company in Sitka bought and renamed the *Bering.* Bennett was here last year, but sailed for Boston on the ship *Ophelia.* "

"He's Bennett's uncle?" said George with surprise. "I know James Bennett. Captain Isaiah Lewis told me that he had once been held for ransom by pirates here. But I've not had a good acquaintance with Captain Bennett. It was he who wrecked the *Bering* on the Kaua'i coast at Waimea and then gave me trouble with Kamehameha's advisor John Young in our efforts to recover its cargo."

"Yes, George, James Bennett is the son of Peter Dobell's sister Ruth and his former partner, Samuel Bennett. Here we think more positively of him, I'm afraid," said Ljungstedt. "I'm sorry you don't like him."

"Well, perhaps I'll meet him again…and meet his uncle too," answered George. "Maybe we'll all become friends…who knows?"

One day walking on the streets of Macau with Filip Osipov, George spotted a ramshackle storefront with paper silhouettes of various people displayed around its curtain-covered door. The silhouettes were of very fine work and the likenesses of the people whose silhouettes were displayed appeared as accurate as mirror reflections.

"Let's go in this shop and have our silhouettes made," George proposed to Filip. "My wife Barbara requested in a letter some time ago that I have one made and sent to her and to my daughter Inga so that she might know what I look like. Inga traced her hand on a piece of paper and I kept the tracing for more than a year until the paper finally wore out."

Filip assented to the idea. They entered the store, pushing the curtain aside, and encountered an elderly Chinese woman and her teen-aged son. George pointed to the silhouettes and held up a few coins. These coins, in fact, represented almost all the money George had left in his possession after his hasty and unprepared departure from Hawai'i. The woman held out her hands, and George gave her all the coins. Then she set to work, closing the curtain again and lighting a candle. Her son held it up as first George and then Filip stood between it and pieces of thick black paper mounted on an easel against the wall. The Chinese woman quickly traced their shadows with an inked quill. Then she took out a tiny scissors and began to cut out the silhouettes, carefully eyeing their faces all the while. Her dexterity was amazing. In short order she turned over to George and Filip her handiwork. George held his up to Filip and marveled, "Mine is so good that you can even see how old I am by looking at it. I didn't realize how my bushy beard and sidewhiskers make me look like an old man. I don't feel that old. And my bald head too. But yours is a fine testament to your robust youth, with your thick neck and thick hair. I'd recognize you from this silhouette at an instant's glance. Anyone would. It's wonderful."

Later George wrote a letter to Barbara and enclosed the carefully folded silhouette into the envelope before he sealed it. He asked his host, Anders Ljungstedt, to post the letter to St. Petersburg through Stockholm on the next ship bound for Sweden. In his letter he wrote:

"September 19, 1817 from Macau, China

My Dearest Barbara and Inga,

My efforts in Hawai'i have taken a negative turn. I was forced to leave the islands by the conspiracies against me and the Russian-American Company by American and English seacaptains who spread the false rumor that Russia and the United States were at war. Our Russian navy Captain Kotsebue and the company of the *Riurik* were of no help to me, and in fact acted foolishly to disavow my intentions there to the Hawai'ian King Kamehameha. Kamehameha's advisors, both native and foreign, of whom the foremost is an English degenerate named John Young, wanted then to imprison or kill me in order to prevent me from maintaining the positive relations I had come to with Kamehameha's tributary king, Kaumuali'i of Kauai. I had to leave the entire party of my Russian and Aleut companions on the island of O'ahu under the command of the able and loyal Timofei Osipovich Tarakanov, a close colleague of Governor Aleksandr Andreevich Baranov, who will now have to see to the party's rescue. I was saved by God's grace and that of a captain I had once treated, Isaiah Lewis of the *Panther,* who transported me and two others, young creole hunter Filip Osipov and the Aleut Toion Grigorii Iskakov, here to Macau, a Portuguese trading settlement on the coast of China, where we are being treated as dignitaries by the honorable Sir Anders Ljungstedt, the Swedish Consul here. My purpose now is to return as soon as possible to St. Petersburg to inform his Majesty, the Tsar Aleksandr, that he should dispatch armed naval ships to the Hawai'ian islands within the next year in order to deal forcefully with these American and English pirates who desire to exclude Russia and its chartered Company from this paradise in the central Pacific. Russia will benefit greatly by taking command of one or all of these islands, no matter how this is accomplished. The central position of the Hawai'ian islands in the Pacific and the bountiful natural resources they possess will give Russia a most advantageous position among its allies and adversaries in the future. Of this I am absolutely sure. I only hope that I will be able to convince the Tsar of this. If I cannot, then all my work on behalf of Russia and the Russian-American Company will be for nothing and I can predict that Russia will be, in the future, only a minor actor in the vast Pacific theater. Anders Ljungstedt has told me about a man he once met here in China named Peter Dobell, an American who claims to be an Irishman, who has traveled via Siberia to St. Petersburg and, acting as an agent of our Russian-American Company, advocates there that Hawai'i and the Philippines should be annexed as Russian trade colonies. Please tell General Tormasov, the Shelikhovs, and anyone else in power who will listen that this man Peter Dobell, at least as far as Hawai'i is concerned, IS CORRECT. His advice should be heeded by all. When I arrive there, I will seek him out and shake his hand in gratitude.

By now I assume that that scoundrel Captain Mikhail Petrovich Lazarev and the *Suvorov* have returned to St. Petersburg and that the charges against Lazarev that Governor Baranov and I and supercargo Molvo sent via Petropavlovsk caused him to be dismissed from command and severely disciplined. A man like that should not be a captain in the Tsar's navy.

But enough business. I know that I have now been gone from you and Inga almost four years. I did not plan to be gone more than the two years projected for the *Suvorov*'s circumnavigation. But Captain Lazarev stranded me in Governor Baranov's care in Novo-Arkhangelsk and the Governor, the Lord bless him, needed me to perform a vital service for him in Hawai'i. This I tried my best to accomplish, and indeed I am still dedicated to accomplishing it, though I now need the armed assistance of the Russian navy to do it. I can only trust that you and Inga are well and that you await my return as avidly as I do. I will return to you now as soon as I am able and we will take up our lives together as before, made even richer by the experiences we have had in this unfortunately extended separation. I am sending you the silhouette you once requested so that Inga can better know what I look like. In Hawai'i there was no opportunity to have a suitable one made. I cherished the tracing of Inga's hand, keeping it with me until the paper deteriorated into shreds. Please hug and kiss Inga for me, give my best regards to all our friends and acquaintances there, especially Aleksandr Petrovich and Nadia, and Nikolai Mikhailovich and Ekaterina and…and know that I love you and that I am now making every effort to get back to you as soon as possible.

Your husband and Inga's father, in love, George."

In October, George formally appointed his new friend Anders Ljungstedt the Macau Agent of the Russian-American Company. An official document George drafted empowered Ljungstedt to act on the Company's behalf in all of China. Not long after this, George heard that the schooner *Lydia*, under the command of Captain William Wadsworth, was anchored at Macau with a cargo of sandalwood from Kaua'i. With the *Lydia* was the ship *Avon*, which old Captain Isaac Whittemore still captained. George asked Anders Ljungstedt to arrest Wadsworth and confiscate the *Lydia* and its sandalwood on behalf of the Russian-American Company. Ljungstedt took George with him to the office of the Portuguese Minister Miguel Arriaga, whom he knew well, and allowed George to present his case against Wadsworth in Portuguese. Impressed, Arriaga decided to order the confiscation of the sandalwood, but refused to seize the *Lydia* or arrest Wadsworth. Nevertheless, George was very happy about his thwarting of Wadsworth's sale of the sandalwood, and he got the chance to let Wadsworth know precisely who had deprived him of his anticipated profits. When Wadsworth was being escorted by Minister Arriaga's police officers out of his office several days later, George was there to inform him.

"You see, Mr. Wadsworth," he called out from across the busy street. "You can't get away with stealing the Company's sandalwood. I have seen to that."

Wadsworth was stunned to see George. His mouth fell open in surprise and he could only utter a few incoherent syllables, "Sheffer, you, you....ah, eh...you..." The policemen were apparently returning him to the *Lydia* after holding him while the sandalwood was unloaded.

George thanked Anders Ljungstedt and Minister Arriaga and he told them that the proceeds from the sandalwood sale should, after the subtraction of appropriate commission and expenses for his and his companions' accommodation, be sent directly to Governor Aleksandr Baranov in Sitka with news of the transaction. Anders Ljungstedt offered to advance to George a considerable sum of money in various cash denominations for his anticipated travel expenses on his way back to St. Petersburg, and George gratefully accepted. He now had in his possession more than just a few coins.

In November George heard that a Mr. Graveford, Captain of an English ship of discovery, had reported to Minister Arriaga that he had taken on board a Russian captive given to him by Captain Alexander Adams of the former *Forester,* now renamed the *Ka'ahumanu.* George knew that this Russian captive had to be that young member of his mission, Ivan Krivoshein, who was captured from Timofei Tarakanov's party on Kaua'i several months before. He went to the port and found Mr. Graveford, requesting that Graveford hand over his man, but Graveford informed George that the man, Ivan Krivoshein, had died a month before and was buried at sea. Later, at Anders Ljungstedt's residence, George, Filip Osipov, and Grigorii Iskakov prayed together for Krivoshein's soul and, at the daily meal, proposed several toasts in his honor.

Through Anders Ljungstedt from Minister Arriaga, George also heard that the grand ship *Luconia* under the command of the Portuguese Fleet Captain Antônio Leão was ready for its voyage back to Lisbon through Rio de Janeiro. He went to see Captain Leão and made arrangements to sail with his two companions to Rio de Janeiro, paying in full for passage with privileged accommodations. Anders Ljungstedt gave George and the others a sumptuous farewell dinner at his residence the day before they departed on Thursday, 4 December, 1817.

Back in Rio de Janeiro:

The *Luconia*'s first port of call was Sydney, Australia, where George had been in August and September of 1814 while on the *Suvorov*, but George was only ashore briefly—only enough to be positively impressed with the city's development in the past four years. He warned Filip and Grigorii about visiting the area known as "The Rocks," where he had been involved in a fight and robbed. During the voyage across the Pacific, the *Luconia* stopped in New Caledonia, in Samoa, and at Nuku Hiva in the Marquesas, at tiny Pitcairn Island, and at Easter Island. Pitcairn Island, only two miles by three miles in size, was populated by the children of the mutineers from the *Bounty* who, in April of 1789, put Captain William Bligh and eighteen of his loyal men adrift in a longboat. Incredibly, Bligh and his men survived. Most of the mutineers were captured on Tahiti and returned to England where three of them were hanged. But nine of the mutineers, including leader Fletcher Christian, escaped justice by sailing with some Tahitian natives in the *Bounty* to the isolated and uninhabited Pitcairn Island. There they burned the ship, made slaves of the Tahitian men, and took their women for wives. By the time their presence on Pitcairn was discovered by an American schooner in 1808, only one of the original mutineers, a man named John Adams, was alive. The number of their descendents on the island, though--several surnamed Christian, numbered approximately fifty.

There was no good anchorage at Pitcairn Island, which rose up out of the sea 1000 feet or more. The *Luconia* dropped sail and hove to with sea anchors while a boat was sent ashore. George went along to converse with the islanders in English and help Captain Leão bargain for fresh water, which the islanders collected in a reservoir they had constructed. George made notes in his journal about the irrigation system used by the islanders to grow yams and other crops.

On Easter Island, where the *Luconia* spent three days provisioning, George and Filip Osipov hiked around and viewed the giant stone statues called "Moai" they had heard about from other sailors. Like others, they had difficulty imagining how the ancestors of the current island natives had managed to carve such huge monoliths out of mountain quarries and move them into arrangements above the sea cliffs. The natives called the island not "Easter Island" as it had been named by the Dutch explorer, Admiral Jakob Roggeveen, who was the first European to encounter it on Easter Day of 1722, but "Rapa Nui." George remembered Governor Baranov at Novo-Arkhangelsk telling him of a conspiracy of his men to kill him and his children, steal a Company ship and make away with a number of native women to this remote Easter Island. Now

George made notes that the native's culture was similar to that of the Hawai'ians. They made kapa cloth from bark by pounding like the Hawai'ians and tattooed their bodies in a similar way. The children played some of the same games as the Hawai'ian children played, but George noticed more than once how the children played games with slender fiber strings, making elaborate patterns on their fingers. On some large boulders were "talking figures"— Petroglyphs like those George had seen in Hawai'i. But George also saw natives with wooden plaques covered with strange ordered inscriptions. It appeared that some among them could read these plaques, which they called "kohau rongorongo," like a European could read a book, though they turned the plaque round and round in their hands as they read it. George made note of this because he was otherwise unaware of any previous evidence of literacy among the Pacific peoples, but he was unable to question the natives about this. They understood some of his Hawai'ian words, but could not communicate with him in any kind of normal conversation. He did, however, manage to purchase one of the inscribed rongorongo plaques from a native leader, giving him a hatchet, a mirror, a pair of scissors, and a bottle of rum for it. George intended to deliver it to the Kunstkamera Museum of Peter the Great in St. Petersburg.

An example of Easter Island's still undeciphered "Rongorongo script" from the "Small Santiago Tablet," from http://en.wikipedia.org/wiki/Rongorongo.

As they approached the southern tip of South America and Cape Horn, the weather grew very cold and windy. The sea became heavy, with high, white-topped waves. Captain Leão explained that traversing Cape Horn was always a hazardous undertaking because of the harsh cold winds, the violent seas, and the rocky island coasts. It was, however, much easier to sail around Cape Horn from west to east, he said, than it was to sail it from east to west. This was because of the prevailing winds, which blew from the west. So the sailors on the *Luconia* did not have to go up to the yardarms and change the sails as often as they would have if they had been tacking around the Horn in the opposite direction. And it was summer in the southern hemisphere. The weather and sea conditions that George and his companions saw as severe and threatening were, in fact, considerably milder than they sometimes got, especially in other seasons. The scenery when they caught sight of Horn Island was very spectacular. On that night there was no moon and the wind had blown the clouds away. George bundled up in his warmest clothes to go out on deck while the ship was running under all its topsails to view the brilliant riot of stars. The night skyscape, including the fiery Southern Cross, was truly magnificent to view. Holding the side rail with the wet sea spume blasting into his face, George thanked God for providing him such a sight and such an experience.

They caught the Falkland currents heading north along the eastern coast of South America and made good time to Rio de Janeiro, anchoring at the port in Guanabana Bay on Wednesday the 8th of April, 1818 after a voyage of four months from Macau. Captain Leão thought that this was extraordinarily good time.

Once ashore, George, Filip, and Grigorii obtained rooms in a hotel near the port. The strikingly beautiful city of Rio de Janeiro had doubled in population since George's visit in May of 1814, four years before. Now there were 120,000 residents, with a larger share than before of Europeans, including even substantial numbers of French émigrés. The city had expanded substantially. Where before had been houses with just one floor, now were substantial buildings four or five stories high. The British had used their trade monopoly to increase the general standard of living, but the cost of most goods had also increased. In 1814 a good lunch could be purchased for 200 reis, but now it cost a milreis…almost a Spanish piastre. Hotels, restaurants and coffee houses had proliferated. The hotel where George and his companions were staying offered delivery of meals to their rooms, maid service, and prostitutes if requested. With astonishment George looked at one street where the gold and silver workers and the jewelers displayed their wares. Such riches, he thought, are not to be found in the markets of Petersburg, Moscow, Vienna, or Constantinople. A cartel of diamond cutters had been founded in Rio de Janeiro, headed by a Dutch Jew named Nathan who prepared gems for the jewels of the royal family.

The ill and aged Queen Maria Francisca had died in 1816, and Dom João the Regent had ascended to the throne as "King João VI of Portugal, the Algarve, and Brazil." Despite the fact that there was now no threat from the French, he did not make any preparations to return to Portugal. George went to the royal palace in the city and tried to make an appointment to see the King, but, despite his insistence that the King would want to see him, he was unable to gain such appointment from the palace administrative staff. They were, in fact, rude to him. But then he remembered that his acquaintance, Dr. João Martinho Flach, was an employee of the royal family. He made some inquiries about where Dr. Flach could be found and went to see him.

"Ah, my good friend, Dr. Schaeffer," said Flach in German. He looked the same to George, perhaps a little heavier in the waist and with some greyer hair. And he looked at George closely and said, "You look quite the same…well, perhaps you are a bit heavier and have now a bit of grey in your beard. How long has it been since we've seen each other? Do you remember our trip around the bay?"

"Yes, I remember, Martin" said George, familiarly. "It's been almost four years."

"Where have you been? What have you been doing? I recall that you were traveling on a ship to the North Pacific with some Russians, is that right?"

"That's right," answered George. "I was on the ship *Suvorov* with the young Mikhail Petrovich Lazarev as its captain. We sailed around the Cape of Good Hope, across the Indian Ocean to Port Jackson and Sydney, Australia, then across the Pacific to Sitka, Alaska. There Captain Lazarev, with whom I and others had conflicts, deserted me. But the Russian-American Company Governor Baranov sent me to Hawai'i. I was there the better part of two years, mostly on the island of Kaua'i. But Hawai'ian King Kamehameha's English advisor, John Young, and the American captains there conspired against me and I was expelled…barely escaped actually. So I sailed to Macau with two companions, and four months ago we found passage on the Portuguese ship *Luconia* to come back here. I'm trying to return home to St. Petersburg to advise the Russian Tsar to make claim on the Hawai'ian Islands as a trading base in the central Pacific."

"What an adventure!" exclaimed Flach. "I hope you've written some of it down."

"Indeed I have," said George. "But I need to prevail upon our friendship with a request. When I was here in 1814, I made the acquaintance of Dom João…now King João, of course, and his sons, Pedro and Miguel. I stayed with them at São Cristovão. I strongly wish to renew my acquaintance with them, but I was not able to get an appointment to see the King from his palace staff. I am sure that the King would want to see me. He gave me permission to seek the hand of the Russian Tsar's younger sister, the Grand Duchess Anna Pavlovna, for his son Pedro. Can you help me get an audience with the King?"

"Yes, I can," said Flach. "But Prince Pedro is now married."

"He's married!?" responded George, disappointed to hear this. "To whom?"

"To a Habsburg…the daughter, Leopoldina, of the Austrian Emperor, Franz I," answered Flach. "King João had his Charge d'affairs in Vienna, Count

Navarro de Andrade, present the idea to Austrian Minister Klemens von Metternich. Then the Marquis of Marialva, his ambassador to France, went to Vienna in a grand parade and made the formal proposal. The marriage took place in Vienna by proxy on King João's birthday, May 13, of last year, 1817. The proxy was the Austrian emperor's brother, the famous Archduke Charles."

George was silent for a few moments. Then he said, "Once, when I was a boy, I witnessed the march of the Archduke Charles' army across Franconia. I thought my own brother might have been in it. He was an Austrian soldier. But I did not see him. That was in 1796. He mused for a moment more, then asked, "But has the new princess come here to Rio de Janeiro?"

"Yes, she is now here and doing quite well," said Flach. "She arrived last November 5th. She's quite young…only born in 1797…though she's a bit older than her husband, the Prince Pedro. Her birthday is the same as mine, January 22nd. So now she's twenty-one years old. She's well educated and very kind. Since I speak German, I have been appointed her personal physician and advisor. We are already very close…she confides in me quite readily."

George shook his head in wonderment. "No matter that Prince Pedro is now married to the Habsburg Leopoldina," he said, "I still wish to see King João."

"I will arrange it," promised Dr. Flach.

Meeting the Kaiserin:

George planned to bring Filip Osipov and Grigorii Iskakov with him to the audience with King João at the palace in the city that Dr. Flach had arranged. Carefully he coached Filip and Grigorii in their hotel room during the days before the audience.

"Grigorii," he told the older man in Russian, "You will be presented as a King in your own right. You are, after all, a grand Toion of the Aleut people of the far north. I want you to dress in your best clothes, even though I know we don't have much finery with us. But you can wear your fur hat."

"But it's far too hot here for the fur hat," protested Grigorii.

"That doesn't matter," insisted George. "You must wear the fur hat, at least when I present you to King João. And try to look comfortable in it, as if it were your crown and you wear it often on ceremonial occasions. I want the King to think that I'm bringing royalty back to St. Petersburg to see the Tsar."

At this Filip Osipov laughed, but ceased immediately when Grigorii shot him an irritated glance.

"And you, Filip, are the Toion's bodyguard and attendant," explained George. "You are to stand immediately behind him at all times. If he should begin to sweat so that he has to remove the fur hat, he will hand it to you and you are to hold it as if it were a crown. And neither of you are to say anything at all to the King. Just bow to him respectfully as I do and speak to each other only in Aleut."

"But the Portuguese King will not understand our Aleut," protested Grigorii.

"That is just what I want," said George. "I will do all the speaking for us in the King's native Portuguese, hoping to impress him with my mastery of it since I saw him last. The two of you are there to give the impression that I am bringing native royalty to an audience with the Russian Tsar…and that is all. Do you understand?"

"I understand," said Grigorii, nodding in assent.

"Oh, all right," agreed Filip.

Dr. Martin Flach was already there when George, Filip, and Grigorii, wearing his fur hat, entered the grand throne room in the city palace where King João sat. In Portuguese he introduced "Dr. Jorge Antonio von Schaeffer" and "an Aleutian ruler from the far north coast of North America, the Toion Grigorii Iskakov, and his attendant Filip Osipov."

King João VI of Portugal (13 May, 1767-10 March, 1826), from:
http://en.wikipedia.org/wiki/John_VI_of_Portugal.

George stepped first into position before the throne and bowed low to the King, saying in Portuguese, "Good day, your Majesty. I earnestly hope you have not forgotten our previous acquaintance. For four years my remembrance of your wisdom during my stay with you and your sons has inspired me. I have brought back with me a King of the far northern Aleuts, the Toion Grigorii Iskakov. He decided to travel with me back to St. Petersburg to convince the Russian Tsar Aleksandr to support his people in their effort to find a source of sustenance in the more temperate Hawai'ian islands. And this is his bodyguard and attendant, Filip Osipov."

At George's gesture, Grigorii stepped forward and bowed. A step behind, Filip did the same thing.

King João, who looked older now to George than he had remembered, said to George and to Dr. Flach, "Does he always wear that fur hat?"

"That is his crown, your Majesty," answered George. "He felt that he had to wear it when he was presented to you."

"Well tell him he can take it off now. It's too hot for such a crown. You may notice that we are not wearing our crown," said King João.

George gestured to Grigorii and, noticing that there were no interpreters of any kind in the throne room, told him in Russian, "Take off the hat!"

Grigorii removed the fur hat and handed it to Filip, who held it forth atop both extended hands as if it were something very important…a king's crown.

King João continued, "We do remember you, Dr. Schaeffer. We remember your opposition to slavery, your proposal to arrange a marriage for our Prince Pedro with a sister of the Tsar, your idea of returning with a great amount of capital to settle here in Brazil someday, and your teaching us a most interesting Russian Orthodox chant."

"Your memory is astonishing," said George.

"We have help in remembering things, Dr. Schaeffer," said King João, looking significantly at Dr. Flach. "But you will notice that there have been changes since you were last here. Our mother Maria has died and we are now ruling as King of Portugal, the Algarve and Brazil. Napoleon Bonaparte is no longer determining the events of our lives, as we once predicted to you. He's now in exile off our shores on the island of St. Helena from which there will be no escape and France is not a threat to us anymore. We still depend upon the British in many ways, but we are not so beset as previously with their advisors. We can now return to our home in Portugal and we plan to do so in the near future. And our Prince Pedro, of course, has married. We are pleased with his marriage and we can only now await an heir."

"I understand that Prince Pedro has taken the Princess Leopoldina of Austria as his wife," said George. "That is a most advantageous match, in my opinion, and I congratulate you on it. I never got the opportunity to present my idea for

Pedro to marry the Tsar's sister. I am only now on my way back to St. Petersburg after more than four years of absence."

"Dr. Flach has told me of your tribulations in the Pacific. You may console yourself that you have enriched your life with a great diversity of interesting experience. We notice that you have somehow learned our language in the meantime. How did this come about? Did you encounter any Portuguese in your travels?"

"When we were here four years ago, two of our crew members abandoned ship in order to remain here in Rio de Janeiro," George explained. "We took on two new crew members from here, the young brothers Rodriguez, and I learned the language from them while crossing the Atlantic, the Indian, and the Pacific Oceans. Sailing a distance like that gives a man much time to learn things."

"Indeed you have learned it well," said King João. "What can we do for you and your company on this visit, Dr. Schaeffer?"

This was clearly an opportunity for George. But he replied, "I have no immediate needs from you, your Majesty. I will have no trouble booking passage from here back to St. Petersburg with Toion Iskakov and his attendant Filip. I only wished on this occasion to make further acquaintance with your Majesty and to offer you what service I can. It is still a possibility that I will want to liquidate my assets in Russia and return here someday. And if I do, I only desire that I be given some position in your court where I may be of real service to you or to your family. You may recall that I got along well with your sons. Your son Miguel and I once planned to climb Sugarloaf together. He liked to collect things and I told him we might find interesting native artifacts on the way up."

"We have been told of this," said King João smiling. "And a position with us at court is a definite possibility for you, should you return here with capital for investment in our country. We can promise you this."

George quickly answered, "That is all I desire, your Majesty. Thank you."

At this moment several people entered the throne room from its other side. There were several women dressed in elaborate dresses and wearing high wigs and much jewelry. Dr. Flach walked over to meet them, saying in German, to George's surprise, "How excellent that you could be with us today, your Highness. I didn't know if you would grant my request."

The women were the attendants of the new Princess Leopoldina, who stepped forth from among them and curtsied to the King. She was a slender young woman of slightly more than average height, unprepossessing in appearance if her finery were disallowed, with gray-green eyes and a long narrow nose. Her high black wig covered hair that was apparently lighter in color judging from her pale complexion, and the open bodice of her colorfully embroidered dress disclosed a flat chest with no visible cleavage beneath a striking ruby pendant. She moved with a lithe agility, however, and spoke up spiritedly in German to Dr. Flach, "I wanted to come and make the acquaintance of another German

28

doctor. The German doctors I know are all such interesting people. And I tire of learning the Portuguese. I want to speak German again with anyone I can." She smiled as she said this, exposing an attractive straight row of gleaming white teeth.

Maria Leopoldina of Austria, Empress Consort of Brazil (22 January, 1797—11 December, 1826) at age 18. Portrait by Joseph Kreutzinger (1757-1829), from: http://en.wikipedia.org/wiki/Archduchess_Maria_Leopoldina_of_Austria.

King João took this as his opportunity to leave, saying that "other important matters need our presence." "I'll leave you in the fine company of my new daughter-in-law," he said as he got up from his throne and exited the room.

Princess Leopoldina then said to Dr. Flach and the others, "Let us go into the banquet room. I have asked that a lunch be prepared there for us and we can talk more freely."

Leopoldina, whom Dr. Flach referred to in German as the "Kaiserin," then began to talk to her attendants. It was apparently her purpose to include only a fraction of them in the banquet room lunch and to dismiss the others. All of the attendants wanted to stay with her and this occasioned her some obvious difficulty. But in a few moments she headed a smaller group of five lady attendants out of the throne room and down an adjacent hallway. Dr. Flach, George, Grigorii Iskakov, and Filip Osipov followed along.

The banquet room was opulent, with golden curtains surrounding tall windows that were shuttered with whitewashed slats. Red and gold tapestries hung from the walls. The high ceiling showed huge dark exposed beams of rough-hewn logs, and a row of five elaborate candle chandeliers hung down from them over a long polished oak table. The chairs were cushioned in dark purple velvet. As George and the others entered the room, a number of white-clad servants were finishing the arrangement of fine silverware and gilt-edged plates and bowls on the table. At each place were several glass goblets and tumblers. There were carafes of both water and wine within reach of every two seat positions.

Filip Osipov sidled over to George as they were invited to take their seats and commented, "This place certainly beats Governor Baranov's banquet hall. I've never seen such a magnificent place. I hope Grigorii and I don't embarrass you in our eating manners. We don't know how to act here."

George whispered, "Just do as I do and don't say anything."

Princess Leopoldina took the seat at the head of the table. Dr. Flach was seated on her immediate right, and George on her immediate left. On George's left was Grigorii Iskakov, the Aleut Toion, and on his left were seated three ladies-in-waiting, the oldest of them seated closest to him. On Dr. Flach's right, across from Grigorii Iskakov, was Filip Osipov, Grigorii's fur hat placed into his lap, and, to his right, were the other two ladies-in-waiting. All the ladies-in-waiting were giggling and speaking discretely to each other.

The lunch proceeded with a rich mixed vegetable soup being served, followed by delicious slices of roasted beef, then a salad of lettuce and carrots and sliced mushrooms, and a dessert of tart dark-purple açai berries in sugared cream. George coached his companions through the meal with sharp Russian commands: "The outside spoon for the soup…no elbows on the table…leave the spoon on the bowl and the servants will take it away…knife in left hand, fork in right"…and so on. While doing this he engaged the Princess in German conversation.

"Do you know, your Highness, that I was in Vienna with my wife Barbara ten years ago, and I found it a most fascinating city. We were on our way to Russia and visited there in 1808 with my brother Wilhelm who was serving in the Austrian army as a provisioner in General Kienmayer's army."

The Princess's face brightened at the mention of Vienna, and she responded, "Thank you for mentioning my home city of Vienna. I didn't realize I loved the city so until I had been away from it for these past six months. I have been telling Prince Pedro about how wonderful it is there in Vienna, hoping to convince him that we should make a visit there. He does not seem very enthusiastic about leaving Brazil, however, and I'm concerned that I may never see Vienna or my family there again." At this ending thought her face darkened and her eyebrows furrowed.

"I am acquainted with Prince Pedro, your Highness, and I am sure that as your language improves and you regale him with stories of the Stephansdom Cathedral and its giant bell, of the Hofsburg, Belvedere, and Schönbrunn residences, of the Hohe Markt and the plague column and all the other wonders of Vienna, he will persuaded to visit it in royal fashion. It's only four months away now with the best transport of ship and coach. You'll be back there soon." George then added, "You might also tell him that the best horses in the world are to be found in Austria."

"Now that is an apt suggestion," said Leopoldina, "I can really use that. The Prince has a real passion for horses. Thank you, Herr Schaeffer."

George continued in his attempt to find common ground. He thought of mentioning to Leopoldina that he had once personally met an uncle of hers, the Archduke Ferdinand III of Tuscany, whose cousin and captain-of-guards he had killed in a duel in Würzburg in August of 1806, but realized that mention of this could only be unpleasant for her and present to her mind a negative impression of him, and so he decided not to. But while he was thinking, Leopoldina asked him a question of her own.

"What did you do in Russia, Herr Schaeffer?" she said.

George didn't know what he should say. Napoleon Bonaparte was actually Leopoldina's brother-in-law, as he had married her sister Marie-Louise in 1810. Could he tell her that he had been involved in a scheme to kill Napoleon from a balloon in 1812?

Dr. Flach took this indecision away from George, interposing, "Dr. Schaeffer managed a secret project of the Russian Tsar to kill Napoleon from a hot-air balloon."

"Really?" said Leopoldina, with apparent genuine curiosity, "How did that project come out? Obviously Napoleon wasn't killed."

George remembered telling Dr. Flach and Dr. Langsdorff about his management of the balloon project four years before. Now he had no choice but to elaborate the story for Leopoldina, whose personal stance toward Napoleon was not obvious to him.

"It was not a hot-air balloon, Dr. Flach," he began. "It was instead to be filled with hydrogen, which is superior to hot air as a means of elevation. The balloon was to be huge in size, shaped like a gigantic ocean shark and able to lift fifty men and their armaments in its gondola. Moreover, the designer, a German-speaking man named Franz Leppich whom Tsar Aleksandr instructed us all to call "Schmidt," built a mechanical device in the gondola that powered rotating wings so that the balloon was not limited in its motion by the wind, but could be steered with a rudder in whatever direction was desired. The plan was to steer the balloon to a position high over Napoleon's head—so high that it was out of the range of artillery or musket-- and drop timed-fuse explosives on him and his other commanders."

"My word!" exclaimed Leopoldina, impressed, "Why did the project fail?"

"It was primarily because we did not have enough time," George related. "We only began the project in June of 1812 as Napoleon and his army were already on Russian soil. We made a heroic effort, and expended tremendous amounts of money, but it was a race against the French advance on Moscow...an advance that only took two months. We had insuperable supply problems. There was insufficient silk for the envelope and so we used taffeta. This, as it turned out, could not be sufficiently sealed with our varnish to prevent leakage of the hydrogen. In the end, the great balloon simply would not rise, and, as Napoleon's army occupied Moscow, we evacuated the entire balloon project to Nizhnii Novgorod and then to St. Petersburg. Further experimentation and different materials might have made a success of the project and who knows what benefits such a device for air travel might have given mankind, but the designer Leppich turned out to be a murderer and fled the country and the Tsar stopped the project's funding after the fortunes of war began to turn to his advantage without it."

"What an adventure! I've never heard anything about this before, and I thought I'd heard just about every story of that war there was to hear from my father and my uncles," said Leopoldina. Then turning to George, she inquired, "What was your role in the project? Were you going to be in the balloon?"

George smiled and answered, "I was primarily the provisioner and the accountant for the project. It was my job to find whatever was needed and supply it immediately. I impressed the needed seamstresses, for example, out of the city's jails. Leppich wanted me to go up in the balloon eventually and I said I would, but I don't know even now if I really would have. I might have gone up in the smaller silk balloon from which we tested the dropping of the explosives, but somehow I was always too busy doing something else."

"Did the tests work?" asked Dr. Flach.

"Yes, spectacularly," answered George. "Just one dropped charge blew to pieces an entire flock of sheep. Napoleon would surely have been killed."

"That's very interesting," said Dr. Flach. "And do you know that only two years ago there was a scheme planned right here in Brazil to free Napoleon from his exile on St. Helena island using a balloon? A balloon to kill him, a balloon to rescue him...what must the man think of balloons by now, eh?"

"What kind of a scheme was that?" asked Leopoldina.

"It was a plot conceived by a young supporter of the Bonaparte royalists in Lisbon, a carioca named Antonio Carlos de Andrada," related Dr. Flach. "King João had him arrested and imprisoned in 1816 after the new French envoy, Duke de Richileu, informed him that de Andrada had engaged a French 'aerostier' to come to Brazil to build a balloon at a secret jungle location which could use the prevailing winds to cross over the ocean and land on St. Helena. There they would overpower Napoleon's guards and take him aboard the balloon. Then they would lift off St. Helena and soar further on to the coast of Africa, where fellow conspirators would harbor Napoleon until he could find a way to return again to power in France."

"To cross the entire Atlantic in a balloon, finding its way to St. Helena?" marveled George. "It was a preposterous idea…impossible, surely. Where is de Andrada now?"

"I think he's in the Aljube prison here in Rio," answered Dr. Flach. "His family is not without political influence here. Somehow they prevented his being hanged."

"Well, I am glad that Napoleon was not rescued," said Leopoldina, revealing her personal opinion of her brother-in-law. "He's certainly caused more than enough trouble in the world."

The lunch ended amicably, with George and Dr. Flach profusely thanking the "Kaiserin Leopoldina" for her hospitality and her conversation. George told the Kaiserin that he had managed to preserve in his medical bag, even throughout all his troubles, a good number of plant seeds that he had collected and carefully described while in Alaska, Hawai'i, and China. Through Dr. Flach, he would give them to her in the hope that they would enrich Brazilian agriculture during her reign. Leopoldina seemed happy with this present to her and told George that she would make sure the seeds were placed into the most competent hands in the realm.

As the guest rose to take their leave, Leopoldina told George that she was most pleased to make his acquaintance and that she hoped she would one day meet him again. From a wooden case held by one of the ladies-in-waiting, she removed a red and white sash with a silver medal attached showing the likeness of King João. She walked up close to George and draped the sash and medal around George's neck, telling him that it was a sign of his being granted membership in an "Order of the Guard" of the Brazilian royal family. She then draped identical sashes and medals around the necks of Grigorii Iskakov and Filip Osipov, both of whom bowed low to her in gratitude. George was very surprised by this gesture, saying "Your Highness, I don't know what to say. I have always dreamed of being a member of some royal order. I assure you that I will henceforth be your most obedient servant. I hope to return here someday and be of genuine, and not only ceremonial, aid to you."

Leopoldina's response only made George blush with pride. She said that he, Dr. George Anton von Schaeffer" could henceforth refer to himself as "Ritter von Schaeffer," a knight with the rank of "Major" of her own Royal Guard. George was speechless.

Despite George's warning Filip Osipov not to say anything, Filip was forced to respond as he could to one of the ladies-in-waiting's persistent efforts to engage him in conversation. She was an attractive young woman with a high pile of unwigged hair as dark as Filip's and she was obviously attracted to him, to his bright smile and to his exceptionally strong physique. She approached close to him as the company was leaving and put her hand on his shoulder, saying something to him that he could not understand, but took as a proposal of some kind of continued contact. "Da, Da…Khorosho!" he said to her in Russian, trying to agree. But George scowled at him, and Princess Leopoldina scowled at the lady-in-waiting, and both parties took leave of each other without further comment.

Dr. Flach left the palace with George and the others. When they got outside onto the street, George asked him, "Did you know that the Kaiserin was going to award us these medals and make me a knight and major in her royal guard?"

"I proposed the idea to her," said Flach. "We are trying to enlist all audience visitors with real support potential into this ceremonial guard. Here in Brazil and in Rio de Janeiro too are many anti-royalists now who want to see King João and his family deposed. It is important that we gain the support of as many powerful friends as we can. I am, by the way, also a knight and major of the Kaiserin's royal guard."

"Wunderbar!" exclaimed George. "And what a good idea! I certainly thank you for this. You are a good friend, indeed."

The Visit to Mandioca:

George wanted to renew his acquaintance while in Rio de Janeiro with Dr. George Heinrich von Langsdorff, the German naturalist who had accompanied Russian-American Company founder Nikolai P. Rezanov on Captain Ivan F. Kruzenshtern's *Nadezhda* during the Russians' first world circumnavigation in 1803-1806. He knew that Langsdorff was now officially the Russian minister to Brazil, but that he lived with his wife Friederike, his young son and a new daughter on a plantation estate he called Mandioca. Mandioca was to be found, George was told, up the Jequitinhonha River from the ocean settlement of Belmonte north of Porto Seguro on the coast of the Bahia State near the place where the Portuguese Explorer Pedro Álvares Cabral first sighted the coast of Brazil on April 22nd, 1500. Belmonte was named after the place in Portugal where Cabral was born. It was nine days journey by sail from Rio de Janeiro, and Mandioca was another day by mule. Dr. Langsdorff, whose memoirs of the circumnavigation George had read, had come to visit with George, together with Dr. Martin Flach, during George's 1814 stay in Rio de Janeiro. At that time, Dr. Langsdorff was departing on an expedition to the Minas Gerais wilderness of Brazil, to territory heretofore unexplored by Europeans.

George asked his friend, Dr. Flach, about going to visit Dr. Langsdorff at Mandioca, but Dr. Flach was not positive about this idea.

"Dr. Langsdorff is not the same man he was," explained Dr. Flach. "After you saw him last he and a small group of colleagues made a very difficult trek into the jungle wilderness in the Minas Gerais region where no civilized person had ever gone before. His purpose was to describe and to gather plant and animal specimens previously unclassified and to make what contact he could with the aboriginal tribes. His wife Friederike thought he was insane to leave Mandioca on such a venture, but she tolerated it at his insistence in the interests of science."

"So how long was he gone?" asked George.

Dr. Flach answered, "The group was gone just over a year. When they came back, Dr. Langsdorff was a broken man. He was physically just a shadow of his former already slender self. His complexion was ghastly pale and he looked as if he would expire at any moment. He was constantly in fever and sweated profusely all the time. He had no appetite. His hands shook and he couldn't hold them steady. His hair had all fallen out and he was as bald as an egg. When I first saw him after his return I could barely recognize him. But the worst thing is what happened to his mind. He can't focus his attention on any topic for any sufficient length of time . And he's lost the ability to speak clearly…at least his power of expression is severely limited. And that's in his native German. He's weaker yet in Portuguese and he can't even respond in the other languages he learned later in his life like French, Russian, and English. It's difficult to have a conversation with him at all."

"Mein Gott!" exclaimed George. "How did that happen to him?"

"Friederike does not know," said Dr. Flach. "Langsdorff's colleagues also had a very hard time of it, and during the journey some of them came to great feelings of enmity for each other. It's strange how shared travail can separate as well as unify people. One of them told me that the final blow to Langsdorff's stability came while they were visiting a very primitive tribe of jungle savages near the Amazon River. These people lived completely without clothing and hunted tapirs and monkeys with traps and birds with poisoned darts blown from long reed tubes. Langsdorff thought he would impress them by donning his full dress uniform and his feathered hat…items the others thought him foolish to bring along."

"That does seem a bit strange," commented George. "Taking a dress uniform and feathered hat along with him into the jungle. But he probably wanted to be prepared for any occasion, I guess. I can imagine that such dress might well have impressed a primitive people who don't wear clothes at all. What did the savages think of it?"

"Oh, the savages were impressed, all right," said Flach. "So much so that they offered him a sacred potion that they had prepared. None of the others were allowed to drink the potion. When Langsdorff had drunk his share, he reported feeling giddy and seeing strange things in the air. And just then a naked female…a very young concubine of a chief…snatched the feathered hat off his head and ran off laughing into the jungle.'

"What did he do about that?" asked George.

Dr. Flach continued, "I was told that Langsdorff became unreasonably angry, ran away after her in chase and did not come back. The next morning the entire group left the savages' village and carried out a search for him and found him sitting up to his chest without any clothes at all in a fetid swamp some surprising distance away. The savages had apparently taken not only his feathered hat, but his uniform also. He is fortunate they did not kill him, but they didn't leave him well. Mosquitoes and other insects had badly bitten the top half of him and some kind of biting fish had badly bitten the bottom half of him. After that his colleagues just led him around on a rope, fed him when he would eat, and finally returned him in miserable shape to his wife at Mandioca. He's been there ever since. He sits all day and stares out at his fields. Friederike tells people that he is recuperating, but, from what I saw, I doubt that he'll long survive. In any case, I don't encourage you to visit him. It will only be greatly depressing to you."

"I respect your opinion on this, Andreas, and I appreciate your concern for me, but I'd like to go see him anyway," said George. "For one thing, I have never met his wife Friederike and I have been told that she is very like my own wife Barbara. And also, I would like to survey the development of his estate there. I want to see what he has been able to build there in these past five years. Does he still have slaves? You might recall that he told us he and Friederike had plans to free them."

"He still has slaves," answered Dr. Flach. "But you might be positively impressed with the transformation of the area that they have wrought. Mandioca is now quite a nice place, and productive too. He has had a thousand fruit and nut trees planted there now."

"I will go then," said George with resolution. "I will leave my companions here in the city at the hotel and go alone. Can you help me find a guide and transportation?"

"Yes, I'll help you," said Flach.

Twelve days later, after sailing north on a small coastal ship, George, riding a mule and following several other pack-laden mules led by the guide, a young man named Jorge recommended by Dr. Flach, approached the main house of the Mandioca estate. For a kilometer or more they had been traversing large plots of sugar cane and lush irrigated fields of tobacco. Closer to the center of the estate they encountered large groves of small trees, some bearing fruit that looked like peaches. At one point, near where a split-rail fence began to delimit the road and a rock-and-mortar bridge crossed a lively stream, George spotted a group of sweat-glistened black men digging to extract a large tree stump. George thought that these had to be the Langsdorffs' slaves, but there was no apparent supervisor of the work.

The main house of the Mandioca estate came into view from some distance away, as the estate was situated on a cleared hill surrounded on the three sides away from the road's approach across the stream by a dense forest of tall vine-entangled trees. It was a large single-storey house made of dried mud blocks that had been dressed with large half timbers to resemble a German merchant's home. It was yellowish in color except for the darker crossing half timbers, and it had a high roof of the dark-colored split-wood shingles and a rock-and-mortar chimney of impressive height at its center. The house's floor level was elevated about two feet on its block foundation and an elevated porch stretched across the front of it, accessed by a wide wooden staircase. To the left of the house in a lower position were numerous lower and unpainted wooden buildings arranged in two parallel rows that George thought might be the slaves' residences. There was a long wooden barn with a sloped shingle roof and several split-timber corrals with cattle and goats in them. Several horses were in another corral adjacent to an apparent stable, and George could see three wagons of different types stationed nearby at the road's approach.

It was a clear and sunny day, but the temperature was not unpleasant and the air seemed dry to George compared to the air in Rio de Janeiro on the ocean coast. As the two-day mule trek was now ending, and the destination in sight, George began to whistle as he was often wont to do. He was whistling a melody from a work of Ludwig von Beethoven that his wife Barbara had particularly admired and played often on the piano. The young guide Jorge, riding a few mules ahead of him, turned around to smile at George, impressed with George's easy ability to render the melody beautifully in a whistle. But then both Jorge and George heard a tinkling distant melodic sound coming from the estate. It was the sound of a piano competently played. George ceased his whistling and listened with deliberate acuity. It was the same melody he had started to whistle…a melody by Beethoven. Jorge turned back and commented to him in Portuguese, "That is indeed amazing! That's the same song you were just whistling!"

George smiled and shrugged his shoulders in wonderment. Was it a mere coincidence or had he already heard the piano at some low auditory level before he consciously realized it and begun his whistling to its lead? Nevertheless it was a remarkable occurrence, he thought. He knew that it had to be Friederike Langsdorff playing the piano inside the estate house. The sound grew stronger as they neared the house and came into its front yard.

George dismounted and walked up to the house. Jorge followed a few steps behind him. On the porch, sitting in a rocking chair, was George's illustrious acquaintance, Dr. George Heinrich von Langsdorff. He leaned forward in his chair as George began to climb the several stairs to reach the level of the porch and said three times, in a loud German, "I know who you are! I know who you are! I know who you are!" Then he asked George, "Don't I know who you are?"

Georg Heinrich von Langsdorff (Grigorii Ivanovich Langsdorf, 8 April, 1774--9 June, 1852) from http://en.wikipedia.org/Grigory_Langsdorff.

The piano sound ceased and a woman came out of the front door and onto the porch. She was a tall woman with reddish brown hair pulled back into a knot at the back of her head. She was very attractive of face, with large brown eyes and narrow high-arching eyebrows. She was slender and appeared very fit, but her skin was quite tan in color and her face seemed extraordinarily weathered, considering that she was, in George's estimation, about thirty years of age. She had obviously done a great deal of work outside in the sun. Her hands also seemed to be the hands of an older woman, with fingers thickened, palms callused, and with rough-trimmed fingernails. George noticed this as she extended her right hand to him. As he brought her hand up to his face in a gesture of greeting, she said in Portuguese, "I am Friederike von Langsdorff. And this is my husband George. Welcome to Mandioca. Have you come far?"

George answered in German, causing Friederike to smile, "I am Dr. and Major George Anton Ritter von Schaeffer of Kaiserin Leopoldina's royal guard at your service. And this young man is my guide Jorge. We have come from Rio de Janeiro to visit you. I met your husband, Dr. Langsdorff, four years ago before his expedition into the great jungle. We have much in common and we got on wonderfully in our previous acquaintance…"

Dr. Langsdorff interrupted George, standing up from his chair and saying, "Dr. Schaeffer, that's who you are. I knew that I know you. You and I met in St. Petersburg. We both know about balloons. We are friends, is that not correct?"

Langsdorff had a short stubble of straw-colored hair growing on his pate and he had grown a greyish blonde beard, trimmed shorter than George's. He did not seem to be as emaciated as Dr. Flach had described him, and his skin, though pale, was dry. He stepped up to George and hugged him firmly, then offered to shake hands as well. His grip was firm and steady. George decided to answer him not in German, but in Russian.

"Da, my druz'ya...Yes, we are friends," he said. "But we did not meet in St. Petersburg. We met in Rio de Janeiro. I was on the ship *Suvorov* traveling to supply the Russian-American Company outpost in Alaska. You had also been on a round-the-world journey on the Russian ship *Nadezhda* and I read your memoirs about the trip. And we do both have balloons in common experience. You raised one up while a captive in Japan, and I managed the construction of one in Moscow, attempting to kill Napoleon in 1812."

Friederike understood the Russian easily and knew instantly that George was testing her husband's mental faculties. She understood that George must have heard already of Dr. Langsdorff's plight. She looked to her husband and smiled.

"Da, ya byl na *Nadezhde*...Yes, I was on the *Nadezhda*," said Dr. Langsdorff in flawless Russian, "i plennikom byl v yaponii...and I was a prisoner in Japan."

"Chudesno!...Miraculous!" exclaimed George, very pleased to hear his comrade speak so well in Russian.

Friederike was also pleased. She said to George, staying with the German, "The pace of his recuperation has been accelerating in the past few months. The fevers have ceased and his physical health has returned. He's eating well now and gaining weight and strength. His memory is still not what it was, and this upsets him. But we have to be patient. I haven't heard him speak Russian for a long time and am pleased to hear it from him. Around here we speak mostly German, but I use Portuguese too to give him practice."

"I don't need any practice in Portuguese," objected Dr. Langsdorff abruptly in Portuguese. " I can speak it well enough. And my French is coming back to me too."

"Wunderbar!" responded George.

George and Jorge were house guests of the Langsdorffs for four days. The Langsdorff's nine-year-old son, Heinrich, whom they called affectionately "Rico," made a boisterous presence, running in and out of the house and shouting for his parents to watch him climb trees or attempt to ride a goat or any of a number of boyish pursuits. George recalled that Rico was actually Dr. Langsdorff's child by a woman other than Friederike, but it was very clear that Friederike considered herself the boy's mother. And young Rico interacted primarily with her. Dr. Langsdorff never disciplined the boy, and almost never spoke to him at all, but only smiled proudly at whatever the boy did. There was also their own little girl, Wilhelmina, who was three years old. She was attended by a slave nanny and was laid down to nap in the afternoons when her mother played the piano.

George had plenty of opportunity to reacquaint Dr. Langsdorff with all the extraordinary commonalities of their lives. Dr. Langsdorff particularly liked to hear George talk about the memoirs he had written. Every conversation about the events that George recited from Langsdorff's memoirs seemed to restore the contained facts to the man's active memory. He liked also to hear George talk about the political events of their time, of Napoleon Bonaparte and of the English-American War of 1812, of Dom João becoming King and the prospects of his return to Portugal, of Prince Pedro's marriage to the Habsburg "Kaiserin" Leopoldina, and of all the countries that were limiting or abolishing slavery. Dr. Langsdorff's attention quickly wandered and he became detached from the conversation when George tried to relate his own adventures in Alaska, Hawaii, and China, however. It was better to stay with issues of personal commonality, George found. It was also clear that Dr. Langsdorff was resolved to make further expeditions into the wild area of Brazil, and that this resolution severely troubled Friederike.

"I swear, Georg, that if you don't give up on such a nonsensical and self-destructive notion," she said firmly, "I'll go back to Europe and take the children with me."

Friederike offered her own views on the situation of their slaves. She had become the active manager of Mandioca during her husband's absence and incapacity, and it was she who had been dealing personally with the slaves for the past three years. She said that the secret of her success at Mandioca was that she treated the slaves as she would treat any other human beings. She allowed them to form their own society, interacting primarily with its chosen leaders. She never punished a slave, allowing them to regulate their own behavior. She directed their projects in Portuguese, which she made persistent efforts to teach them. She allowed them time to build their own houses, allowed them the majority of food from the livestock they raised and slaughtered and from the food crops they harvested. Mandioca's main source of external income for the Langsdorffs came from the tobacco, which the slaves themselves did not understand as none of them could be induced to smoke the leaves in the European way. They just worked to grow, harvest, pack and ship it at Friederike's direction. When several of the slaves ran away, she made no effort to find them, and, as it turned out, most of the runaways returned voluntarily to her after they found that they could not make lives for themselves in freedom at large in Brazilian society. Twice she had purchased lots of female slaves to balance the genders in her slave population. And she helped with the subsequent births and began a project with her female house slaves to teach the slave children to read and write in Portuguese. She did not feel threatened by the slaves on the Mandioca estate at all, but in fact felt protected by them.

"If I announced to our slaves today that they are all free and can go where they want," Friederike said, "they would not go. Of this I am now quite sure. The slaves' griot, a kind of story teller and keeper of their history, tells me that their memories of life in Africa are filled with terrible hardships and cruelties, even from their own. Their enslavement there and their journey here was indeed a hell for them, but their lives here with us are a kind of heaven on earth now for them, they say. Indeed we can already say that we've freed our slaves by our treatment of them. And they remain with us, sharing our lives."

"Unfortunately, the institution of slavery is not universally practiced as you practice it," said George. "Slavery is an evil wherever it occurs and should be abolished by all mankind."

"I agree with that view completely," said Friederike. "But George Heinrich and the children and I could not survive on this estate without them. And if we freed our slaves, just let them go on their own without recompense for them, and returned to Europe as George Heinrich sometimes says he wants to do, the slaves would also not survive. We would be doing them a favor either to sell them or give them to someone else who views the practice of slavery the way we do."

"If you left here, you could give them Mandioca under some terms of purchase," said George. "That might assure not only their survival, but your continued prosperity."

"Indeed you are correct, George," said Friederike. "We have discussed this and that is exactly what we would do. There are some laws here that need to be changed so that this could happen, however. As Minister of Russia to the new King, George Heinrich could advocate such changes for the good of Brazil…if he were able."

"I understand," said George.

Friederike was curious about George's acquaintance with the new Princess Leopoldina, whom she had not had the opportunity to meet. George told her all about his experience at the palace with the "Kaiserin Leopoldina," extolling the young woman's intelligence and sincerity in learning all she could about her new realm.

"But can she make a marriage with young Pedro?" asked Friederike. "He's involved, as I hear it, in constant debauchery. Apparently he takes after his mother. He's extremely self-centered, thinking only of himself and doesn't seem to have a head for politics at all."

"I don't know what kind of a marriage they will have," answered George. "But to me Leopoldina has many of the attributes that Pedro lacks, including an adept sense of how to gain political advantage by enlisting others in their cause. I know she certainly enlisted me. I'd do anything to help her now."

"And we will do the same when we get the chance," said George Heinrich forcefully. "If you think her right for Brazil, then so do we. It's only right that we should take the same side in such matters, given our commonality of background and understanding."

One evening Friederike played a selection of melodies for her husband, George, and Jorge on the piano after the children had gone to bed. She said the piano had fallen somewhat out of tune, but George could not discern any shortcomings in the music. Friederike's roughened fingers fairly flew over the keys, and the result was thrilling to her three avid listeners.

"Wunderbar!" exclaimed George when Friederike ceased, after a half hour or more, her playing. "I haven't heard such virtuosity since my wife Barbara last played for me at home in St. Petersburg. How I wish that you could meet her, Friederike. You have so much in common with her."

"I would like that," said Friederike.

When George and Jorge packed up to leave, George Heinrich was most effusive in professing his feeling of kinship for George. "We simply must get together again in this life, my dear brother," he said. "If you do manage to return here from Europe, be sure to visit us again. And try to write us when you can. I will write to you in St. Petersburg and to others there too, recommending that they heed your advice on matters of the Hawai'ian islands and other things. You clearly have the best interests of Russia in mind, and I will try to help you convince the Tsar and his government of this. I am not without influence there still, you know. Indeed I would like to return there myself and apply for financial support for another expedition...if I can convince Fredike to tolerate my absence again, that is. And if you return here to Brazil with your wife and daughter, then Friederike and I will do whatever we can to help you here too. We are two ships on the same seas, George…two ships on the same seas."

George embraced George Heinrich and Friederike warmly and thanked them for their hospitality. Then he and Jorge mounted the mules that Jorge had saddled and packed and departed. As they crossed the bridge onto the road away from the Langsdorffs' Mandioca estate, they could hear again Friederike playing on the piano. It had been a fine visit.

Filip Falls in Love:

Back in Rio de Janeiro with his traveling companions after three weeks away, George found that Filip Osipov had recently spent two days and the intervening night away from the hotel room in the company of one of Kaiserin Leopoldina's ladies-in-waiting. He had, he said, "fallen in love."

"But how do you even speak with her?" asked George.

"We communicate mostly with our eyes," Filip answered. "And with our hands. But I've already learned a few Portuguese phrases, and I'm sure I'll learn more very soon. Lucinda has been very patient in teaching me."

"She just came to the hotel in a carriage and her driver came in and inquired about Filip," explained Grigorii Iskakov with wry amusement. "So Filip went out to meet her. And now he says he's in love."

"I see," said George smiling, speaking still to Filip. "But she's Portuguese royalty and she's catholic and you are bound to St. Petersburg with me. So how will you deal with these problems, given that you are communicating only with your eyes and hands?"

"I'll come back here for her after we complete our mission in St. Petersburg," said Filip. "We'll be together then no matter what. Either she will convert to orthodoxy and come with me, or I'll convert to Catholicism and stay with her. There is no problem that love cannot conquer. We were meant to be together and that's all there is to it."

"Have you met her family?" asked George. "What is her family's name?"

"The name is Arriaga. Lucinda's uncle is the Portuguese Minister in Macau who confiscated at your request the sandalwood from Captain Wadsworth."

"That is an astonishing coincidence," George replied, but then he repeated the question about Lucinda's family, "Have you met the Arriagas?"

"I met her mother and her sister," answered Filip. "And they seemed very nice, although the mother kept fainting and crossing herself all the time. She told Lucinda she didn't know what the father would say. But he will have to be convinced, that's all."

"I don't think that you will have the time to convince him, Filip," said George. "We'll be leaving here this week or next. I have Dr. Flach making inquiries to find us a ship to Europe as soon as possible."

"Well, if I don't have the time to convince him, then Lucinda will have to do it while I am gone," said Filip.

George looked Filip in the eyes seriously, shook his head and said, "I can only wish you success in this, my young friend. It has become my opinion that acting on love in this world is never a mistake."

The Journey Homeward:

Dr. Martin Flach reported to George that a Russian merchant ship, the *Natalia Petrovna* under Captain Andrei Sinelnikov, was departing for Rotterdam in the next week to deliver a cargo of Brazilian cane sugar and rum before returning to its homeport of Riga. George went to the port and found Captain Sinelnikov's mate, a Dutchman named Ulrick van Gelder who was in charge of arranging paid passage. In a brief negotiation, George reserved places aboard the *Natalia Petrovna* for himself and his companions by paying van Gelder in advance. Filip and Grigorii would have ordinary seamen's bunks, but in exchange for his services as onboard physician, George would be assigned a middle-deck corner in which were a desk and a curtained berth. His living arrangement on board was to be like he had had on the *Suvorov* five years before. Van Gelder estimated that the trip to Rotterdam through the Canary Islands, Lisbon, and London would take five months so that they would be back in Europe in September of 1818.

At the hotel Grigorii Iskakov had taken ill. He had stomach pain and said that he felt extraordinarily fatigued without reason. He didn't want to get out of bed. George interrogated him about what he had eaten, and concluded that a laxative might be the appropriate remedy, but it did not help. Only after two days of bedrest did Grigorii rise to dress himself and come to breakfast with George and Filip.

"He's never told me how old he is," Filip said to George in confidence. "But it's clear that he's quite a few years older than you are…and that's OLD."

George regarded this comment with amusement. He was thirty-nine years old and did not feel the least antiquated. But Filip was only twenty-six and anyone over thirty-five seemed old to him. George reckoned Grigorii to be in his late fifties, but he thought he might take the opportunity of their breakfast together to ask him.

"Grigorii, do you know how old you are?" George inquired.

"I don't know exactly how old I am in the Russian years," answered Grigorii. "But I was already a grown man in Unalaska when the first Russians came there. I remember meeting Aleksandr Andreevich Baranov in those days and thinking that I was a few years older than he is, but I might be wrong. He looks older than I do now, I think you would agree."

"Indeed I would agree," said George. "But Governor Baranov is nearly seventy years old, the Lord bless him. That makes you older than I thought. Filip and I will have to start taking better care of you."

"It is I who will take care of the both of you," joked Grigorii.

As the men ate, George noticed a spry young man in a blue-striped sailor's jersey coming toward them from the door. Suddenly he recognized the man. It was Esteban Rodriguez, one of the two brothers the Rio de Janeiro crew brokers had supplied to the *Suvorov* in 1814.

Esteban strode rapidly to the table where George and the others were sitting and said "Dr. Schaeffer, I heard that you were here and came to find you. How are you?"

George stood up and hugged his young friend warmly. "Esteban Rodriguez. It's so nice to see you again. I have to admit that I didn't expect to see you after the *Suvorov* left Novo-Arkhangelsk and stranded me there. It's been four years."

George introduced Esteban to Filip and Grigorii, telling them about how Esteban and his brother Rodrigo had come to serve as sailors on the Russian ship captained by "that scoundrel Lazarev" he had told them about. He joked about how he and Esteban and Rodrigo had been involved in a bar fight in Australia and about how Esteban had bitten a man's ankle "like a cannibal." Esteban smiled at this and remarked laughing that "my brother Rodrigo bit a ear off another man, so he also was a 'cannibal'."

"It was Esteban and Rodrigo who taught me Portuguese," George told his companions in Russian. Then he turned to Esteban and said in Portuguese, "You may be interested to know that your new King João was most complementary about my speaking of Portuguese. I spoke with him personally three weeks ago and he wanted to know where I had learned to speak his language so well. I mentioned your name to him as my teacher."

"My name means nothing to him, the fat usurper," said Esteban grimly, looking around himself to see that no one inappropriate heard his opinion of the King. "May the pox take him."

George had momentarily forgotten that the Rodriguez brothers had been incarcerated in the Aljube Prison after resisting the confiscation of their land by João's police officers in a tax dispute. He said to Esteban, "I can understand why you might be opposed to King João. But are you against just him or Kings in general?"

"I'm against all such arbitrary rule, and I'll be fighting with all my strength to end it," answered Esteban. "It's past time for the country to be free of this tyranny."

"So you're a rebel then," said George. "And Rodrigo also?"

"Absolutely," answered Esteban.

"My position is that most rebels haven't given enough serious thought to what kind of government they will install once they do away with the monarchy," said George. "They get caught up in a life of violence in the process of destroying the old order and then inflict that violence on the people once they are in power. I think that a monarchy tempered by constitutional assurances of rights and a constituent assembly to consider the laws is a better form of government. And I think there is a possibility that this kind of monarchy will take shape here in Brazil if the people are patient."

"I've long ago run out of patience, Dr. Schaeffer," said Esteban. "But I didn't come here to discuss political philosophy with you. I came because you owe me and my brother money."

"Oh, I understand," said George. "That scoundrel Captain Lazarev cheated you out of your share of the *Suvorov's* fur profits, didn't he?"

"That's it," said Esteban. "He said that you, as the agent of the Russian-American Company that chartered the Russian navy ship, had agreed to pay us an advance on these profits when he returned us here after the voyage from Alaska. You would then recoup the money when the *Suvorov* returned to St. Petersburg. He said it was not his fault that you had left the ship and that we had to find you to get paid. Either that or continue on the ship to St. Petersburg and make our claim there. We weren't about to do that. Do you remember the flogging of the clerk Krasilnikov?"

"Yes," said George. "How could I forget?"

"Well we witnessed more of the same on the *Suvorov* when it was sailing here out of Lima, Peru. Some of the crew objected to Lazarev's trading part of the fur there for items of cargo that would only benefit him…so he had them flogged. Rodrigo and I resolved to get ourselves off that ship as soon as we could and to stay off it. No amount of money would induce us to sail on it further to St. Petersburg, especially after we were back in our homeland. But now I've found you. I think of you as a friend despite our differences. I think of you as a fair man. I think you will give Rodrigo and me our money."

"You should know that I have, with Supercargo Molvo and Governor Baranov, sent to St. Petersburg documents of indictment against Captain Lazarev for his abusive actions and incompetence," said George. "I imagine that by now he is no longer a naval captain. He might even be in prison. I certainly hope he is. And it WAS his fault that I did not complete the voyage back to St. Petersburg with the *Suvorov*. He deliberately stranded me in Novo-Arkhangelsk and he knows it. But it is true that I agreed to pay you and Rodrigo an advance on the fur profits when you were returned here. The problem is that I don't know what those profits were and I'm not in a financial position just now to pay you in full. What I can do is to give you now what I can spare and promise to return through here…as such is our plan to do on Russian naval ships bound for Hawaii…and give you the rest then. Is that agreeable to you?"

Esteban looked at George seriously and spent a few moments in thought. "I think you are a man of your word, Dr. Schaeffer," he said. "So that is agreeable to me. How much can you give us now?"

As we are very soon leaving Rio, we will not need any more of our reis. I'll give you all the réis we have…600 réis, some in paper, some in coin."

"That will be satisfactory," agreed Esteban. "I will give Rodrigo his portion of that. When do you think you will be back here with the rest?"

"I think I'll be back before the end of the next 1819 year," answered George. "And when I return here, I will find you and pay you whatever you are owed." He extended his arm to shake Esteban's hand in agreement. Esteban smiled and shook his hand.

When George, Filip, and Grigorii were in the act of leaving the hotel for the ship *Natalia Petrovna*, their bags already sent on board, there occurred the difficult good-bye of Filip with Lucinda Arriaga, the Kaiserin Leopoldina's attendant. She appeared at the entrance of the hotel, as beautiful a young woman as they had seen, draped her arms around Filip's neck and began to kiss him on the face with a shameless vigor that embarrassed George, Grigorii and all others who saw it. Filip responded fitfully, separating himself slightly in a minute or so to ask George in Russian to "Tell her I promise to come back for her. Tell her."

George did his best in Portuguese to assure Lucinda that Filip would be coming back without fail to marry her and become her life's partner. "He loves you and promises to be back soon for you. It won't be long…just a few months. Surely you can wait that long. Your family members need that time to reconcile themselves to Filip as a husband. You and he will be together in a short time. Don't worry."

Lucinda was unconsoled. She obviously did not want Filip to leave at all. She told George, "You can let him stay. You don't need him. He's not your servant, after all. I need him to stay with me. I love him. We should be together now, right now."

This caused George to think a bit. He hadn't realized that in Lucinda's perception, HE was the obstacle to Filip's staying with her and advancing her marriage plans. But then he continued in Filip's behalf, saying, "No, he has to leave. It's his duty. He's sworn to accompany me back to St. Petersburg and he wouldn't feel right with himself if he did not. But he will be back. His promise is good and a return here is already in our plans. You'll be reunited in a short time. You have to let him go now."

Filip kissed Lucinda one last time and pushed her away from him. He and George and Grigorii got into the taxi carriage and the driver urged the horses onward. Lucinda remained on the hotel veranda waving forlornly in Filip's direction.

"That was hard," George said to Filip in the carriage. "Are you sure you want to go on with us? I could release you from your duty to accompany me to St. Petersburg now. I'm in no real danger anymore. Grigorii can take care of me easily. You could stay here with Lucinda."

Filip thought for a moment, then smiled at George and Grigorii and replied, "I'll go on with you. What would you do without me?"

The voyage to Rotterdam on the *Natalia Petrovna* with short stays in the Canary Islands, in Lisbon, and in London was an interesting and pleasant experience for George and especially for young Filip. But Grigorii Iskakov, despite George's best efforts at remedy, sickened severely during a brief becalming near the equator in the middle of the Atlantic Ocean. He went to sleep one night in his bunk after drinking one of George's herbal teas and in the morning he was found to have died in his sleep. George and Filip were saddened immensely by this, so had they come to love the old man. That evening George had Grigorii, wearing his fur-hat "crown," sewn into a weighted canvas bag and, accompanied by a reading from scripture, dropped over the side of the ship into the still sea.

Back in Europe:

In Lisbon, George posted a letter to Governor Aleksandr Baranov in Novo-Arkhangelsk. He thought that the letter would reach Alaska through Rio de Janeiro and Macau, the reverse of his own journey…but that it might be routed through Petro-Pavlovsk as well. He wrote:

"August 26 on your calendar, 1818

Sixth anniversary of the Battle of Borodino

Esteemed Friend and Governor Aleksandr Andreevich,

By now you have likely had Timofei Osipovich Tarakanov and the group of Russians and Aleuts I was forced to leave on O'ahu rescued and returned to you. I trust that Timofei, whose version of the matter you can trust, has acquainted you with all the facts of our efforts in the Hawai'ian islands. I assure you that, despite the obvious setbacks caused by our competition there, these efforts have not yet come to failure. I am now in Lisbon on my way back to Rotterdam and then to St. Petersburg. It is my plan to petition his Majesty the Tsar to send an armed naval fleet to the Hawai'ian islands and annex one or all of them by force, subduing Kamehameha and expelling the American and English pirates who advise him. When this is done your dream of having a provisioning outpost in those climes will be realized and Russia will become a powerful force in the Pacific. The Tsar will be most grateful to both of us for this and we will be able to retire in the wealth and peace we deserve.

When I was in Macau I made the acquaintance of an extraordinary man, Sir Anders Ljungstedt, who is the Swedish Consul there. It was Ljungstedt who helped me take back from the trecherous Captain Wadsworth the shipload of sandalwood he stole from the Company while on Kaua'i. By now you may have received the money from the sale of this sandalwood and an accounting of the matter from Consul Ljungstedt. You should know that I appointed him official agent of the Russian-American Company in Macau and he will, I am sure, be valuable to us in this capacity. You may rely upon him absolutely. He is acquainted as well with another agent of the Company who worked in Petro-Pavlovsk. This agent's name is Peter Dobell and you may know him. I understand that he is now in St. Petersburg advocating Russian annexation of land in the Hawai'ian islands or the Philippines for purposes of advancing Pacific trade. I can only hope that he has had success in advancing this argument, since it clearly supports my own argument that Russia should make a more forceful presence known in the cental Pacific…i.e. in Hawai'i.

I have heard from a former crewmember of the *Suvorov* that Captain Lazarev sold in Lima some of the fur cargo he took away from your base in the Pribilovs for trivialities. He had some of the company aboard who objected to this flogged. I can only think that he must have had quite a tax to pay for his sins when he returned to St. Petersburg. It included not only our mutual charges against him, but others as well from his own crew. Well, it serves him right.

I have the sad duty to inform you of the death of the Unalaska Toion Grigorii Iskakov, who was accompanying me and creole hunter Filip Osipov on our voyage. He took ill from some kind of stomach ailment and, on July 15, died while asleep in his bunk on our Russian ship *Natalia Petrovna.* We buried him with honors at sea in the Atlantic south of the Canary Islands. I think he was about seventy years of age. I know that he was a long-time friend of yours and that you know his family and can inform them of his death. Please tell them that as his commissioner I commend him for his constancy of support and his bravery.

Please pass on my highest regards to your son Antipatr and to all the members of my former company you may encounter, especially Timofei Tarakanov. In my prayers I ask the Lord to bless them, for their efforts in my service and in yours was superb.

With great respect and affection, I am yours sincerely,

Yegor Nikolaevich, RAK Commissioner and

Major George ("Jorge") Ritter von Schaeffer, now of the Brazilian Princess Leopoldina's personal guard."

In London, George was informed at the Russian embassy that Tsar Aleksandr was not in St. Petersburg at that time, but was visiting a number of other cities in northern Europe. He thought that he should try to arrange a meeting with the Tsar himself, but the embassy officials could not tell him exactly where the Tsar would be on any particular date. Aachen, Berlin, and Riga were on the Tsar's posted itinerary, but the order or dates of his stay in these cities was not precisely known to the embassy. George would have to attempt to intercept the Tsar in one of these cities and obtain a meeting with him. He told Filip that the Tsar's being in Europe was a fortuitous coincidence. He would not have to wait until arriving in St. Petersburg to talk to him, and getting an audience with him might be easier in Europe than it could be in Russia. They would, he said, leave the *Natalia Petrovna* in Rotterdam and make their way by coach to Aachen instead of staying on the ship as far as Riga. He went to see Captain Sinelnikov to tell him about this and request a refund of a portion of their prepaid passage money. Captain Sinelnikov assented to this request, even saying that he would regret parting with George and Filip earlier than he expected to. But George was elated, so optimistic was he about the prospects of success in their mission.

From Rotterdam, George and Filip set out by coach for Aachen, hoping to find the Tsar there. George remembered that it was near Rotterdam that Franz Leppich, the fugitive balloon-master murderer he had called a friend and associate in 1812, was born, and that it was in Aachen, called by the French Aix-la-Chappele, where Leppich had grown up. As he related to Filip the story of his strange acquaintance with Leppich, George could not help wondering if he might encounter the man again by some chance in the city he had called home. He wondered if Leppich might still have family there. He knew that Leppich's father had been a watchsmith in Aachen, and this fact gave him some small basis to make inquiries. But he would make these inquiries only in the most discrete and confidential ways. He was sure that he did not desire to meet Leppich face-to-face again.

In Aachen, George and Filip found a hotel room and spent a day walking around the city seeing the sights. In a German-language newspaper, George read an article about how the visiting Russian Tsar and his party were preparing to leave for Berlin. They were, the article said, occupying almost half of the city's most luxurious hotel and providing a real boon to local merchants and provisioners. A sketch of Tsar Aleksandr, captioned "The Conqueror of Napoleon," appeared in the newspaper. George was not used to seeing such illustrations in a newspaper and wondered about the technology that made it possible. The sketch made the Tsar look younger and more handsome than George remembered him. He was depicted in his full dress uniform, complete with a multitude of medals and awards.

The next morning George and Filip paid a visit to the hotel where the Tsar and his party were staying. Immediately they encountered armed Russian soldiers in the hotel lobby who were interrogating all unrecognized visitors and guarding the central staircase leading to the upstairs rooms. Some "unpleasant occurrence" had transpired...a failed attempt to abduct the Tsar, and the guards were clearly on edge. George approached their apparent commander and addressed him in Russian, saying, "I am Dr. Yegor Nikolaevich von Sheffer, a commissioner of the Tsar since the campaign for Moscow in 1812. I have important matters to report to him and would like to have an audience with him as soon as possible."

"His Majesty is not granting audiences now," the guard commander said "All his business here is now completed and he is moving on to Berlin. You will have to apply for an audience to see him there."

"How do I accomplish this?" asked George.

"You'll have to see the special secretary at the hotel registration desk."

George looked over to the registration desk and noticed a uniformed officer at the far end of the desk, apart from ordinary hotel operations. The man seemed to be without other petitioners, and so George, followed by Filip, approached him directly and stated his identity and his case for an audience with the Tsar.

"Please tell the Tsar that I am that same Dr. von Sheffer to whom he personally entrusted a secret balloon project in July of 1812, the same one his brother, the Grand Duke Konstantin, commended for developing a supply of laudanum for his armies, and the same one who has spent the past three years as an agent of the Russian-American Company advancing the Russian cause in the vast Pacific. Please ask if it might be possible for him to see me here in Aachen before he leaves for Berlin. The matter is important."

The uniformed secretary took quill in hand and wrote on a piece of paper an outline of what George was telling him. He recapitulated the relevant facts as he wrote them down, saying, "Your name is Dr. Yegor Nikolaevich von Sheffer, a Russian citizen with the rank of Collegiate Assessor, who was born in Germany…Commissioner of a balloon project in July of 1812…Developer of laudanum for the army…Russian-American Company agent in the Pacific ocean…has personally met both His Majesty and the Grand Duke Konstantin. And the audience is to concern the government's role in the Hawai'ian islands. Is that it?"

"That's it," said George. "Will you be able to present these facts to His Majesty?"

"Yes, I will," answered the secretary. "Come back to see me here tomorrow morning early and I will inform you about the possibility of an audience."

"Khorosho…Fine!" said George. "Uvidimsya zavtra…We'll see each other tomorrow."

George left the Tsar's hotel buoyed by his optimism. He told Filip, "I'm sure I'll be seeing the Tsar tomorrow. You will come with me and I will endeavor to get you admitted to the audience as well. Almost any knowledgeable person in the world would consider meeting Tsar Aleksandr of Russia a once-in-a-lifetime event…a historic opportunity. I would ask that you stay silent unless I ask you for confirmation of the facts I present."

"Don't worry. I will," said Filip.

Traces of Leppich:

The first citizen of Aachen George asked about a watch shop owned by a man named Leppich gave him the location of the shop. It was now owned by a man named Andersen who had once been the old man Leppich's apprentice. George and Filip went to the shop and entered it. Herr Andersen was alone in the shop, sitting behind a glass vitrine filled with a display of watches. He was a man in his late sixties, bald and heavy.

"Guten Tag," said George. "Are you the proprietor of this watch shop?"

"Yes, I am," said the man. "My name is Andersen…Fritz Andersen, and I've owned this shop for fifteen years. Are you interested in a watch?"

"Actually no," said George. "My name is Dr. George von Schaeffer. I am originally from Franconia, but I have been a commissioner of the Russian Tsar for the past several years."

"Oh yes," said Herr Andersen. "I've heard that the Tsar is visiting here. You must be here with him."

George did not deny that he was with the Tsar's party in Aachen, but continued, saying, "I am interested in the whereabouts of the son, Franz Leppich, of this shop's former owner. I made his acquaintance in Russia six years ago, but I've been out of contact with him since and would like to know where he is. Can you help me?"

"I don't think so," said Andersen. "I don't know where he is and haven't heard anything about him for five years or so. His mother has died and he has no family left here anymore, but I knew him when he was a boy. He was musically gifted and mechanically too. His father wanted him to take over this shop, but Franz was more ambitious. He went out in the world instead, inventing mechanical pianos and trying to make air balloons into weapons of war. He even tried to make one to kill Napoleon Bonaparte in Russia. But it didn't work, and he disappeared."

"I was one of the directors of his balloon project in Russia," said George. "It was a secret affair then. We called him 'Schmidt'."

"Yes, I've heard that too," said Herr Andersen. "My daughter Hannalore married one of Franz's closest friends and associates. She and her husband and son went to Russia with him. But her husband was killed there and now she's back here. You might ask her about Franz. She lives in the apartment above this shop."

"I would very much like to speak with her, Herr Andersen," said George. "Indeed I may have met her already. What was her husband's name?"

"Dieter…Dieter Schneider," was the answer.

"I did know Dieter Schneider in Russia," said George. "I remember his death well. It was in the explosion of our trial balloon in Mozhaisk. It was I, in fact, who spoke the words over his grave at Vorontsovo. I'm sure your daughter will remember this. Please let me speak with her."

Herr Andersen reached up over his head and tugged sharply on a sash that extended up through the shop ceiling. A muffled bell could be heard from above. In a few seconds the bell sounded again. "She'll be right down," said Andersen.

George turned to Filip and explained to him in Russian who it was they were about to meet. Filip said, "What an astonishing coincidence it is to find her here now. I hope you can find out from her what you want to know."

A door opened above a rear staircase in the shop and down walked a svelte and pretty dark-haired woman of about thirty, dressed in a white apron and followed by a blonde boy about nine years of age.

When his daughter and grandson got to the bottom of the stairs, Herr Andersen said, "Hannalore, there is a man here who wishes to speak with you. His name is…"

Hannalore, seeing George, finished her father's sentence. "…Dr. Schaeffer. Mein Gott, it's Dr. Schaeffer." She stepped quickly up to George and hugged him warmly, continuing, "I know him from Russia, father. He was in Moscow when we were there, and in Nizhnii Novgorod too. This is just such a surprise. I can't believe it."

George knew that if he had encountered the woman on the street he would not have recognized her. He did not know her that well. But seeing her now gave him a realization of her familiarity to him. He had indeed seen her before…at Dieter's grave, and queuing up with her baby son in arms for winter food aid from Barbara and the other women at the refugee camp in Nizhnii Novgorod. She had shared much of this very hard experience in life with him.

"Hannalore, I remember well what we went through together," George said. "Those were trying times indeed. To find you here in Aachen now with your father and your son is very pleasing to me, I assure you. You look so fine and happy. God has truly blessed you." He then introduced her to Filip, who just stood by silently enjoying this reunion vicariously.

"And this is little Fritz, my son," she said, introducing the boy. "You may recall him as a mere baby, but now he's such a big boy…almost grown." She reached over to the boy and tousled his unruly shock of light blonde hair. Then, to little Fritz, she said, "This man held you and examined you when you were a baby. He is a famous doctor. His wife Barbara was a great help to us when we were in danger of freezing and starving in a camp we lived in outside Nizhnii Novgorod. Can you shake his hand and tell him thanks?"

Little Fritz extended his hand to shake George's and said quietly, "Danke."

George did not specifically remember examining the boy, but replied, "It's nice to make your acquaintance now that you've grown, young fellow."

George and Hannalore spent the next hour in conversation renewing their acquaintance and elaborating on their respective paths to this extraordinary meeting. Hannalore's father engaged in the conversation as well, but little Fritz soon left them with his mother's permission to go outside and play with friends. Hannalore would occasionally direct her conversation to Filip as well. She realized that he could not understand what she was saying in German to the others, but she wanted to be polite. Filip, recognizing her consideration, would simply smile back at her and nod for her to continue.

After a while, George thought the time opportune to bring up the topic of Franz Leppich. "Do you know anything about what has happened to Franz Leppich, my dear?" he asked. "Have you heard from him?"

"No, I've heard nothing from him after he disappeared from Oranienbaum," Hannalore answered. "The St. Petersburg police interrogated me about him. And later some Russian soldiers asked me about him too. But I don't know where he is or how to find him. In truth I think that he is dead."

"Why do you think that?" asked George.

"Franz was a man who so stood out from the rest that he would be noticed and accounted for anywhere he happened to be," she said. "The very fact that he has remained invisible for so long now means that he is most likely dead and buried where he can't be found. Otherwise we would have heard of him in some other scheme or adventure by now. But that isn't the only reason."

"What do you mean?" asked George.

Hannalore, noticing that her father had removed himself temporarily from the conversation to begin taking the watches out of the display case, suddenly switched from German to Russian. Filip's attention was instantly seized by this.

"Frants, po-nastoiashchemu, otets malenkogo Fritsa…Franz is actually little Fritz's father," she confided. "Dieter always thought himself the father, and he named the boy Fritz after my father and his close friend, Fritz Bauman, who was also killed in Moscow. But I knew that Franz was actually the father, and he knew it too. We planned to tell my husband this, but we kept postponing the telling…until we didn't have to. But there is no possibility that Franz would not have by now reestablished contact with us if he could. He must be dead."

George and Filip looked at each other understandingly. "I see," said George. Then he repeated, "I see."

Later, after taking their leave of Herr Andersen and his daughter Hannalore Schneider at the watch shop, Filip asked George about Franz Leppich. "Didn't you tell me that Leppich seduced the wife of a Russian General friend of yours? And now we find out that he had his way with the wife of his friend Dieter Schneider. And both affairs left children too. You have to wonder how many other such affairs the man may have had. He must be quite a rake, eh? Do you think that he might really be dead?"

"I have to say that when I was working with the man, I did not notice that he gave any more than ordinary attention to women at all," said George. "He was completely consumed by his efforts to make the balloon project successful and to put an end to Napoleon, whom he hated. But he was a handsome fellow and very prepossessing, even charismatic, with abilities in music as well as mechanics. Women are clearly attracted to such men. And men too. The men in his company, including Dieter Schneider, would have followed him into hell. And I know that he had high regard for Dieter too."

"But he didn't respect him enough to stay away from his wife," said Filip.

"I guess not," agreed George. "He seemed to lack some kind of moral control when he was pressed by circumstances that hindered the realization of his desires. In that way he resembled Napoleon, the very man he so opposed. When the Vorontsovo estate manager Demidov became an obstacle to him, he killed the man."

"Yes, you've told me about that," said Filip. "But do you think that Hannalore Schneider is right about his being dead?"

"When I left there, Leppich's fate was to be the result of a contest between the St. Petersburg police and General Tormasov's army agents," said George. "I imagine that the army agents found him first and that he's dead. I think Hannalore is correct that he would otherwise have turned up again somewhere into public view."

"Do you think the General is right to have the man killed for seducing his wife and leaving her with child?" asked Filip.

"That's a very difficult question and I've thought a lot about it," said George. "You have to imagine what you might do if such a thing happened to you. In your case, what would you do if you discovered…the Lord perish the thought of it…that another man had gotten his way with Lucinda and left her with a child? Even if you could forgive her and take the child as your own, you might still want to find and kill the man who gave her this child, don't you think?"

"Yes, I do," said Filip. "And I have to admit that I do think about possibilities like that, especially since I am to be away from Lucinda for so long. She has such a passionate nature and is so attractive to other men. I can't help worrying. That's why I want to get back there as soon as I can. But what about you, Yegor? You have been away from your wife for five years. Don't you worry that something like that might have happened to her too?"

"The thought has entered my mind more than once, Filip," admitted George. "But Barbara and I were raised in religious families in a strict Catholic tradition. We believe that God is watching our behaviors on earth and that these behaviors affect our possibilities of getting into Heaven. This gives us an advantage in resisting temptation and achieving fidelity in our marriage. Also, in Moscow five years ago I was accepted into the world's oldest and largest fraternity, the brotherhood of freemasons. I had time to advance within it beyond the status of apprentice, and this means that I am one of the world's builders, resolved to improve the world for others in whatever ways I can. One of the ways I try to improve the world is to deal with everyone in my life on the basis of honesty. As a freemason and a builder of the world I never cheat anyone, and that especially includes my wife."

"Well, I can say that I don't remember you ever fornicating with any of the Hawai'ian wahines," said Filip, "…and sometimes they were very tempting, you have to admit. Certainly they were too tempting for me to resist. Surely you must have been tempted too, weren't you?"

"Once I thought Kamehameha's sacred queen Keōpuōlani wanted me to spend the night in her hale," related George. "And I was thinking about how she might be difficult to refuse, and about what Kamehameha would think about it if he found out. She was most attractive and even reminded me of my wife. But it turned out that she always planned to sleep elsewhere and I didn't have to refuse her. Apparently I misunderstood her intent. And later I rubbed noses with Kekaiha'akulou, the young wife of Kaumuali'i."

"Now there was a beauty," remembered Filip. "And a saucy one too."

"But nothing came of it," said George.

"And a good thing for you it didn 't," said Filip. "The savages might have strung you up for torture instead of Charles Fox-Bennick. That was a time, wasn't it? With Captain Wadsworth foaming at the mouth and leaping overboard and all? What a crazy day that was."

"Indeed it was," agreed George. "Indeed it was."

Later, before they turned in to sleep in their hotel, Filip asked George, "Yegor, when you married your wife Varvara, did you receive money from her family?"

"Yes I did," said George. "It's called a dowry. I didn't get it right away after our marriage, but it was a lot of money and it made our life together easier. Why do you ask?"

"Grigorii told me that Lucinda's family might give us a great deal of money if we marry. He said that such is the custom among his people too, especially if a man marries the daughter of a Toion. He said he had given his daughters' husbands fine baidarkas, spears, and many furs when they married."

"Well, I hope it isn't just the possibility of a dowry that makes you want to marry this Lucinda, Filip," said George. "A marriage can't be based on money. You'll both be unhappy if it is."

"I know," said Filip. "Lucinda and I will be happy with or without money. I'm sure of that."

"Hm-mm," mumbled George as he fell off to sleep.

Parting Company:

The next morning, George and Filip, dressed as finely as they were able, came to the Tsar's hotel and presented themselves to the uniformed special secretary at the registration desk.

"The Tsar will not see you here," the man told George. "You'll have to apply for an audience in Berlin…perhaps in Riga or even St. Petersburg."

"But did you explain my case to His Majesty? I can't believe he would not want to see me as soon as possible," protested George.

"I gave the Tsar all your information just as I wrote it down before you," said the officer. "But he does not want to see you here. He's going on to Berlin. You may apply to get an audience with him there, but I have to tell you that such an audience is not likely. His Majesty is not inclined to see you at all."

George was crushed by these words, but he persisted. "That is impossible," he said. "What I have to tell him is of vital importance to Russia. How do I apply for an audience in Berlin?"

"You'll have to travel to Berlin and see me again there," said the officer. "But if I were you, I wouldn't. I would go on to St. Petersburg and wait for his return there. Then I would try other means to gain an audience…some important contact, perhaps, or sponsor. That's the best advice I can give you. You'll have to decide."

George and Filip left the Tsar's Aachen hotel in a much worse mood than they had entered it. George was resolved to go to Berlin and try again to gain an audience with the Tsar while he was still in Europe. His opinion was that he should try again in Riga if Berlin did not work, and then again in St. Petersburg if that did not succeed. One way or another he WOULD see the Tsar. But Filip disagreed with this, saying that such persistence might irritate or anger the Tsar and predispose him against George's ideas no matter how well reasoned they might be. The better course, he said, was to go directly to St. Petersburg and take the matter to the Russian-American Company directors. "Let them figure out how to approach the government on it," he urged. For the first time in their acquaintance they quarreled, and this upset George.

The next day George and Filip were still in disagreement. Filip did not want to spend any more time than was absolutely essential in getting to St. Petersburg. Traveling to Berlin in what appeared to be a futile effort to speak to the Tsar would only prolong his journey back to Lucinda, he said.

"Yegor, a direct return to St. Petersburg is clearly the more sensible action to take in this situation," Filip maintained. "We could be there in a month at most and I could then be on my way back to Rio de Janeiro."

"So you don't plan to live with me and my family in St. Petersburg until we can arrange to return with an armed fleet, is that it?" asked George, measuring his young friend's intent. "Apparently you plan to turn around and sail back to Rio as soon as you get there."

"It is my intent to sail back as soon as you and I are together in St. Petersburg," stated Filip. "That is what I pledged to do…to see you back to St. Petersburg. I didn't pledge to stay there waiting for you to deal with the Company directors, the government, or the Tsar. That would take too long for me. I can start back on my own. Surely you would not begrudge me that, would you?"

George thought seriously about what Filip was saying. Then he proposed, "Filip, I think you should go directly to St. Petersburg from here and I will follow the Tsar to Berlin and to Riga if necessary. I will give you enough money for the journey and a report to transmit to Vasilii Grigorievich Shelikhov and the Company Directors. You could prepare the way for my return to them. And, of course, you will meet my wife Barbara and tell her that I am coming home to her and Inga as soon as I have had a chance to speak with the Tsar. When I arrive there then, I will help you arrange passage back to Rio de Janeiro immediately and pay your way."

"But I promised to be your bodyguard for the entire trip home," said Filip. "Can't you just give up on the Tsar here in Europe and we'll continue traveling together to St. Petersburg? The mission to return to the Pacific with a Russian navy fleet would not be compromised in any way, but might even be advanced."

"It is clear that I don't require a bodyguard anymore, Filip," insisted George. "And it is vitally important to the mission that I speak with the Tsar. My estimation is that it is precisely here in Europe where the best chances of doing this are. I release you from your duty to accompany me every step of the way. There is no doubt that I will now get there safely, thanks to you. I want to give you the opportunity to return to your beloved Lucinda as soon as possible. Please agree to go on to St. Petersburg on your own. I'll be there too as soon as I can, and both our purposes will be served. What do you say?"

Filip could only bow his head and say, "I agree, Yegor. I'll go on without you as you say."

Berlin, Riga, and an Old Friend:

In Berlin two weeks later, George was again unsuccessful in his attempt to gain an audience with the Tsar, but he felt that his persistence had apparently earned him some sympathy with the Tsar's traveling staff members so that he had hopes of seeing the Tsar in Riga. All he could do was to follow Tsar Aleksandr's intinerary and keep trying. Filip, he knew, would be in St. Petersburg in the first days of December of that year of 1818. Filip Osipov would be reporting to Vasilii Grigorievich Shelikhov and the Russian-American Company directors. He, Filip, would be meeting with his wife Barbara and seeing before he did his daughter Inga. How would Barbara and Inga understand why he had not rushed to stand first before them himself? He had given Filip a letter for Barbara explaining the reason for the delay in his return. And he had given Filip instruction in what he should say to Barbara. But would she understand the importance of his reasoning the way he did? He could only doubt it. It was all, he came to think, Tsar Aleksandr's fault. Why would the Tsar, who had once so readily given him an important commission, not now want to see him? Did the Tsar not trust his judgment of what was important? Or did the Tsar suspect his motives for other reasons? Was he still subject to investigation or, perhaps, arrest?

Portrait of Tsar Aleksandr I of Russia (12/23 December, 1777—19 November/1 December, 1825) from http://general-history.com/three-tsars-three-Alexanders.

In the lobby of the Tsar's Riga hotel quarters, George was informed that Tsar Aleksandr would still not see him, but that he had suggested that George take up his concerns with the "appropriate new administrators" back in St. Petersburg. George was very discouraged by this latest rebuff, even though it appeared that the Tsar had made a kind of response directed to him personally. And he had run out of traveling money, having given too large a portion of his remaining funds to Filip. He was forced to leave the cheaper hotel where he was staying. But, with nowhere else to go, he returned to the grand hotel where the Tsar was staying. In despair he went in and took a seat on a luxurious sofa in the hotel's waiting area. He was thinking that he had nowhere to stay the night and no way to pay for further travel. He wondered whether he might find a way to request some financial help from the Tsar. He might again, he thought, capture the attention of the Tsar's uniformed special secretary and ask if he, "a loyal commissioner of His Majesty since the campaign against Napoleon," might be granted the funds to pay for his travel back to St. Petersburg. But just then he spotted a trio of men entering the lobby, one of whom was familiar to him. It was Semyon Pavlovich Tarasov, his medical colleague and partner in the laudanum venture who had become the Tsar's personal physician. George called out to him, "Semyon Pavlovich, moi staryi drug...my old friend. How nice to see you here!"

Dr. Tarasov excused himself from the others and came over to George, saying, "Yegor Nikolaevich, what are you doing here in Riga? I heard you were somewhere in the Pacific Ocean?"

George and his old friend spent a half hour in conversation. Tarasov told George that Tsar Aleksandr was not "his old self." He had, Tarasov said, become strangely disengaged from the matters of his rule as if he "didn't want to be Tsar anymore." Tarasov was not surprised to hear that George had been unable to see him. "He doesn't really want to see anyone these days," he said. "He delegates everything he can to others."

When George explained his mission to Dr. Tarasov, Tarasov gave his opinion that George would have a better chance of success presenting his case to the new Minister of Foreign Affairs Nesselrode in St. Petersburg. At that point George could only agree. But how could he even get back to St. Petersburg without any money? He shared his financial dilemma with Tarasov too. And here his friend gave him the help he needed.

"I can request the Tsar's secretary to issue you a voucher for passage on any Russian ship," Tarasov said. "All you have to do is go down to the harbor and find one going to St. Petersburg."

That very evening, George, with the voucher in his possession, found a ship bound for St. Petersburg. It was that same *Natalia Petrovna* he and Filip had left two months before in Rotterdam. Captain Sinelnikov and mate van Gelder were happy to see him. They were leaving the next day for St. Petersburg to take on a cargo of hemp and honey bound for England. George would be home before Christmas. But what would await him there?

Chapter Nine-- Barbara in St. Petersburg

Friends:

In the months after George's departure in October of 1813, Barbara's mental well-being depended heavily upon her friends, the Tormasovs. General Aleksandr Petrovich Tormasov was a powerful man, a widely recognized hero and military advisor to the Tsar's command staff. His much-younger wife, Nadia Konstantinovna, was Barbara's closest confidante and ally in all things. After Nadia gave birth in February of 1814 to little "Varochka," named "Varvara Aleksandrovna" in Barbara's honor and with Aleksandr's patronymic, they became even closer, like sisters of nearly the same age and situation. As soon as Nadia recovered from the childbirth, she and Barbara began to make appearances at social and charitable functions, always accompanied by the formidable Aleksandr. They especially enjoyed concerts and ballets, attending all of them that they could. Both musically talented, they played many duets at home, with Barbara on the grand piano and Nadia on her violin, much to Aleksandr's pleasure.

Barbara and Nadia liked also to attend the literary salons to hear poetry readings. Gavriil Derzhavin and Vasilii Zhukovsky were favorites with them, and they stayed as guests in the salons until almost morning listening to robust old Derzhavin, whom George had once met at the Shelikhovs, read his lyric poetry and to the charming Zhukovsky read his romantic narrative poems. Aleksandr had less patience for the poetry, and would frequently slink off to one of the salon's hosts' separate rooms to sleep. There was one young poet, still in his mid teens and a recent graduate of the Tsar's Village Lyceum, who even irritated Aleksandr with his sharp epigrams ridiculing prominent citizens and with what Aleksandr called his "anti-autocracy prattle." This young poet's name was Aleksandr Sergeevich Pushkin. He was too brash for Aleksandr's taste. There was that story about his performance at the public final examination at the Lyceum. When the noted professors asked him questions about mathematics, science, and philosophy, he gave jocular answers in French and in Russian verse, spontaneously composed. But Derzhavin, who had been present, defended him when the Lyceum administrators tried to kick him out, saying, "Leave him in peace. He is a poet! Here is the one who will replace me!" And young Pushkin's physical appearance was a bit too strange for Aleksandr too. He was a short young man, with bristly black hair and a prominent flat nose and thick lips on a swarthy face. His maternal great grandfather had been an African black man, a human curiosity purchased in Constantinople, it was said, by Count Peter Tolstoi for Tsar Peter the Great in the late 17th century.

It was much harder for Barbara after the Tormasovs left. Aleksandr was asked to replace Moscow Governor-General Fyodor Rostopchin in the rebuilding of the burned older city. Rostopchin's intent was to retire from the Russian government service and travel with his wife and daughters to Paris, France, where he said he could offer the French "recuperative advice." General Tormasov had recovered most of his health and thought that this final service to his country might eventuate in his being given formal nobility with the same rank of Count that Rostopchin had always had. His position in Moscow began on September 1, 1814, but he commuted back and forth to St. Petersburg often because Nadia and Varochka were to remain with Barbara until he could make a grand restoration of their former residence in Moscow so that Nadia and Varochka would be able to join him in convenience and comfort. When the day of their parting finally came in January of 1815, Barbara and Nadia shed many tears and promised to stay in close touch by their letters.

A likeness of Barbara Schaeffer at 35 years in 1820

Barbara found her closest domestic support in the company of Inga's primary nanny, Lara. Lara was only a year or two younger than Barbara, and was very bright, despite her lack of a formal education. Barbara taught her to read and write in Russian at the same time as she taught Inga, and even began to give Lara piano lessons too. And she taught Lara as much German as she could, since Inga spoke German as well as Russian.

Lara was an attractive young woman, shapely and with long brunette tresses, but she never expressed any interest in men. She had one discolored eye that she was unable to control. It wobbled off on its own when she tried to direct its gaze in any direction, providing a distraction to those with whom she spoke. For that reason she was very shy in the presence of strangers. But little Inga, so bright and exuberant and effusive in her many enthusiasms, dearly loved Lara, who sang songs with her, told her Russian folktales, and praised her constantly. Gradually, Lara became the de-facto head of the staff of servants. She told the cooks what to prepare and when to prepare it. She gave orders to the stable hands and the coach driver, telling them when to have the carriage ready to transport Barbara where she told them to go. And she managed the laundresses and the house cleaners as well. Only the nominal house steward Porfirii and his wife Aniushka did not look to her for instructions, but they refrained from any conflicts with her out of respect.

Natalia Alekseevna Shelikhova, Barbara's senior neighbor, was always kind in her support of Barbara and always delighted to see little Inga. How she would exclaim, "Kakaia krasavitsa! Chudesnitsa!…What a beauty! What a miraculous one!" whenever she saw Inga, and would kiss Inga three times on the cheeks and hug her warmly and caress her hair. She liked to comb Inga's hair and to braid it, just clucking with joy as she did so. But Natalia was slipping ever more into senility. She would nod and say "Da, Da…Yes, yes" to whatever Barbara said to her, even if such a response was clearly inappropriate. Her son Vasilii Grigorievich, who, at a year younger than Barbara at twenty-seven years of age was now the principal director of the Russian-American Company in his mother's stead, was very supportive of Barbara and Inga. He was a small, but corpulent, man, who was prematurely balding. But he was very energetic, both in his work and in his family life. He told Barbara that he had to instruct the servants to watch his mother at all times, and that she was no longer allowed to go out by herself. Vasilii was responsible for much of Barbara's financial sustenance, making sure that George's Russian-American Company salary and his stock dividends were deposited into her account and that she received a generous cash allowance from it, which he personally delivered to her monthly. He often told Barbara that he considered himself "her brother," and that she could rely upon him for any needed aid.

As an extrordinarily beautiful woman, and a very wealthy woman without a husband in immediate attendance, Barbara often had to fend off male suitors. One of the first of these was Dr. Dmitrii Ivanovich Volkov, who was depositing George's share of the laudanum income—a quite large amount—into another bank account to which Barbara had access through Vasilii Shelikhov, who was the listed surrogate signatory, since Russian bank policy did not allow women direct power of withdrawal. Dr. Volkov was a bachelor of almost fifty years of age who thought that he should provide for Barbara in more ways than the mere financial. One week after Nadia and Varochka Tormasov left for Moscow in late January of 1815, he came to the mansion to propose an "arrangement of mutual convenience." Barbara was outraged by this proposal, exclaiming indignantly, "I can't believe you would make such an offer to me. How could you possibly think that I would stoop to such behavior? Get out of my house right now, and don't you ever come back."

Dr. Volkov, seeing Barbara's anger, strode quickly to the door, but replied, "You know I only wish to comfort you in this hard time with your husband Yegor Nikolaevich gone. In a few months or so, you may change your mind…and if you do…"

"I will not be changing my mind, Dr. Volkov," said Barbara as she shut the door after the man, "I will be faithful to my husband whether he is here or not."

She did not see Dr. Volkov personally after that, and he gave her no further trouble, but continued from an interpersonal distance to provide her with the accustomed substantial flow of income. She decided not to write George about Volkov's offer, not wanting to cause him worry.

Barbara was aware that the sum of money from the Russian-American Company and from the laudanum factory's increased revenues was growing well beyond her needs to enormous size in the accounts to which she had indirect access. Sometimes, but always through Vasilii Shelikhov, she would disburse large sums to charities for the sponsorship of soup kitchens for the poor or to the Catholic Church of St. Catherine of Alexandria on Nevskii Prospekt, that had just been taken over by the order of Dominicans. It was there that she planned to have Inga confirmed. Or she would purchase residential lots on the outskirts of the city, having them deeded as the Russian law required in her husband's name. But mostly she just let the money accumulate. George, she thought, would be very happy with their finances when he returned home.

The Karamzins, Nikolai and Ekaterina, had returned to their Ostafievo estate near Moscow. The estate had required significant reconstruction, and Nikolai was engaged in the continuing work on his History of the Russian State. After the Tormasovs were once again in Moscow also, Ekaterina Karamzina began to write letters to Barbara in which were included parts written by Nadia Tormasova. In one of these letters, written in December of 1815, Ekaterina informed Barbara about the death the previous month due to scarlet fever of their three-year-old daughter "Natasha."

"…My dear Varvara, I can't remember if you know that Nikolai and I lost our first baby together, the infant Katia soon after birth, so we named our next child, the daughter you know as Katia, to replace her. Then, as you know, we lost Andriushka in Nizhnii Novgorod. That was harder, because he was no longer an infant, but was our little boy, Nikolai's first hope for carrying on his name. So last year when we had another son, we named him also Andrei. And then, earlier this year, another son Aleksandr was born, restoring yet more joy to us. But now we've lost little Natasha to the scarlatina at the age of three. It's terribly difficult for both Sofia and Katia…the loving older sisters…and for their father Nikolai. He wrote a letter to his brother Vasilii and another to Aleksandr Turgenev saying that he can only look at everything now in an 'omnis morior' manner. He's very sad and depressed…inconsolable now."

64

Ekaterina Andreevna Karamzina (Kolyvanova/Viazemskaia…5/16 November,
1780—1851), from http://www.kljaksa.ru/

Nikolai Mikhailovich Karamzin (1/12 December, 1766—22 May/3 June, 1826),
portrait by Vasilii Tropinin (1776-1857) from:
http://en.wikipedia.org/wiki/Nikolay_Karamzin.

Nadia Tormasova had added lines in her hand to the letter.

"Varvara, you can't imagine how sad things are here after the death of little Natasha. I don't know how Ekaterina bears it. She busies herself taking care of the other children. She is even telling Nikolai that they will have still other children, that they won't quit trying. But Nikolai now says that they must leave Ostafievo. He is finishing the latest volume of his history and he has resolved to move them all to St. Petersburg at the first signs of spring. So you will be seeing them soon. Also, I understand that Ekaterina's younger stepbrother, Prince Pyotr Andreevich Viazemskii, has been reciting his poetry in the St. Petersburg salons. He is a friend of the young poet Pushkin. Have you heard him read? I miss attending such events with you and I miss our musical evenings and our duets. Aleksandr is working so hard here as Governor-General that it seems I rarely see him. When I am lonely, I console myself by thinking of how hard it must be for you, not having seen Yegor for so very long. Ekaterina and I speak of you often and we wish for you all the world's happiness. Please give hugs and kisses to Inga. Sometimes I think that Varochka misses her too. We must somehow get them together again in the future. They will be like sisters. I embrace you. Good-bye. Nadia."

Barbara broke into tears when she read this letter, so deeply did she sympathize with her friends. "Why was life so hard?" she asked herself. "Why does God deprive us of the ones we love?"

Peter Dobell:

Vasilii Grigorievich Shelikhov introduced Peter Dobell to Barbara on Saturday, February 5, 1814, at a royal charity ball in the grandiose Winter Palace where Barbara had attended the previous month's New Year's Ball. There was a large crowd of dignitaries, both foreign and native, there in attendance and all were dressed in their best formal attire. Barbara had gone to the ball together with Aleksandr Tormasov only, since Nadia was in bed at home recovering from the birth of daughter Varochka. But she separated from Aleksandr for a time to stand with Natalia Alekseevna Shelikhova while Natalia's son Vasilii circulated among the other guests. A few minutes later Vasilii brought this man back to meet his mother and Barbara. Vasilii explained that Peter Dobell was an agent of the Russian-American Company who had recently arrived in St. Petersburg after a harrowing journey across Siberia from Petropavlovsk at the end of the Kamchatka Peninsula north of Japan. He had traveled by dog sled, reindeer cart, and horse through Gizhiga, Okhotsk, Yakutsk, Irkutsk, Krasnoiarsk, and Perm. He was, Vasilii said, writing a book about his many adventures entitled Travels in Kamchatka and Siberia; with a Narrative of a Residence in China. The problem was that he was writing the work in English, since he was an "Irishman," and, although he spoke Russian passably well, formal written Russian was still relatively uncomfortable for him. Excerpts of his work were to be translated into Russian as he wrote and they would be published in St. Petersburg's popular journal, Son of the Fatherland.

Peter Dobell looked like what an "Irishman" was supposed to look like, Barbara thought. He was tall and well formed, with broad shoulders, muscular arms, and a narrow waist. Barbara guessed him to be in his late thirties, a bit older, she thought, than George. His face was speckled with light orange freckles and he had a thick head of very red hair. Even his eyebrows were light red in color and his smile, with straight white teeth, seemed to radiate a brightness into the already brightly illuminated palace hall.

"So you have been in China, Mr. Dobell?" asked Barbara to begin the conversation. She was dressed in a dark purple velvet gown and wore a spectacular diamond pendant around her neck. Her black hair was gathered at the back and held by a diamond-encrusted barrette.

A likeness of Peter Dobell (1775-1852) at 39 years in 1814

"I spent a decade there, my Lady," Dobell responded. "I lived in Macau, ran a tavern in Canton, and traded there in tea after I got my ship, the *Sylph*, four years ago."

"You have your own ship?"

"Yes, my Lady," said Dobell. "It's a small two-master, a brig of two-hundred tons about thirty meters in length."

"Where is it now?" Barbara asked.

"It's plying the Pacific out of Petropavlovsk," Dobell said. "I've loaned it under a lease agreement to the Russian-American Company while I am here advocating that the Russian navy establish provisioning outposts in the Philippines and in Hawai'i for the Russian-American Company's Alaska fur enterprise."

"Do you know that my husband is right now on a mission to provision the Company's settlement at Novo-Arkhangelsk?" said Barbara. "He's the surgeon on the navy ship *Suvorov* that left here four months ago."

"Vasilii Grigorievich has told me about him already. But what is his name again? I'm sorry that I have forgotten it."

"He is Dr. Yegor Nikolaevich von Sheffer," Barbara answered. "We came here to Russia together from Franconia in Germany, and lived for a time in Moscow. But we evacuated from Moscow just as Napoleon was occupying it and came here after a hard winter in Nizhnii Novgorod."

At this point, Aleksandr Tormasov came back from another room into the long windowed hall where he had left Barbara with Natalia and Vasilii. He had another man with him whom he introduced to the three of them as Levett Harris, "the first Consul to St. Petersburg from the United States of America." Consul Harris appeared to be about fifty years of age. He was particularly well dressed in his formal attire, with a stiffly starched white shirt contrasting sharply with his black waistcoat and a striking red-white-and-blue bow tie. He took Natalia Shelikhova's hand in his and, bowing gracefully to kiss it, said in Russian "Ochen' prijatno...Very pleased to meet you."

Vasilii Shelikhov, realizing that neither General Tormasov nor Consul Harris was acquainted with Peter Dobell, introduced him by saying, "This is Peter Dobell. He's an Irishman who's been sailing the China Sea. He spent the past year traveling overland across Siberia to get here from Petropavlovsk. He's one of our Russian-American Company agents."

Peter Dobell bowed politely and said in Russian to Aleksandr, "So, General Tormasov, these ladies tell me that you've just become the father of a new daughter. I congratulate you."

"Thank you," said Aleksandr. "Of course I'm a first-time father at a grandfather's age, but that only makes me happier about it. I'm very blessed."

Then Dobell, speaking in English, asked Consul Harris, "How long have you been a Minister of the United States?"

Harris corrected Peter by explaining, "I don't have the title 'Minister.' I was appointed by U.S. President Jefferson in 1803 and accepted here only as 'Consul' to the city of St. Petersburg. The United States has only been allowed a 'Minister' to the whole of Russia since President Madison's appointment five years ago of the former President Adams' son, John Quincy. So he is the 'Minister,' and I am merely the 'Consul'. But since I've been here eleven years, and he only five, I wind up helping him quite a bit. Because his Russian is not as good, he doesn't like to attend formal events…so that's why I'm here and he's not."

"I see," said Peter Dobell, discerning a bit of bitterness in Consul Harris's explanation of his status. "But I hope that both you and Minister Adams are at work to settle the war with England's King George. I can tell you that it is a real obstruction to sea trade all over the world. The American ships are forced to find sanctuary where they can and can't conduct any business at all. I've been told that Tsar Aleksandr and his Ministers of Foreign Affairs are urging the British allies to settle the matter. Are you involved in that effort?"

"Indeed we are," said Consul Harris. "In only a month or two Minister Adams will be leaving for Ghent in East Flanders to meet with the British delegation to negotiate a peace treaty. We hope to have this concluded by summer. When that happens, hopefully, maritime trade can resume." Then, changing topic, he said to Peter, "Do you know that you speak English with an American accent? You don't sound to me like an Irishman at all. I'm from the city of Philadelphia myself and from your speech I would swear you were a close neighbor…that is, not a Virginian like President Jefferson, or a Massachusetts man like Minister Adams, but an actual Philadelphian. It's remarkable."

Peter seemed rattled by this observation, and responded by saying, "Well, I have spent some time in Philadelphia. I was courting a young woman there and, trying to impress her parents, I imitated their manner of speaking. But I think that out of consideration for the others here we should keep to speaking in Russian."

Consul Harris gave a glance to the others around him and quickly agreed, saying in Russian, "Konechno…Of course, we must only speak in Russian so that everyone can understand us."

Aleksandr Tormasov then asked in Russian, "How did you come to live in China, Gospodin…Mr. Dobell?"

Peter answered, "How did I come to live in China? I traveled there on a tea ship in 1798 and then returned there on another tea ship in 1803. But that time I didn't sail back home, but stayed in China until 1812. I was involved in the tea trade there, at first for others and then for myself after I acquired a ship of my own. But now I have the ship leased to the Russian-American Company and have become one of their agents here. My purpose is to propose that Tsar Aleksandr annex strategic territory in the Pacific to serve as provisioning and trading centers for the Company and for Russia itself."

This stated purpose definitely raised Consul Harris's level of interest, and he asked, "Just what territory in the Pacific do you think Russia should annex?"

Peter answered matter-of-factly, "I think Russia should annex territory in the Philippines or in the Hawai'ian Islands…either or both. The problems of doing so would be small, in my opinion, and the advantage of doing so would be great."

"What about the claims of Spain on the Philippines, or of England on the Hawai'ian Islands?" asked Harris.

"Spain isn't in a position to contest a Russian claim to some island or two in the giant Philippine archipelago," said Peter. "And King George of England has not approved Captain Vancouver's idea of claiming the Hawai'ian Islands...so that means there is no claim. A few Russian navy ships could easily make one, however, and the matter would be settled. British, Spanish, and American ships...and French too, if they have any left...would then be paying harbor fees and taxes to Russia in order to use the only land in half a world of ocean. The claim would result in future profits beyond our current dreams."

"Is that what you plan to tell Tsar Aleksandr?" asked Harris.

"Indeed it is," answered Peter. "But, of course, it now looks like I'll have to chase him into Europe to do it. I understand he's just now leading the Russian army into France."

"God be praised," interjected Natalia Shelikhova.

"And he'll lead them down the Champs-Elysées in Paris," said General Tormasov proudly. "And what a blessed day that will be...amen."

Consul Levett Harris nodded affirmatively to this, then said to Peter Dobell, "I would like to introduce you to Minister Adams. I'm sure he would like to hear your ideas about Russia's annexations of territory in the Pacific. Would you permit me to arrange a meeting?"

"Yes," said Peter. "I'd like to meet Minister Adams. When would it be?"

"I'll ask Minister Adams if he and his wife Louisa could receive you for the mid-day meal on Monday, two days hence," said Harris. "If that idea is acceptable to him, I will send a courier to inform you. Where are you staying?"

"I'm staying at the Hotel de Londres," answered Peter. "And if I'm not in, just have the courier leave word for me at the reception desk. And, of course, I'll need to know where to go."

"The Minister and his family and staff have quarters in the nearby Hotel de l'Europe...the Evropeiskaya...on Nevskii. Do you know where it is?"

"I can find it," said Peter. "Just let me know."

On Monday, February 7th, Peter Dobell was the luncheon guest in the dining room of the Hotel de l'Europe of United States Minister to Russia John Quincy Adams and his wife Louisa. Consul Levett Harris had met Peter in the hotel reception area so that he could escort Peter into the dining room and introduce him...then he excused himself and left. John Quincy had returned from walking his young son Charles Francis to school. He was a slightly portly man of less-than-average size, forty-one years of age. He had a bald front pate, framed by reddish brown patches of hair above his ears and around the back of his head, and he had a matched set of whiskers extending from his sideburns down his face almost to his chin on both sides. His wife Louisa was a pleasant-looking woman, with brown eyes, though very pale of skin, and with brunette hair arranged in fringing ringlets that hid her ears from view.

A portrait of John Quincy Adams (11 July, 1767—23 February, 1848) in 1818 by Gilbert Stuart (1755-1828), from :
http://en.wikipedia.org/wiki/File:John_Quincy_Adams_by_Gilbert_Stuart_1818

After the initial introduction and Consul Harris's departure, Minister Adams asked Peter in English, "Did you walk here from your hotel, Mr. Dobell?"

"Yes, I did," answered Peter. "It isn't far enough to justify paying for a ride."

"That's very sensible," commented Adams. "But I simply like to walk. I walk almost everywhere, just for the exercise…even if it's cold or wet. I keep a record in my daily diary of the time it takes me to get to diverse places. I know, for example, that it takes me precisely thirteen minutes to walk from here to the Hotel de Londres where you are staying. Now you, with your longer legs, can probably make it faster…ten minutes, I would say. Do you agree?"

Peter thought for a second, then agreed, "Yes, I would say it took me ten minutes to walk here."

"Tsar Aleksandr also likes to walk," said Minister Adams. "And he often does so alone, without guards or servants or anybody at all. Of course he's now chasing Napoleon Bonaparte and his army back into France. But when he was here, we would occasionally meet and walk together. I feel that I've gotten to know him quite well in the course of our walks together. We speak mostly of ordinary things…history, science, art…even pets… I can tell you that he is a complex man…at once rational and yet very superstitious, ruled by both thought and notion. But what he wants most now, after the millions of dead are buried and memorialized, is simply to see the whole world just get along, to proceed in some vaguely defined state of harmony, rejecting any further interactions of force. He speaks of bringing about a 'Holy Alliance,' including all the European powers in a kind of borderless union. I would venture to say that he will now reject anyone's proposal that Russia annex anyone else's territory. I can predict that he will not even make territorial claims in Europe, where his armies are now disestablishing Napoleon's dominion. You have no chance of convincing him to send Russian naval ships to the Pacific to make any such remote territorial claims, no matter the commercial advantages of doing so. You're wasting your time."

Peter marveled at the abrupt directness of this statement by John Quincy Adams. "It's my time," was all he could say, letting the Minister know that he would not be deterred from trying.

"Now that we've gotten that unpleasant matter out of the way, let's eat," said John Quincy. "Louisa has ordered such a nice meal for us."

The meal was a tasty fish soup accompanied by Russian black bread and slices of hard cheese. As they ate, Louisa asked, "Are you married, Mr. Dobell?"

"No, Madame, I'm not married," he said. "I guess I've not yet met the right woman."

"I'm sure the right one will come along," said Louisa. "John Quincy and I have been married seventeen years now and are quite happy, aren't we, dear?"

John Quincy could only agree with an "indeed we are, Mrs Adams" as he dipped some of the bread into his soup.

"Do you have any children?" asked Peter.

"Yes, we do," said Louisa. "Our son Charles Francis is with us here and is a constant source of delight to us and to everyone else. Even the Tsar's family agrees that he's a special little boy. You should have heard their cheers when we brought him to the November Tsar's Children's Charity Ball dressed as an American Indian with a feathered head-dress and carrying a bow and a quiver of arrows. All the Grand Duchesses and the royal children dote on him."

"Is he an only child, then?" asked Peter.

"No," answered Louisa, saddening. "We have two older sons, George and John, living with family in Massachusetts. We haven't seen them in four years.

And we had a daughter Louisa, my own namesake and my joy, born to us here after several unsuccessful pregnancies. But a fever took her to heaven after only one year. That was two years ago and I still weep to think of it. Life is hard…and harder still, I sometimes think, here in St. Petersburg. But ours is a life of service, and we can only hope that someday, when we are together in heaven with little Louisa, our people will be grateful for our service to them.”

“Well put, my dear,” said John Quincy. “Very well put.”

Peter asked John Quincy, “How long have you been a Minister of the United States?”

John Quincy replied, “For twenty years. I was previously the United States Minister to the Netherlands, then to Portugal, and then to Prussia. I’ve been here in St. Petersburg as Ambassador since 1809. But I was here previously as a teenaged youth. In 1781 I accompanied plenipotentiary Francis Dana to the court of Catherine the Great and had quite a memorable visit.”

“So you’ve seen a lot then,” said Dobell.

“Indeed I have,” answered Adams, and then he repeated, “Indeed I have.”

Louisa said very little more during the meal. But John Quincy asked Peter, “So you’ve captained a ship in Chinese waters?”

“Yes, I have,” said Dobell.

“Did you ever encounter pirates? I’ve heard that the Chinese seas are rife with pirates.”

“Indeed I have had to deal with pirates in the Chinese seas, Minister Adams,” replied Dobell, “They were a constant problem for us there. In 1809, the Chinese pirates of the notorious Admiral Apo-tsy took the ship *Atahualpa* by force, slaughtering its crew and holding its captain, my own sister Ruth’s son, captive, so that both he and the ship had to be ransomed. In 1812, my own ship, the *Sylph,* was boarded by pirates under the command of the woman Ching Shih.”

“The pirates were commanded by a woman?” asked John Quincy. “What did you do?”

“After her pirates had subdued my crew, killing two of my best men, she made the mistake of coming on board herself. Feigning that I had been seriously injured, I managed to seize her by the throat and threatened to run her through with a sword if she and her men did not leave my ship,” said Peter.

“Did they then leave the ship?”

“Yes, they did, thank God,” said Peter.

“I’ve been told that you are writing a book and that excerpts from it are to be published in the Russian journals. Is that one of the stories you are writing in your book?” asked John Quincy.

“Indeed it is,” answered Peter.

"Well, it's quite a story, all right," observed John Quincy, and then he repeated, "It's quite a story indeed."   "

Peter Dobell soon had several invitations to reside during his stay in St. Petersburg with members of the Russian-American Company Board of Directors. Venedikt Venediktovich and Anna Maria Germannovna Kramer were the first to invite him, a result of the fact that Venedikt Kramer, very facile in English, had some private commercial dealings with Consul Levett Harris, who told him that Peter was staying in a single room of the Hotel de Londres and might appreciate more space and amenities as Company agent. The Shelikhovs also invited him, but, after much discussion among these parties, it was decided that he would move in as a guest with Mikhail Matveevich and Avdotia Grigorievna Buldakov. Mikhail was one of the original members of the Russian-American Company's board of directors, a one-time rival of Nikolai Petrovich Rezanov for control of the Company after the death of Grigorii Shelikhov, the founder. Mikhail had married Grigorii and Natalia's older daughter Avdotia, while Nikolai had married the younger daughter Anna. But Anna had died very young in 1802, leaving the children Pyotr and Olga with husband Nikolai, and, after his death four years later, with their grandmother Natalia and their Uncle Vasilii. Despite his senior status, Mikhail Buldakov had become reconciled to first Natalia's and now Vasilii's leadership of the Company. He and Avdotia were frequent visitors at the Shelikhov mansion on Nevskii Prospekt, and Peter Dobell began to come with them. For this reason, Barbara, who lived next door and frequently visited Natalia and Vasilii also, had occasion to see Peter Dobell and to talk with him numerous times in the next several months. She came to like him, being impressed, she told Aleksandr and Nadia, with the way he related to the children, not only thirteen-year-old Petya and eleven-year-old Olga, but also with Inga. Inga went right to him without reservation, and laughed and laughed as he would set her on his knee to hold his hands as reins and "ride a horsey to Dublin town."

One day during the late summer of 1814, not long before Aleksandr Tormasov left to take up the Governor-General's post in Moscow, he told Barbara that he had learned some "interesting facts" about Peter Dobell that he thought she should know.

"You might have heard that United States Minister John Quincy Adams left St. Petersburg in late April for Europe to help negotiate a settlement to the war between his country and Great Britain. But as it turns out, he had several encounters with Peter Dobell before he left and became quite curious about Dobell and his purposes here. So he made inquiries and drafted a report on the man."

"Minister Adams from the United States made a report on Peter?" Barbara asked, astonished.

74

General Aleksandr Petrovich Tormasov (11 August, 1752—13 November, 1819) in a portrait by George Dawe (1781-1829) in the "Military Gallery" of St. Petersburg's Winter Palace, from
http://en.wikipedia.org/wiki/Alexander_Tormasov.

"Yes, he did," answered Aleksandr, "And I've had it translated and read to me. This report says that Peter is not an 'Irishman' at all. He was born and raised in the United States in a place called Bucks County in the State of Pennsylvania. He was a soldier there in the Bucks County Dragoons where he won decorations for his ability at fisticuffs, horsemanship, and marksmanship. His gift for winning fights subsequently attracted the attention of one of the richest men in the United States, Stephen Girard of Philadelphia, who employed him despite his youth as a kind of guard and agent. It was on a ship of Girard's that Dobell first sailed to China."

Barbara was perplexed to hear that Peter Dobell was not an Irishman, as he had been introduced to them. "Why would Minister Adams have some report made about Peter?" she asked.

"You know that Peter Dobell is advocating to the Tsar and government ministers here that Russia become more active in the Pacific, that we establish outposts in Hawai'i and the Philippines to help develop Russian-American Company, and therefore Russian, interests on the northwest coast of North

America," Aleksandr related. "Minister Adams sees that as a potential threat to United States' interests. His view is that Russian development as far south as Spanish California will conflict with the United States' own plans for expansion there after consolidation of their Louisiana Purchase. So he decided to make some inquiries about Peter's background and his activities."

"How did he do that?" Barbara asked.

"He just posted a few letters back home to some of his associates in United States political circles and waited for their responses. He had little difficulty discovering, for example, that in 1800 his employer Stephen Girard requested that the United States' current President James Madison, who was then their Secretary of State, appoint Peter Dobell the United States' Commercial Consul to Bourdeau, France."

Barbara was impressed by this, saying, "Peter was a Consul to Bourdeau France for the United States' government?"

"Well, he was appointed to that office," related Aleksandr, "But for some reason Peter did not long serve in that capacity. Instead he disassociated himself from Stephen Girard and returned to China, where he became wealthy enough in his own right to purchase the ship *Sylph*. The ship was previously registered in New York to the Pacific Fur Company owned by another of the United States' wealthiest men, John Jacob Astor. And do you remember him telling about how his sister's son was the captain of the *Atahualpa* and had to be ransomed from pirate captivity? Well, the story was true, but the ransom was paid by the United States' Consul to Canton, Benjamin Wilcocks. Interesting, isn't it, what details he left out of his story."

"All that does not discredit Peter," Barbara said. "But I don't understand why he would lead us to believe he is an Irishman."

"Minister Adams says that his wealth in the China trade is not limited to tea," Aleksandr continued. "He was the first, on his *Sylph*, to smuggle opium directly from Turkey to China, and now that a large market for opium is being created there, he instructs others in how to avoid Chinese regulations against its import. During the on-going war between England and the United States, the British navy ships are seizing all United States' ships in the Pacific, so Peter's trade on the *Sylph* was threatened. He avoided this threat by disguising the *Sylph's* ownership by flying a Russian flag on it and claiming to be Irish. He'd rather continue business as usual than see his ship taken by the British, and this is his strategy for doing so. It might not be patriotic, but it is clever."

"You know that a large share of Yegor's wealth derives from the importation here of Turkish opium," said Barbara after a few moments of thought. "So I can't fault Peter Dobell with bringing Turkish opium into China. Opium clearly has both positive and negative uses. Peter can't be blamed for what the Chinese do with it, can he?"

"Not under our law he can't," answered Aleksandr. "And I suppose the Chinese laws don't mean much to him, especially now that he's here. I only tell you this for your own protection. I believe that you've come to like Peter Dobell and to trust him. Indeed I have come to like him myself, as have the Shelikhovs. But as a man, a soldier, and a mason, I believe that human relationships should be based upon honesty, and Peter Dobell has not begun his relationship with us on an honest basis."

"What should we do about this?" Barbara asked. "Are you going to tell all this to Natalia and Vasilii?"

"I have no doubt that the American Consul Levett Harris will be sure to tell Vasilii about it as soon as he can, thinking to discredit Peter to the Company directors," said Aleksandr. "Like Minister Adams, Harris does represent the United States here, you know. And I suspect he would like to be named the Minister here, succeeding John Quincy Adams."

"Yes, of course you are right," replied Barbara. "The Shelikhovs deserve to know the truth about him and decide for themselves whether his advice to them should be trusted. And that applies to me too. The next time I see Peter Dobell, I will ask him directly what he has to say about all this."

The next time Barbara had the opportunity to speak to Peter Dobell was at a public auction of royal horses and carriages arranged in November of 1814 under the auspices of Tsar Aleksandr's younger brother, the Grand Duke Nikolai Pavlovich. Barbara was interested in both horses and carriages, wanting to bring the quality of her estate's means of transportation up to the highest levels. Also, the proceeds of the auction were to benefit an orphanage to which Barbara had donated previously. Barbara went to the auction with Vasilii Shelikhov, driven by their coachman in a fine white sleigh. When they arrived at the auction site, Barbara soon noticed that the Kramers, the Buldakovs and Peter Dobell were also in attendance. Avdotia Buldakova called out to Vasilii and Barbara to join them in an inspection of the horses and carriages to be sold. Vasilii and Mikhail had gone through the process of registering as eligible bidders, since only registered male citizens were legally eligible to bid.

"We are not really very expert judges of horses, Varvara," Avdotia said. "And these horses are the ones the Grand Duke has selected to cull from his own stables. They may be old or sick, or lame, or may have other problems we can't easily detect. That's why we've asked Peter to come here with us. He knows a great deal about horses. Someone in his family, an uncle I think he said, owned a world-famous racehorse sire named *Messenger.* With his advice, we may be able to pick a gem from the rubble."

Barbara had already spoken at length with Vasilii Shelikhov about Peter Dobell's hiding from them his true background. Aleksandr Tormasov, who was then in Moscow, was correct that the United States' Consul Levett Harris had shown a detailed report about Peter Dobell to Vasilii, to Venedikt Kramer, and to Mikhail Buldakov of the Russian-American Company, as well as to a number of Russian government ministers and even the Grand Dukes. But Vasilii was surprisingly undisturbed by the report. The only aspect of it that varied from the truth, as he saw it, was Dobell's claiming to be an Irishman. And he didn't really care about that, saying "Yankee, Irishman, Chinaman...what does it matter what he calls himself if his advice to us is good? He may have left some details out, but his stories are apparently true, aren't they?"

For a time during the inspection of the well-stabled horses, Barbara did not come close enough to Peter Dobell to engage him in conversation. But soon Peter called the attention of the group to a horse he thought was promising.

"Do you notice the color of this horse's coat?" he asked. "Even with its winter shag it shows a fine bright black. Its confirmation is superb, its teeth are all there, straight and unmarred. This is definitely a mare worthy of purchase, whether for transportation or for breeding. This is the best one...number 29 in lot 3. Make a note of it. It'll bring the orphanage plenty."

But Mikhail Buldakov said "I'm looking for a stallion," and Vasilii said "I came looking to buy another carriage...a two-seat surrey for my mother."

"What about you, Varvara?" asked Peter. "It's a horse one could be proud of, I assure you. In fact, it reminds me of you."

"This last comment jarred Barbara. "How so?" she asked.

Peter smiled as he thought a moment, then he answered, "You and the horse are both female, both of you have the same color hair, the same straight bright teeth, the same regal bearing and sense of confidant dignity. The mare has been given the number 29. Isn't that now your age? And her lot number is three. Aren't there three people in your family? You and this horse are both numbered 29 among three. This just has to be the horse for you."

Vasilii, Venedikt, and Mikhail laughed at this surprising analysis, whereas the women, Anna Maria and Avdotia, gasped in vicarious embarrassment, covering their mouths with their hands.

"Varvara Wolfgangovna, you'll surely have to bid on this one," said Vasilii.

"I might consider asking you to bid on it for me, Vasilii, if the advice hadn't come from an American who claimed to be an Irishman," Barbara snapped.

Peter Dobell's smile disappeared. "Please let me tell you all something important," he said. "I'm very sorry now that I allowed you people to think that I am an Irishman. I started saying I was an Irishman in China because of the war between England and the United States so that I could stay in business. It was a simple convenience based upon the fact that many of my ancestors were Irishmen and therefore I looked like an Irishman. And so it was as an 'Irishman' that I first became known to Russian navy Captain Ivan Fyodorovich Kruzenshtern, and to all of your Russian-American Company officials in Petropavlovsk. Many subsequent Russians I met had already heard that I was an Irishman, and I didn't see the sense of telling them otherwise and thus discrediting the good people they had heard it from. In time I stopped directly telling people I was an Irishman, but I continued to let them believe it, never correcting them. Now I must apologize to you, and tell you that which you already know, that I am not an Irishman. I am an American, born and raised in Philadelphia. As a schoolboy there I marched in the funeral procession of Benjamin Franklin. I survived the yellow fever epidemic there in 1793, and served in the Pennsylvania militia as a Bucks County Dragoon."

Barbara could see that Peter was sincere in his apology. "I just like to have honest relationships with all my acquaintances," she said. "So I accept your apology." Then, she said after a delay of two or three seconds, "And I'll ask Vasilii to bid for me on the mare you suggest. Thank you."

"You're very welcome, my dear Varvara," answered Peter, "I assure you that you are the person I most regretted deceiving about my being an Irishman. I really want to be your friend."

Barbara looked around at the faces of Anna Maria and Venedikt, Avdotia and Mikhail, and Vasilii. They all seemed to be awaiting her response.

"Since I forgive you, my friend you can definitely be," she said to Peter. "But," she added in caution, "that's all."

"Dogovorilis...Agreed," said Peter. "Now let's go to the auction pavilion. It's warmer there and they have the samovars for tea. The bidding is about to start."

An hour later the horses of lot 3 were being auctioned. When the mare number 29 came up for bid, the auctioneer began at a higher-than-usual price...50 rubles. Vasilii was the first bidder. But the mare had attracted the attention of other bidders too, and quickly the bidding passed 100 rubles, then 200.

"Now we'll see some of the others drop out," observed Venedikt. "Stay in it, Varvara. It's all for charity, in any case."

Barbara nodded affirmatively at Vasilii and he continued bidding competitively. The amounts hit 300 rubles, and soon thereafter 400. It was now apparent that there were only two other bidders left in the contest. Then, at 500 rubles, one of these dropped out and there was only one competing bidder left. Barbara could easily see who it was, but she did not know him. He was a stocky man with thick and curly black hair. He had a prominent jawline and thick dark eyebrows. He was surrounded by several male friends and was obviously enjoying himself. When he made his bids, his friends would congratulate him and slap him on the back, and he would laugh.

Barbara asked Avdotia, "Do you know who he is?"

"Yes, I know who he is," she answered. "He's Count Fyodor Ivanovich Tolstoi—the 'American'."

"How could a Count Tolstoi be an American?" Barbara asked.

A sketch by Russian Poet Aleksandr Sergeevich Pushkin (1799-1837) of his much-storied acquaintance, Fyodor Ivanovich Tolstoi (aka "The American," 6/17 February, 1782--23 October/5 November, 1846) from http://en.wikipedia.org/wiki/Fyodor_Ivanovich_Tolstoy or from the relation from the Russian website of the Tolstoy Family estate at Kologriv at http://kologriv.com/index.php?options=content&task=views&id=20&Itemid=10

"He isn't really an American," Avdotia explained. "He is only called the 'American' as a sobriquet or nickname. He was with my brother-in-law Nikolai Rezanov on the *Nadezhda* during Russia's first circumnavigation ten years ago. He was actually dismissed from the crew in Petropavlovsk and had to make his way back overland through Siberia...just like Peter Dobell, but for other reasons. He now tells people that Nikolai had him marooned on one of 'America's' Aleutian islands where he almost starved to death. He says he survived by eating a monkey companion that was marooned with him, and that the Aleut people on this island asked him to become their king."

"So I'm bidding against a liar and a cannibal, is that it?" asked Barbara with a smile.

"Yes," said Avdotia. "He's a very unpleasant person...but a very rich one. His family owns thousands of serfs on their estates."

The bidding went back and forth between Count Tolstoi and Vasilii Shelikhov, acting on Barbara's behalf. Barbara was focusing her attention on Vasilii, so she did not notice that Peter Dobell, Venedikt Kramer, and Mikhail Buldakov had left their adjacent seats and circulated around to the side of the pavilion where the Count Tolstoi and his friends were seated.

"725 rubles," called out the Count Tolstoi, responding to Vasilii's previous bid of 700 rubles. The auctioneer shouted out the standing amount, and asked "Is that all now? Is that all?"

Barbara nodded to Vasilii again and he called out,"750!"

Count Tolstoi did not immediately respond to this bid. He seemed to be discussing the matter with a few of his companions. The auctioneer looked in his direction and shouted out to him "Is that all now? Is that all?"

Still Count Tolstoi did not respond. The auctioneer shouted out the final call, "750 rubles going once. 750 rubles going twice. SOLD for 750 rubles to the honorable Vasilii Shelikhov! And what a fine donation to our beneficiary orphanage. The Grand Duke Nikolai has informed us that he will present this horse's documents to the new owner personally. Congratulations, Mr. Shelikhov. Please come to the registration table for the presentation."

The auction then continued to sell other horses of lot 3, but Vasilii, Avdotia, and Barbara all made their way to the registration table where the Grand Duke Nikolai and several other men were waiting. The Grand Duke was a tall slender young man of about twenty years of age. He was wearing a military uniform festooned with orders and decorations and he wore a feather-trimmed formal officer's hat. He knew Vasilii and, as Vasilii approached, he extended his hand and said, "Thanks and congratulations to you, Vasilii Grigorievich! This is Director Matvei Maksimovich Shapkov of St. Andrei's Orphanage. He has some papers for you to sign, and the mare will be yours. I think you have purchased the very best horse being sold here today."

But Vasilii quickly introduced Barbara to the Grand Duke, saying, "Your Excellency, as a registered bidder I was acting upon the instructions of another. This is Varvara Wolfgangovna von Sheffer, my neighbor and friend. It is she who will actually purchase the mare in her husband's name."

The Grand Duke Nikolai looked at Barbara, and said warmly, "Then I congratulate you, Madame von Sheffer, and thank you for your substantial contribution to St. Andrei's Orphanage. Director Shapkov has the papers for signature."

"Thank you, Your Excellency," said Barbara, curtsying to the Grand Duke, who then took her hand in his and bowed to take it to his lips. As he did this, she said, "I've made previous donations to St. Andrei's Orphanage and think it's a good cause. You will surely be blessed for your patronage of it."

Grand Duke Nicholas Pavlovich Romanov (25 June/6 July, 1796—18 February/2 March, 1855…Tsar Nicholas I of Russia from 1825-1855), in his portrait as a young soldier by George Dawe (1781-1829) from: http://www.hermitagemuseum.org.

"And who is your husband, Madame?" the Grand Duke asked. "Do I know him?"

"He is Dr. Yegor Nikolaevich von Sheffer, Your Excellency," Barbara answered. "He was the Tsar's commissioner on the secret balloon project against Napoleon and once received a commendation from your brother, the Grand Duke Konstantin, for his work to manufacture laudanum for the military. He's now the ship's surgeon on the *Suvorov* on a journey around the world to provision the Russian-American Company outpost at Novo-Arkhangelsk in Alaska."

Looking more closely at Barbara, the Grand Duke responded, "How very interesting, my dear. When will your husband return?"

"He's been gone thirteen months and is scheduled to be away another eleven months or so. The voyage was planned to take two years."

"Well, we all wish him a prompt and safe return," said the Grand Duke. "And if there is any way I can be of help to you in the meantime, please let me know."

"I will, Your Excellency," said Barbara. "And I thank you for your offer of support."

"Good day to you, then," said the Grand Duke. He nodded at Vasilii, Anna Maria, and Avdotia, and walked away into the crowd. Director Shapkov laid out two copies of the mare's ownership papers on the registration table. Barbara wrote out a bank account request for the 750 rubles, had Vasilii Shelikhov sign it, and gave it to Director Shapkov. Then Barbara wrote their address and signed George's name on both copies of the ownership documents, with Vasilii signing as a witness. Then, keeping one copy for her legal records, she left the area of the registration table with Vasilii and the women to look for Venedikt, Mikhail and Peter in the crowd.

When they found the men at the samovar station, Mikhail was most excited about Barbara's winning the bidding for the mare. "Do you know why Count Tolstoi stopped his bidding at 725 rubles?" he asked. Then he answered his own question, "It was because Peter told one of the Count's friends that the mare had a record of losing foals and that the winning bidder would become the object of the Grand Duke's mirth. We then watched this same friend speaking with the Count, and the Count stopped bidding right at that point. It wasn't so much the matter of the time and expense in trying to breed a deficient mare that stopped him. It was that he couldn't stand the prospect of being ridiculed. He now thinks that the Grand Duke will be laughing at Vasilii. But Varvara has the mare."

Barbara looked at Peter, who was standing quietly at her side as Mikhail spoke, and asked, "Peter, is that true? Did you tell the Count's friends such a falsehood?"

Peter answered smiling, "We don't know it to be a falsehood, Varvara. It could very well be true. I just placed the thought into the Count's mind at the right time."

"So you did," said Barbara. "And I thank you for it."

The Return of the *Suvorov:*

After the November 1814 horse auction, Barbara allowed Peter Dobell a larger presence in her life. If she wanted to attend some public event, she would inform Peter through the Buldakovs and he would attend also. There he would accompany her closely as a friend and a kind of male sponsor so as to ward off the unwanted attention of other men. He did not usually come to call at her residence but they saw each other often at the neighboring Shelikhovs. When people asked her about his frequent presence in her company, Barbara would always say, "He's a dear friend." And although Peter was clearly a most eligible bachelor in the St. Petersburg social circles, he was never seen with anyone else, nor did he mention seeing anyone else to Barbara or her acquaintances. Bolstered in the decision by the advice of Avdotia Buldakova, Barbara did not mention Peter in her letters to George or to her mother, though she felt less than comfortable about not doing so.

In May of 1816 Nikolai and Ekaterina Karamzin moved back to be near St. Petersburg, taking a fine large residence for themselves and their children, Sofia, Katia, Andriusha, and the baby Sasha in an area called the "Chinese Village" in Tsarskoe Selo ("Tsar's Village"), a kind of administrative center some forty kilometers from the capital where two of the Tsar's palaces were as well as many of the grand residences of members of the nobility, court officials, and government ministers. For the time they needed to spend in the city of St. Petersburg itself, they took up residence in the well-located grand residence of Nikolai's friend Aleksandr Nikolaevich Turgenev at number 20 on the Fontanka Embankment in the heart of the city. Soon they began hosting there the literary salon called "*Arzamas*," where poets and writers of a more European liberal political and social inclination would recite their works in a kind of competition-of-influence with the participants of another popular literary salon called the "*Beseda*" or "Colloquy" of Lovers of the Russian Word hosted by either the poet Gavriil Romanovich Derzhavin at his St. Petersburg mansion located only a few residences away from the site of the "Arzamas" at number 118 on the Fontanka Embankment or by the conservative Slavicist Admiral Aleksandr Semyonovich Shishkov, the Tsar's State Secretary. For Barbara the Karamzins' return was the restoration of another sisterhood. Ekaterina was such a kind and supportive person, so bright and always positive that just being around her made Barbara feel better about herself. And Ekaterina was a wonderful confidante, older and worldly wise, with whom Barbara could share her most intimate feelings.

On Monday, July 8, 1816, Gavriil Derzhavin, the poet known to the Shelikhovs and to the Karamzins, died at his rural estate called Zvanka near the city of Novgorod. Barbara had met him more than once, and she knew that George had also become acquainted with him. So she attended a memorial service for Derzhavin at his mansion on the Fontanka Embankment. There Derzhavin's last poem was read, about how "The River of Time in its ceaseless coursing,/ Carries away all the affairs of men,/ And drowns in the abyss of oblivion/ All peoples, kingdoms, and their kings..." It was said that he had been contemplating the poem for a long time, and was finally writing it when he died. His servants and friends found it under him on his desk. Barbara felt sad that a man should die with the thought that what he had created in the world was only fated to perish and be forgotten, as if he had never lived. She asked Nikolai Karamzin about Derzhavin's reputation as a poet and whether he thought that Derzhavin's work would be forgotten. "Never," was Nikolai's response. "In another poem, written when he was younger and more optimistic, he wrote that 'As long as the universe honors the race of Slavs, my glory will keep growing, never to fade away'. In that poem, which he called his 'Monument,' he had the correct appraisal of his poetic worth."

One day, a week after Derzhavin's memorial service, Ekaterina Karamzina came to see Barbara at the Nevskii Prospekt mansion, bringing Andriusha and Sasha with her to show Barbara and to introduce them to Inga, who was Ekaterina's goddaughter. It was a delightful visit, with Ekaterina meeting Lara and praising Inga's "wonderful vocabulary in both Russian and German, her playing the piano already at the age of four, her beginning to read." And Barbara could only praise in return Ekaterina's two young boys, baby Sasha being only several months old, for how they "looked just like Nikolai," and "how happy and healthy" they seemed. But then another visitor arrived unexpectedly and was announced by the house steward Porfirii. It was Peter Dobell, who had come to see Barbara with "important news."

When he entered the parlor where Barbara was and saw that she had guests, Peter did not know what to say. But Barbara quickly introduced him as her "dear friend" to Ekaterina and assured him that he could tell her whatever news he had for her in Ekaterina's presence. "Ekaterina is like a sister to me," she said. "And I have no secrets from her."

Peter decided to give the news in the most direct terms. "The *Suvorov* is at Kronstadt and will be docked in the city in a few days. Your husband Yegor Nikolaevich is not on it. Mikhail has been told that he left the ship in Novo-Arkhangelsk and remained there. He was apparently alive and well when he did so. We are trying to find out more about it from the ship's officers."

Barbara was so shocked by this news that she became unsteady on her feet and started to fall to one side. But Peter sprang agilely closer and caught her in his arms. He hugged her tightly to his chest for a second or two, trying to console her, then guided her over to the sofa where Ekaterina was sitting and placed her alongside her friend. Then he went to little Inga, who was upset by her mother's reaction to the news, picked her up into his arms and took her hand into his.

"Varvara, I'm so sorry about this," Ekaterina said. "But I'm sure Yegor is all right. No doubt he'll be coming home soon by other means. That's all there is to it. You'll see."

"That's what Vasilii and Mikhail also think, Varvara," said Peter. "They'll find out more in the next few days."

A half-hour later Peter excused himself and left. Ekaterina stayed for three hours more, trying as best she could to console Barbara and give her positive hopes to cling to at such a time. Before she left, however, with Barbara in a calmer state at last, she asked Barbara about her relationship with Peter Dobell. "Forgive me for asking you this, dear Varvara, and don't worry about me sharing with anyone else what answer you give," she said, "but have you and your 'dear friend' Peter had intimate relations? Obviously there is a great deal of affection between you."

"No we haven't had intimate relations," answered Barbara. "Not even a kiss. I am resolved to be faithful to my husband no matter how long he is away. But Peter has become important to me, and I won't tell you that this is not very difficult for me at times."

"I understand, Varvara," said Ekaterina. "And I can certainly sympathize with you in this. Whatever happens, you know I'll always be your friend. You can talk to me."

"I know," said Barbara. "And I'm very grateful for that."

In the next week Vasilii, Mikhail and Peter were able to tell Barbara that the *Suvorov's* mission was being considered a success from the point of view of the Russian navy. The ship had made the voyage around the world in the new direction in quite respectable time, delivering the essential provisions to the Company outpost at Novo-Arkhangelsk as the charter agreement specified. And the Russian-American Company, it appeared, would have sufficient returned goods, including a good number of seal and sea otter hides, to make the charter profitable. Shares of the proceeds would be paid to the navy officers and crew. But there was a disagreement concerning the absence from the returned mission of supercargo Germann Nikolaevich Molvo, feldsher, former servant and courier Larion Afanasievich Trifonov, and the ship's surgeon Dr. Yegor Nikolaevich von Sheffer. Captain Mikhail Petrovich Lazarev and his officers claimed that these three had left the ship voluntarily in violation of their crew obligations, thereby forfeiting their shares and increasing those of the rest of the crew. But the Company clerk, Fyodor Fyodorovich Krasilnikov, whom the officers discredited as a "flogged drunk and malcontent," reported to his Russian-American Company superiors that George and the others had been deliberately stranded in Novo-Arkhangelsk as a result of a conflict between Captain Lazarev and Russian-American Company Manager and Governor of Russian America Aleksandr Andreevich Baranov, with whom George and the others had sided in the conflict. Krasilnikov depicted Captain Lazarev as a villainous bully whose behavior jeopardized the purposes of the mission more than once. The Russian-American Company directors decided to await further communications from Manager Baranov in Novo-Arkhangelsk, since it was their judgment that the *Suvorov* had been able to return to St. Petersburg faster than any other communications could have reached them from the Russian north Pacific. Barbara would also have to await such communication from George.

In the next month the awaited communications arrived. The Russian-American Company directors received the packet containing the formal complaints against Captain Lazarev by Manager Baranov, supercargo Molvo, and surgeon von Sheffer. And Barbara received a separate letter from George in which he described Captain Lazarev's irresponsible acts, both professional and personal, and the situation of his being stranded in Novo-Arkhangelsk. He was about to depart for Hawai'i on a separate mission for Company Manager Baranov and he assured Barbara that he was safe and sound and would be returning to St. Petersburg as soon as possible on another ship. These communications caused Vasilii Shelikhov, Venedikt Kramer, Mikhail Buldakov, and the other Company directors to register a formal request with Admiral Ivan Ivanovich Traversé and the navy Admiralty that a court-martial be convened to investigate the allegations of misconduct on the chartered mission of the navy ship *Suvorov* by its Captain, Mikhail Petrovich Lazarev.

The Admiralty did not answer the Russian-American Company's request for more than a month. From personal contacts among the members of the State Council of the Russian Empire's Military Advisors, including Governor-General of Moscow and General-of-the-Army Aleksandr Tormasov, Vasilii Shelikhov was irritated to find that the Russian navy's leading admirals, including Admirals Traversé, Chichagov, and Shishkov, were opposed to convening such an inquiry. They reportedly felt that the navy should not be swayed to consider disciplining one of its commanders by civilian requests. Vasilii told Barbara that Captain Lazarev apparently had "friends in high places." But he was persistent. He asked Barbara to allow him to make and circulate to selected others a copy of George's letter to her in which Lazarev's scurrilous personal actions were described. He thought that this would make the admirals realize that Lazarev was a liability to the navy's positive reputation and thus ineligible for further command.

In early September of 1816, Barbara received a letter from Nadia Tormasova informing her that General Aleksandr Tormasov had been granted hereditary nobility in his own right by Tsar Aleksandr for his achievements in the military and in the rebuilding of Moscow, with which the Tsar could only be positively impressed. "He's 'Count Tormasov' now," Nadia's letter read, "and I'm a Countess, as will be your namesake Varochka when she grows up. The nobility separate from that of his father and brother is something Aleksandr has dreamed of all his life. But now, strangely, he seems to take only little joy in it. It's the rebuilding of the city that consumes him now and gives him pleasure. He says he's been involved in too much destruction in his lifetime, and now he has a chance to build something lasting. The new Moscow will be his legacy, he says-- an ideal one for both a general and a mason. I can't help but worry about him, however. He turned sixty-four years of age on the eleventh of this month of August and he comes home every evening very tired from working so hard."

In early September of 1816, the Russian Admiralty decided to convene a Commanders' Court to consider Captain Mikhail Petrovich Lazarev's conduct of the Russian-American Company's charter mission to circumnavigate the globe and provision the outpost in Novo-Arkhangelsk. This was a closed court and no outside spectators were allowed. Vasilii Shelikhov was called as a witness, as was Company clerk Fyodor Fyodorovich Krasilnikov. The official complaints of Governor Baranov, Supercargo Molvo, and Dr. Sheffer were admitted into evidence. But the ship's log, authored by Captain Lazarev, was admitted, as was the testimony of the Second Officer, Lt. Semyon Iakovlevich

Unkovskii, and of Lt. Pavel Ivanovich Povalo-Shveikovskii. Lazarev, in order to discredit George and his written allegations of his misconduct, pointed out the log entries from the *Suvorov's* passage through the southern Indian Ocean in July of 1814 in which George reported seeing with others nine mysterious airborne objects in the sky...flying "lampshades" that started to glow at dusk and flew off out of view in formation at unfathomable speed... objects that he later explained as being the vehicles of time travelers who were our own progeny. And, in the end, the Commanders' Court exonerated Captain Lazarev of the charges against him, writing that the mission was completed successfully in a reasonable term without loss of life and even profitably for its client, the Russian-American Company. Lazarev was not to be reprimanded for his disregard of Australian Governor Macquarrie's restrictions on the sale of alcohol, for his flogging of clerk Krasilnikov, his departing Alaska without three of the ship's company due to "disagreement with a civilian official about the role of the Russian navy in civilian commerce," for trading away some of the cargo of furs for less-valuable Peruvian handicrafts, or anything else. He was declared "eligible for future command responsibility." The only navy concession to the Russian-American Company's case against Captain Lazarev was the court's recommendation that the Company's contractual payment of profit shares to the crew include, as Lazarev opposed, shares to Supercargo Molvo, to Larion Trifonov, and to Dr.von Sheffer.

Vasilii Shelikhov was very disappointed about the Commanders' Court decision. But, he told Barbara, "at least they recommended we pay Yegor and the others. Of course, I would have seen that done anyway."

Mikhail Buldakov, who had read George's letter to Barbara about Captain Lazarev, was outraged at the decision. He told Barbara and Peter Dobell, "A man like Lazarev shouldn't be in command of any ship, no less a Russian navy ship."

In the next month, Vasilii Shelikhov reluctantly assented to sending another Russian navy ship, the *Kutuzov*, under Lt. Leontii Andreianovich Hagemeister around the world to Novo-Arkhangelsk with the mission of replacing at last Governor Aleksandr Baranov. He had, Vasilii told Barbara and others, "suffered there for us long enough. It's time to bring him home."

Raising Public Interest in the Pacific:

In late 1816 and early 1817, Barbara received the first of George's letters from Hawai'i. His description to her of the islands' beauty and of the life of these islands' people was very fascinating to her. She purchased maps of the world and had Peter Dobell mark the place on them where these islands were located so that she could show the place to Inga. It was a providential coincidence to her that George should be on a mission to the Hawai'ian islands, one of the two places in the Pacific Ocean where Peter Dobell was advocating that Russian colonies be established for provisioning and trade purposes. Soon she came up with the idea that she could help Peter's efforts, and, she imagined, George's too, by doing what she could to raise St. Petersburg's public interest in Hawai'i, the Philippines, and other islands of the Pacific. She would sponsor a series of free public lectures on the islands of the Pacific, paying the speakers and advertising the lectures well in advance by printed posters and newspaper announcements. She would pay for new editions of the travel logs of the previous Russian Pacific explorers to be printed and sell them at these lectures. Carefully selected influential ministers or other government officials would be individually invited to attend the lectures as announced "special guests," who might be asked at the lectures to give their comments and opinions concerning the advantages of Russian trade in the Pacific.

All Barbara's friends were enthusiastic about her idea, which soon developed into her "project." Natalia Shelikhova was now quite infirm with age and unable to communicate reliably with others. She was entirely homebound, well cared for by Vasilii, young Pyotr and Olga, and the household servants. But Barbara remembered her mentioning the memoirs of the participants of Russia's first circumnavigation by the ships *Nadezhda* and *Neva* from 1803 to 1807. There were those of Captain Ivan Fyodorovich Kruzenshtern, whom Peter Dobell had met and befriended in China, of Lieutenant Yurii Fyodorovich Lisianskii, of the Russian-American Company supercargo Fyodor Ivanovich Shemelin, of Lieutenant Hermann Ludwig von Löwenstern, and of Dr. Georg Heinrich von Langsdorff, whom George had met in Brazil. Natalia had also mentioned the memoirs from the Pacific of Captains Leontii Andreianovich Hagemeister and Vasilii Mikhailovich Golovnin, who could, like Langsdorff, relate about a period of captivity in Japan, though Golovnin's period of captivity was more recent. All these memoirs, some of which had gone out of print, recounted adventures in the Pacific islands and could be republished in new editions. And there was that actual Hawai'ian Natalia had once mentioned to Barbara and George named Kane'ohe who had come back to St. Petersburg on the *Nadezhda* and been adopted by the former State Councillor for Naval Affairs, Count Vasilii Fyodorovich Moller. This native Hawai'an had reportedly flourished in Russia and even graduated from the Tsar's Village Lyceum under the name of Vasilii Vasilievich Moller. If he still lived in or near St. Petersburg, he could be found and asked to participate. Barbara especially wanted to meet and speak with him herself.

In March of 1817 after the first thaw, the first lecture, entitled "Adventures in Hawai'i, the Philippines, and China" by "Agent of the Russian-American Company Peter Dobell" took place in one of the largest lecture halls of the Main Pedagogical Institute, the successor higher-educational institution after the 1803 disbanding of the St. Petersburg Academy, founded by Peter the Great in 1724. All of the books Barbara wanted to have for sale were not yet available in their reprinted versions, but many of the former versions that were available were sold. And they were sold to a packed house. The posters and the newspaper announcements had worked wonderfully, and there were people standing

89

without seats. Many were attracted primarily by the lecture hall's warmth on a very cold day, and by the word "free" describing the lecture on the ubiquitous posters and flyers. Peter's booming and dramatically recounted stories about the custom of the Hawai'an Ali'i requiring their subjects upon threat of immediate death to prostrate themselves on the ground in their presence, and of the tribes in the Philippines who wore no clothes and knew nothing of the wheel nor of beasts of burden, but ate insects and occasionally each other, and especially of his personal combat in the China seas with a woman pirate drew thunderous applause. And the very aged Count Vasilii Fyodorovich Moller was there with his adopted son, Vasilii Vasilievich Moller, formerly known as Kane'ohe, to answer questions from the audience. Vasilii Vasilievich was a very handsome young man of medium height with a very tan complexion and very black hair who had impressed Barbara when she met him with his polite manner and his knowledge of the world.

"Young Vasilii, did you ever have to put your face into the ground when a nobleman came near you?" one fellow shouted out.

"In truth I never saw an Ali'i in my Hawai'ian life," answered Vasilii. "So I never had to put my face into the ground. But I was told about the necessity to do so by my Hawai'ian parents and relatives."

"Is it true that Hawai'ians don't have to work in order to live...that the fish and fruit are in such abundance that they don't need to be harvested, but just fall into the people's nets, and the weather is so kind that warm clothes or warm houses aren't necessary?" asked another man.

"The weather is indeed very kind all the year through, but there are storms sometimes," answered Vasilii, "and people do build their own kind of houses. Food is indeed abundant, but Hawai'ians do work to grow and harvest it. Even in Eden there is work."

The audience broke into laughter at this last remark.

"Can you say something for us in the Hawai'ian language?" another man shouted.

"In greeting we always say 'Aloha'," answered Vasilii. "It means 'love'. And for 'yes' we say 'Ae,' and for 'no' we say 'A'ole'."

"Count Moller," shouted another man, addressing the older man, "Do you think we should make the Hawai'ian islands a Russian colony?"

"Yes, I do," answered Count Moller. "Some day we'll be sorry if we don't."

"Would you like to go to the Hawai'ian islands and visit young Vasilii's natural parents?" asked the same man.

"Of course I would, young man," answered the Count. "But I'm afraid I'm too old now to undertake such a travel adventure. I encourage Vasilii, however, to return to his homeland and his parents at any time he wants."

Barbara, who was sitting together with Ekaterina Karamzina in the front row of spectators near the speakers' rostrum, noticed a look of apparent recognition on young Vasilii's face. She turned to look in the most recent questioner's direction and recognized him herself. It was Aleksandr Pushkin, the young poet who had irritated Aleksandr Tormasov at his readings in the literary salons. She realized that Aleksandr Pushkin and young Vasilii Moller had recently been classmates together at the prestigious Tsarskoe Selo Lyceum. She wondered if the similarity of their atypical complexions had engendered among them any similar feelings of identity among their noble classmates. Both were "foreigners" of a kind, she thought, but both were clearly specially gifted people.

1827 Portrait of Russian Poet Alexander Sergeevich Pushkin (26 May/6 June, 1799—29 January/10 February, 1837) by Orest Adamovich Kiprensky (1782-1836), from: http://en.wikipedia.org/wiki/Alexander_Pushkin.

After the lecture and questions were over and the audience was leaving the hall, Barbara's friends gathered round her to congratulate her on the success of the event. Ekaterina Karamzina complemented Peter Dobell on his lecture, saying that she had "rarely heard such an exciting presentation." Peter was then beseiged by a number of post-lecture questioners for some time. He had come to the event with the Buldakovs and they waited patiently for him so they could leave together.

Aleksandr Pushkin had also remained in the hall after the event to speak with Vasilii Moller. Barbara watched as he slapped Vasilii on the back, shook his hand, and said, "I thought I would embarrass you, Vasya, by questioning your old man in that way, but he was too sincere for me. What a good man he is! I wish I had such a father."

"What a strange thing for him to say," thought Barbara to herself. But then the young man walked over to Ekaterina Karamzina and hugged her quite vigorously, asking, "So where is Nikolai Mikhailovich this evening, my dear Ekaterina?" Obviously, young Pushkin was well acquainted with Ekaterina.

"He's working with some of the professors of your alma mater in the Tsarskoe Selo Lyceum to publish some textbooks on language and history, and it's too far away for him to get back for a single evening's event," answered Ekaterina rather sternly. "But he wants to have a serious talk with you."

"About what?" asked Pushkin.

"About your recent behavior and your participation at *Arzamas*," said Ekaterina.

"I see," he said. "Well, perhaps I will travel there and have a visit with him."

"That would be fine," she said. "I wish you well."

Pushkin then walked away and out of the hall. The hall was now empty and Barbara walked over to Ekaterina so that they could collect their coats at the cloakroom and leave together. They had both come in Barbara's coach and the coachman would be waiting for them outside.

"So what was that scene with our young poet about?" asked Barbara.

"You would never believe it, Varvara," replied Ekaterina, "but he's become quite enamored with me in the course of his reading his poetry at our *Arzamas* salon. I love him dearly, and he's an enormous talent, but he's still just a boy. He's only a year or two older than Sofia. In the salon we call him the "cricket" for his annoying little epigrams. But now, I'm afraid, his obvious attentions to me have annoyed Nikolai. Nikolai will be having a word with him about it."

"Does he have a good father in his life?" asked Barbara, recalling Pushkin's comment to his classmate Vasilii Moller.

"His father is quite selfish and doesn't seem to care a great deal about him," answered Ekaterina. "In fact I would say that Nikolai is a better kind of father figure to him. So I hope the talk will have some positive effect."

"I'm sure it will," said Barbara.

The Count Tolstoi:

One bright spring afternoon, Porfirii came to find Barbara in her kitchen and announced to her that a gentleman had come to call. It was, he said, "The Count Tolstoi."

"Have him wait in the parlor, Porfirii," she said. "I'll need a few minutes to change into different clothes and fix my hair."

"Very good, Madame," answered Porfirii, and he went back toward the entrance to admit the guest.

When Barbara came into the parlor several minutes later, she found Count Fyodor Ivanovich Tolstoi just as she had remembered him from the horse auction two and a half years before. He was approximately her age, perhaps a bit older, and was a stocky man of just under six feet of height with dark and curly hair, thick eyebrows and heavy whiskers on the side of his face. He had a prominent jawline and chin, and he was smoking a pipe.

"Count Tolstoi," she said. "You are welcome as a guest in my home, but I don't allow smoking here. You'll have to douse the pipe or have my steward Porfirii take it back out to your coachman."

Tolstoi was apparently surprised by this, but he gave up his pipe to Porfirii who took it away immediately. "I'm sorry, Madame," he said. "Everyone smokes where I live or visit elsewhere. I didn't imagine that you would object to it."

"I think it unhealthy and can't stand the smell of it," said Barbara. "So I avoid smoking and smokers whenever I can, and don't allow smoking in my house."

"Such is your right, of course," said Tolstoi, "and I don't want to offend you. Instead I wish to help you by offering you my services."

"What kind of services do you have in mind?" asked Barbara cautiously. She had been told of Tolstoi's reputation as a womanizer and for being very forthright in his offering such "services."

"I wish to be a speaker in the lecture series you are sponsoring," he said. "I have attended the first two lectures, the one by Russian-American Company Agent Peter Dobell and the one by Captain Vasilii Golovnin about his being held by the Japanese for more than two years, and found them very interesting."

Barbara thought it strange that she hadn't noticed him in the audiences of these lectures, but, as there were quite large crowds in attendance for both, it was entirely possible that he attended without her noticing him.

"You must be aware," she said, "that these lectures support the purposes of the Russian-American Company, for whom my husband is currently employed."

"Yes, of course I am aware of this," he said. "And I have gone to the trouble to find out who your husband is. I know about his management of the balloon project against Napoleon, and about his beginning the manufacture of laudanum for the military. I know that he was supposed to return on the *Suvorov*, and that his return has been delayed by a mission to the Hawai'ian islands for the Company Manager Baranov in Novo-Arkhangelsk. When you next write to him, you should tell him that I am an admirer of his. You might tell him that I once went up in a balloon myself...back in 1803."

"That's nice of you, Count Tolstoi," Barbara said. "And I will write this to my husband. But I had in mind the difficulty of your previous relationship with the Russian-American Company and its directors. By this I mean the matter of your being expelled from the retinue of the Company's Charterer and Mission Head, Nikolai Petrovich Rezanov, and from the crew of the *Nadezhda*, ten years ago in Petropavlovsk. Rezanov has since died, of course, but I am very close to his children, to his mother-in-law, his brother-in-law, and his sister-in-law. The Shelikhovs live immediately next door to me and they have been very supportive of both me and my husband Yegor. The Kramers and the Buldakovs are my friends. I would certainly not feel comfortable about selecting someone they might oppose for my lecture series. I just could not."

"As you say, Madame von Sheffer, all that was ten years ago," responded Tolstoi. "I was young then and very rash. And Director Rezanov was also a rash man then. It was because of his instruction of subordinates to make attacks upon the Japanese that they then imprisoned Captain Golovnin, you know. But that has apparently been remedied and Golovnin is preparing to depart to the Pacific again on the *Kamchatka*. He's a rather too serious fellow, but he's happy. Didn't he say that he recently became engaged to marry?"

"Yes," said Barbara. "He told me that he has asked his intended, a Evdokiia Stepanovna Lutovskaia from Tver, to wait until he returns from his voyage to marry. And that will likely be more than two years. This is something I understand, as you know. It will be difficult for both of them."

Tolstoi did not respond to this, but continued on his former topic.

"In the years since I was on the *Nadezhda*," he said, "I have come to appreciate from a more mature point of view the Russian-American Company and its purposes. Indeed I would now invest my own funds into the Company if the directors would so allow...and you might inform them of this. I have never done anything to offend Natalia Shelikhova or her son Vasilii. Two years ago I found myself bidding against him at a horse auction, in fact, and decided in the interests of reconciling with the Shelikhovs to let him have the horse. And that's not like me. It was a fine mare and not an easy prize for me to surrender."

Barbara kept her knowledge of the horse auction's results to herself and asked the Count, "What kind of presentation do you propose to give?"

"I would not talk about what happened in the north Pacific at all," said Tolstoi. "I would make a presentation instead about the south

Pacific...specifically the Marquesas and the island of Nuku Hiva. I still maintain an acquaintance with an old Frenchman living in Oranienbaum named Jean Baptiste Cabri that we took on board the *Nadezhda* from Nuku Hiva in 1804. How he came to be there is really still a mystery, but he now claims that he knew young Napoleon Bonaparte as a military cadet in the French army, and that both he and Napoleon applied to join the Pacific Expedition of the Comte de La Perouse in 1785. He was accepted, he says, and, by some work of the Devil, Napoleon was rejected. So he says that he was on the French ship *Boussole* in the south Pacific, but abandoned the ship without permission in the Marquesas because of a native woman he met there. He lived on Nuku Hiva for many years, learning the native language to the point where he says he forgot French, had several children there, and had himself tattooed all over his body in the fashion of some of the native chieftains. In fact it was he who then, on the *Nadezhda*, tattooed me in a similar manner. He could appear with me as the 'special guest.' We could both exhibit our tattoos. And I have a number of artifacts from Nuku Hiva as well—carved toys, woven mats, a war club, a drum, and a few other things."

"I have to admit that such a presentation sounds attractive to me," said Barbara. "It would surely be entertaining and would raise interest in the Pacific as I intend. Natalia Shelikhova once told Yegor and me about this fellow Cabri. He's sure to be of interest to many people. But how would you both exhibit your tattoos? Surely you know that I can't have you entirely disrobing in public."

"Of course not, Madame," Tolstoi assured her. "Allow me to tell you just how it might be done. We would only disrobe so that our upper bodies, from the waist up, would be exposed to view, and also we would pull up the bottoms of our pants to show the patterns on our legs below the knees. Here, let me give you some idea..."

As he said this, Count Tolstoi pulled his shirt sleeve up to his elbow. He also quickly unbuttoned and pulled aside his collar, exposing to Barbara's view the dark criss-cross patterns permanently tattooed into his arms and neck. Involuntarily, Barbara opened her eyes wide to stare in curiosity at the strange adornment of his skin.

"If you want, I can show you more, Madame," he said, smiling.

"That won't be necessary," said Barbara. Then she asked him, "Did the tattooing hurt you as it was done? And how was it done? Do the natives have some special kind of ink?"

"The ink is made of the soot collected from the burning of a native nut called the 'kukui.' Cabri then mixed this soot into the liquid from a coconut. He used a needle made from the hollow wing bone of an albatross bird to pound the ink through my skin with a kind of mallet, rubbing in the ink with a cloth where it bled," answered Tolstoi. "It took months to do it all. It did hurt terribly, but I mostly stayed drunk during the actual needlework, so I didn't feel it so much. And it took a long time to heal. But now my tattoos are in better shape than

Cabri's. He has more, even on his face, but they are fading with age. He's got to be close to eighty years old."

Barbara thought in silence about what she should say. Count Tolstoi's proposal was timely for her in that she did not have another lecture actually scheduled.

"You wouldn't have to pay me, Madame," coaxed Tolstoi. "Or I could agree to contribute my speaking fee back to you to help pay the fees for others."

"Please allow me to consult about your proposal with the Shelikhovs and the other directors of the Company," she said. "Then, in a week or so, I'll let you know."

Vasilii Shelikhov told Barbara that she should be careful in her dealings with the Count Tolstoi. "He's characteristically a cheat," Vasilii advised. "So that many card players won't gamble with him anymore. He chases women of all classes ruthlessly, claiming to entrance them with a kind of 'human magnetism' of the Mesmer type. He's a rumormonger, telling untruths about himself and others without consideration of the consequences. And he's dangerous, quick to challenge others out to fight on the slightest provocation. He claims to have killed eleven men in duels. I don't know of any in particular, but I don't doubt he's killed some. He's continually involved in some conflict or scandal."

Vasilii admitted that Count Fyodor Tolstoi had served bravely in the military in campaigns against the Swedes and the French and that, since he was known to be a most entertaining story teller, his proposal to lecture on Nuku Hiva with Jean Baptiste Cabri as a special guest was a viable one for the lecture series' purposes. Tolstoi's widespread notoriety would even help attract a larger, and different, audience. What Barbara told him about Tolstoi's desire to reconcile with him and the Russian-American Company after all these years, however, merely amused him, as did Barbara's mention of Tolstoi's version of the horse auction.

Peter Dobell did not have much to say about the Count Tolstoi. "If you want to have him speak in the lecture series, Varvara," he said, "then go ahead and inform him he can speak. Tell him that if he gives you any trouble, he'll be dealing with me."

"I don't think I'll be telling him that, Peter," said Barbara. "But I do think I'll ask him to speak. And I'll pay him just like everyone else. My thought is that his lecture could be a major success for the series."

Barbara saw Count Tolstoi on two occasions prior to his lecture. He came again to her mansion to discuss the financial aspects of his presentation and to discuss the place, time, and time constraints. On this occasion he met Lara and was charming in his manner with Inga, showing her the tattooing on the back of his forearm and inviting her to try to rub it off. And he and Barbara met again at the lecture hall two days before the lecture. This time he brought with him his Nuku Hiva artifacts for the exhibit accompanying the lecture and he brought Jean Baptiste Cabri. Cabri was a wizened old man, completely bald and without whiskers of any kind. His forehead and cheeks were discolored with faded tattoo patterns. Count Tolstoi had helped him find a career for himself teaching the sailors at Kronstadt how to swim, and, as a result of this physicality, he was surprisingly spry and quick of movement. He gave Barbara a toothless smile when Tolstoi introduced him and spoke to her in a French-accented Russian, "I thank you so very much for giving me this possibility to earn a few rubles at this lecture, Madame. I don't earn much most of the year when it's too cold for the sailors to swim. And what I earn in summer doesn't last through to the next one, I can assure you of that. I have to depend on charity, eating at the soup kitchens. And somehow I've gotten so very old. I don't know how that happened."

Looking significantly at Count Tolstoi, Barbara asked Cabri, "Don't your friends give you any help?"

Cabri looked also at Count Tolstoi and answered, "Now and then they do, Madame. But life is not a walk across a field."

The Count's lecture, given at the Main Pedagogical Institute's lecture hall, was entitled "Tales of the South Pacific with Count Fyodor Tolstoi: Nuku Hiva and the Tattooed Frenchman." There were more than three hundred people in attendance, including many ministers, government officials and members of the nobility. Even the Grand Duke Nikolai Pavlovich was there with his wife and daughters. And the Count Tolstoi was superb. His description of the voyage to Nuku Hiva, the natural beauty of the island and its resources, and the curious customs of the people there enchanted the St. Petersburg audience. His voice was strong and his manner of narration kept the listeners' attention focused on him every minute. When he described at one point how the natives of Nuku Hiva swam fearlessly among sharks to dive and pick shellfish off the ocean floor, the audience involuntarily gasped in unison. And he repetitively made the point that Russia should develop a more prominent trading presence in the Pacific. "This is the earth's largest ocean, the largest source of natural resources on our planet," he said. "We should not exclude ourselves from it while it washes our eastern shores. We should send as many of our ships and men there as we can and establish more Russian outposts and even colonies there. We should teach the natives all across the Pacific our language, teach them our Orthodox Religion, and better their lives. They will then enrich us in return, and our grandchildren will thank us."

After his lecture, Count Tolstoi introduced Jean Baptiste Cabri to the audience, telling them the man's fascinating story. Then he explained the Pacific custom of tattooing the skin as an overt sign of social role or of prominence. He told the audience he had seen young men, guards or servants of the native chiefs, who had tattooed patterns covering large portions of their bodies, including even their eyelids. Then he described the process by which

Jean Cabri had tattooed him, and he and Cabri partially disrobed as planned to show the audience the patterns tattooed into their skin. The increased murmur of the audience revealed an even more heightened interest. The difference in the men's physiques was striking, with the robust and muscular Tolstoi's dark chest hair partially obscuring the tattooing there, contrasting with the sagging hairless chest of Cabri, revealing the tattoing's age distortion. And the tattooing on Tolstoi's chest was quite different in comparison to Jean Cabri's Polynesian tribal patterns. Tolstoi's chest and stomach showed the likeness of a large

Figure 1. Portrait of Jean Baptiste Cabri, engraving by R. Cooper, from Voyages and Travels, vol. 1, by G. H. von Langsdorff (1813). Courtesy of the Bancroft Library, University of California, Berkeley.

1810 Engraving by R. Cooper of a sketch from Georg Heinrich von Langsdorff's <u>Voyages and Travels</u> of the tattooed Frenchman Jean-Baptiste Cabri (ca. 1740-1820), from:
http://wiki.bmezine.com/index.php/Jean_Baptiste_Cabri

firebird from Russian mythology, bursting up into flight to free its feet from the entanglement of writhing serpents. And on his back he had a remarkably detailed picture of the ship *Nadezhda* at full sail. Barbara noticed that some of the women in the audience covered their eyes at the sight of the disrobed men, but that most of them were peeking through their fingers. Tolstoi and Cabri turned around slowly so that people could view them from all sides. Then they dressed themselves again as Tolstoi invited questions from the audience.

"Did the tattoos hurt?" was the first question.

"Yes, they hurt when they were put in and for some time after," answered Tolstoi. "I don't recommend being tattooed to others."

The questioning went on for an entire hour. Almost all of the questions were asked by men, but one woman addressed a question to Jean Cabri.

"Monsieur Cabri, you left a native wife and children behind on Nuku Hiva more than ten years ago," she said, "Do you miss them?"

"Every day," answered Cabri.

"Did you ever think of remarrying?" she continued.

"No, never," he said.

After the audience had finally departed, Barbara came forward with Peter Dobell, with whom she had come to the event, to speak with Count Tolstoi and Jean Cabri.

"Count Tolstoi, your lecture was outstanding," she told him. "I certainly want to thank you for so helping our cause."

"You're very welcome, Madame von Sheffer," he said. "But I think we might now become friends. Please begin to address me by my first name as 'Fyodor.' And may I call you 'Varvara'?"

Barbara reflexively replied, "Yes, you may. And I'll be glad to address you as 'Fyodor' from now on. How do you want to be paid?"

"A bank draft will do," he answered. "I'll send a courier to your residence on Monday to pick it up. And don't worry, I'll now be taking better care of Jean Baptiste."

"I'll have a bank draft for him too," Barbara said. "And I'll trust you to dispense it to him and not gamble it away."

Barbara then turned to speak with Jean Cabri. Tolstoi turned to Peter Dobell and said, "I thought that your lecture was also outstanding, Agent Dobell. I commend you on it." He offered his hand to Peter.

"Thank you," answered Peter tersely, looking Tolstoi in the eyes, but he did not extend his hand.

On Monday Count Tolstoi came to see Barbara in person to collect the bank drafts.

"My usual courier is ill, and so I decided I might as well come myself," he said after Porfirii had announced him. "I have a gambling engagement and could use the money for that."

Count Fyodor Ivanovich Tolstoy, ca. 1815, from
http://en.wikipedia.org/wiki/Fyodor_Ivanovich_Tolstoy.

"That is all right," Barbara said. "I have the bank drafts ready. They are drawn on an account I had Vasilii Shelikhov deposit, and he signed them for me on Saturday."

After she had given him the bank drafts in their separate envelopes, Count Tolstoi said, "What can I do, Varvara, to become even closer friends with you? You must know that I find you most attractive, and I think that you could easily learn to like me a great deal. I know how to entertain single women even better than I entertain groups of spectators at a lecture, you know."

Barbara was shocked. "And you know, Count Tolstoi, that I am not a 'single woman'. And I am not in need of any such entertainment as you might intend to provide. I ask you to leave immediately, and if we ever see each other again, I'll thank you to address me as 'Madame von Sheffer' as before."

But Tolstoi did not immediately leave. Instead he asked, "But what about Peter Dobell? Do you mean to tell me that he is not offering you such entertainment? And what advantage do you see in associating with him? He's a foreign rogue without substantial position. He's here today, but tomorrow he'll be gone. You would be much better off with me. Just think about it. I have much more to offer you."

This angered Barbara, and she said, "I'll not discuss Peter Dobell with you. And whatever you have to offer me, I'm not accepting. Get out of my house!"

100

"All right, I'll leave for now," said Tolstoi. "But I haven't given up and I think that after you think it over, you will be inviting me back. If you don't, you'll be making a serious mistake."

"Are you threatening me now?" asked Barbara loudly, showing Tolstoi to the door. "Get out!" She slammed the door behind him, then went back into the parlor, sat on the sofa and broke into tears.

The Card Game:

The third night after his unpleasant scene with Barbara, Count Fyodor Tolstoi was gambling by playing cards with five other prominent gentlemen in the center of the large main reception room of the Dutch Embassy. The host was the Dutch Ambassador's first officer, who had reserved the room for an after-hours gathering that stretched on beyond midnight. The men were smoking as they played, and drinking heavily both Russian vodka and French cognac. The accumulated tobacco smoke made the entire room seem foggy, with luminous auras emanating from around the candles in the chandelier over the men's heads.

"I'm having a good night, my friends," said Count Tolstoi, looking around the table. "The cards are smiling upon me and I seem to be taking all your wagers."

At that moment one of the embassy's uniformed guards walked into the room. Another man was walking with him, holding a pistol to his head. It was Peter Dobell. When the two men approached the table, Peter said to the guard, "I'll just keep your pistol for a bit, but you can sit down over there." He motioned for the guard to take a seat on a sofa along the wall farthest from the door. On the wall above the guard's head was a framed oil portrait of the Dutch Ambassador.

Count Tolstoi was surprised to see Peter Dobell come walking into the room at that hour with the guard and the guard's pistol in his hand, but he remained calmly seated and said, "Gentlemen, let me introduce to you Mr. Peter Dobell. He and I have been sharing the affections lately of a certain lady, and he is, perhaps, upset about that. Is that what this is about, Peter?"

"I'm glad to see you keeping such an air of arrogance about you, Fyodor," Peter said, deliberately using the first-name address. "Because it will give me great pleasure to take it away from you."

P.A. Masse's etching "Hard Hit: Losing Badly at Cards" from: http://cardshark-online.blogspot.com/2010/05/19th-century-etching-of-gamblers.html.

"And just how will you do that?" asked Tolstoi with a scoff. "Are you going to shoot me in front of all these gentlemen witnesses?"

"If I had planned to shoot you, I would have brought my own pistol," said Peter, coming closer to the place where the Count was seated until he stood just at Tolstoi's left shoulder. The other players around the table focused their eyes on Peter and the pistol, but they did not stir from their seats and did not move. "I only took this one from the guard because he tried to stop me from coming in here. But I'm willing to give you a demonstration of my skill with it, crude and unfamiliar to me as it is."

A split second later a pistol shot erupted with a ringing BANG just a few inches from Count Tolstoi's left ear. A cloud of white smoke covered the gambling table. Count Tolstoi winced in sharp pain from the rupture of his eardrum and ducked away to his right. The other players recoiled from the blast, ducking their heads toward the table, and one then dropped to the floor and crawled under the table.

"Gentlemen, did you notice that I fired that shot left-handed and from the waist under rather hurried circumstances?" asked Peter. "But you will notice where the ball has struck." He pointed in the direction of the guard sitting on the sofa. The guard was looking up at the portrait of the Dutch Ambassador, whose likeness had a half-inch hole directly between his eyes.

"But now you've fired your only shot," said an enraged Count Tolstoi, jumping up to his feet and confronting Peter. "So now I'll give you a lesson you won't forget." He pulled back his right hand in a wide arc and aimed a wild punch at Peter. Peter instantly took a short step to his left, dodging the blow adroitly, and came swinging up from below his waist with a crisp right uppercut to Tolstoi's solar plexus at the point of his breastbone. Tolstoi bent over with a gasp, squeezed his elbows inward as if sickened, and dropped to his knees on the floor.

While Tolstoi was on his knees trying to recover, Peter said, "You know, Fyodor, the city of St. Petersburg is not big enough anymore for both of us. It's time for you to visit your residences in other cities—Moscow, perhaps."

Peter threw the pistol, which he still held in his left hand, onto the table. He looked at the gentlemen card players, who were all looking at him. He raised his eyebrows at them, signaling his readiness to deal similarly with any of them who wished to come to Tolstoi's aid. None of them did, and Peter reminded them, "You all heard Fyodor say he was going to teach me a lesson, gentlemen. You all saw him attack me first."

Count Tolstoi had struggled back to his feet. He rushed drunkenly at Peter, swinging again with his right fist. Peter moved out of the punch's way to the right this time, then hit Tolstoi in the face with three punches in quick succession, two left jabs and a hard right cross. Tolstoi fell again to the floor face-first, but then rolled over onto his back and looked up at Peter with an angry expression on his face. His nose began to bleed.

"You son-of-a-bitch," he growled. "I'll kill you for this."

"Now you've all heard him threaten me, gentlemen," said Peter to the other card players and the guard. He reached down and pinched Tolstoi's bleeding nose very strongly between the thumb and first finger of his right hand. Then he pulled Tolstoi up off the floor by his nose. Tolstoi grimaced in pain and humiliation, crying out, "aaaaa-hhhhh."

In about twenty seconds, after leading him this way and that around the room with his head at waist height, Peter let Tolstoi's bloody nose go and allowed him to stand upright. As Tolstoi was rubbing his nose with his hand, Peter wiped his own hand on the back of his pants and said, "Fyodor, this is just a taste of what is going to happen to you every time I see you from now on. I really think you should take a vacation from this city, don't you?"

But Count Tolstoi was not done. Spying one of his fellow gambler's knob-topped walking cane leaning against the back of a chair, he seized it by the bottom and swung the heavier top of it viciously at Peter's head. The cane made a whooshing sound in the air, but Peter adroitly ducked under it. He then hit Tolstoi with another right uppercut, but this time under the chin. Tolstoi hit the floor again, on his back first, then rolling over onto his stomach. In his right hand, extended ahead of him, he still held the cane in a vise-like grip.

"Taking up weapons now, is it?" Peter said. "Well, I think I can make that quite a bit more difficult for you." He strode quickly over and stomped as hard as he could with his boot heel directly down onto Tolstoi's hand where it held the cane. There was an ugly crunching sound, and Tolstoi screamed in pain, pulling his crushed right hand under him and holding it in his other hand. The cane's lower shaft was shattered. "I think handling a pistol will be a challenge for you for quite some time," Peter said. "But I certainly wouldn't advise pistol duels to you in any case. You're just too slow and inept for such contests, and especially with a real 'American' like me. You could easily wind up dead."

Tolstoi stayed on the floor this time, saying nothing and quivering involuntarily in shock and pain.

"I think I'll be leaving you gentlemen now," Peter said. "But I am trusting you to remind Fyodor of what will happen to him if I see him again in St. Petersburg."

Then Peter turned and walked out of the room and the Dutch Embassy into the cold dark night and disappeared.

Peter Dobell Meets Tsar Aleksandr:

On the first of June 1817, at the same time as George Schaeffer, a communication-year or more away, was struggling to maintain his mission in Hawai'i, the Board of Directors of the Russian-American Company in St. Petersburg, acting partly upon George's letters and at Peter Dobell's constant urging, sent a proposal to Tsar Aleksandr and to several of his ministers that the Russian government undertake measures to assure that the Russian-American Company's operations in the northern Pacific be supported by provisioning posts in more temperate and fertile climates. The two sites mentioned for the intended "provisioning posts" were Hawai'i and the Philippines.

A week later Peter Dobell came to see Barbara. He had "important news" to tell her, he said.

"Tsar Aleksandr has requested that I meet with him about the issue of a Pacific provisioning site for the Company's settlements," he said. "I think your lecture series may well have had some influence in bringing the matter to his attention."

"I wouldn't be so sure of that," said Barbara, "but it's nice of you to say so. When will you be seeing the Tsar? Will you be seeing him alone, or will Vasilii and Mikhail also be going?"

"Strangely, they weren't asked to come. Only I was. I'm to meet the Tsar next week on Saturday the fourteenth," answered Peter. "I'd like your advice on what I should wear. Mikhail and Avdotia think I should wear a green waistcoat—the color green symbolizing fertility, they say, like the places I am to recommend for annexation. But I think a formal black waistcoat would be more appropriate and respectful."

"No," protested Barbara, "not black. That's the color of mourning and death. That's no good. I think you should wear gold, the color of wealth. It will look striking with your red hair and the Tsar will not be able to deny you his full attention as you speak. Yes, I'd say you should wear gold...with light tan breeches and white stockings. Wear the brown brass-buckled shoes instead of your boots. They will complement the gold coat. And wear the ruffled white shirt."

Peter thought about it a moment and then said, "I'll dress just as you say, Varvara. And I thank you for the fine advice." Then he asked, "Where is Inga?"

"She's upstairs with Lara. They're painting some artwork today," said Barbara, smiling. "I'll call her. She is always so very happy to see you."

Barbara went out of the parlor to the bottom of the staircase and shouted up the stairs, "INGA! Peter is here. You can come down and see him."

In a few seconds Inga came running down the stairs, followed closely by Lara. Little Inga's long dark hair wreathed her bright face as she skipped from the bottom of the stairs into Peter's kneeling embrace. He picked her up, holding her in his arms. But she was wearing a white smock that was bespattered with various colors of paint from the artwork she had been doing, and several of the colors smeared onto Peter's waistcoat and shirt.

Barbara and Lara simultaneously cried out, "Inga, you're getting paint on Peter."

Inga stopped her cheerful laughter and recoiled in embarrassment. "I'm sorry, Peter," she said. "I didn't mean to paint YOU."

Barbara said, "Inga, why don't you go back upstairs with Lara and change your clothes? Then you can come back down and visit with Peter as a clean little girl."

Peter reassured Inga, joking, "Inga, I am most flattered that you would make a painting of me. I've always wanted to be in a portrait."

Lara and Inga quickly retreated back up the stairs, whispering and giggling between themselves.

"She really does like you, Peter," said Barbara. "You are very good with her. You'll be a fine father, I'm sure."

"I'll have to be a husband first," said Peter. "And that hasn't gone as well in my life."

Peter Dobell holds little Inga Schaeffer in his arms

Barbara didn't want to pursue this line of conversation any further. She had something else on her mind.

"Peter, is it true that you beat up the Count Tolstoi? People are telling me that you hit him and injured him at a card game in the Dutch Embassy. It's the scandal of the city, I assure you. The nobility is exempt from corporal punishment and so the physical beating of a count by a foreigner is a shocking matter...and especially to the Count himself, I'm sure."

Peter did not deny it. "I think the Count was shocked all right enough," he said. "But he isn't permanently injured. I'm reliably informed, however, that he has left St. Petersburg and gone to Moscow to recover. I don't think you'll have any further trouble with him."

"But you might," said Barbara. "He's a dangerous man and prone to violence. People say that he's killed eleven men in duels. He'll either return to shoot you himself or he'll hire others to do it for him. His reputation is at stake and he'll have to revenge himself on you in some way."

"To salvage his reputation, he will have to vanquish me personally in a duel or some other physical confrontation," said Peter. "And I think I've convinced him that any such course against me will only further damage his reputation. If I am attacked now by anyone else, he knows that he will be suspect. He's a hotheaded man and strong-willed, but he isn't stupid."

"It was Avdotia Buldakova who told you that he had proposed to 'entertain me,' wasn't it?" asked Barbara. "I shouldn't have told anyone about it, but I told Natalia Shelikhova, Ekaterina Karamzina, and Avdotia. It was Avdotia, wasn't it?"

106

"It was Avdotia," admitted Peter. "But your servants Porfirii and Lara knew about it too. You either told them or they were witnesses to it. They also might well have been the ones to tell me. All of these people love you and care for you. If you are insulted or injured, then they are insulted or injured...as am I."

Barbara was silent at this, but nodded in assent. Inga and Lara were coming back down the stairs.

On the afternoon of Saturday, the fourteenth of June, 1817, Peter Dobell, wearing a gold waistcoat with a white ruffled shirt, tan breeches with white stockings and brass-buckled brown shoes, was ushered into an office room in the Winter Palace to find Tsar Aleksandr sitting behind a magnificent carved wooden desk. The Tsar stood up to greet him. He was almost as tall as Peter himself, slender and quite trim of physique. He had a pleasant face below a balding pate fringed with some grey hair, with a sharp nose, giving Peter the impression of intelligence. And he was wearing a military uniform with golden epaulets.

"Mr. Dobell, it's nice to meet you. Thank you for coming," said the Tsar, extending his hand.

"I'm very pleased to be of whatever service I can to you, Your Majesty," answered Peter as he shook the Tsar's hand. The hand was soft, he thought, and the grip not forceful enough to assure him of the Tsar's enthusiasm about meeting him. "I'm a great admirer of your achievements and your policies, which I can only hope to advance."

Tsar Aleksandr motioned Peter to a seat in front of the desk, then took his own seat behind it. Looking Peter in the eyes, he said, "I've heard enough about you to conclude that you are an extraordinary man. I know about your background in America and your adventures in France, in Turkey, and especially in China. I've read the parts of your journal about crossing Siberia in the Son of the Fatherland. And I've heard about your recent conflict with Count Fyodor Ivanovich Tolstoi. That's essentially why I asked you here to represent the Russian-American Company's proposal. I simply wanted to meet you in person."

The Tsar smiled as he said this, and Peter smiled back. "So have you decided what course you will follow with regard to the Company's proposal?" he asked.

1809 Portrait of Tsar Alexander I of Russia by Stepan Semyonovich Shchukin
(1754-1828), from
http://en.wikipedia.org/wiki/File:Alexander_I_of_Russia.PNG

The Tsar's face turned more serious as he spoke. "I now rule more of the world than anyone else," he said. "And this entails a great human responsibility that weighs very heavily upon me. I have decided to commit myself to ruling with minimal use of force. Too much force has been expended upon people in our time, as you know, by other rulers of dubious intentions. My intention now, after so much strife and struggle, is to impart accord among people and among their nations. I do not wish to impose Russian rule by force upon anyone who does not desire it. This is why I have not, as I surely could have, made myself the ruler of all of mainland Europe as well, supplanting the governments there in the wake of Napoleon's demise. This commitment of mine to accord will extend even to the Pacific Ocean. Assuring a provisioning outpost for the Russian-American Company in the Hawai'ian Islands will require Russian naval force against competing interests from our British allies and from the United States. That will not be done and I will not listen further to those who advocate it. The Philippine Islands are an established colony of Spain, where I now have very persuasive influence. I have recently placed an ambassador there, Dmitrii Tatishchev, who will gain the needed territorial concessions from the new Spanish government by mere diplomacy and without the need for any more force."

"Indeed that seems quite reasonable to me, Your Majesty," said Peter. "I think that the Russian-American Company directors will be well pleased with a decision to find them a provisioning outpost in any more temperate climate. And the Philippine climate is definitely more temperate. Moreover, the Phillipines are closer to China, where there is an appreciable market for whatever else the provisioning outpost might produce. The outpost could well become most profitable for the Company and for Russia as well."

"The Philippines are closer to Kamchatka and the rest of the Russian mainland as well," said the Tsar. "Hawai'i might easier support the Company's operations in North America, but I think that operations there are over-reaching and that the Company should withdraw from there. It's just too far away to govern effectively from here, and trying to do so will inevitably cause trouble."

Peter did not agree with this opinion, but he was not about to argue with the Tsar. He asked, "What can I do to help in the establishment of the Philippine outpost?"

"You can serve as Russian Consul to the Philippines and establish it there yourself," said the Tsar. "If you are willing, I will have Ambassador Tatishchev present your credentials to the Spanish crown. You would be provided with a generous government salary in addition to whatever the Company might pay you."

Peter was surprised at this offer of a Russian government position in the Philippines, and responded, "But I'm not a Russian citizen."

The Tsar only laughed at this and said, "I've heard that you can't decide whether you are a citizen of Ireland or the United States. But that doesn't matter. If I say you are to be the Russian Consul to the Philippines, and you are willing to serve, then that is what you will do and no one will object. But are you willing? THAT is the question."

"I am willing," said Peter. "How long would the appointment's process take? When would I leave?"

"The appointment will take several months to finalize. It will require approval from the Spanish, after all," answered Tsar Aleksandr. "But I don't doubt that it will be approved. You could leave as soon as you can be ready. I'm sure you'll need to arrange things with the Company also. You will clearly need an advance of travel funding and I will see that such is provided right away."

"Very good," responded Peter. "I'll make what arrangements I must and be off to the Philippines. It may take me a year to get there, you know."

"I know," said the Tsar, standing up to signal the end of the meeting. "And I'll be waiting to hear reports of your success."

Leaving Barbara:

Three days after his meeting with Tsar Aleksandr, Peter came with Mikhail and Avdotia Buldakov to visit the Shelikhovs. In speaking with Vasilii he found out that Barbara had already been told about the Tsar appointing him Russian Consul to the Philippines. He very shortly excused himself from the Shelikovs', saying that he would be visiting "next door."

Barbara hugged Peter warmly upon his arrival, congratulated him formally on his appointment, and then asked the question foremost in her mind, "When will you be leaving?"

"I'll leave sometime next month," he said. "I'll be going overland to Petropavlovsk, and so it's best to get as far as I can before the Siberian winter sets in.

"Oh," said Barbara in a wan voice. "It's sad for me to think of you going away. You've been such a good and close friend. I'll miss you terribly. And so will Inga."

"I tell you truthfully, Varvara," said Peter, "that for three days I've been trying to conceive of some real way of possibility that I could stay here anywhere near where you are...or that I could ask you to come away with me, even faithfully to await your husband's fate from wherever else we would be...Petropavlovsk, the Philippines, the Moon...no matter, just so long as I could continue to find time together with you. The plain truth is that... I love you."

Barbara's eyes began to tear. Struggling not to convulse into crying, she said, "And I love you. That is also the truth. But you know we can't be together...not as long as I know that my husband is alive and coming back to me and to Inga. And I do know that. Where he is now in far-away Hawai'i, whatever may be happening to him, I know he'll be all right. My prayers are keeping him safe."

"God help me, I've even dreamed of seeking him out and killing him, so consumed am I with possessive feelings for you," admitted Peter. "But in wakefulness I know that that would only destroy what possibility of love we might have together. Your faithfulness to him is an essential part of my admiration and love for you. You and he were truly made one by God, and I, only a man, am not meant to separate you."

Barbara took a deep breath and stepped into Peter's embrace. He held her close to his chest and buried his face into her hair. The scent of her permeated his entire being and etched itself indelibly into his memory. The urge to kiss her almost overpowered him, but he forced himself just to remain as he was, holding her close and stroking the back of her shoulder.

"Peter," she said, "we've got to stop this. It isn't right."

"More of the truth," he said, reluctantly releasing her from his embrace and holding her by the shoulders at arms length. "But how am I going to survive away from you?"

"You'll have to find someone else--someone who will be even more to you than I could be," said Barbara. "That is truly what I wish for you. And I'll be praying for that too."

Peter dropped his hands from her shoulders to his sides. Looking downward he said, "When I was a young man in Philadelphia, I thought I had found the woman of my dreams. Her name was Mary Emlen and I thought we were in love. But her family rejected my proposal of marriage to her and she could not bring herself to defy them. So I sailed away on a ship to China and began the long path of life that brought me here. The memory of her is still painful to me and it causes me doubt about whether I'll ever find marital happiness."

"But in all those years, has there never been another?" asked Barbara.

"I admit to being with others I didn't consider worthy of marriage," said Peter. "But only one woman since has struck me as a possible wife. In Tobolsk on my way here across Siberia I met a merchant's daughter named Daria Andreevna. She was very attractive to me, and she had many admirable qualities. But I left her in order to do my duty to the Company and get to St. Petersburg."

"Do you know that I am also a merchant's daughter?" asked Barbara.

Peter involuntarily chuckled. "Your descriptions of your life in Würzburg are far removed from Daria Andreevna's life in Tobolsk, I assure you," he said. "But even so, you and she do have some similarities. She is musically talented and plays any stringed instrument superbly. And she sings like a nightingale...so that even the wind stops blowing to hear her."

"You should definitely go back through Tobolsk on your way to Petropavlovsk," Barbara said. "Find Daria again and see if you can't find a wife in her. Take her with you to the Philippines and onward through your life. Take her with you wherever you go and never leave her alone. Someday we'll visit each other. You and Yegor will be friends and I'll joke with Daria about our earlier affection for each other. You'll have children with her for Inga and our other children to play with."

Peter was profoundly touched. "Varvara, you're trying so hard to make this easier for me, and I adore you for it. But I have to go now and not come back. You'll have to tell Inga for me. And we really shouldn't write. We'll hear about each other through the Shelikhovs or the Buldakovs."

"That's the right way, Peter," said Barbara. "But I won't forget you."

"And I won't forget you," said Peter. He raised two fingers to his lips, kissed them, and placed them without her objection onto Barbara's lips. Then he left.

Aleksandr Tormasov Visits:

Barbara's emotional state was precarious for some time after the departure of Peter Dobell for the Philippines. All through the fall of 1817 and the winter of early 1818 she was subject to a depression that she could not escape. She couldn't sleep well, but then did not want to get out of bed in the morning. Dressing and fixing her hair was a trial for her. The St. Petersburg winter darkness did not help. She began to wonder if she would ever see the sun again. Vasilii Shelikhov, sensing her emotional trouble, increased the frequency of his visits to her, inviting her to various activities he thought she would enjoy. But more and more often, Barbara would refuse to go, making up excuses to stay home. She did come with Inga to the Shelikhovs' New Year's celebration, but, having observed the Catholic Christmas earlier, she declined to accompany the Shelikhovs to Orthdox Christmas mass at the Aleksandr Nevskii Cathedral in January.

Inga began to attend a Catholic kindergarten in the fall at the Church of St. Catherine. After the inital weeks, Barbara entrusted to Lara the task of taking Inga to the church school in the morning and picking her up afterwards in the afternoon. Inga liked school very much, greeting each day with evident enthusiasm and bubbling over with excited reports to her mother about each day's activities. Inga's coming home was the high point of Barbara's day, the only part of it she now enjoyed. And she would talk at length with Inga, sometimes like she would talk to an adult friend. And Inga would often startle her with surprisingly mature offerings of conversation.

"I think Papa is on his way home now," Inga began to say consolingly. "And it will be so nice to see him every day and tell him what I'm doing in kindergarten. I can't wait for him to see the pictures of him I've drawn there. I have a picture of him on a great big ship, and a picture of him in a huge balloon. He's sure to like them. I think I draw better than anyone in the class except Fedia. He's already a real artist, the teachers say. But even he says that my picture of Papa in the balloon is outstanding. It's hanging on the classroom wall, but soon I'll get to bring it home so you can see it. We'll save it for Papa, won't we?"

"Yes, we will, darling Inga," said Barbara. "We'll have it framed and put up in the parlor even."

The kindergarten had both girl and boy pupils and Inga was soon friends with everyone in her class of a dozen. The Dominican nuns who taught the children were full of praise for Inga. Barbara started to make plans for Inga's further elementary education, scheduled to begin the next fall. Above the kindergarten level boys and girls were separated, and the best educational opportunity for the girls was the exclusive and expensive school at the Smolny

Institute not too far from their residence. And so Barbara made an application for Inga there, and, in February of 1818, she received a notice of acceptance.

In February of 1818 also Barbara received a visit from General Aleksandr Tormasov, who was in St. Petersburg on business. On his arrival he explained to Barbara that he would be staying with his former aide, General Kaminskii, and his family instead of staying with her. To Barbara, he looked tired and ever thinner...and yet older.

"You know, Aleksandr—or should I say 'Count Tormasov'?-- that you are certainly welcome to stay here," she said. "This will always be your home away from home, you know."

"I know, Varvara," said Aleksandr, smiling. "But I'm alone here now without Nadia and Varochka, who, by the way, send their greetings to you...and I've got to deal with some military matters here too, so that staying with the Kaminskiis will be convenient for me. But I wouldn't come to St. Petersburg without looking in on you. Ekaterina Karamzina has written to Nadia that you have withdrawn from the social scene and that you don't leave your house for weeks at a time. We are becoming worried about you. Is there anything we can do?"

"No," said Barbara seriously. "I don't think there's anything you can do. I've been suffering from some gloomy moods these past few months. I begin to wonder if it will always be dark, always be cold...and if Yegor will ever come back. It's four and a half years now."

"I can't help thinking that he'll be back soon," said Aleksandr. "What's the last you've heard from him?"

"In the most recent letter I've received from him, dated early last summer, he was having trouble on his Hawai'ian mission with American and British sea captains and the king of an island called Kaua'i. He wrote that he had become an actual ruler of part of that island, and that he was planning to build a grand residence there...a 'palace in paradise', he called it, and that he'd soon travel here to get us and take us there."

"I see," said Aleksandr. "That sounds quite grandiose and exciting. Do you have doubts about it?"

"No, I don't doubt what he writes," answered Barbara. "But I don't know if I want to travel to some Pacific island to live. What would I do there? And what about Inga? What kind of life would we all have there?"

"Surely, Yegor has also thought of that," suggested Aleksandr. "And he must have concluded that life for all of you there will be better than life for all of you here. Since he has now experienced life both here and there, he is a better judge of that, don't you think?"

"I know I should trust him in this without question," said Barbara. "I did pledge to go 'wither he goes,' wherever it is. And I would have, but he left me behind...so that now I've been four and half years without him. And lately I haven't been so happy here in St. Petersburg, I have to admit."

"But you have quite a lofty station here, Varvara," said Aleksandr, looking around them at the art on the parlor walls, noting with a raised eyebrow the elaborately framed pencil-drawn sketch Inga had made of a stick-figure man in a basket under a large balloon. "And, more importantly, you have many good friends too. Nadia and I consider you a part of our family even, as you know. While we were here you seemed to be happy enough. But now your patience is wearing out, is that it?"

"That's it, I guess," said Barbara. "How long am I expected to wait?"

"Until Yegor comes back, Varvara," answered Aleksandr. "...or until you are sure he isn't coming back."

"You're right, Aleksandr, you're right," said Barbara. "It's just that these past few months have been very hard for me."

Aleksandr then asked, "Is that because of Peter Dobell?"

Barbara didn't know what to answer and remained silent, with uncomfortable surprise showing on her face. But Aleksandr continued, saying, "If you gave yourself to him and he then also left you to travel to the Pacific like Yegor, I can understand how you might feel badly about yourself and come to a state of despair. But I, who once took your advice to forgive Nadia, tell you now that you should forgive yourself. Forgiveness is the better way. Nadia and I and Varochka are clear evidence of that. And I think I can assure you that Yegor will feel the same way. He'll forgive you also."

Barbara came closer to Aleksandr and hugged him. "My dear Aleksandr," she said, "it's clear that you've heard about me and Peter Dobell...how we grew so much closer after you left here. That's all true. Out of love for me, he defended my honor by giving a scandalous beating to Count Fyodor Tolstoi, who proposed to offer me 'entertainment' in my husband's absence, assuming that I was somehow capable of it. When the Tsar appointed him Consul to the Philippines, Peter came to me and confessed to me that he was in love with me. And I confessed to him that I loved him too. But somehow we managed to part without my giving myself to him. We embraced. He placed a kiss on my lips with his fingers. And then he left. As God is my witness, I swear to you, Aleksandr, that I did not give myself to Peter, though I powerfully wanted to. I stayed faithful to Yegor...at least physically."

Aleksandr was quiet for some time, thinking. "Then you are a very strong person indeed, Varvara. I admire that and I apologize for assuming otherwise."

"I accept your apology, but I'm not blameless, Aleksandr," said Barbara. "I was emotionally involved with Peter, and his absence even now pains me as much as Yegor's absence. That's what makes my days so miserable, I think. It was so nice when Peter was here just to know that the possibility of love and romance was waiting for me in his arms. But it didn't happen. And that had to be awfully hard, harder yet, on Peter."

"Yes, I would have to say that Peter Dobell is a better man than I thought," Aleksandr remarked.   "It's easier, in fact, to understand the Count Tolstoi...especially given your obvious attractions—great beauty, great character, great wealth. I talked with him in Moscow's English Club only last month. He is, after all, a military hero. He was in the campaigns of 1808 and 1809 against Sweden as an aide to General Dologorukov and as a mounted scout for Barclay de Tolly. And, of course, he fought most bravely against the French from Smolensk and Borodino to Paris, finishing his service at Colonel's rank and with the cross of St. George. So I've a certain respect for him. His right hand is now apparently deformed as a result of the beating he took. He still has it wrapped so you can't tell. Knowing of our relationship, he made a point of telling me about you and Peter Dobell. In his version you were undoubtedly 'entertaining' Peter. He claimed that it was his letter of complaint to the Tsar and his influence with the new Foreign Minister Nesselrode that got Peter sent out of St. Petersburg to the Philippines. He called it not an appointment, but an exile, and laughed about it. Indeed I've heard since that the Spanish have rescinded their approval of Peter Dobell's appointment as Consul. I don't know how Dmitrii Tatishchev, an old acquaintance of mine who is now the Ambassador in Spain, might be involved. He's also an acquaintance of Count Tolstoi's. But in Petropavlovsk Peter will be lucky to have the word reach him that he won't be welcome in the Philippines before he sails there on his ship."

Barbara was very angered by this, saying, "So Peter Dobell left here for nothing then? And Count Tolstoi had something to do with it? That means he took his revenge on Peter at the expense of the Russian-American Company's plans to find a provisioning outpost in the Pacific. As I think about it, he's likely happy about fouling those plans too. The Company once affronted his pride by seeing him expelled from the crew of the *Nadezhda*. He lied to me when he told me he now wished the Shelikhovs well and wanted to buy stock in the Company. His lecture supporting Pacific ventures for Russia was nothing more than a ploy to seduce me. Peter was right to thrash him! I tell you, Aleksandr, the Tsar ought to hear about such actions. And if I ever see that Count Tolstoi again, I just don't know what I'll do. I swear I'll pray for his damnation!"

"I don't think you'll see him again soon, Varvara," said Aleksandr. "He's taken up with a renowned Gypsy dancer, Avdotia Tugayeva, in Moscow. I've seen her dance myself and can easily understand his attraction to her. What she can do with her stomach and hips...well, I won't describe it to you further. She kept his name off the English Club's blackboard of shame by paying his gambling debts when he was short of cash with money she got by selling all the many presents he had given her. And now she's pregnant with his child. He claims he loves her and will marry her despite his family's threat to disown him for it. It's just another example of the way his life is—one scandal after another."

Count Fyodor "The American" Tolstoi in his later, married, years. Notice the tattoo barely showing out of his left sleeve, his scrimshawed pipe and his dog. From: http://en.wikipedia.org/wiki/Fyodor_Ivanovich_Tolstoy.

"Well I, for one, pity that poor Gypsy woman," said Barbara. "If she marries him, she'll be 'reaping the whirlwind,' to be sure."

Vasilii Brings Barbara Guests:

Barbara's depression eased as the spring of 1818 turned into summer. She had begun to visit the Shelikhov residence more while Inga was in school in order to help take care of Natalia Alekseevna. Natalia was ill and mostly bedridden now and was very forgetful. Barbara could tell her the same story over and over, with only slight changes of detail, and Natalia seemed to love it. "Oh, thank you, thank you, Varvara," she would say, "for telling me that delightful story." And Natalia would tell her own stories over and over the same way, forgetting that she had told it to Barbara only two or three visits ago. "When Grigorii was alive..." she would begin, "...and we were in Petropavlovsk...or in Alaska...or..." And Barbara would always listen patiently, carefully reacting as if she'd never heard it before.

Sometimes, when Inga had already come home from school, Barbara would bring Inga with her to see Natalia. Natalia still loved to see Inga, repetitively expressing great surprise when she was told that Inga had just come from school. "What?! You're in school already?!" she would exclaim to Inga with a smile, "You must be such a smart little girl. Soon you'll be reading and writing and ciphering like our genius Lomonosov. No doubt you'll figure everything out. I know you will." She had a box on her bed table that her teen-aged grandchildren Petya and Olya had given her as a birthday gift. Natalia treasured it and saw that her servants kept it filled with small hard candies. Whenever she saw Inga, she reached for the box and took out a candy to give her.

In early September of 1818, Barbara received the letter that George had written from the Portuguese colony of Macau, China, on the 19th of that same month of 1817, the previous year. When she saw that the envelope included a folded silhouette of George's profile, she was delighted and called Inga to come see it.

"Just look what your Papa has sent you, Inga," she said, holding up the carefully unfolded piece of paper. "This is just what he looks like."

Inga smiled broadly as she looked at it and said, "Papa has really bushy whiskers, doesn't he, Mama? He looks like 'Ded Moroz'...the Russian Santa Claus."

Barbara couldn't help laughing. "Yes, I guess he does," she said.

Later Barbara took the letter to the Shelikhovs to let Vasilii read it. She discussed with him George's information about having to leave Hawai'i with only two of his comrades, about the failure of Captain Kotsebue on the *Rurik* to support him there, about the false rumor spread by the British and American sea captains that Russia and the United States were at war, and about his presence in Macau with the Swedish Consul Anders Ljungstedt. But the most astonishing thing, that caused the most discussion, was George's mention of Peter Dobell. Barbara read this part of George's letter out loud to Vasilii, and also to Natalia: "Anders Ljungstedt has told me about a man he once met here in China named Peter Dobell, an American who claims to be an Irishman, who has traveled via Siberia to St. Petersburg and, acting as an agent of our Russian-American Company, advocates there that Hawai'i and the Philippines should be annexed as Russian trade colonies. Please tell General Tormasov, the Shelikhovs, and anyone else in power who will listen that this man Peter Dobell, at least as far as Hawai'i is concerned, IS CORRECT. His advice should be heeded by all. When I arrive there, I will seek him out and shake his hand in gratitude."

"Isn't that remarkable that George has heard in far-away China about Peter's efforts here to get the government to establish a provisioning post in either Hawai'i or the Philippines?" she asked.

"Indeed that is a remarkable coincidence," agreed Vasilii. "And it's a shame that Peter had to leave here before Yegor can return to meet him."

Barbara didn't say anything to agree with this. Just the thought of George meeting Peter in person troubled her with a certain uncomfortable feeling of guilt. "When Yegor returns he can help you and the Company get that provisioning outpost established after all," she said. "Though I imagine he'd rather see it in Hawai'i."

"According to Peter," Vasilii responded, "the Tsar is against the Hawai'i alternative and won't hear further proposals to that purpose."

"Well, Yegor is very persuasive and clever. So maybe he can change the Tsar's mind about Hawai'i in some way Peter could not. But the most important thing to me is that he is definitely on his way home," Barbara said. "and he may now have been on his return journey almost a year. That means he could arrive any day now. I'm very excited by that news, I can tell you."

In late September Vasilii sent his nephew Petya over to ask Barbara if she would come to the Shelikhov mansion that evening for dinner to meet a guest.

"I haven't been going out much socially, Petya," Barbara told her young neighbor. "But if your uncle thinks it important, then I'll be there. Do you know who the guest is?"

"No, I don't know," answered Petya. "But Uncle Vasilii said you would definitely want to meet him. He told me to tell you that."

"All right, then, Petya," said Barbara. "What time should I be there?'

"Seven o'clock," was the answer.

At the Shelikhovs at seven, Barbara encountered with Vasilii a young man in a naval cadet's uniform. He was a wiry youth of about twenty years of age, with a dark complexion and a slightly asiatic cast of face. When he saw Barbara, who was wearing a dark purple dress with a necklace of Baltic amber beads, his face brightened. He was already holding his cadet's cap in his hands, but he acknowledged her presence with a quick bow of his head.

"Varvara Wolfgangovna von Sheffer, allow me to introduce to you a young man who was with Yegor Nikolaevich in Alaska and in Hawai'i. This is Antipatr Aleksandrovich Baranov, our Company Manager's son," said Vasilii in a formal introduction.

"My heavens, Yegor has mentioned you more than once in his letters," said Barbara, extending her hand to shake that of Antipatr's. "I'm so very glad to meet you."

"And I you, Madame," said Antipatr. "Yegor often talked of you, and always with such positive praise that I welcomed the chance the meet you."

"But how have you come here?" asked Barbara.

"I have always wanted to become a sea captain," explained Antipatr. "Even as a small boy I imagined myself commanding a ship someday. And my father controlled several ships that he either had made for the Company in Alaska or purchased from foreign traders. But he advised me to learn modern navigation and seamanship 'from the bottom up' in the navy in St. Petersburg before taking on a command. 'It's always best to be the best,' he would say. And so, after Yegor Nikolaevich sent me back home from Hawai'i two years ago, I asked father to arrange an appointment for me to the St. Petersburg naval academy. At

118

his request, Captain Vasilii Golovnin agreed to be my sponsor. So I sailed here and enrolled earlier this month."

"I know Captain Golovnin quite well," said Barbara. "He gave a lecture in a series I created on his captivity in Japan. But he's gone now. He sailed off last fall to the Pacific on the *Kamchatka*."

"That's true, Madame," said Antipatr. "And I don't think I'll see him here for quite some time. But his sponsorship with the academy was registered before he left. I'm trying to do well in the academy in order to make him proud of me."

"How is it going?" asked Barbara. "And please call me Varvara."

"It's going well in my classes," answered Antipatr. "And I've made several friends already. I haven't been on a ship as an officer yet, but that will come later."

Over a meal of soup and beef stew, Antipatr shared the details of his life with Barbara and Vasilii. He told them about his mother Anna and his sister Irina. He told them how he had learned to hunt seals as a youth, paddling a baidarka. And he had several colorful stories about his father, the illustrious Governor Baranov of Pacific North America, that Barbara had not heard before.

"But what are some of your memories about Yegor?" asked Barbara. "I'm very curious about his activities and his acquaintances while he is away from us."

Antipatr thought a bit, then began to relate, "When I first met him in Novo-Arkhangelsk, he was our guest, stranded by Captain Lazarev of the *Suvorov*, with whom my father had a violent disagreement. He was working, however, at my father's suggestion as our Company physician with a feldsher named Larion Trifonov. While in our home, he taught me to play chess, to make a 'monkey's fist' knot like a sailor, and to fling a knot into the end of a weighted line. He told my father he had once shot and killed a rival for your hand in a duel. He told me and my sister about his effort to construct a balloon from which to kill Napoleon Bonaparte. He said he once treated the hero of Borodino, Prince Bagration...but that Bagration died because he allowed himself to be bled."

"That's Yegor, all right," said Vasilii. "He's a fine story teller."

"I was very grateful to him for agreeing to include me in his retinue when father sent him on the mission to Hawai'i," continued Antipatr. "Father was not sure I was old enough yet for such a mission, but Yegor told father that he would take care of me...and that's what he did. With him on the big island of Hawai'i I climbed high enough into the sky on a mountain called Mauna Kea to look down on clouds of ash spewing from an erupting volcano. While we were on top of the mountain Yegor whistled melodies he said you could play on the piano. His whistling is remarkable, as you likely know."

Barbara affirmed this, saying, "Yes, he whistles often...sometimes so quietly that you can barely hear it, but very well."

Antipatr continued, "Then, on the Hawai'ian island called Mau'i I watched him leap from a high cliff into the ocean surf. It was a place where the Hawai'ian nobles, called Ali'i, jump to prove they're worthy to rule, and Yegor felt that he should jump there himself. On the island of O'ahu we hiked together with the O'ahu governor and his two daughters to a battleground in the Ko'olau Mountains where King Kamehameha's warriors pushed the opposing king's forces over a cliff. And, he helped the governor's daughters teach me to swim on a beach in a place called Waikīkī. On the island of Kaua'i he made grand agreements with the King there—a man named 'Kaumuali'i, who wanted to be called 'George' also. And I was at the celebration feast, called a 'luau,' where we drank some kind of pepper brew called 'awa' and ate roast dog.

"I couldn't believe it when Yegor wrote to me that he had eaten roast dog," said Barbara. "How could you stand to do it?"

"Yegor said we shouldn't offend our hosts," explained Antipatr. "But the way they roasted the dog in an underground oven, it was quite tolerable, even tasty to the hungry. But then, after that, two years ago this month, Yegor sent me home to Novo-Arkhangelsk on the ship *Avon*. He gave me a magnificent Ali'i's cape of red and gold feathers to give my father as a gift of respect from the King. I was supposed to convince my father to purchase the ship *Avon* for the King, but my father wouldn't do it. I think that probably caused Yegor some trouble with the King Kaumuali'i on Kaua'i, but I don't know. Nevertheless I failed him in that, and after he was so good to me. With him I had so many memorable adventures. With him I grew up and became my own man in the world, so that my father felt it was time to send me here."

Barbara felt warm inside as she listened to Antipatr Baranov talk about his memories of her husband. "Do you know, Antipatr," she asked, "that I fell in love with Yegor when he was teaching me to swim?"

"And I fell in love with the O'ahu Governor Homa's daughter Hannah while she was teaching me to swim," said Antipatr. "Perhaps there's something in the water, don't you think?"

Both Barbara and Vasilii laughed at this. Vasilii said, "Varvara, I've told Antipatr that Lt. Leontii Hagemeister has been sent on the *Kutuzov* to relieve his father of command in Novo-Arkhangelsk. The plan is for Governor Baranov to return here as he has been requesting for several years. When that happens, he and his father and Yegor also will likely be reunited. Won't that be a fine time? I'd like to propose a toast to that reunion—to that of Governor Baranov, his son Antipatr, and Varvara's husband Yegor..."

"To the reunion!" they all said as they raised their glasses and drank.

More than two long months later, in late November on a rare clear and sunny day at noon, Vasilii Shelikhov came to Barbara's mansion accompanied by a very fit and handsome young man of dark hair and complexion. Vasilii was brimming with excitement in the entry foyer as he announced to Porfirii and to

Barbara, "This is Filip Osipov, Yegor's bodyguard and companion since Hawai'i. He's just arrived by coach from Europe. He says that Yegor will be here very soon too...that he was trying to arrange a meeting with Tsar Aleksandr in either Berlin or Riga and sent Filip on ahead to inform us. He has a letter from Yegor for you."

Barbara shook Filip's extended hand, but then gave him a welcoming hug. "Please come into the parlor," she said excitedly. "You've got to tell me all about this. I've got so many questions for you that I don't know where to start."

In the next several hours, Filip answered question after question about how he had come to know George, about their many adventures in the Hawai'ian islands, and about their escape to China, the voyage back across the Pacific and through Rio de Janeiro, where he detailed the matter of his need to return with dispatch to his beloved Lucinda, then about the death of their companion Grigorii Iskakov, and finally George's attempts in Europe to obtain a meeting with the Tsar. Filip also mentioned George's promise to pay for his way back to Rio de Janeiro.

When Inga came home from school as this was happening, she and Lara both came into the parlor to meet Filip Osipov and hear his news about George's impending arrival.

"When will my Papa be here?" asked Inga simply.

"I think he will be here within two weeks...three at the most," answered Filip. "I have a letter from him for you and your mother." He took an envelope out of his pocket and handed it to Barbara.

Barbara opened the envelope, removed the letter, and read aloud to the others, translating the German into Russian for Vasilii and for Filip:

"My Darlings Barbara and Inga,

I am sending this letter to you from Aachen with my faithful bodyguard and heroic young companion Filip Osipov. I have instructed him to find first Vasilii Shelikhov and give to him a report that I have written. But this man Filip should be extended every courtesy of a place to stay and food to eat until I get there. I would be there with you as he is except for the importance of my mission to meet here while he is in Europe with Tsar Aleksandr and convince him of the need to send Russian naval ships to annex the Hawai'ian islands as a Russian colony and a provisioning outpost for the Russian-American Company. But as soon as I have met with the Tsar, I will hurry there to you as rapidly as I can. I think that I will be there within a month's time. I am looking forward to our reunion after such a long time apart with real excitement. Barbara, I love you dearly and can't wait until we are together again. Inga, my little daughter who has been deprived all her years of her father, I want so much to hug you and kiss you and restore myself to you. I am proud of you and can't wait to see how you've grown.

With warm hugs and kisses, husband and father, George"

Barbara was fighting back tears as she finished reading. "I'm so happy that he's finally coming home," she said, patting Inga on the top of her head. "We've missed him so much." Then she said, "Filip, you will be staying with us. We have plenty of room, and you will have access to a coach and driver to go anywhere you want."

"But," Filip said, "Vasilii Grigorievich has already invited me to stay for a time with him, and I could only think that I should accept his invitation, since I have no resources of my own...no money, that is. I've used all the money Yegor Nikolaevich gave me just to get here. So I don't know what I should do."

Barbara turned to Vasilii, saying, "Vasilii, I know that you want to be hospitable, but I must ask you to allow Filip to stay here with us. He can have the room Aleksandr and Nadia once had, and I promise to see that he is well provided for. You will be able to see him at any time, since you are only next door. But if he stays here, that will give me more opportunity to talk with him about Yegor and all that has happened to him while he was away."

Vasilii was content to agree, telling Filip, "You should stay here with Varvara. I will have ample opportunity to speak with you, and if you need anything from me, just tell me. And don't worry, I will get you some money until Yegor Nikolaevich returns to instruct how we should settle things."

"Soglasno...ochen' prijatno...Agreed...very nice," said Filip. "I'll just go back to your house to get my bag."

"No need," said Vasilii. "I'll have a servant bring it to you right away."

"Then let me show you your room," said Barbara to Filip. "But first you should get to know Porfirii here. He is the steward in charge of the house and the stable. If you need a carriage and driver to go anywhere or you need anything, just tell Porfirii what it is. And this is Lara, our lead nanny and supervisor of the other domestic servants. You can ask her to have your clothes washed or to have food or drink brought to you at any time. She will inform you of the times when we will be eating meals together."

Filip nodded to Porfirii and Lara, saying to each, "Ochen' prijatno...pleased to meet you." Then he said, "You'll have to pardon me in advance for not knowing how to interact with servants in a house like this. I grew up in a hut on a frozen Aleutian island and became a hunter of walrus and seal. I've never ridden in a carriage, but only paddled a baidarka. Since I've grown up, no one has ever washed my clothes but me...and I haven't always washed them regularly anyway."

Lara, addressing Filip as "Gospodin Osipov...Mr. Osipov," said, "We will make every effort to make your stay here pleasant for you. That's the most important thing. You can ask us about anything at all and we'll try to help you."

Filip smiled and said, "Well, can you just call me 'Filip'? I'd feel better about that than 'Mr. Osipov'."

"It will be as you wish, Filip," said Lara. Porfirii nodded in agreement.

Barbara then showed Filip to his room overlooking Nevskii Prospekt from the second floor. Seeing the chandelier and the art on the walls impressed Filip.

"Heated water comes by pump to your room's wash-stand through a pipe, and drains away also through a pipe inside the wall. All you do is pump the handle and use the stopper. There is a bathtub and shower in a room in the hallway that works the same way. The toilet is at the end of the hallway to the rear," Barbara explained. "All you do is pull the chain after using it and everything will be carried away."

"Very nice," said Filip, amazed. "Yegor told me about this. No outhouse, eh?"

"No outhouse," said Barbara, smiling.

Filip was a fine guest. A tour of the city of St. Petersburg in the carriage with Barbara and a driver impressed him greatly and he began to request carriage tours to different parts of the city every other day or so. Since Barbara had more than one carriage and more than one driver, this did not inconvenience her, and she enjoyed talking with Filip about his impressions of the city. Once he came to understand Lara's daily schedule, he asked to go along in the carriage with her to take Inga to school and afterwards to visit with her the port or the shopping center at Gostinyj Dvor. Both Inga and Lara came quickly to like him. Lara told Barbara that "this Aleutian was a better gentleman than many of that title she had met. He's said nothing at all about my eye and acts at all times as if I were an attractive and desirable woman."

"But Lara, you ARE an attractive and desirable woman, no matter the eye, and you should expect to be treated as such by such a young man as he is," commented Barbara. "Of course he says that he is engaged to some Brazilian woman and can't wait to return to her. Are you aware of that?"

"Yes, I am aware of it," said Lara. "He's mentioned his 'Lucinda' to me several times already."

Once during their conversations, Barbara had the opportunity to ask Filip about George's relationship with the Hawai'ian women.

"I've heard that the Hawai'ian women are very careless with their affections, Filip...that they dress very immodestly, with bare breasts even, and that they give themselves readily to the officers and sailors on foreign ships. Is that true?"

"Yes, it is true, Varvara," answered Filip. "And I have to admit that my friends and I fell to their temptation more than once. But Yegor always said we shouldn't have such relations with them. He feared the possibility of disease. And he was a fine example for us. He never dallied with any wahine that any of us ever saw...and I know that he had several opportunities to do so, even with one or more of the native queens."

"With queens?!" asked Barbara.

"Yes, with queens," repeated Filip. "And they were beautiful women, to be sure. One of them, he told me...King Kamehameha's sacred queen Keōpuōlani...reminded him powerfully of you."

"Kee-o-pu..." Barbara started to say, then asked. "What was her name again?"

Filip sounded it out several times until Barbara could say it, "Keōpuōlani."

"And nothing happened between her and Yegor?" she asked.

"Nothing," Filip assured her. "And there was also one of King Kaumuali'i's queens on Kaua'i...Kekaiha'akulou. She was such a sight to see...so beautiful. The men couldn't take their eyes off her. She once asked Yegor to rub noses...and he did, but that's all that happened."

"They rubbed noses?" asked Barbara.

"The Hawai'ians rub noses and share breath as a sign of affection," explained Filip. "And this was an important queen...one that Yegor did not want to offend. She was the one who later acted to save another one of our company's life when the natives were torturing him on the shore at Waimea and we were thinking to fire at him one of the ship's cannon to put him out of his misery. Yegor would shortly have given the command to fire had Queen Kekaiha'akulou not suddenly come forth to order the man spared."

"My goodness," exclaimed Barbara. "You really did have some adventures together, didn't you?"

"Indeed we did, Varvara," said Filip. "And Yegor was our leader. He was very, very clever in everything he did...the smartest man I've ever met. He learned to speak Hawai'ian so well that he could communicate like a native with the Hawai'ian Ali'i...confounding other foreigners who had been there for years. Only their jealousy and treachery kept us from being successful in establishing a colony there. And through all of it, Yegor was faithful to you."

"You really are kind to tell me that, Filip," said Barbara. "I'm sure you can imagine how I must have been thinking about such things in his long absence. It's been a difficult time for me."

"It's the truth, Varvara," said Filip. "Yegor is the kind of husband I dream of becoming with my Lucinda. And I also dream that she will be so faithful to me while I am absent from her."

This thought discomfitted Barbara slightly, but she said in answer, "I'm sure she will, Filip. Why wouldn't she?"

George Returns:

On December 16th, 1818, Porfirii opened the front door in response to a knock to see George standing on the stone stoop. He had walked all the way from the port without any of his things, not being able to afford a taxi carriage.

"Porfirii, my good man," George said. "Will you please tell Barbara that I have returned?"

In a minute Barbara was at the entry, hugging George and saying to him, "At last you're home, my dear husband. At last you're home. How good it is to see you."

"I've been thinking of what to say to you after being gone for so long, Barbara," he said. "But I just haven't been able to come up with anything appropriately clever. All I can say is 'I love you.' I've missed you terribly all these five years, two months, and three days that I've been gone. My desperate hope is that you still love me and that we can take up our lives together again as if we had never parted. Whatever changes in our lives there have been, I want to assure you that all my time away has only made stronger my desire to be your husband and little Inga's father. Please, please, assure me that this will be a possibility."

"Oh, yes, George, yes, I do assure you of this," answered Barbara. "We'll be together as if we'd never been apart. There haven't been any changes in my love for you."

George took a deep breath of relief, and so did Barbara. Then, stepping back to look at him, she said, "George, you're a bit thinner, and somehow harder of body than I remember. You've got some gray now in your hair and beard. And there's a wrinkle now on your forehead above your eyes. But, my word, you must be frozen. It's cold out and snowing, and you're only wearing a waistcoat."

"What things I have with me...surprisingly little," he said, "are still at the port. We'll have to arrange to go back there and pick them up. Where is Inga?"

"Inga now goes to the church kindergarten," said Barbara. "Lara has gone to get her and will be back here with her very shortly. She'll be thrilled to see you."

"Did my young companion Filip Osipov get here? Did he come to see you?"

"He's upstairs even now taking a nap after lunch," Barbara said. "He's been staying here, getting accustomed to life in the capital city. Last night he and Vasilii were out late playing cards. They planned to go by the Naval Cadet Academy to see if Antipatr Baranov might be able to go with them."

"Antipatr Baranov is here?!" exclaimed George with surprise. "How did that come about?"

"His father sent him here to attend the Naval Academy so he can become a sailor and ship's captain," said Barbara. "He's been here to the house once or twice now. He'll be very happy to see you."

"All right," said George. "Of course, I'll want to see Vasilii too...but all in good time. Inga is first. Just let me sit down to wait."

Barbara helped remove George's waistcoat, handing it to Porfirii. Then she accompanied George into the parlor and sat down beside him on the sofa. "Are you tired?" she asked.

"Yes, I am tired, my dear," he said. "I sailed in on the *Natalia Petrovna* from Riga, the third city in Europe where I attempted unsuccessfully to arrange a meeting with Tsar Aleksandr. I had run out of money there, but my former colleague and friend, Dr. Semyon Pavlovich Tarasov, who is now the Tsar's personal physician, helped me get passage to St. Petersburg. When I was set ashore I couldn't afford a carriage for my things. So I walked here. Along the way I couldn't help but notice all the changes in the city. I saw that they've now begun to build a huge new cathedral...to be called St. Isaac's."

"My, my...you walked all the way from the port?" sympathized Barbara. "And in this cold? No wonder you're tired. After you see Inga you can just go up to bed. You can sleep for a week, if you want. I'll see that your things are retrieved from the port. And you won't have to worry about not having enough money ever again. You have definitely been getting richer and richer all the time you've been away."

"I do notice some new art on the walls," said George with a smile. "I especially like that one there." He pointed to the framed pencil sketch of a man in a balloon that Inga had drawn. "It goes well here in the parlor."

Barbara knew that the drawing was jarringly at variance with the other classical art in the parlor and that it attracted immediate attention. "Of course, it's Inga's portrait of you in the great balloon," she explained. "She did it in her kindergarten class and was so proud of it that I had it framed and hung here in the parlor."

"So she will likely become a famous artist," said George. "I can easily see exactly what it is."

At that moment, Lara and Inga came into the hallway outside the parlor, coming forward from the kitchen. They had entered through the rear door, having come from the stable a half block away. When she saw George, Lara gave an audible gasp. "It's your father, Inga," she said.

Inga's eyes widened and she stood stock still, looking at George. She didn't know how to react. She put her hands to her mouth, but said nothing. George also said nothing, but just looked at little Inga with a smile of admiration. She was so beautiful to him that his voice was lost.

"Come here to me, Inga," said Barbara.

Inga took several strides to the sofa and was quickly enveloped by her mother's warm embrace. "How was school today, my darling?" asked Barbara. "Did you draw anything today? Your Papa has been admiring your picture of him in the balloon. He thinks it's wonderful."

Inga looked up out of her mother's arms at George. He was close enough, seated by her mother's side, to touch her. But he did not. "Are you my Papa?" she asked.

"Yes, I am your Papa, Inga...home at last to be with you," said George. Then he asked her, "Can I give you a hug?"

Inga looked briefly at her mother, then at Lara...then she took the step into George's outstretched arms. He hugged her close, giving her a squeeze, and said to her, "I've been dreaming of doing that for a long, long time. Thank you so much for allowing me to hug you. I know that you will have to get to know me as if I were a stranger to you. You were only a baby when I left, and now you are a beautiful little girl. I promise you that I will be a nice Papa for you from now on. You will see."

Lara took out a handkerchief and was dabbing her eyes. George, noticing this, stood up and walked over to her and hugged her warmly. "Dear Lara, it's nice to see you again too. I know how well you've taken care of Barbara and Inga while I've been gone. I hope you know that you've become a member of our family now and that we'll be trying to take care of you as well."

"Oh, Yegor Nikolaevich," said Lara. "It's wonderful to have you home safe and sound."

In the next month, George settled with Filip Osipov and got him passage to Riga, London, and Rio de Janeiro on the same *Natalia Petrovna* they had been on before and on which George had arrived home to St. Petersburg. When they said good-bye, George told Filip that he would see him again in Rio de Janeiro. He would be coming, he said, on a Russian naval ship bound for Hawai'i.

Antipatr Baranov was relieved when he met George again that George was not angry at him for not being able to convince his father to buy the *Avon* for King Kaumuali'i. "That was just one blow of the many that finally knocked us down," George said. "And I'm sure you did your best to convince your father. It wasn't your fault."

Antipatr told George that when he became a qualified sea captain he would return on a fine ship to Hawai'i to find and marry Hannah Holmes, O'ahu's governor's daughter. "I'm like Filip Osipov in that way," he said. "I'm in love and I can't wait to get back to where I met her."

"Have you written about this to her?" asked George.

"No," admitted Antipatr. "She doesn't know about it. I only realized how much I love her after I left there. And how am I to communicate with her now?

She understands English and Hawai'ian, while I am confined to Russian and Aleut. And how do I send her anything?"

"You could have a letter translated into English and send it to Honolulu via the Russian Embassy in England," said George, matter-of-factly.

"But such a letter would take more than a year to get there," said Antipatr. "By that time I might be there myself."

George realized that this was highly doubtful, given the length of the Naval Cadet Academy's course of training and the fact that even a highly placed naval lieutenant was not generally able to determine his own assignments of destination. But he did not want to admit negative thoughts into his young friend's dream.

"Have you ever thought, Yegor," asked Antipatr, "about what exact time was the high point of your life? What were you doing, and where were you doing it, when you were able to say to yourself 'That was my finest hour...that of which I dreamed and after which all subsequent events represented a decline'?"

"I have had such a thought, Antipatr," said George. "It was when we were together in Hawai'i. It was that sunny day on Mau'i when I jumped off that black-rock cliff into the surf and we saw that breaching humpback whale. That was, I thought then and I still think now, the apex of my life so far....my magical moment, when all my future possibilities seemed positive. I thought I was infallible, immortal even, at that moment. But, of course, my life isn't over."

"My magical moment was also in Hawai'i when I was with you, Yegor," said Antipatr. "It was on Waikīkī beach learning to swim with Hannah and her sister. I can still see their slender bronzed bodies, their bare breasts and their long light hair gleaming wet in the sun. We ran on the sand and splashed and swam together in the cooling surf. Do you remember them teaching me to ride the waves standing up on those surfing boards?"

"Yes, I remember laughing and laughing as you kept falling off," said George. "But then you mastered it and I was proud of you. I never was able to do it myself."

"Well, it was then, one morning when Hannah took me out to ride at a place called Kalehuawehe...'where the flowers fall off you.' That was the moment. It was heaven...and it stays living in my mind ever since. I've got to get back there. That's all there is to it."

"We should live every hour, Antipatr, as if our best one is yet to be," said George. "If your future includes you returning as a sea captain to O'ahu and marrying Hannah Holmes, then surely that will become your magical moment, don't you think so?"

"Yes, I do," said Antipatr.

"So that is why you should work as hard as you can in the Naval Academy to see that future become a reality."

"That is what I am doing," said Antipatr. "I'm even trying to take my examinations ahead of schedule, so that I can get on to the seaman-apprentice stage."

"Molodets...That's the way," said George. "I'm sure that some day you and I will both be living in the Hawai'ian islands with our families. We'll get together then and reminisce."

"So do you plan to take Varvara and Inga away with you to Hawai'i, then?" asked Antipatr.

"That is the plan," said George. "I couldn't really leave them again so soon. So I'll be taking them with me, and we won't be back. We'll be leaving St. Petersburg for good, I'm afraid. I'll have to start immediately to turn all my assets here into transportable cash, gold, and jewels, like I once did before evacuating from Moscow. I'll have to sell the mansion and the land Varvara has purchased. And I'll sell the Russian-American Company stock, my rights in the laudanum factory, and everything else."

"But that's a lot of money, Yegor," observed Antipatr. "It's obviously a great fortune. What will you do with all that money in Hawai'i? When we were there, I didn't think we used much actual money at all?"

George laughed. "My father, who was a good businessman, used to say 'Whether you are rich or poor, it's always nice to have a little money'. So, when we get to Hawai'i I'll use the money buy a ship or two so you can captain one of them when you get there."

"Molodets...that's the way," said Antipatr. "That's what I like to hear."

Barbara managed to convince George that he had nothing to fear from an investigation of the balloon project's finances or the death of Anton Antonovich Demidov. Franz Leppich was now, in his absence, clearly understood by all concerned parties to be the one to blame. And nothing at all had been heard from Leppich since his disappearance five years before.

George was very happy to revive his friendship with Nikolai and Ekaterina Karamzin. Nikolai was enchanted by George's tales of his adventures during the past five years, and told him, "Yegor, when I finish my History of the Russian State and get it into publication, I think I'll write a biography of you. You can help me with it and it will be my masterpiece."

George and Nikolai transferred together their memberships from the Moscow masonic lodge to a more convenient one in St. Petersburg called the "Lodge of Elizabeth's Virtue" under the leadership of Nikolai's acquaintance, Sergei Lanskoi. George confided in Nikolai that he wanted to sell all his St. Petersburg holdings, asking Nikolai to help him find people who might want to buy his mansion and other assets. Nikolai agreed to this and also to help George convince the Tsar and his government to annex territory in the Hawai'ian islands as a colony and Company outpost. George said that he would function as the Russian Governor there as well as the Company outpost manager.

"When I'm governor of a Russian colony in Hawai'i," George told Nikolai, "then you and your family will be among my most honored guests. How I would enjoy showing you around the world's closest thing to paradise."

"I think I'm getting too old now to make such a journey, Yegor," protested Nikolai. "Sea journeys are for the young. I have enough trouble surviving the coach ride from Tsarskoe Selo to St. Petersburg. My back aches and I worry continually about how I will be able to relieve myself."

In January and February of 1819 George commenced his activities to convince the government that it should act as he desired in Hawai'i. He gave two presentations in the lecture series Barbara had begun. He wrote articles and letters and sent them to the St. Petersburg News and to several journals. When, in early February, he heard that Tsar Aleksandr had returned to St. Petersburg from Europe, he wrote a letter to the Tsar describing all the commercial advantages to be obtained from the annexation of Hawai'i. He mentioned the multifarious agricultural attributes of the islands, the sandalwood, the fish, taro, and salt ponds. He stated that fruit of all kinds could be dried and imported to Russia, as well as sold to foreign sailors and traders. He mentioned that control of a port there could result in a source of great revenue from fees paid by foreign ships for services and repairs. Hawai'i, he said, had a unique advantage of position—the only land for a thousand versts in the world's largest span of ocean—that could easily be used to unprecedented mercantile advantage by Russia.

George asked again in his letter for a meeting with the Tsar, disregarding what Vasilii Shelikhov had told him of the Tsar's position as he had earlier communicated it to Peter Dobell. But the Tsar would still not see George. Instead, he referred the matter to his new Department of Manufacturing and Internal Trade under the administration of the Minister of Internal Affairs, Osip Petrovich Kozodavlyov. Since Kozodavlyov was known to be a member of the Beseda literary salon as a poet and writer, George asked Nikolai Karamzin to have a few words with him in an attempt to influence him to act positively. But Minister Kozodavlyov sent George a brief response indicating that all commercial advantages of territory in Hawai'i should be the concern of the government-chartered Russian-American Company, which was already fully empowered to obtain such advantage anywhere in the north Pacific. This response caused George to write a second letter to the Tsar on March 2, 1819 expressing his dismay at having his idea for external trade advantages referred to a department of internal trade. Before he got an answer to this, on March 18, Vasilii Shelikhov and the Russian-American Company Board of Directors issued a position statement on the issue to Minister Kozodavlyov and the Department of Manufacturing and Internal Trade, in which the need for the government's military support was described as a prerequisite to gaining commercial advantages in Hawai'i. Meanwhile George had written up a series of invoices for his services already rendered to the government. His intent was to send them to the Ministry of Foreign Affairs.

When George told Vasilii Shelikhov about the invoices and his intention to take the matter up with the Ministry of Foreign Affairs, Vasilii expressed his doubts. "After the aged Count Nikolai Rumiantsev retired as Minister of Foreign Affairs, the Tsar appointed two other prominent Counts to take that position," he explained. "When he was asked about why he had essentially named two Ministers of Foreign Affairs, the Tsar is reported to have joked that 'Russia has more than one man's share of 'foreign affairs'. But unfortunately, the two ministers don't always act in concert."

"Who are they?" asked George. "In Moscow I had a very positive personal relationship with former minister Rumiantsev. He was a lodge brother and I once treated his ears with wine to help his hearing. But now I have to deal with TWO ministers?"

"Well, I think you should choose one," answered Vasilii. "One is Count Ioann Kapodistrias, a man of Greek heritage in his early forties. The other is Count Karl Vasilievich Nesselrode, a man a few years younger than Kapodistrias. Nesselrode is a little man of German heritage with a Jewish mother who strangely chose to raise him in the Anglican protestant faith. They say he's an admirer of the Austrian diplomat Metternich. Also, it was he who processed Peter Dobell's appointment as Consul to the Philippines, but we don't know if he truly supported Peter's proposals or if he was doing it as a perceived exile at the behest of the Count Fyodor Tolstoi. It's difficult to discern."

"Assuming that he speaks German," said George, "I think I would prefer to deal with him."

"Nesselrode's a diplomat, but he can be abrupt in his dealings with people," said Vasilii. "He doesn't suffer fools. The Tsar's other bureaucrats fear him and call him 'Kissel-vrode'...meaning 'like a fruit drink that has a tart bite to it'."

"I'll send him the invoices and request a meeting with him," said George. "It sounds like he is already familiar with the issues, and I can relate to him as a fellow German."

George's copiously detailed invoices represented such a large and imposing bill that Minister Nesselrode sent a courier to inform George that he should come in and arrange a meeting about his "demands." At this meeting, the irritated Minister Nesselrode did not appear, but George was confronted by a representative of the Police—an organization under the ministry of Internal Affairs Minister Kozodavlyov-- who threatened to have him arrested for fraud pending a comprehensive investigation of his Hawai'ian activities if he did not withdraw the invoices. George expressed his outrage, punning angrily that Kozodavlyov was a man who would "strangle a goat," but then withdrew them.

George's continued inability to see the Tsar and his negative exposure to the government ministers at last convinced George that the Russian government was not going to act to advance the interests George perceived for it in Hawai'i. His dream of returning to Hawai'i, revenging himself on the American and British captains and advisors to its King Kamehameha, and becoming its governor was clearly not going to be realized.

George was pleased to find that Barbara was easy to convince that they should sell their assets and leave St. Petersburg. "We really should go back to Germany, George," she said. "My mother is getting older there now, and I'd so like to see her while she's still alive. She should be able to see her only granddaughter. And knowing her will be good for Inga too."

"We can go back to Germany, Barbara," agreed George. "But not to stay. There is no life there for us like I want us to live. We should go on from Germany to Brazil and settle there. It's a grand new country with a vital spirit and a very temperate climate. It's almost as beautiful and fertile as Hawai'i, and it now has a European-style monarchy where I am already known and well regarded. With our wealth, we will be able to live there like royalty ourselves. We can even take your mother with us."

In April of 1819, George offered his Russian-American Company stock to the current officers and directors and found a group of buyers for his rights to the proceeds of the laudanum production. His attitude was just to sell out as rapidly as possible, accepting any total cash offer made. With this attitude as a guideline, Vasilii Shelikhov found a compatible buyer for the Schaeffers' mansion, including its stable, furnishings, and art. The land quickly sold also. No matter the haste of the process and the resultant bargain amounts accepted, by the end of the month the amassed sum for conversion into transportable form amounted to two million, eight-hundred-fifty thousand rubles. Barbara was deeply impressed by such a sum, but George said that it would have totaled five million rubles if they had taken a longer time to find buyers at the appropriate prices for all that they had accumulated. As it was, George joked that the sum was approximately the same as the Tsar spent on each year's end-of-summer public celebration with its pageants, parades, grandiose buffets, and fireworks entertainment. But, be that as it may, the Schaeffers were ready to leave.

Part Ten—Brazil

Back in Germany:

George and Barbara returned to Germany through Livonia and Prussia in a suite of four luxurious coaches with paid drivers and armed mounted guards. They took their time, staying in the best hotels in each city, where George would endeavor to meet the city's mayor or other leading citizens. Their nanny Lara had decided to leave St. Petersburg and stay with them as a member of the family—going where they went, and taking continued care of little Inga, now seven years old.

The Schaeffer party arrived in George's birthplace of Münnerstadt in late May of 1819, having added the requisite twelve days to their calendar. Their arrival and presence at the town's best inn created a local sensation. The citizens were duly impressed with how well their "local boy" had done in life. "Just imagine," many said, "George Anton Schaeffer—one of us—coming to such a station in life." "His wife is such a beauty," they said, "They say he's been all around the world," "I wonder what he paid for those coaches and horses," "Have you ever seen a private citizen with that many guards?" All of them found it important to mention to others their personal connection with him: "I went to school with him," "I remember when he was our pharmacist," "He and I never liked Napoleon and his lackies," and so on.

As they were being driven to the family estate on the Lauer River to pay their respects to George's parents at the family grave site, Barbara told George that she wanted him to be kind and respectful toward his brother Jacob, who had taken up residence there after the deaths of the parents, Nicholas and Margarita Kantz Schaeffer. "In your dealings with your brother, George," she said, "I want you to show the world that you are the bigger man. Be nice to him...magnanimity will become you."

When George encountered his brother Jacob, the man's apparent age surprised him. He looked quite like their father Nicholas had looked as he neared his death. Though fifty-five years of age, fifteen years more than George, Jacob appeared to be sixty-five. Long a stranger to physical work, his stomach protruded prominently and hung low over his belt. His hands had long lost their calluses, and his arms seemed thin and weak. His hair was gone and several of his front teeth were decayed almost into absence. Evidently he had continued his disrespect for medical care. But George strode up to him briskly and hugged him warmly, saying, "Brother Jacob, how nice to see you again after all these years. I can see that you've done well. Thank God for that."

"And I can clearly say the same about you, George," answered Jacob. "Father and mother would be very proud of you. They always told me that you were special...extraordinary...and it turns out that they were right. I'm glad to see you here."

George introduced Jacob to Barbara, Inga, and Lara, then asked him, "Do you know what has become of our brother Wilhelm? Barbara and I once found him in Vienna, but I have had no word since. And do you ever hear from sister Julia?"

"Wilhelm is no longer a soldier. He has returned here whole, thank God, and married a woman from here you may remember—Anna Karlson. They have a young son and live in the city, though pretty poorly. Things have been hard here in the past several years. There is no work and it's tough to make a living. Wilhelm and Anna sell baked goods from the stall that Anna once worked with her late mother. And he helps us out at harvest time. I pay him what I can. Julia lives here now too. She is a teacher in the new secular school, but that's not much more than volunteer work. I keep her from starving."

"But what about the Church?" asked George. "Is Julia no longer a nun?"

"No, she's not," Jacob answered. "She and the Dominicans parted company somehow in Spain after she claimed that certain of the priests were abusing some of her pupils. She's been back almost three years now and hasn't set foot in the Church in all that time. And she's still not married. Potential suitors just don't know how to regard her, I'm afraid."

In the coach on the way back to the inn, George told Barbara that he had once considered Wilhelm's wife Anna a candidate for marriage. But her Lutheran religion and her status in the community as an "experienced woman" left her without his proposal.

"Likely you were just not ready to marry at that time, George," said Barbara. "And I'm very grateful for that."

The reunion with Wilhelm in a small Münnerstadt apartment was very warm. He and George hugged very tightly and slapped each other's back until sore. And George hugged Anna warmly too, saying, "I'm so glad you've taken up with my brother Wilhelm, Anna. He's been such a hero to me all his days, and I hope he is to you."

Anna was an attractive woman of forty, with dark ungrayed hair, and gleaming dark eyes under prominent dark eyebrows. "He is indeed my hero, George," she replied. "And do you know that he named our son 'George Nicholas'...in your honor and to honor your father too?"

George looked in wonder at Wilhelm, and Barbara smiled, her eyes tearing. Wilhelm was still taller than George, though more slender, and he still moved with athletic grace. His face was quite weathered and wrinkled, but his eyes gave it a very pleasant animation.

"You named your son after me? Where is he?" George asked.

"Georgie," Wilhelm called into another room, "Come here and meet your Aunt and Uncle."

At this a tousle-haired boy ran into the room and attached himself to his mother's skirt, peeking out at the guests from behind it.

134

"How old is he?" asked Barbara.

"He's four...born this very month in 1815," answered Anna.

George came closer to Anna and the boy, kneeled down and asked him "Do you know who I am? I'm your Uncle George."

The boy protested sharply, "NO...you not George. I'm George."

Anna patted the boy's head and explained to him, "Now Georgie, you both...you and your Uncle...are named George. We named you George in honor of him."

But again the boy protested, "NO. He NOT George. I'm George."

Wilhelm laughed at his son's vigorous protests at encountering another "George" in his life. "He thinks he's the only George," he chuckled. "And who can blame him? He's always been our only George...all his life."

In subsequent conversation, George and Barbara learned that the politics of 1812 had resulted in Wilhelm serving in Napoleon's *Grande Armée,* a mounted officer in the cavalry. So Wilhelm had been a combatant at the Battle of Borodino outside Moscow while George was trying to raise a balloon to kill Napoleon, the French commander-in-chief. As Wilhelm was ordering cavalry attacks on the Bagration fleches, his own horse shot out from under him, George was with Franz Leppich waiting on word from Dieter Schneider's ill-fated trial balloon detachment sent to nearby Mozhaisk. On that fateful day they had been only a few kilometers apart...brothers on opposing sides in the most intensely bloody conflict in human history.

"And we're both alive and well and here together," said Wilhelm, shaking his head in wonder. And then he asked George, "And do you know who else in our family was there?"

"No, who?" said George, his curiosity definitely piqued.

"Our cousin Michael from Munich," answered Wilhelm. "He was with General Karl Wrede's army of young men from Bavaria, more than thirty thousand of whom died in Russia. Somehow he too survived, though he was wounded at Maloyaroslavets and frozen so that it him took two years to recover his health."

"I remember him well from my pharmacy school days in Munich," said George. "But how do you know about him?"

"Jacob got some letters from him, informing us of the deaths of Uncle Anton in 1813 and Aunt Anna three years later. I wrote him back and we began a correspondence. He came here to visit us last year and is quite well now, though, like everyone else, he hasn't been able to find a good livelihood in this Post-Napoleonic Europe. The economies are still wrecked, business is bad, and the crops don't bring anything. It's very tough to make a living. We can only wonder what we were all fighting about for so long. Certainly our struggles didn't result in a better standard of living."

"We can only have faith that things would have been worse under Napoleon," said George. "I believe this even now that he's been exiled to a South Atlantic island and has no further opportunity to rule anyone at all. And, I can tell you that there are other places in this world where a man's work will be rewarded, and richly. You can own land, work it, and gain that better life you seek...no doubt about it. All you have to do is move there."

"Where is that, George?" asked Wilhelm. "I'd move in a minute if I just knew where to go."

"Brazil, my brother," answered George. "You should move to Brazil. That is my present intent. And I can promise you that you will find life there substantially more rewarding. The climate, both natural and political, is very favorable there now. I've been there twice. I know the rulers personally."

"But it's so far away, George," said Wilhelm.

"It's only a few months of travel by land and sea...a minor adventure, to be sure, compared to what you've seen in life." said George. "And you're still young and fit. Anna and little George would be your helpmates in building a better life, a legacy for your children and grandchildren too."

"But how will we pay for our passage to far-off Brazil? What would we do there? How could we afford to buy any land?" Wilhelm was full of questions and doubts.

An idea suddenly occurred to George. He thought a moment, then said, "You can come with me. I will pay your passage there and buy the land. You would help me build a large plantation estate there on which you will have your own estate as well. It's as simple as that."

"Lord, that's something to think about, that's for sure," said Wilhelm. "Do you have that much money?"

"Yes, I do," answered George without elaboration.

Sister Julia lived in a room in a house owned by one of Jacob's bank employees. Jacob paid the rent, as Julia's work at the municipal elementary school paid only well enough to keep her fed. And she was very, very slender...almost emaciated in appearance. When they met her, George and Barbara both noticed that her every movement was quick to the point of seeming frenetic. "You'll have to excuse me," she said, "I'm used to running after children. You have to be quicker than they are."

In Julia's austere appearance George could still see subtle evidence of the attractive girl Julia had once been. Her arms and hands, legs and feet, were supple and graceful. Her skin was smooth and unmarked by blemish. Her teeth were straight and white and when she smiled her entire surroundings seemed to take on an aura of light. But she seemed generally tired, so very tired...and disappointed in life.

When all the basic facts of their lives apart had been recanted, George bluntly asked Julia, "Julia, have you ever been in love?" Barbara was aghast that

George had asked his sister such a question and grimaced in embarrassment, though she had had the thought herself that Julia's apparent disenchantment with life might be due to her loneliness in it.

"I've dreamed of being in love," Julia said. "And I may have had some opportunities for love in the past. But I was committed to serving Christ and the Church, and men don't approach nuns with the idea of love and marriage. Then I was forced to realize that the Church was itself not following the example of Christ and that I had served a corrupt organization for my entire marriageable youth and more. Since I moved back here the men still don't see me as an eligible person for marriage...once a nun, always a nun, they may think, or worse. Maybe they fear someone they know opposed the Church and left it. I don't know. Maybe I need to find somewhere where my personal history isn't known to one and all."

"Indeed I may have just the place for you, Julia," said George.

"Where is that?" asked Julia.

"Brazil," answered George. "Barbara and I are taking Inga and our family there, and we would gladly include you."

"But Brazil is a country even more Catholic than here, isn't it?" asked Julia.

"The Europeans in Brazil are predominately Catholic in faith, that is true," said George. "And they are working to convert all the natives to Catholicism. But I assure you that people of many faiths now live there amicably. A person's religion does not so determine his life in the new world as it does here in the old. You could practice what religion you want, especially on the plantation estate we plan to build there—or you could hold no religion at all."

"When do we leave?" asked Julia.

In the next week George invited his entire Münnerstadt family to meals at the inn so that they could become reacquainted with him and acquainted with Barbara and Inga. At each of these meals the topic of relocating to Brazil came up, and, somewhat to his own surprise, George found himself praising Brazil as a place to live and advocating that any of his relatives who desired might accompany him there to help him build the plantation estate of his dreams. He would, he said, pay their passage to Brazil in exchange for their help in building his estate and he would see that they had ample chance to acquire their own land and build their own estates. Soon Wilhelm and Anna and Julia were talking seriously about the prospect and asking George pointed questions about it. Only Jacob was persistently dismissive of the idea.

"The grass always seems greener on the other side of the fence," said Jacob at one of these inn meals. "But when you get to the other side of the fence, all you find is nettles. I've heard that Brazil is a vast jungle, teeming with snakes, every kind of bug, and even hostile cannibal tribes. Building a successful plantation there will be more difficult than you can now imagine. Farming is tough enough here in land already cleared and surrounded by civilized people. What will it be like there?"

George fought with himself to stay patient with Jacob.

"I have seen plantations flourishing there," George said. "But I don't deny that building the kind of plantation estate I plan to build will take a great deal of work. No one should come with me to Brazil who is not willing to work."

Barbara was eager to move on to Würzburg to see her mother. George asked Wilhelm to send a letter to their cousin Michael in Munich inviting him to come to Münnerstadt to hear the proposal that he also might emigrate with George to Brazil. He told Wilhelm and Julia that he and Barbara would also be extending an invitation to Barbara's mother. He asked them to make firm decisions in the matter by the time he and Barbara returned to Münnerstadt in two month's time. Moving so many members of the family all at once to Brazil would take much preparation. George would have to decide on a port of departure and charter an entire ship.

On the way to Würzburg in the lead coach, Barbara and Lara tried to prepare Inga for her first meeting with her grandmother.

"Do you know that you have a grandmother named Ingrid Hindernacht who lives in the city we are traveling to?" asked Lara. She was speaking German all the time now and doing quite well in it thanks to her daily practice with both Barbara and Inga.

"Yes, I know," said Inga. "And my first name is really Ingrid. I was named after her. Her last name is Hindernacht because that was my mama's name before she married my papa. My grandfather Hindernacht died and now lives in heaven with my Schaeffer grandparents."

Barbara could only comment, "Inga, you are so smart. Everything is just as you say it is. And I'm sure you will like your grandmother. She's very kind and she always asked about you in all her letters to us."

"I'm sure I'll like her, Mama," said Inga, but then she asked, "Is she very old?"

"She is sixty-seven years old," answered Barbara. "And that is quite old. She's the oldest member of our family now, and I pray that she is healthy and well. We haven't heard from her in some long time. And she doesn't know we're coming to see her."

In Würzburg they found Barbara's mother, the widow Ingrid Hindernacht, living in a room in the rented house of a construction project administrator for the new municipal government named Johann Phillipp Henning. Johann and his wife Sylvia had taken Ingrid in from quite destitute circumstances. She had become homeless after her former rental properties had been condemned so that Henning's construction project could proceed. But in the course of the condemnation process, that resulted in Ingrid's receiving only a pittance of payment insufficient to sustain her, Henning had become personally acquainted with her and impressed by her history of wealth and her network of personal contacts among the city's former elite. So he and his wife decided to provide

Ingrid with a room, asking her only to help in the preparation of meals and in doing laundry.

It took Ingrid several moments to realize just who had come to see her. She seemed puzzled by the attention given to her by her daughter Barbara and son-in-law George when they came to her room accompanied by the Hennings. She recognized that she knew them, but couldn't immediately decide how. Only when her granddaughter Inga was presented to her did it all become clear. Inga looked to her as her daughter Barbara was most firmly impressed into her memory. In those first instants, she saw Barbara in Inga. But then she thought to herself, "Barbara is much older now. She must be the mother, here to see me again." She threw herself at all of them in a group and burst into tears. "Mein Gott, Mein Gott," she said, "I've lived to see you again, my dear daughter Barbara...and to see you again George...and to meet my darling granddaughter. How sweet life has now become to me. God is rewarding me for what I don't know. But how I thank him."

Ingrid looked good, but George and Barbara quickly detected in conversation with her that a certain deficit of mental acuity had crept into evidence. She couldn't find words easily, and this bothered her, so that she would occasionally just stare away with an irritated look on her face. It was clear that George and Barbara had already met the Hennings when she saw them all together at her door, but Ingrid introduced the Hennings to George and Barbara again anyway as "new members of her family."

George was soon very positively impressed with Johann Phillipp Henning. He was thirty-seven years old, having been born and raised in Wertheim am Main. His parents had both died when he was young and he had been taken care of by his maternal grandparents. His grandfather was a prominent builder of bridges and belonged to a constructors' guild, in which he enrolled Johann as an apprentice at the age of fifteen. As he grew and matured in the construction profession, Johann came to prefer to build public buildings of considerable size. After his grandfather died when he was twenty-two, he became the construction assistant to the renowned German architect Reinhard Mainz and worked for two years on the construction of an annex to the Wertheim Municipal Administration Building. He began to seek construction contracts on his own before he was thirty. "I have a gift for fixing and fabricating things. I'm a builder. Whatever you can conceive, I can build it or get it built," he said. "I've built apartment buildings, administration buildings, a hospital building, and part of a prison. Here in Würzburg I'm building a city warehouse and its office center."

"Do you work on this project personally?" asked George.

"Yes, I do," answered Johann. "But mostly I manage the labor...telling other men what to do. Of course, you have to know what to do yourself. Material supply is also a big problem, especially these days. Finding the needed building materials and getting them to the site in a timely manner is no easy task."

"I understand that," commented George. "Once, in the summer of 1812 in Moscow, I was in charge of supplying materials to a project to build a hydrogen balloon to drop explosives on Napoleon from the sky. And I can tell you that it was a real trial to find the things needed and get them into place before Napoleon's army reached the city itself. In fact, the project was, unfortunately, a failure...and partly because of the supply problems."

"Just how did a German physician become a provisioner to a Russian balloon project to kill Napoleon?" asked Johann.

"It's a long story," replied George, waving his hand to signal his desire to change the topic to something else.

Johann's wife Sylvia was thirty years old. She was born in Hannover and met Johann when he was working on a construction project there. It was clear that Johann had not chosen her for her appearance. She was short and stocky of frame, and swarthy of complexion, and she had a too-prominent square jawline that drew attention to her large lips. Her frequent smile somehow showed only her bottom row of teeth. But she was very friendly and gregarious, eager to engage anyone she met in conversation. She and Barbara got on wonderfully from the start, especially inasmuch as Sylvia had such care and affection for Barbara's mother. Sylvia's own mother, now fifty-five years old, lived alone in Hannover.

During the next month, George discharged all but three of the armed guards who had accompanied their coaches all the way from St. Petersburg, giving each of them a substantial severance bonus in gratitude. One of the guards who wanted to stay with him, and even declared that he would go to Brazil too, was Vyacheslav "Slava" Petrov...a huge man who had to shave twice a day to keep his face free of beard. Slava was as strong and tough a man as George had ever seen, and he was an expert with weapons as well. But he was a gentle giant, always polite and kind. What motivated him to want to remain with the Schaeffers was Lara. He had become attracted to her in the course of their travel from St. Petersburg, bowing low whenever he saw her and smiling at her until at last she engaged him in conversation at first trivial and then, by degrees, more comiserative, until at last, as they entered German-speaking territories, Lara told Barbara that she "liked Slava the guard very much."

In Würzburg, Slava Petrov asked George for permission to court Lara.

"I know you are not her father, nor her owner, Gospodin von Sheffer," he said in Russian. "But still I think that proper protocol demands that I get your permission to seek her hand in marriage. Could you please give me your opinion on this?"

"I think that since Lara has no other senior male in her family to speak here in her behalf, I am the proper one," admitted George. "I am the head of the household that employs her. So you've done the correct thing. But I have to tell you that my way is to allow Lara to decide the matter. I will report to her that you have asked me for permission to court her. And I will ask her what I should tell you in answer. If she allows your courtship and the courtship results in marriage, then you, just like she, will be considered a member of my family.

We will be kin. But if she says that she doesn't want to consider you as a suitor, then I think that you should leave us under the same terms as the others I have discharged and return home to St. Petersburg. Are you agreed, Slava?"

"Yes, I agree," said Slava. "But can you tell me Lara's full name? I don't yet know her 'familia'...her last name, and I think that I should know it."

"She is Lara Petrovna Ivanova," answered George. "Her last name is 'Ivanova.' She has told us that both her parents are deceased and her only brother was killed at Smolensk."

George soon told Lara in German that he wished to speak with her about "something personal." Then, changing to Russian, he said, "Our guard Slava Petrov has asked me for permission to court you. He wants to marry you. I have told him that the decision is yours. What do you say?"

Lara's gasp and her instant covering of her face with her hands gave George the answer he expected. "Is that a 'yes'?" he asked.

"Da...that's a 'yes'," she said. "I think he's a fine man and that he will be a good husband...and perhaps father. He wants to come to Brazil to start a new life there too...so his marriage plans won't keep me from staying in Inga's life...and in yours and Barbara's."

"That's the way I see it, Lara," said George. "I'll tell Slava he can begin his courtship, and I will leave the terms of it to you."

There were some problems in convincing Ingrid that she should emigrate to Brazil. The idea was just too foreign to her, too strange and daunting. She had endless objections. "What about my marmelade kitty cat Tommie?" she said. "Who will take care of Tommie?"

"You can bring Tommie with you, Mama," said Barbara. "We'll help you take care of him. That isn't a big problem."

But the Hennings were the real problem. George soon realized that he would have to include them in the emigration plans or Ingrid would never agree to go. And the Hennings were not, like others of his family, dissatisfied with their current lives in Germany. Johann was doing well in life. He was clearly a man of great ability that others recognized. He was ambitious and had a positive future looming in front of him.

George held forth to Johann the "vast potential" that awaited such a builder as he was in Brazil...that "new frontier of the world where all the materials were already in abundance and all that was needed was a constructor extraordinaire to wreak miracles in the building of entire cities." He told Johann that he and Barbara wanted to live on a large plantation estate on land in Brazil that would approximate Eden...the fertility of it simply transcending a European's ability to imagine it. He offered Johann twice his Würzburg salary for two years to come with him and commence the building and the physical management of his Brazilian plantation estate. Like with the others, he told Johann that he would provide him with subsequent opportunity to gain his own estate. He would draw up a legal written contract with these terms clearly specified if Johann so desired.

"George, that's a very fine offer," said Johann. "But it's two birds in the bush for me when I've got one in my hands already. I don't speak a word of Portuguese. How would I instruct anyone there how to build anything?"

"I will personally teach you to speak Portuguese," offered George. "You will be amazed at what you can learn just during the voyage there."

"You are a doctor...and a really intelligent person," Johann continued to object. "And I believe Ingrid and Barbara that you are especially gifted in the acquisition of foreign languages. But it's always been German only for me...and, in Brazil, there aren't many Germans."

"But, even if after my instruction you have language problems in Brazil, we will simply hire an interpreter for you. That's not a large problem," countered George.

George's most persuasive tactic was his offer to bring Sylvia's mother along too.

"Sylvia can go by coach to Hannover right away to bring her back here. And we'll take her with us too...and even her pets, if she has any. She will be there in Brazil living with you in abundance and helping to raise her grandchildren in a land with a bright future," said George.

In the end, Johann Phillipp and Sylvia Henning agreed to accompany George and Barbara and Ingrid to Brazil under the terms of a contract that both Johann and George signed before a Würzburg notary public. Johann resigned his construction administration position immediately and sent Sylvia to Hannover to get her mother, Frau Martha Kemmer.

On the Ship to Rio:

The Schaeffers' emigration party had swelled to a surprising forty-seven people by the time the ship *Argus* departed Amsterdam for Rio de Janeiro. The core group comprised George's brother Wilhelm with his wife and son, sister Julia, Barbara's mother Ingrid Hindernacht, Johann Phillipp and Sylvia Henning, and Sylvia's mother Martha Kemmer. Michael Schaeffer, George's cousin from Munich, had decided not to go with them, since, as a result of a fortuitous marriage, he had recently been appointed to head his father's former department as Inspector of the new Bavarian King Maximilian I Wittelsbach's "Rechnungshof," or Tribunal of Accounts. In a letter to Wilhelm and George,

Michael expressed his "feeling of close kinship and his wish that this great adventure they were embarked upon might show the way for many others."

George had traveled ahead of the others to Amsterdam together with his brother Wilhelm and the guard Slava Petrov to make arrangements to charter the passenger ship. The *Argus* was large enough to transport many more people than were in the Schaeffer party. It was designed to carry as many as two hundred in a situation of "close contact." But George wanted everyone to have the most comfortable possible accommodations, and so he chartered the ship exclusively. The only passengers would be members of his group. And he demanded that the ship stock the best food available and that it have competent staff apart from the sailors to attend to the passengers' needs. "These are my family members, after all," he told Conrad Meyer, the ship's owners' agent. Meyer had agreed to sail on the ship himself to see that all went well. The captain, Bernhard Ehlers, was reputed to be the best captain sailing out of Amsterdam, and his second-in-command and navigator, Peter Zink, was highly regarded for his competence. George was very pleased also when he discovered that all three of these men, Agent Meyer, Captain Ehlers, and Navigator Zink, were members of the same Amsterdam masonic lodge. They were, he said, his "brothers."

After all the passengers were gathered together in Amsterdam, there was still a period of local residence needed while George worked to sell his coaches and his horses. He got a large sum of money changed by the Amsterdam banks to pay his drivers and give Conrad Meyer a deposit on the ship's charter. George was trying to keep accurate records of all his expenditures. He was deeply impressed at how the number of people who were eager to relocate themselves and their families to a distant new country grew upon his description of its merits and his relieving them of immediate expense. Just in a turn of conversation he had invited his brother Wilhelm, dissatisfied with his life in post-Napoleonic Germany, to join him in emigrating to Brazil...then he invited his sister...then his mother-in-law...then... One person needed to bring another: a husband would be accompanied, of course, by his wife and child, a daughter wanted to bring her widowed mother too...and another sibling, or cousin, or just a friend. Clearly there was some kind of latent, but very powerful, impetus for Germans to leave their distressed country to find residence in another. They were activated by hope and by faith in a better future elsewhere...a future George was adept in describing.

The *Argus* left Amsterdam on September 10, 1820. Every day on the deck George would tell his company members about life in Brazil and teach them Portuguese. He enjoyed the teaching, and most of the company aboard enjoyed it too. The children were the most able students of the language, George found. They were not afraid to "babble" in their attempts to say the words, phrases, and sentences George asked them to say. The older people were embarrassed to say things inaccurately or wrongly and would decline to speak or merely mumble, to George's consternation. But in three weeks time, the *Argus* hove to in Lisbon for almost a month's stay. George encouraged everyone to go ashore and practice speaking Portuguese. He wanted to assess the popular attitude in Lisbon with regard to the prospect of the ruler's, Dom João VI's, personal return from Brazil to Portugal, a return he thought was overdue. George believed that Brazil would be better off with Dom João's son, Prince Pedro d'Alcantara, as regent, especially inasmuch as he had been married to the Archduchess Maria Leopoldina Josepha Karolina of Austria...a German-speaking Habsburg. He was very proud to be personally acquainted with her from his 1818 visit to Rio de Janeiro and to be a Major in her personal guard.

George found that the people in Lisbon were quite dissatisfied with Dom João's British proxy, General and Viscount William Carr Beresford, whom Dom João had designated the 1st Marquis of Campo Maior. Popular dissatisfaction had resulted in the rise of dissident movements, some of which were antimonarchist in character, and in riots and uprisings. George's thoughts were confirmed that he should, if he got the opportunity, urge Dom João, whom he had described to his group as his personal friend, whom he had once taught a Russian Orthodox chant, to return to his native Portugal with all possible haste.

The passage across the Atlantic on the *Argus* was a pleasant one. There was only one mild storm, and the area of frequent becalming relented and granted the ship enough wind to cross it without delay. George, remembering how the young Captain Lazarev of the *Suvorov*, had challenged his entire ship's company to a chess game, asked the ship's carpenter to set up a chess board with pegged pieces on the aft deck, and issued a similar challenge of his own. "Something to pass the time," he said. But there was no one aboard with chess abilities sufficient to make winning difficult for him, and after he had won three matches against the company's aggregate efforts, he stopped playing. The Portuguese lessons continued and George gradually became satisfied with the results. His very best student was his own daughter Inga. She constantly impressed the others with her ability to respond in Portuguese and to express herself in it more and more facilely. Obviously she had inherited George's ability to acquire foreign languages.

The need for George to exercise his medical training was very slight, limited only to the extraction of a crew member's tooth and to making an herbal tea to quiet Conrad Meyer's persistent stomach upset. Seasickness had made Ingrid and some others ill early in the voyage, but, as George had said it would, it lessened with time and became manageable with other elixirs from George.

Meals were a fine time for the passengers to gather together around the mess table and talk. The ship's crew prepared and served hearty meals twice a day—at "ten bells" and at "eighteen bells." At each evening meal, the adults were served wine, or, if they requested it, a drink of rum or vodka. This resulted in frequent toasts—"To Brazil and a fine future for all of us," was one, or "To Captain Ehlers and his crew, may they ever sail in peace." But one day, soon after the ceremony they observed when Navigator Zink calculated that they had crossed the earth's equator, Slava Petrov rose at the evening meal to announce that he and Lara had decided to be married on the ship. Captain Ehlers would marry them, he said. His long-time friend and fellow guard Misha Arbuzov would serve as his best man. Barbara would be Lara's maid of honor, and Inga would serve as flower girl and ring bearer. George would be the one to give Lara away. John Henning would say a blessing. And the ship's head cook would make a cake large enough for the entire company and crew to share in celebration. At this announcement, a round of multilingual cheers resounded through the dining room.

"So now you and Lara will need married quarters, is that it?" asked Captain Ehlers with a smile.

"Da," answered Slava loudly when Captain Ehlers' question had been translated for him.

So Slava and Lara were married on the deck beneath a spectacular sunny sky filled with soaring cumulus clouds, and in a fine sea breeze that made the sails strain and the lines creak. Lara wore a beautiful white dress borrowed from Martha Kemmer's trunk of keepsakes, and Slava wore his heavy dark topcoat for dress purposes, even though it was inappropriate to the equatorial temperature. After the celebration dinner and cake, they moved into a stateroom together that Captain Ehlers had had decorated as a "honeymoon suite." They were therafter seen more rarely until the *Argus* reached the port of Salvador on a promontory into All Saints Bay in the Bahia State of northeastern Brazil. Then they went ashore together with the rest of the passengers and crew to meet their first Brazilians.

The people of Bahia were very diverse, but they were equally as welcoming and hospitable. It appeared that they all loved to swim, fish, eat, and drink. One day's late evening celebration was succeeded by an even more salubrious occasion to celebrate the next day. Food and drink seemed plentiful and quite inexpensive. Lively music came to the ears from every inn, park, and public square. And yet, the Catholic Church had a strong presence, with many church buildings and all manner of priests and nuns visible on the streets at any time. George couldn't help but comment to Julia that the Church was not as restraining a factor in the Brazilian people's lives as she had been used to in Europe. "Here the people see God in a different way," he said. "They figure 'God and I are friends, as evidenced by his granting me this beautiful place in which to live. The Church may be a spiritual guide, but it doesn't rule my life. I only need the church as a place to meet other people who see it the same way'. It's a place of social function."

"And is converting the native tribes to Catholicism also a 'social function'," asked Julia.

"Yes, it is...and that primarily," answered George. "The natives will have to live compatibly with all these European newcomers to their land. The Church gives the natives the rudiments of our European civilization, explains to them why and how we do things, aiding our communication and our relations with them and theirs with us."

A Map of Brazil's Regions and States, from:
http://www.ecobrazil.com/into/maps/regional_map.html. George Anton
Schaeffer's activities most importantly involved the Rio de Janeiro, Bahia, and
Rio Grande do Sul States.

"I'm not so sure you are correct about this, George," said Julia. "The Church
is primarily a spiritual organization. It WILL convert the natives spiritually to
see God the way the Church sees him, and ONLY that way. Those who do not
convert are damned in the Church's eyes...and this will inevitably lead to
persecution and harm for the natives. The Church is, unlike Christ, quite
intolerant. I'm surprised you don't understand this."

"I've seen priests, albeit Russian Orthodox priests, expend their lives...every
waking minute...trying to convert the Alaskan natives to a spiritual commonality
with Russians," explained George. "Indeed the Orthodox Church's dogma is as
intolerant as the Catholic Church's, and the priests TRY to enforce this dogma
on the natives, but it doesn't work. The natives retain their former relationship

with their own God...at least in the first generation. But the priests do manage to educate the natives in non-spiritual ways too, and this serves to make the natives compatible partners with us in many ways—military allies, commercial employees and partners..."

"And slaves," interjected Julia.

George was discomfited by this, but continued patiently. "Yes, there are slaves here in Brazil...some native, but even more very harshly imported from Africa. But it isn't primarily the Church that is to blame for slavery. It's secular commerce...the critical need for labor to clear the land, plant the crops, work in the factories. Development depends upon labor...and this labor must be affordable and allow a profit to be made. This is what causes slavery. But we will create our own social conditions here in Brazil, Julia, and we just won't allow slavery in it. It's up to us. We'll make our plantation work...make it profitable...without slaves."

"I'm very glad you see it that way, George," said Julia. "I wouldn't want to be part of a plantation that used slave labor."

The Terms of Land in Brazil:

In Rio de Janeiro on the 5th of January, 1821, George went ashore ahead of the group to request that they be given a royal welcome. He managed through the impression of his formal dress, complete with his medal and sash signifying his officer status in the Princess Consort's personal guard and a great amount of bluster in both Portuguese and German, to gain an audience with the "Kaiserin Leopoldina" on the same day he arrived, and to his great pleasure she was very warm and hospitable. She was clearly pregnant, so that George praised her "radiant" appearance, saying that "mothers-to-be have a kind of glow about them." She told George that she had, since she last saw him, been almost continually pregnant. Daughter Maria da Gloria was already nearing two years of age and was at that active stage which causes all parents to lament it. A son, named Miguel after Pedro's brother, had tragically died on the same day he was born the previous April. And now she was pregnant again, expecting another child in March.

"The death of a child can have lasting effects on a mother," said George. "I can confide in you that my own dear wife has had miscarriages where we lost children soon to be born. She can't ever completely forget these terrible experiences and I am unable to console her when thoughts of the children lost come to her on occasion."

"But I held my little son in my arms," replied Leopoldina. "We had to rush to have him baptized before he passed away. It was very difficult. Pedro was thrilled to have a son, but then he suddenly had none. So now we're trying again."

"And I'll have everyone in my company praying that the birth is successful and that the child born is a joy to both of you," said George. "And can you please tell me the date of your daughter Maria da Gloria's birth? I have recorded in my journal for prayers and toasts that your own birthday is January 22nd...so that you will soon be twenty-four years of age. But I'd like to write in my journal the little princess's birthdate as well."

"Maria's birthday is April 4th," said Leopoldina. "And I like the thought that someone might be praying for her on her birthday. Thank you."

George explained to Leopoldina that he had come back to Rio de Janeiro with that "large amount of capital" that he had told Dom João and the other members of the royal family about during his 1818 visit. And, he told her, he had come on the ship *Argus* that now sat in the harbor with forty-seven other citizens of the German principalities and of Russia who had come with him. His intent was to found a colony that would have a plantation estate at its core on land he hoped Dom João would designate to him in ownership. He dreamed of a kind of titled barony, he told her...one that he could pass on to his heirs and constitute part of his legacy.

"How much capital have you brought with you, Major von Schaeffer?" Leopoldina asked.

George responded, "I don't know what it will come out to in your réis...but certainly more than two million...maybe three."

"Three million?" repeated Leopoldina. "I think I can assure you that Dom João will take such an investment of capital very seriously. I'll arrange to have you talk with him and Pedro too about it soon."

"Do you think that I could get some kind of royal reception for my company on the ship?" asked George. "They are excited about coming to Brazil, thinking that they will have more pleasant and rewarding lives here in the colony I hope to found. After they help me build the core plantation estate and get crops into regular harvest, I want to grant them land of their own to develop. That is the plan."

"And it's a fine plan," said Leopoldina. "You may know that a Frankfurt compatriot of yours, a naturalist named Georg Wilhelm Freyreiss who was an associate of the Russian Consul von Langsdorff and participated in expeditions to our unexplored territories five years ago, is also founding a colony of Germans here in Brazil. He's calling his colony " Colônia Leopoldina," after me. It's in the south part of Bahia on a river inland from the town called Vila Viçosa. That is a very productive area and might be suitable for your plantation estate as well."

"I have heard of Freyreiss, though I haven't met him as I have Langsdorff," said George, "but I didn't know he was founding a colony of Germans. The idea pleases me, of course. The more Germans there are in an area, the more we'll feel at home. Can you get Dom João or Prince Pedro to pay a visit to the ship *Argus* and give a welcome to my company of colonists?"

A formal portrait of Dona Leopoldina of Habsburg, Queen Consort of Brazil, by Luis Schlappriz, date unknown, from:
http://en.wikipedia.org/wiki/Archduchess_Maria_Leopoldina_of_Austria.
Notice that Dona Leopoldina could well be pregnant in the portrait.

"I'll visit the ship myself," said Leopoldina. "And I'll do so tomorrow so they won't have to wait long before coming ashore."

"That's most gracious of you, Your Highness," said George. "I didn't imagine that you would be doing such things in your pregnancy. But I'm very glad to see that you feel healthy and strong enough to do it. I'll return to the ship now and inform the Agent and Captain to expect you tomorrow. When will you visit?"

"I'll be there at noon," she said.

Princess Consort Leopoldina and several of her ladies-in-waiting with an accompaniment of four uniformed guards arrived on the *Argus* a few minutes before noon on January 6th. George, dressed as the day before in his finest apparel and with his medal shining on his chest, introduced Agent Meyer, Captain Ehlers and Navigator Zink to her, saying in German, "Your Highness, allow me to present to you our ship's owners' agent, Herr Conrad Meyer, our ship's Captain, Herr Bernhard Ehlers, and our able Navigator, Herr Peter Zink." Then he turned to the assembly on deck of passengers and crew and said, "And these are the entire company, passengers and crew, of the ship *Argus*. I have told them of your own coming to Brazil from Vienna in marriage to Prince Pedro, the son and heir of Dom João, now by grace of God ruler of Portugal, the Algarve, and also of Brazil. They are waiting to hear a few words from Your Highness."

Leopoldina spoke in a crisp, clear German, saying: "I know that most of you are my compatriots in that we speak the same language and call the same area of Europe our birth home. But now, after only four years here, I am a Brazilian, and am proud to be one. This is a fine land and it has fine people inhabiting it. And there is plenty of room for you. Indeed we need you to help in our country's further development. I assure you that you will have the opportunity here to realize your dreams. All it takes is hard work...something I'm sure you know. In the next week or so your place of settlement will become known to you and you will move yourselves there to begin your new lives. But for now let me suggest that you enjoy your stay in Rio de Janeiro. Please remember that our government is trying to serve you as best it can. I'm hoping that you will all become loyal to it. Major von Schaeffer tells me that you have been learning Portuguese, and that you already speak it commendably. I think you'll find our citizens very eager to speak with you and to help you in whatever ways they can. Thank you all for your patience in waiting to hear me. Now you can go ashore."

As Leopoldina smiled, the passengers and crew cheered loudly and broke from their places into a milling crowd. Leopoldina stepped closer to George and asked him, calling him by his first name, "George, will you introduce me to your family?"

George motioned heartily for Barbara to come over to him and to bring Ingrid and Inga with her. He also motioned for Wilhelm, Sylvia, and Georgie to come, and to Julia. Then he motioned for Sylvia's mother, Martha Kemmer, and to Lara and Slava Pyotrov. All ten of these people, George's "family," quickly approached George and Leopoldina. As George introduced each one, Leopoldina had some particular question to ask. She asked Barbara how she had met George and laughed when Barbara responded that George had been her swimming instructor in Würzburg. When Wilhelm told her that he had served in the Austrian army, she asked him if he knew her uncle, the Archduke Charles...but Wilhelm said he did not, being only a "rank and file soldier." When she asked little Georgie if he was eager to leave the ship, Georgie ignored the question and asked, "Are you really a princess?" Leopoldina told him, "Yes, I am. And now you've met a real princess. But I'm sure you'll meet many more in your lifetime." She asked Slava Petrov if it was the Russian food that caused him to grow so big. When George told Slava what she had asked, Slava grinned and nodded affirmatively, "Da, russkoye blyudo ochen' khoroshee...Yes, Russian food is very good."

Leopoldina spotted Ingrid's cat Tommie on the deck and went over to reach down and pet the thoroughly spoiled pet of the entire ship's company, causing widespread positive commentary from the watching company and crew. She then came back to George, who was standing with Barbara, and asked, "George, what has happened to that handsome young man you had with you in 1818...the one who proposed marriage to my lady-in-waiting, Lucinda Arriaga? I think his name is Phillip."

George was taken aback. "His name is Filip Osipov, and I assumed that I would find him here married to the Lady Lucinda. He couldn't wait to leave St. Petersburg as soon as we got there in December of 1818. So I paid his way back to Rio de Janeiro on the ship *Natalia Petrovna* and he departed in January. Did he not get here?"

"Lucinda has not seen him," said Leopoldina. "For more than a year she suffered waiting, hearing nothing from him, much to the distress of her family. Now she's married someone else and worries about what she'll do if this 'Filip' should now appear."

"Well, I just don't know what to think about this," said George. "I can tell you, and Lucinda if you want, that his love for her was sincere and that he was making every effort to return here to marry her. Of that I'm very sure."

"And I am also sure," vouched Barbara in Portuguese. "He was a good young man, and he thought only of his Lucinda all the time he was with us."

George then said, "I think I will go to the port and check the record of arrivals to see if the *Natalia Petrovna* ever got here. It should have arrived in May or June of 1819...July or August at the latest."

In the next two weeks George had two audiences with Dom João. In the first meeting he renewed his acquaintance with Dom João, reminding the ruler of the circumstances of their previous meetings. Dom João had gained some weight and his face looked a bit wan and pale. He introduced George to "one of our designated advisors." This was Jose Bonifacio de Andrada e Silva, whom Dom João described as a "Santos-born savant," having been educated in France, Germany, and Italy...an expert in metallurgy and mining who had been named the "Perpetual Secretary" of the Lisbon Academy of Sciences and who had come back to Brazil in 1819 to become active in matters of government.

George was pleased to hear Dom João relate that Jose Bonifacio de Andrada e Silva spoke not only German as a consequence of his study in Freiburg, but also English, French, Italian, and Spanish. Jose Bonifacio was wearing European-style breeches and a powdered wig, and was a man of approximately George's height, and well proportioned. George guessed him to be in his middle fifties of age. Dom João told George that he had assigned Jose Bonifacio to be Prince Pedro's closest political advisor, tolerating in his son's tutelage, a "democrat, an abolitionist, and liberal who thinks that Brazil should be an independent constitutional monarchy." This description impressed George and he was surprised that Dom João would engage the services of such a man to advise his son. And he wondered how the tempermental and authoritarian Prince Pedro would consider such a man's advice.

Jose Bonifacio de Andrada e Silva (13 June, 1763—6 April, 1838) in a portrait by Oscar Pereira da Silva (1867-1939), from: http://en.wikipedia.org/wiki/Jose_Bonifacio_de_Andrada_e_Silva.

After George gained Dom João's agreement to meet more substantively later in the week about the terms of his investment of capital into Brazil, he had the opportunity to speak with Jose Bonifacio. Just as he was wondering whether he should speak to the man in German instead of Portuguese, Jose Bonifacio said to him in good German, "I notice the ring on your finger, Herr von Schaeffer...how it's turned around so that the medallion is concealed in your hand. Does that mean that you are a mason?"

George was suddenly embarrassed and did not know how he should answer. He had heard that Dom João had banned masonry in Brazil as a subversive organization. But Jose Bonifacio, perceiving George's consternation, continued, "I am also a mason. I was initiated in Europe and have been working secretly here to organize a lodge in Rio. I'm gradually trying to persuade Prince Pedro that masonry isn't incompatible with Catholicism and that it has much positive to contribute to the development of a new society. Yet I would advise you for now to put the ring in your drawer, if you know what I mean."

George was grateful for the advice. "Yes, you are correct, my good friend," he said, "I have been a mason since I was in Moscow several years ago. I had not worn the ring for some time, but put it back on while on the ship here, since the owner's agent and the ship's officers are fellow masons. I know that Dom João is against masonry, so I would never wear the ring to an audience with him. I just forgot I was wearing it. Thank you for cautioning me about it."

"Very good," said Jose Bonifacio. "And from now on, let us be on a first-name basis. Do you mind if I call you 'Jorge' in Portuguese? You can call me 'Jose'."

"That would be fine," said George. "But please allow me to ask you if you are related to the Antonio Carlos de Andrada who was imprisoned here for conspiring to free Napoleon Bonaparte from St. Helena in a balloon. Is he a relative of yours"

"He is my brother," answered Jose Bonifacio with some discernible discomfort. "And he is no longer in prison. My father managed to persuade Dom João that the plot was too implausible to be believed and that he should be released. The whole episode was an embarrassment to my family...an embarrassment we blame on the French...and we don't like to talk about it."

"I understand," said George.

The second and more substantive meeting with Dom João included Prince Pedro. Both father and son treated George quite cordially, especially when George signed over to Dom João's royal account in the *Banco do Brasil* a promissary note in the amount of a million réis. George was confident he could come up with that number of réis in private commercial exchange in Rio for an appreciable part, though not nearly all, of his gold bullion and jewels. This would take some time, they agreed, and George would have to establish bank accounts of his own as well. Dom João referred George to a firm of financial advisors, with British principals named Timothy Wolf and Raymond Kelsey, and suggested that he consult as well with Leopoldina's German-speaking consultants, Dr. João Martinho Flach, with whom George was well acquainted already, and Johann Natterer, a Vienna zoologist who had come to Brazil in Leopoldina's party in 1817 and had already begun a large collection of bat, fish, and insect specimens on expeditions into the Brazilian wilds.

Dom João agreed to transfer to George unencumbered title to a square legua...two and a half kilometers on a side...of royal land upstream near Vila Viçosa from where Georg Wilhelm Freyreiss was being allowed to situate the Colônia Leopoldina. The site was in the extreme southern Bahia State of Brazil, about 750 kilometers north of Rio de Janeiro...six weeks travel by mule overland along the shore with its many ferries and fords, but only a week away from Rio de Janeiro by ship if the wind was right. This was, he told George, a particularly fertile area, suitable for a plantation, and with river access to the sea to enable transportation of crops to more populous markets. His lands director assured him, he said, that this square legua of land had quite a large portion of it already arable...that is, free of the very dense jungle indigenous to the area. On a central hill strategically overlooking the river in it was a recently abandoned military outpost, now bereft of soldiers who were already billeted in Rio de Janeiro preparing to ship back to Portugal with Dom João.

"So, your Majesty, you have decided to return to Portugal," commented George. "I remember that seven years ago in 1814 you told me that you were like a salmon, yearning to return to the stream where it was spawned. But this is a wise decision also in the political sense. When I was in Lisbon only a few months ago, I learned that the people are very dissatisfied there without you."

"We are indeed returning to Portugal," said Dom João, using his customary royal "we." "We tell you, and this is in confidence, that we'll be sailing in late March or April. Prince Pedro will be a loyal and able regent for us here. As you know, his wife is expecting another child in March, and it would be nice to hold our grandson and heir in our arms before we depart. Pedro tells me that if the child is indeed a son, he will name him João Carlos after us."

George wanted to gain agreement from Dom João and from Prince Pedro also that the square legua of land he was being granted for his colony could thereafter be expanded to allow for the creation of future estates for the others in his company. "My dream," he told them, "is to develop much more land than a square legua. I can walk around a square legua of land in a half day. Certainly my investment with you in the future of Brazil is worth many times the value of a square legua of land. I dream of developing an area equal to that of the principality of Franconia where I was born or more. Have I been dreaming in vain?"

"No, not at all," said Dom João. "The square legua is just the beginning. You are correct that an assessment of its value is far less than a million réis. We like to accomplish things in stages. We will set up an agreement...a written contract if you want...that specifies a set price you may always pay for more of our royal land surrounding the legua, territory we believe to exceed the size of Franconia. This way you will be able to pay for an expansion of your legua from the profits made on it without diminishing the amount of your initial investment, which we will be using for other purposes as well. And we will grant you a worthy title too, when your services in development of our country are in a more advanced stage. Surely you know that the development of a plantation on a square legua of land is not worthy of such a title...and not even that is yet accomplished. Rewards will come with accomplishments...we will see to this."

George told Dom João and Prince Pedro that he was satisfied with these arrangements and requested only that they give him some kind of documentary evidence of it, specifying the particulars of the option to purchase more land at a prescribed price. He was assured that a kind of charter, signed by both of them, would be forthcoming. He was to show this document and its appendices to the military authority in Vila Viçosa and an official there would accompany him to the outpost and record his ownership locally. All George's doubts and concerns had vanished. He was immensely pleased. To Prince Pedro he said, "I'll have all my company praying that your child with the Kaiserin Leopoldina is a son. I know that you already have a delightful daughter, the little Princess Maria."

1816 portrait of Prince Pedro da Braganza of Portugal, Brazil, and the Algarve (12 October, 1798—24 September, 1834) by Jean-Baptiste Debret (1768-1848), from: http://en.wikipedia.org/wiki/Emperor_Pedro_I.

"The Princess Maria is indeed a delight to us," said Pedro. "And I thank you for praying for us to have a son. That is very good of you."

George had rented a villa in Rio de Janeiro to house his company ashore, and all members of it were delighted to make the acquaintance of the city and its inhabitants. Both the place and the people were so overwhelmingly beautiful, so filled with opportunity and encouragement at every turn. "Could this really be January?" they asked George. "It's so sunny and warm. The air simply caresses us." When George reminded them that January was summer to the subequatorial Brazilians, they said, "But it isn't really hot either. And the rains are tolerable on us every day, causing only rainbows for us to admire." The rife abundance of vegetation also impressed them. Every manner of fern, shrub, bush, cactus, and tree seemed intent on taking over those other plants around it, and the flowers and fruit were in such easy abundance that they could only thank George repetitively for bringing them to such a place.

The *Argus* waited in the harbor, replenishing and advertising for passengers and cargo bound back to Amsterdam. George had gotten along very well with his fellow masons, Conrad Meyer and the ship's officers. When he settled with them for the voyage he included substantial bonuses, telling them how grateful he was for giving him and his company such a trouble-free trip to Rio. Conrad Meyer told George that he would welcome future opportunities to provide transportation for whatever purposes George might have. He said he was "masonically" acquainted with the principals of many shipping firms in Rotterdam, Amsterdam, Hamburg and Bremen, so that he could, if needed, arrange the chartering not only of individual ships, but entire fleets. Captain Ehlers said that he would recommend George's employ to all the captains he knew. "I've never worked for a more generous and reasonable man," he told George.

Meetings with Old Friends:

Within the first week, George renewed his acquaintance with Dr. João Martinho Flach. Dr. Flach, who looked to George as if he hadn't aged at all, was quite effusive when he first came seeking George and encountered him on the street outside the villa George had rented.

"My good friend," he boomed, "Princess Leopoldina told me that you have come back here to Rio...and that you've brought your whole family with you. She says you've invested a great sum of money into the royal accounts and that you'll be starting a colony here. What wonderful news! What wonderful news indeed! How happy I am to see you again."

"And I you, Martin," responded George, embracing the man. "Please come with me into this villa so that you can meet my family. My wife and daughter are inside...my brother, sister, and others too."

Dr. Flach, after he had been introduced to everyone, was especially taken with Barbara. He engaged her in conversation, and, at her request, spoke to her in Portuguese. When she had difficulty understanding him, he patiently repeated what he had said. She responded to him in German. In this way Barbara could increase her understanding of Portuguese, while not sacrificing conversational facility because of her still more limited ability to speak it.

"What did you think of our Princess Leopoldina?" Dr. Flach asked.

"She impressed me very positively," said Barbara. "Coming onto our ship at George's request to welcome us was a very fine gesture...especially since she's expecting a baby in only two months time. Everyone felt better about transplanting themselves to Brazil when she said that she already considered herself a Brazilian after only four years here. But then she spoke personally to several of us. She asked me how I came to meet George...just like a friend or a sister would do. As a result of this, I already feel that she is 'my princess,' and not just some distant member of the royalty I might hear about."

"She is indeed an extraordinary young woman," said Dr. Flach. "I also have become more and more impressed with her as I have gotten to know her better."

"George tells me that she lost a baby son only last April," said Barbara. "And that now she's expecting another baby in March. As her physician, do you think that is wise? I would think that she should have more time to rest between pregnancies...even more so if she is going to be carrying out official duties so late in them."

"Indeed I have told her that she should have at least six months rest between pregnancies...a year even," said Dr. Flach. "She doesn't say it, but I think she just doesn't feel that she can deny Prince Pedro's demands on her. She is grateful that he even makes such demands, since he has never stopped consorting with other women. One mistress in particular is well known. Her name is Domitilla Marqueza de Santos...but it's a name not to be said in the Princess's presence."

"That's shameful," said Barbara. "To have a wife of such quality and to treat her with such disrespect. I don't think it bodes well for Brazil to have such a man as Pedro ruling it."

"Well, Prince Pedro isn't all bad," said Dr. Flach. "He's a man who is accustomed to being given whatever he wants, and he is powerfully attracted to female beauty. Princess Leopoldina is, at least in comparison to some of Pedro's mistresses, quite plain. So he strays. That is a fault that that he won't, or can't, change, and his wife will just have to live with it. So that is what the Princess does. Despite Pedro's unfaithfulness, I think that Leopoldina sees something positive in him and has even come to love him."

"Really?" said Barbara, "How very sad for her."

Dr. Flach introduced George to Johann Natterer, the zoologist, who was one of Princess Leopoldina's closest confidants and had come with her from Vienna. Dom João had suggested that George consult with Natterer about financial matters, but this recommendation was a mystery to Natterer, who told George, "Sometimes Leopoldina needs money to do certain important things she wants to do...to buy diapers for poor babies, to circulate books among her literacy centers, to buy food to attract people to her educational gatherings, and to accomplish all kinds of charity. And her royal allowance simply isn't sufficient. And when she tells Prince Pedro this or Dom João they tell her there is just no way that her allowance can be increased. This is why she enrolls people like you into her personal guard. You are not only a guard, but a possible source of revenue to pay for the things she wants to do here. Just wait and you will see. She will be asking you for money. Maybe Dom João knows that I've become the Princess's banker, managing the account she draws from for charitable purposes."

A drawing of Johann August Natterer (9 November, 1787—17 June, 1843) from: http://en.wikipedia.org/wiki/Johann_Natterer.

"Has she asked you for money?" George asked Natterer.

"From time to time I have given her some money for causes I thought were good," answered Natterer. "But, of course, I don't have that much money. I have some inheritance left in a bank account of my own, and I have a stipend on which to conduct my collections."

"I wouldn't have imagined that a royal Princess would have such need to ask private citizens for money," said George. "I thought that Princesses like Leopoldina had all the funds they would ever need and more. So please tell me this-- When you give her this money, is it considered a loan, or is it just a gift?" asked George. "And if it's a loan, does she ever pay it back?"

Dr. Flach answered for Natterer, saying, "She pays us back for whatever we give in honorifics—awards and titles and opportunities she can give for us to develop other sources of income. I earn, for example, a small salary to be on a hospital board. Johann has a similar position, obtained upon Leopoldina's recommendation, to administer a museum that Dom João commissioned. Also, he has a salary as her supervisor of secretaries. She got him that."

"So you don't get the money back?"

"Never," said both Dr. Flach and Natterer in unison.

One day to the villa came Esteban and Rodrigo Rodriguez. They were also very cordial when they met George again. And George was happy to see them. He introduced them to his family and many of his company and invited them to a meal served in the central veranda. The brothers were obviously impressed by the wine and fare, a richly seasoned vegetable soup and roast beef carved off a spit by a burly waiter.

"How did you find out that I am here?" asked George.

"Rodrigo works at the port now," said Esteban. "He noticed your name as the charterer of the Amsterdam ship *Argus*. It just has to be our friend the Doctor 'Jorge von Schaeffer,' he said. So we made the effort to find out...and here it IS you. No doubt you remember that you told me three years ago that you would be back here two years ago with the rest of the money you owe us. Do you have it now? It would certainly appear so."

"Indeed I do," said George. "And I'll be paying you with interest. You are my friends and you certainly earned it."

"How much are you talking about, Jorge?" Rodrigo asked.

"The share for a sailor on the *Suvorov* turned out to be six hundred and fifty rubles," explained George. "That would be approximately one thousand réis...about two year's wages, I would think, for a Rio de Janeiro port worker. So I would owe you two milréis...a thousand each. Now I have already given you, when I was here in 1818, six hundred réis...three hundred each. That means that my debt to you now would be fourteen hundred réis...seven hundred more each. But, I think it fair to pay the debt with interest, thanking you for your patience in waiting for me to return here as I said I would. So, I will now give you a milréis each. I will give it to you as you desire...in paper or in gold or diamond equivalents."

"We'll take the gold," said Esteban, speaking for his brother as well.

"Then we'll need a formal assayer's assessment of the amount at the current rate of exchange," said George. "Can you give me three days to get this? Also, Rodrigo, I could use your help...just a minor favor. Will you make an inquiry into the port arrivals' record to see if a ship out of Riga called the *Natalia Petrovna* arrived here. It was supposed to be here in May or June of 1819. I was once a passenger on it myself. The Captain's name is Andrei Sinelnikov."

"We've waited three years for our money now," said Rodrigo, smiling. "I think we can wait another three days. And we thank you for treating us so fairly. We'll be back here then. And I'll find out what I can about the *Natalia Petrovna.*"

In three days George had the proper amount of gold ready for the brothers Rodriguez when they came back to the villa for it. Rodrigo gave George the bad news that the *Natalia Petrovna* was presumed lost in the central Atlantic in April of 1819.

Dr. Flach informed George that Dr. Georg Heinrich von Langsdorff, the Russian Consul to Rio de Janeiro, was in the city seeking a ship to travel to St. Petersburg. He had, Dr. Flach related, been planning a large expedition into the Brazilian Amazon basin to investigate the geography, flora, fauna, and peoples. He had already received commitments from a host of prominent scientists who would be joining him if he received the funding that he had applied for from the Russian Academy of Sciences. He intended on his trip to St. Petersburg to petition Tsar Aleksandr himself for support.

George eagerly sought out Dr. Langsdorff, finding him in the tavern room of a central city hotel. When he caught first sight of Langsdorff he noticed that the man had gained weight since he saw him last at his plantation estate of Mandioca, but he was still a slender man.

"My dear colleague, Georg Heinrich," he said as he approached the tavern table where Langsdorff was sitting alone, "I hear that you are planning another expedition. Was the earlier one into Minas Gerais not enough for you? What about your insanity?"

Langsdorff looked up in surprise, and, recognizing George, replied, "George Schaeffer...as I live and breathe. Our paths cross again. Where have you been for these past three years? What are you doing here now?"

"I've been in Germany," answered George. "But I've come back with my wife Barbara and my daughter Inga, as well as a quite large party of family and friends to found a plantation estate like yours at Mandioca."

"Where will it be? What will you grow?"

"It'll be in Bahia, but south of you, near a town called Vila Viçosa on the Rio Peruípe," said George. "There was a military settlement of some kind there, but it has been abandoned now. I'm told it's a quite nice location. I'm thinking to grow coffee there, sugar cane, and perhaps pineapples."

"All those take years to develop as crops," said Langsdorff. "You can't get a marketable bean out of a coffee tree in less than four years from planting. Sugar cane takes substantial processing ,to make what you ship economical. Pineapples are easy to grow from tops, suckers, or slips...and they proliferate. But you'll see no pineapples for two years. In the meantime you should plant cotton. That's what I did, and it worked out well."

George already knew this, and, smiling, he said, "Actually, I think we'll be growing a number of things...cotton and flax included. I've always had an interest in medicinal plants and we may try some of those. I've got a large collection of seeds that I've been gathering for years. Dom João tells me that the land I'm getting is quite fertile and that much of it has already been cleared of forest."

"Your description of where it is sounds like it's quite near where Freyreiss is planning a German colony he calls 'Leopoldina'. Is that where it is?" asked Langsdorff.

"Apparently so," said George. "Do you know him?"

"Oh yes. I know him quite well. He was on one of my earlier expeditions, in fact...though he left it before things became difficult."

"But those difficulties haven't dissuaded you from trying another expedition?" asked George. "Our friend Flach says you're traveling to St. Petersburg to get funding for another one."

"Indeed I am," said Langsdorff. "And I haven't forgotten that I should advance there your idea of annexing territory in the Hawai'ian islands. I'll certainly advocate that most strongly for you."

"There's no longer any need," said George. "I've given up on that idea. The Tsar's ministers convinced me that it's futile. Russia will never claim any part of Hawai'i, even though it well should. Tsar Aleksandr is quite resolute about not annexing any more territory, especially in the Pacific. The Pacific fur enterprise in North America is too far away to sustain as a Russian possession, he says. It's too expensive, not worthy of supporting with the annexation of more temperate provisioning outposts or trading ports. It's a short-sighted mistake, but I'm now convinced there's nothing we can do to correct it. So you can spare your efforts."

"All right, George," said Langsdorff. "But isn't it interesting to consider that the Russian Tsar Aleksandr will support the exploration of the Amazon basin in almost-as-distant Brazil...at least I think he will. It's likely that this just does not entail an annexation of any kind...but only exploration, the description and collection of socially valuable data of all kinds. And this will be a grand expedition indeed. My intent is to map the watersheds from São Paulo well north into the Pará Territories of the Amazon Basin. Have you heard of the scientists Ludwig Riedel, or Edouard Menetries, Christian Hesse, or Nestor Rubtsov? They've all written that they want to come. And the inventor Karl von Drais...a brilliant young man. And the artists...just imagine having Hercules Florence, Johann Moritz Rugendas and Adrien Taunay on the same expedition. Tauney has done illustrations in Hawai'i where you've been. There's no end to what such an expedition could accomplish."

"I've heard of some of these men," said George. "But I've been somewhat out of touch in the past few years and don't know about the others. It sounds like a important undertaking. And if I were the Tsar I would definitely give it all due support. But I worry about you, my friend. Leading such an expedition into the unexplored Amazon basin jungles can be, as you well know, dangerous. Your own experience in this should be a lesson to you. Did you not lose your mind for some prolonged period of time as a result of the fevers and the stress of such a journey? What does your wife Friederike say about this? Don't I remember her strong opposition to such an idea?"

"Indeed you do," answered Langsdorff glumly. "She's already left me in reaction to the idea. She went back to Europe, taking Rico and Wilhelmina with her. I've leased Mandioca to a man under the condition that he treat the slaves as we did, and share the profits with them too. That's all I could do legally. Of course the insanity I suffered on my previous expedition was a terrible trial, but without perseverance through such trials science will not advance. And I am a scientist, first and foremost."

"But to give up your wife and children," said George, shaking his head negatively, "That seems too high a price for what scientific advancement you might accomplish."

"I haven't given them up, George," said Langsdorff. "I'm only enduring a separation from them for a time to do what I must do. You did the same when you signed onto that Russian circumnavigation in 1813."

This thought gave George pause. For what accomplishment did he leave Barbara and Inga in foreign St. Petersburg for over five years? It was a thought that was bitter to him. But, thinking of Barbara and a wife's sometimes hard lot, he asked, "Does Friederike understand it this way?"

"Perhaps not yet," Langsdorff said.

There was a pause in the conversation while Langsdorff finished a drink that had sat untouched in front of him since George had approached him. Langsdorff put the mug down and said, "Do you know, George, that I have a piece of mail for you? It came addressed in care of the 'Russian Consul in Rio de Janeiro,' but it has your name on it. I've had it more than two months, even though I didn't really know if I'd ever see you again."

"Who is it from?" asked George.

"It's from Vasilii Grigorievich Shelikhov in St. Petersburg," answered Langsdorff. "It was sealed with the Russian-American Company stamp."

It turned out that Dr. Georg Heinrich von Langsdorff left Rio de Janeiro in late January of 1821 on the same ship *Argus* that had delivered George and his party to Brazil. George had recommended the ship to Langsdorff and then introduced him to Captain Ehlers. Amsterdam would become a stop in Langsdorff's way back to St. Petersburg.

The letter from Vasilii Shelikhov read in Russian as follows:

"March 12, 1820

St. Petersburg

Dear Yegor and Varvara,

Greetings from wintry Nevskii Prospect in St. Petersburg. I'm sending this letter in care of Consul von Langsdorff, hoping that you do wind up in Rio de Janeiro as you planned. My news for you is likely to make you sad. I have to report to you that some people you know have passed away in the past year. The first was our Company Manager and Russian-America Governor Aleksandr Andreevich Baranov. At our instruction Lt. Hagemeister relieved him of command in Novo-Arkhangelsk and he was then rather amicably replaced by our man Iankovskii who even married his daughter Irina. On a ship bound for St. Petersburg, he died off the coast of Java on April 16, 1819 and was given to the sea. What a pity that he didn't live to see his son Antipatr qualify as a naval officer. Antipatr has passed his exams and is scheduled for a ship's assignment soon. He is taking his father's death very hard and is frequently ill. I worry about him. Within a month of Manager Baranov's death, on May 8th of last year, King Kamehameha of Hawai'i died, and his succeeding son Liholiho is facing some problems with the people there. Our agent Peter Dobell is on his way there now. Dobell's position as Consul in the Philippines was not approved as we feared. But I'm informed that he has married a woman from Tobolsk named Daria and has her with him on his ship, the *Sylph*. Your friend and our Russian hero, General Aleksandr Petrovich Tormasov, a truly great man as you know, died on November 13, 1819 and is buried in Moscow's Donskoi Monastery Cemetery. Nadia and little Varochka and the infant son 'Count Kolyusha' they had together, as you might imagine, are heart-broken. The General's death is such a loss for us all. But the worst for me is my mother, Natalia Alekseevna Shelikhova, who passed away only days ago, giving me the resolve to write this letter to you. You will recall how she always so adored your Inga. Please give Inga a consoling embrace from me.

Your house is being sold again already by the current owner...one of the Merkulovs, I think...who bought it from that fellow we found who purchased it from you. Apparently you sold it too cheaply and these people are all taking profits from successive rapid sales. We never even got to know any of them as neighbors. That first fellow didn't even move in, but just sold it right away to someone else.

Everyone else is doing fine. Petya and Olya transmit their greetings to you, and so do the Buldakovs. Ekaterina and Nikolai Karamzin have asked about you and send their best wishes also.

With warmest regards,

Vasilii."

Frankenthal:

When the time came to depart by mule caravan with the purchased livestock along the coast to Bahia, several of the company decided that they wanted to stay in the city of Rio de Janeiro...so enchanting and filled with opportunity did they now consider it. This did not surprise George and he tolerated well the loss of these people to his intended colony. He couldn't deny that life building a rural plantation in a remote undeveloped region would be quite different than that they were experiencing in the country's largest city. He could only be grateful that his closest core of family members and friends...precisely twenty adults and seven children...were happily resolved to travel with him to begin their new plantation life in Bahia.

As George and Wilhelm and Johann were working to pack all manner of agricultural supplies onto the mules George had purchased, a courier from Princess Leopoldina came to give George a written request that he come to the palace to see her. He went immediately and was admitted without a wait to see her in an official reception room near the entrance.

Leopoldina was dressed very casually in a tan shift that resembled a Russian "khalat," and with felt slippers on her bare feet. Her natural reddish blonde hair was falling down her back, bound only by a piece of yarn, and her face was not covered by any powder or creams. To George she appeared as an ordinary young woman such as he might encounter in any village or town in Austria or Germany or Switzerland. But her swollen belly was clearly evident beneath her shift. Her delivery date was only weeks away now.

"George, I know that you and your family are about to leave for Bahia," she said. "So, I wanted to come to an agreement with you about your continued services to me as a Major in my guard."

"I will always be at your service, Your Highness," replied George. "All you have to do is summon me and inform me of what you need done, and I'll do my best to see that it is done."

"That is very kind of you, George, and I appreciate it very much. But I would like to give you a special kind of status here in the palace—the position of chamberlain, so you can enter the palace whenever you want and we can communicate more easily."

George didn't know quite what to make of this offer. "In Russia the court chamberlains are quite powerful people who usually have the rank of 'Count'," he said. "Will that be the case here? What duties will I have? What pay?"

"There is no rank nor pay for now," Leopoldina said. "I don't have the power yet to confer such. But I can foresee that I may gain such power in the near future...after Dom João leaves and Pedro becomes the official regent, or more."

"What do you mean by the phrase '...or more'?" asked George.

"I mean that Pedro could become the ruler of Brazil independent of his father in Portugal," said Leopoldina. "Does such an idea shock you?"

"It surprises me to hear it from you," admitted George. "Will you be advocating such independence after Dom João returns to Portugal?"

"Yes, I will," she said. "And I'd like to know if you will you help me in this."

George thought for a second or two and then said, "Yes. I believe that Brazil will be better off as an independent country, and I will help you."

"For now, of course, we will have to keep such a cause a secret among us," said Leopoldina. "But it is for that reason that I need your services. So you will be appointed an official palace chamberlain. And you won't have anything regular to do, especially since you are about to leave the city to begin your colony in Bahia and may be gone for some time. It's just that I need to have very resourceful people around me, people who understand me and with whom I can speak openly...people I can trust."

"I am certainly one of those people," George assured her. "I'll be returning as often as I can to Rio de Janeiro, and I'll always come to see you to see how I may be of service to you. You can rely upon me."

"Then good luck to you in building your colony in Bahia," she said. "What will you call it?"

"I will name it 'Frankenthal,' as any good Frank would," said George.

The journey to the site of Frankenthal was quite a trial, with thirty-five mules, five horses, twenty head of cattle including a recalcitrant bull, a dozen sheep, and a dozen goats with two wonderful shepherd dogs named "Fitzli" and "Putzli" to herd them. There were also crated chickens, and pigs that needed frequent removal from their carts. Tommie the cat was carried in a fabric-screened cage and allowed exit from it only on a leash. The route followed the beautiful beaches along the coast northward from Cabo Frio, needing to ford or be ferried across a number of ocean-entering rivers. Progress was slow. The summer weather was hot and there were frequently soaring towers of cumulus clouds boiling up above them and hitting them with powerful driving rains that soaked the new settlers to the skin. Yet spirits were good, and everyone, even the elders like Ingrid and Martha, and youngsters Inga and Georgie, made what efforts they could to help. The people in the settlements they passed through, including the port town of Vitória in the Esprito Santo State, were very friendly and helpful.

After seven weeks of this trial, the caravan reached the entry into the ocean of the strongly flowing river Peruípe and the seaside community of six hundred residents called Vila Viçosa. The beach there was broad and magnificent, with golden sloping sand entering the brilliantly azure ocean as it contrasted with the rust-brown silt poured into it by the Rio Peruípe. An impressive number of boats and small ships had found harborage in the river above its last meandering turn into the ocean. Vila Viçosa was a fine port for shallow-draft craft. This meant that, although the journey of 750 kilometers overland from Rio de Janeiro along the beach route took the mule caravan seven weeks, the sea journey from Vila Viçosa to Rio de Janeiro only took seven or eight days, depending upon the wind. This fact pleased George immensely as he considered what a trial the overland journey had been.

The official in Vila Viçosa who registered George's ownership papers and who agreed to guide them to the site of the granted square legua of land...a recently abandoned military outpost that had been the residence of fifty Portuguese soldiers...was Arthur Mason, a colorful Brazilian of English heritage, who, in addition to functioning as the royal land representative, functioned as the community's mayor. He also was the owner of one of the larger ships in the harbor, a two-masted schooner about twenty meters in length called *The Pilgrim*. Twice a week to Vila Viçosa came a larger ship from Rio de Janeiro for purposes of cargo and mail.

"We'll be treading along the Rio's north bank to get to the outpost," Arthur told George. "It's about forty kilometers away, but there's a pretty good rut worn as a path for us. The young soldiers were terribly lonely there at the outpost, and they used to come as often as they were allowed to Vila Viçosa just for the sight of a female. They could get to town faster by boat on the Peruípe than it took them on foot or mule in this rut, but going back upstream takes much longer and is a lot of work."

"How long will it take us to get there?" asked George.

"With such a moving menagerie it's likely to take us three days, I would say. It'll only take me a long day to get myself back on this mule. If there are any boats still left there, I could leave the mule and use a boat to get back faster. But there may not be any kind of boat there, and you'll have to loan me the mule for later return.'"

"Whatever is most convenient for you," said George.

Arthur nodded and continued, "We can stop one night at the place where Herr Freyreiss plans to build his 'Colônia Leopoldina'. There isn't much there yet...only a few people in some shacks they've put together. The outpost you are getting is a much superior site. Much of the land around the outpost is clear and arable, with a vegetable garden that was likely left to you. There are buildings intact and a number of pens and corrals."

"So why were there soldiers stationed there?" asked George. "Are the natives dangerous? We are not very well armed. We only have a few firearms and swords."

"The natives in this area were once very dangerous," explained Arthur. "We had the Waitacá and the Aimoré...both fierce and merciless cannibals. The Waitacá were well organized and their warriors fought in groups well on both land and sea. They made canoes out of hollow reeds that float   The men could run down wild boars, and in the water they killed sharks with sharpened sticks. A Waitacá family's status was determined by the size of the pile of bones of enemies they had eaten stacked outside their common hall. But we haven't had an attack from the Waitacá in anyone I know's memory. They seem to have been driven inland. They are at war not only with the Portuguese, but with other tribes. The Aimoré are also cannibals and they tend to fight in smaller groups from clever ambush. But many years ago when Vila Viçosa was still called 'Campinho,' a large group of Aimoré massacred and ate most of the residents, leaving only few survivors. Their hostility threatened even Porto Seguro to the north, so that the Portuguese built a number of military outposts all along the coast—at Belmonte, Prado, Alcobaça...and on the Peruípe above Vila Viçosa where you will be."

"So is it the Aimoré we have to fear?" asked George.

"No, over the many years the soldiers have successfully exterminated them," continued Arthur. "Now the only possible threat is from the Bodocuds south of the Rio Mucuri, or, in this area, the Pataxó. But neither of these tribes has given us much trouble for years. I think the Portuguese no longer needed the outpost for defense against the natives. They might have been thinking in recent years about the possibility of foreign invasion, I don't know."

"Do you think we will encounter any of these Pataxó?" asked George.

"I'm sure you will," answered Arthur. "They're living in the jungle all around the outpost and throughout this part of Bahia. But I don't think they'll attack you in any organized way. They may pilfer some livestock from time to time, that's all. Yet if I were you I wouldn't antagonize them."

"What do they look like?"

"They're a short bronze-colored people...agile like monkeys. The men remove all the hair from their bodies except for a topknot of long hair. They run around almost completely naked, only putting on robes or wearing feathers for adornment on special occasions. The men put flat stones into their earlobes and lower lips, and have tattooed stripes on their arms for every enemy or jaguar they've killed in combat."

"And the women?"

"The women are very small with mud-caked hair in braids, and whenever you see one she seems to be pregnant," said Arthur.

"Does anyone know their language and speak with them?"

"Yes, we have some people in Vila Viçosa who can speak to them pretty well," said Arthur. "We even have a Pataxó or two living there. One of these is a 'curandeiro' who knows how to cure illness with jungle herbs. Even I have gone to him when I was sick and he gave me cures. We call him 'Doctor Anko'. He speaks a kind of primitive Portuguese with us, but understands us when we speak to him."

"Is he a cannibal?" asked George.

"He says he isn't," said Arthur.

In the middle of the second day out of Vila Viçosa, the caravan came to Georg Wilhelm Freyreiss's "Colônia Leopoldina" site. There were about a dozen people there living in mud-brick houses surrounded by wattle fences. They had pigs and chickens in abundance, but no sheep, goats, cattle or horses...and only a dozen mules. A man named Dingeldein from Darmstadt was in charge, and he was very happy to see George and his entire party arrive, especially since George shouted out his initial greeting in German.

"Gott im Himmel!" exclaimed this Dingeldein. "How fine it is to see you here. You'll like it here. Did Freyreiss send you?"

"Nein," explained George. "We aren't staying with you, but only visiting for the night. I'm Major and Doctor George von Schaeffer and this group of people is accompanying me to the former military outpost where we will form our own colony and build a plantation estate called 'Frankenthal'."

Dingeldein was disappointed. "Oh," he said, "I thought that maybe you had all come at Freyreiss's direction to join us. How did you come to take possession of the outpost? It's a great place to settle. Much of the work we are doing here is already done for you there. But it's further from the sea."

"The outpost was deeded to me for my estate because of my service to the crown," George said. "Herr Mason here will vouch for the legality of it."

Arthur Mason nodded affirmatively to Dingeldein.

"So what will you grow on your plantation, Herr von Schaeffer?" asked Dingeldein.

"Coffee will be the main crop," answered George. "What are you growing?"

"Cotton for sale...everything else to eat," said Dingeldein.

The night passed very well, with all the combined groups of Germans sitting around a huge bonfire that the Colônia Leopoldina men had built. They sang songs together and talked about their homes and what people they might mutually know. Dingeldein gave George a variety of plant cuttings and seeds, and George unloaded from one of his mules a European style horsehair mattress and gave it to Dingeldein, who said, "I thank you for this, George, but my wife is even more grateful, I'm sure. I can see now that it's going to be nice having you, so to speak, 'in the neighborhood'. We fellow Germans should be good neighbors, don't you think?"

"Yes, I do," said George. "I'm sure we'll have opportunities to help each other in many ways. We already are grateful to you for your hospitality. We'll return the favor when you come our way."

Within two hours of their arrival late the next day at the military outpost overlooking from a north-side bluff the confluence of the Rio Peruípe and the much smaller but clearer Jackarander Stream, Johann Phillipp Henning was able to give George his inspection report.

"There are fifteen buildings in all, George," Johann said. "Ten are the same, arranged in two rows of five, and they are solid, made of sunbaked mud bricks with thatched roofs. They were obviously barracks with large open interiors. They still have the soldiers' metal bed frames in them. And they have nice windows with shutters that still work well. Behind them on the outpost edge is a large communal outhouse. One building has a nicely equipped kitchen and a dining hall with a very long table and chairs, and another, the largest building, has an administrative office in it and a two-bedroom apartment in the back of it. There is a barn of considerable size with sixteen separate stables for horses. It has a large workshop with a forge in it with even the tools left. Then there are two other wooden sheds for the animals. There are also several wood-railed pens, chutes, and a large corral. All in all, I'd say we are in very good shape here. Only the exterior fence is not in very good condition. Many of the slats are missing."

"Is there a well or do we have to trek to the stream for good water?" asked George.

"There are three wells, two with bucket lifts and one with a pump that works, and the water seems quite good," answered Johann. "And there is a kind of dock down on the Peruípe with four dugout canoes left to us."

"Wunderbar!" exclaimed George. "It's even better than I imagined it would be. Dom João hasn't cheated us. Let's get the animals contained and find places for the night. Tomorrow we'll start our new colony as we see fit. We should have some kind of ceremony in the morning. I'll be signing the possession papers for Mr. Mason for sure."

Starting the Plantation:

In the morning George had a long red-and-gold embroidered streamer run up the military outpost flagpole as the "banner of Frankthenthal." The men saluted it and fired three musket shots into the air. George, holding a German Bible, addressed those gathered around to say, "My dear family and friends, we are beginning this morning a new life. We ask the Lord to bless our efforts and reward them. We promise to work together as brothers and sisters following Christ's example of tolerance and love for one another. Amen."

All the company responded with a loud, "Amen."

Arthur Mason then stepped forward with some papers in his hands and said to George so that the others could hear what he said, "Major von Schaeffer, if you sign the last of these papers, it means that you are formally taking possession of this outpost and the square legua of land that surrounds it. Your name will then be entered into the rolls of land ownership in the Vila Viçosa prefecture of the municipality of Mucuri in the State of Bahia in the Portuguese colony of Brazil. Your ownership is perpetual and subject only to your payment of the required taxes."

The quill was already in George's hand. With a flourish he signed the document, and the company heartily applauded.

Arthur Mason told George that he would not trace with George, as a regulation-bound land agent ordinarily would, the outline of his square legua of land around the outpost.

"You are the only people for miles...except for the Freyreiss group and the savages," he said. "So there's no one to dispute borders with. You can just use what land you need. No one will say anything about it. For as far as you can see, the place is yours. Good luck in your development of it."

George and several others then accompanied Arthur Mason down the winding dirt path from the top of the bluff to the rough log dock and the bare dirt shore-patch on the Peruípe where the four dug-out canoes had been dragged up high above the rushing water line and tied to trees. They found him a paddle and helped him launch the canoe. In only a minute or two Arthur was out of sight downstream on his way toward the ocean.

The birth date of Frankenthal was Wednesday the 4th day of April, 1821, the second birthday, George pointed out to the others, of Princess Maria da Gloria, the Kaiserin Leopoldina's first child. With the exception of a month's horseback and mule-train tour with Wilhelm south into Minas Gerais and back around north to Georg Heinrich von Langsdorff's estate of Mandioca, where he purchased from the absent Langsdorff's manager a number of coffee trees, a steel plow, and departed wife Friederike's piano for Barbara...an acquisition that took great effort to cart back to Frankenthal, George spent every day of the next seventeen months in the outdoor sun working on Frankenthal's protective fence, its buildings and their roofs, and in its surrounding fields. Brother Wilhelm quickly became the leader in the agricultural effort, devising an irrigation system from the pump well for the largest vegetable and herb garden, and directing the tilling and the weeding and the preparation of the soil with manure from the barn, pens, and corrals for planting. Johann Henning was the leader of all construction, revising the shop, equipping it as best he could with the tools they had brought, and getting the forge lit and functioning. He soon constructed a

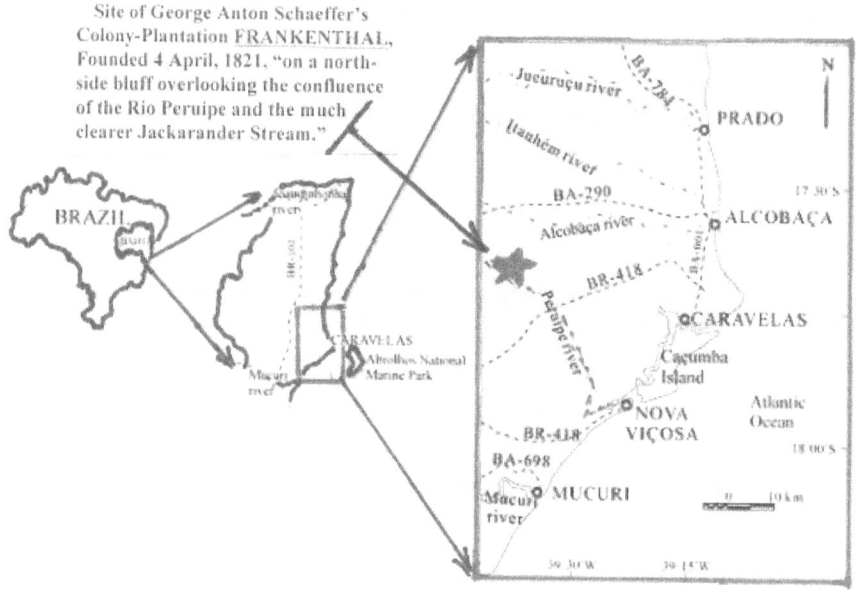

A Map of the Southern Horn of Brazil's Bahia State, adapted from
http://www.scielo.br/img/revistas/aabc/v75n3/a08fig01.gif. In George Anton
Schaeffer's time, the current city of Nova Viçosa was named Vila Viçosa. Refer
also to the Regions and States Map of Brazil on p. 144.

mill, with a large two-man saw they had brought, for making logs into planks.
Sasha Petrov and his Russian friend Misha Arbuzov were the loggers, axing
down tree after tree from the surrounding forest, trimming the branches into
firewood, then stacking the firewood in one of the unused barracks to dry it, and
dragging the cut tree into the outpost using chains they had brought pulled by
teams of mules. No matter that the weather was quite warm, the forge and the
kitchen stoves required a continual supply of firewood. Yet Slava and Misha
soon filled a second barracks with firewood and had a large number of thick
trimmed logs ready for the mill. Molds were made to begin the manufacture of
bricks made of mud and clay brought up from the riverbanks by periodic
evening bucket brigades. Anna and Barbara headed the kitchen effort to keep
everyone fed. Lara and Sylvia schooled the children and worked on making
mattresses and bedding to fit the soldier's metal bedframes, some of which had
been strapped together by Johann.

George, Barbara, and Inga lived in the two-bedroom apartment in the back of
the large administration building. Each other family had a barracks building to
itself, with the single men in one separate barracks and the widows Ingrid and
Martha and three other single women, including sister Julia, in another, in which
curtains were used to screen off areas for individual privacy. This was a

temporary arrangement, George maintained, until individual houses could be built on individual plots of the surrounding land.

In the early morning and in the evening, the entire company ate together. After the long table was cleared and the plates and utensils all washed and put away...a chore that everyone helped perform...the men would play checkers or chess or card games and the women would sit around in a circle and talk while they knitted or sewed. After George and Wilhelm brought the piano from Mandioca, Barbara, who had it placed in the dining room, would often play and the company would sing. There was only the light of torches or candles, and so darkness caused the company to go to their beds. After the day's work, no one had trouble sleeping, even though it was sometimes uncomfortable in the humid heat of summer or there were thunderous storms with howling winds. All of the men rotated in four hours of sentry duty each throughout the night.

The outpost had a fruit orchard, with peach, cherry, apricot, and apple trees. There were coconuts and figs in abundance. Men hunting in the forests were always quickly rewarded with game...wild boars, tapirs, and turkeys were the most desired. And the river was easily fished by hook-and-line, net, or fish-trap, providing a wide variety of tasty fare. There was plenty of rich grass pasturage on the slopes of the bluff for the livestock, and the thickness of the surrounding forest kept the animals manageably contained. Since they could not get to the stream or the river, they were attracted back to Wilhelm's irrigated garden to drink...so he provided them a number of troughs for that purpose.

One day Slava Petrov came to tell George that he and Misha were being watched from the forest by savages as they worked to cut down trees.

"They are dark men," he said, "with no clothes and no hair. Three or four of them."

"Are they armed? Did they approach you?" asked George.

"We can't tell if they are armed. We just catch glimpses of them from time to time in the dense foliage, but then they disappear. It seems like they are just watching us for now. But we'll start taking the muskets out to do the logging...in case they attack us."

"What I'd like to do, Slava, is try to tame them and make them our friends," said George. "So please don't do anything to scare them. Don't do any shooting unless you absolutely have to."

A few days later, Misha came running to tell George that the savages had come out of the forest near them and were standing in plain sight. He was quite excited and was out of breath.

"There are...a dozen or more of them," he said. "And they are armed with bows and spears. Slava has two muskets and a pistol loaded and ready to shoot, but he hasn't fired because of what you told him."

An aerial photo of the Rio Peruipe as it approaches the coastal city of Nova
Viçosa (formerly Vila Viçosa) in Brazil's southern Bahia State,
from:http://oceanfrontproperties.com/property/brazil/jardim/...

George quickly rounded up Wilhelm and Johann to accompany him along
with Misha to "see the savages." Barbara and Anna, who happened to hear from
the kitchen what George told Johann, cautioned them, "You men be sure to take
weapons with you," but the men were already loading pistols and putting on
swords.

In fifteen minutes of hurried walking, George, Wilhelm, Johann, and Misha
came within sight of where Slava Petrov, naked to the waist, stood with two
mules attached to a drawbar-and-chain rigged to pull away a large tree they had
cut down and trimmed. Two muskets were leaning against the fallen tree, close
to Slava's possible grasp. He had a pistol tucked into his belt.

Fifty meters away at the edge of a dense copse of foliage was a group of
twelve small bronze-colored men. They were almost completely naked, with
their only body coverings being a conical bark codpiece over their penises.
Some were smeared with different colored pigments, and the larger men had
wooden disks inserted into their earlobes and lips, giving them, to the
Europeans' taste, a fiercely disfigured appearance. All of them had bows or
spears in their hands.

"Why are they just standing there?" asked Slava. "They just popped into sight about a half hour ago, and none of them has moved much since."

Wilhelm said, "I guess they are just letting us know they are here. Perhaps they are displeased about our coming into their territory."

"We have to convince them that our coming into their territory is a good thing for them," said George. "I am going to try to approach them and give them an axe. That should signify to them that our presence is positive for them."

Slava said, "As you go, I'll be ready with the musket," and he handed George one of the axes.

George walked slowly forward toward the savages. In his first steps he held the axe high over his head so that they could see it clearly, but as he got closer he lowered the axe to his waist level, holding it forth horizontally as an offering to them. As he approached to within a few meters of them, they moved to rearrange themselves into a semi-circle around him. George noticed that he was sweating heavily as he eyed the lean little men. He was unable to discern their intentions from any of their faces. They all just stared blankly at him. But none raised a weapon. George knew that if one did, Slava would shoot him. But then what would happen? It was a precarious moment.

When George was only steps away from the man in the center of the surrounding semi-circle...and this man was the most distinctive by his physical size and relative adornment...he put the axe down at his feet and took one step back from it. He pointed at it and then waved his arm at the man, trying to indicate that it was a gift and that the man should pick it up. But the man did not move.

George thumped his hand on his chest and said, "George. I am George." Then he rubbed his two hands together and said, "I want to be friends."

The central man handed his bow and spear to the man next to him. He then stepped forward, bent down, and picked up the axe. His face then brightened into a smile, and he put his hand to his chest and said, "Pah-tah-CHO. Pah-tah-CHO."

George also smiled. He realized that the man was telling him that he was a Pataxó tribesman. He motioned his arm around to include the group of his company behind him and said, "Ger-mans. We are Ger-mans."

The man looked at George's compatriots and repeated, "Ger-mans."

George then repeated his identification of himself, thumping his chest and saying, "George. Ger-man George."

The man looked at the group and said, "Ger-mans," and then looked at George and said what sounded like, "Doud." George knew that the man was trying to repeat his name. Then the man thumped his chest just as George had and said, "Ah-nip." George was most pleased. He looked at the man and repeated, "Ah-nip. You are Ah-nip."

George turned away from the man and motioned with his arm for the entire Pataxó group to follow him back to the other men. Led by the man George called "Ah-nip," they did this. In a minute they were standing face-to-face with Wilhelm, Johann, and the others. Ah-nip made so bold as to walk right up to Slava, reach up and touch his arm. The others made a gutteral kind of sound in unison and broke out in smiles.

Johann said, "I think they're fascinated by your size, Slava. You're certainly an unimaginable giant to them."

"You may have made us some friends, George," said Wilhelm. "Good work."

For a half hour the two groups of men awkwardly mingled. One of the Pataxó men came up to Misha and pointed to his leather belt, which had a brass buckle. Misha took it off and handed it to the man, who smiled broadly as he took it and then began making some strange gestures with his hands. It appeared he was acting out the making of some object he wanted to give to Misha. But at this point, the leader Ah-nip grunted abruptly and began to walk away. The other Pataxó followed him and in a minute they were gone.

For a week there was no sign of the "savages," but then they reappeared near the settlement fence where the path began toward the Jackarander Stream. George asked Slava and Misha to take them out a roasted turkey the women were preparing for supper. When the two Russian loggers came back, Misha had with him a rolled-up sleeping mat woven out of flat waxen leaves. "It was that man I gave my belt to," he said. "He gave me this mat."

The next week Wilhelm found a well roasted boar blocking the outside of the rear fence gate when he went to investigate Fitzli's and Putzli's barking. The Pataxó were returning the favor for the roast turkey. Before another month elapsed, a group of twenty Pataxó men were helping Wilhelm harvest the fruit trees in the orchard so that he would give them a share of the crop. In another month, Johann was able to bring Pataxó men inside the fence into the living compound to lift and carry planks and bricks to his building projects. They turned out to be marvelous brick makers, mixing just the right amounts of dirt and clay into the molds after hauling it up from the river in the company's buckets, some of which they took to their own use.

The Pataxó men were clearly awed by the size, appearance, and dress of the company's women, who were in turn embarrassed by the men's nakedness. None of their women had yet been seen by any of the company, but George remembered that Arthur Mason had described them to be quite small. Anna and Barbara gave the workmen cookies still warm from the kitchen as pay for their labor. At first they didn't know what to make of these cookies, but soon they clearly craved them and horded what they were given to take back with them to their families in the jungle.

George made his best effort to learn to speak with the Pataxó. He did find out that "Ah-nip" was not that first-contacted man's name. It was his title...something like "Chief." The Pataxó did not say their names to others.

And they were to George's perception simply a taciturn people who only reluctantly spoke to anyone. But George and the others communicated with the Pataxó by gesture and example. These "savages," they found, quite intelligently understood what they should do...and they seemed to have a sense of fair exchange—gift for gift, goods for work.

After a year of protracted hard labor, Frankenthal had made dramatic progress, and George couldn't help bragging to his sister Julia that, "It's all been done without the sweat of a single slave." The buildings were all in good shape, stuccoed, whitewashed, and with leak-proof roofs. The fence around the living compound was solid and impenetrable. The barn and shop, the pens, and the corrals were the equals of any seen in Europe. The gardens were green with a second year's crop of edible produce and medicinal herbs. The outlying fields were being expanded with the help of the Pataxó labor for the growing of cotton and flax. The coffee trees were flourishing beautifully, as were the pineapple plants that had grown out of the suckers George had brought. George was already anticipating treating his family and friends to their first taste of this wonderfully tasty fruit, remembering his own first taste on the island of O'ahu. Things were going well...not only for the buildings and the fields, but also for the people. Barbara pointed out to George how fit and healthy they all were, and how their population was soon to grow. Anna, Sylvia, and Lara were all pregnant and expecting babies in the same coming month. Several of their first crops looked good, and a method of preparing log rafts for one-way delivery of these crops to Vila Viçosa and from there to larger ports had been devised and tested.

Barbara was happy.

"I just love the way you and I and Inga are working hard, each day in our own way, to build our own place together, George," Barbara said. "And 'together' is the key word. I was so unhappy without you in St. Petersburg, even though we had a fine stone mansion. But here it's so beautiful and warm and...and...encouraging. My mother is genuinely enjoying every day. She loves it here. Inga is learning to cook and to play the piano so very well. And our friends here are all so warm and well meaning. There isn't a single troublesome person here. Even the savages are helpful to us. Everyone is working every day for the common good. And it IS good...a real Eden, don't you think?"

"It is very nice here now, my dear," said George. "But it's still a long way from what I've dreamed of. I want to have Johann start the construction of a mansion for us here. It should have piped plumbing like we had in St. Petersburg. And a system to heat the water for both baths and showers. And we'll light it with whale oil lamps so we can stay up and read all night if we want to. We'll need to improve the rut to get here into an all-season road...and get some nice carriages to travel on it. There's just so very much yet to do. And we need more people. We'll have to attract many more people here...more Germans like we are. Frankenthal should become a city with a hospital and a library, and where Inga can see operas and plays and play the piano in concerts."

"George," said Barbara sharply. "We don't need another stone mansion like we had in St. Petersburg. We already have a plantation anyone would envy. And more people might be nice, but they might not be nice people. I worry that your dreams are too big for us. We should be happy now as we are."

"I am happy, Barbara," said George. "But I'll be even happier when we have our own plantation completed and the others are at work on theirs."

George told Barbara that he should travel back to Rio de Janeiro for a number of different important reasons—supplies, banking, assuring a market for their produce and such. And he was anxious to meet again with Princess Leopoldina to see if she needed anything from him in his capacities as Major in her personal guard and as a palace chamberlain.

"There are some important services you need to render here, George," Barbara pointed out. "You can't leave until after Anna, Sylvia, and Lara all give birth. What if something goes wrong in any of these births? You've just got to be here."

George knew that Barbara was right. He postponed traveling back to Rio de Janeiro until after all three births, which blessedly went well in July and August of 1822. Baby sons were born to Slava and Lara and to Johann and Sylvia, and a baby daughter to Wilhelm and Anna. While he was attending Anna, a party of the Pataxó laborers suddenly gave Slava and Misha an opportunity to follow them back to their village in the jungle. They reported that the village was about an hour's hike away and that it had a population of over one hundred people, with women and children, which none of the Frankenthal company had seen before, in abundance. They said that the villagers lived in thatched huts of some size and had a central cooking fire heating a large metal kettle. When Slava and Misha gave attention to this kettle and made motions to try to determine where it had come from, the Pataxó laborers who had brought them there pointed off to the east and said "Ah-ta Ma-son" until Slava at last nodded that he understood them. Arthur Mason, the royal land agent and Mayor in Vila Viçosa, was somehow the source of the metal kettle.

Duties for Brazil:

George traveled back to Rio de Janeiro with Arthur Mason on Mason's ship *The Pilgrim.* Within sight of the ship at sea was a great multitude of humped-back whales showing their flukes above the water, leaping high into the air above the waves, and gamboling in groups with their calves. In all his sea travels, George had never seen so many.

In the course of their journey together, Arthur related to George how he had come to give a metal kettle to the Pataxó.

177

"Our local curandeiro, Doctor Anko, is a kind of runaway from that particular group of Pataxó," Arthur said. "A family of friends of mine found him injured and took him in...adopting him in a way. After several months, when he had healed and was able to communicate pretty well in Portuguese and had shown his use in curing people, a party of warriors from the Pataxó came looking for him. They were skulking around on the edge of the town near my friends' house, and when Doctor Anko saw them, he told us that their intent was to bring him back or, failing that, to kill him."

"So you gave them the kettle as payment for their healer, is that it?" asked George.

"That's it," said Arthur. "It was Doctor Anko for the kettle, with me negotiating on behalf of the town. Doctor Anko was my interpreter, of course."

After only a few days in Rio de Janeiro doing his business, George went to the palace to see Princess Leopoldina. He obtained access without trouble and was shown into the antechamber of her night suite. He waited only a short while until she came to see him. She dismissed the lady-in-waiting who accompanied her and sat down onto the sofa where George was already sitting. She reached out and grasped his arm and asked, "My dear George, how are you? It looks like you have been working in the sun. You seem leaner and your skin is quite tan. Your hair and your beard seem lighter in color. Is your colony doing well?"

"Yes, Your Highness," said George. "It's been a great deal of work, but we now have Frankenthal operating well and the people are happy there. It's a beautiful place...a paradise of a kind. But it's a long way from the city and I sometimes feel as exiled from things as Napoleon."

"Do you know that Napoleon is dead?" Leopoldina asked. "He died at St. Helena on the 5th of May last year."

George shook his head in amazement. "Napoleon Bonaparte has died? And more than a year ago? That is truly astonishing."

Leopoldina said, "I haven't really heard what my sister's reaction to his death is. In some ways I'm as out of touch as you have been. I think she admired him more than loved him. And now I don't know what she'll do."

"It's hard for me to realize that such a giant figure of our time is no more," said George. "But I'm glad he's gone and there is now absolutely no chance that he'll be restored to power anywhere. I always said that he was like a stone thrown into the waters of the world and causing ripples of disturbance and deaths everywhere. In Europe it was Napoleon. In Russia it was Napoleon. In Africa, Australia, Alaska and the Pacific it was Napoleon. Even in China people were concerned about Napoleon. And now he dies and I don't hear of it for more than a year? That really does show how out of touch I've been. What else don't I know about?"

"There is much," answered Leopoldina. "Since I last saw you I gave birth to a son and heir for Pedro...the blessed João Carlos...of such is the kingdom of heaven. But he lived for less than a year, dying of fever this past February. My grief was terrible and I don't know how I survived it, especially since I was heavily pregnant again by the time he died. I gave birth to our daughter Januaria the next month and she is doing very well. But Pedro wants a son so that he can have a male heir. So, as you can likely tell, I'm pregnant again and expecting in February of next year."

"No I couldn't tell," said George, not wanting to admit he hadn't noticed her new slight heaviness as a pregnancy. "And I can only grieve now on your behalf myself about your lost son. What terrible news. Was there nothing the doctors could do?"

"They tried everything, but..." Leopoldina couldn't finish the sentence.

"Pedro has a great deal to worry about," continued Leopoldina, dabbing her eyes with a handkerchief. "Late last year the Portuguese government demanded that he also return to Portugal, but in January he made the public statement to all here that 'he will stay.' Now he's agreed at last to have himself crowned Emperor of an independent Brazil. He plans to announce this next month. But what kind of a government will he have? He's working with Minister Jose Bonifacio de Andrada e Silva on that. Jose Bonifacio advocates that he accept a constitution, and in the future he may. Jose has been showing him drafts of one. But the main task is to assure Brazil's independence from Portugal and to keep it safe from other countries who may wish to take Brazilian territory. Dom João may just send soldiers to take Pedro to Portugal, where his brother Miguel has already gone, and force Brazil to remain a colony."

"I see," said George. "And Pedro has no army he can trust to oppose the Portuguese. Most of the soldiers in the country are Portuguese and will take their orders from Dom João, even though he is far away."

"Pedro thinks he can establish our independence without having to fight Portuguese soldiers," Leopoldina said. "And he has won the loyalty, he thinks, of many. But the situation is far from sure. We desperately need an army that never pledged its allegiance to Dom João. And that's where I would like to request your service...to raise us an army from the German-speaking countries of Europe."

"But Your Highness," said George. "How would I do that? I've never been a soldier."

"You have brought Germans here by telling them about Brazil, George. And I am told...you have told me...that there are many, many Germans who want to leave their country and move to someplace else like Brazil. They could come here and be soldiers in our army. You could convince them to come. And you could find a way to enable them to come."

George was a bit distressed to see how simply Leopoldina apparently thought the idea was. He protested again, saying, "But I paid the passage for the

Germans I brought here, and I promised them land of their own on which they could build their own estates after they helped me build mine. And I brought only forty-seven people here, and you will need thousands."

"George," Leopoldina said in a pleading voice. "I know it's a big job and that it will take a great effort to accomplish it. But that's why I'm asking you. Please tell me that you will speak to Minister de Andrada about it."

"I will speak with him," said George.

By the time George was able to speak with Jose Bonifacio de Andrada, he had thought considerably about how Prince Pedro, soon to be Dom Pedro I, Emperor of independent Brazil, might attract an army of German mercenaries from Europe. But Jose Bonifacio had thought considerably about it too.

"We have been aware for some time of the desire of the German-speaking peoples of Europe to come here to Brazil, Jorge," explained Jose in Portuguese. "In 1818, before I returned to Brazil from Europe, 165 families from Germany came to the Bahia State to settle in Ilheus. That same year Dom João permitted several hundred German-speaking people from the Swiss Canton of Freiburg to settle in the mountains northeast of here. The place is now called Nova Friburgo and is doing well. The next year 200 German families came to live in São Jorge in the Rio Grande do Sul State. Are you aware of any of these groups? The Ilheus group is not all that far from your colony."

"I don't know anything about them, Jose," said George. "And Georg Heinrich von Langsdorff, whose estate of Mandioca is closer to Ilheus, never mentioned them to me."

"Well, we are now trying, as Leopoldina has told you, to take advantage of the German desire to leave Europe for other places. This is especially important to us now because of our need to raise an army independent of Dom João and Portugal. So we have begun a project to inform large numbers of Germans about the virtues of Brazil."

George couldn't help wondering who the "we" was as Jose used this pronoun as a subject for his personal actions.

Jose continued, "We asked Consul von Langsdorff before he left to do what he can while he is in Germany. He informed us that he will write a treatise on the reasons why Germans should consider coming to Brazil, and I'm sure he will write a good one. Georg Wilhelm Freyreiss is going to do the same thing. And we've gotten another two German-speaking physicians to agree to recruit Germans to Prince Pedro's foreign battalions. One of them you know well— Dr. João Martinho Flach. He says that he would be glad to accompany you to Germany and help you as you direct. The other, a Dr. Kretzschmar who has correspondents among my acquaintances here, lives in Frankfurt am Main in Germany. He has been authorized to make offers on our behalf to former soldiers there."

"What kind of offer is he making?" asked George.

"He's telling able-bodied men with military experience that the Brazilian government will pay their passage to Brazil and give them free eight-acre-sized plots of land that will be tax exempt for eight years in exchange for eight years of service in Prince Pedro's army. We're calling it the 'Triple Eight Offer'."

"Does that mean that a man from Frankfurt must pay his way here in the hope of reimbursal, or does this Dr. Kretzschmar pay in advance for the man's travel? And is he to serve his eight years in the army before he gets his land?"

"Those, of course, are real problems, Jorge," admitted Jose. "Some adventurous and resourceful souls might get here on their own. I once went to Europe to get an education. You took yourself to Russia to practice medicine. But we were adventurous and we had certain resources that many of these people don't have. Their destitution is the very reason they would read a treatise on Brazil or to come to hear Dr. Kretzschmar. But unless we can find a way to pay their travel in advance, we won't be bringing here the numbers of Germans we need. Dr. Kretzschmar does not have the resources to pay their way in advance. And we don't have the ships to go get them ourselves. It's a matter of money, as most things are."

"And I have the money, is that it?" asked George.

"Yes," answered Jose. "You have the money."

George took a deep breath. "I'm mean you no disrespect, Jose, but I want to speak directly as well with Prince Pedro on this matter. Are you able to include him or not?"

"I can include him...and will," answered Jose.

In three days George was speaking with both Jose Bonifacio de Andrada e Silva and Prince Pedro, whose planned announcement that he would become the Emperor of Brazil was only weeks away. In seeing Pedro again...how he had apparently aged into physical maturity, George consciously reminded himself that Pedro was a man not much older than the century...that until October 12 he was only twenty-three years old.

"Princess Leopoldina tells me that you will help us recruit German soldiers from Europe, Major von Schaeffer. Is that true?" asked Pedro.

"I do want to help Brazil become an independent country...and to stay one," George said. "But in order for me to take on such a project, I will need to have a strong agreement from you on the terms."

"The terms are simple," said Pedro, looking significantly at Jose, "You help us and we'll help you. That has not changed since you spoke with my father."

"Your father deeded to me a square legua of good land in a good place so that I could found my colony of Frankenthal," began George. "And I am happy. But I want to have much more land, and I want to bring many more people to it...and not all soldiers. So I will want you to deed to me another square legua of land or give me its value equivalent in gold for every man I bring from Europe who becomes a soldier in your foreign battalions. And in order to entice these soldiers to come here we will need to enable them to bring their families with them...and give them better terms than the Frankfurt Dr. Kretzschmar's 'Triple Eight Offer' that Jose has described to me. They should get seventy hectares or more, and exemption from paying tax while their family member serves in the army. In this way the families can already be settled on the land and working it while their soldiers serve. And the term of service should be less than eight years. I would say four."

"How about six?" said Pedro.

George smiled, saying "All right, agreed," and continued. "I will go to Europe and pay to bring not just individual soldiers, but whole families of Germans here. Each of these families will have at least one able-bodied male member who will sign a contract to enroll for six years service in your army...assuming normal army pay. But each of these families will, upon arrival, receive free deed to seventy hectares of land and be exempt from paying tax upon it as long as their family member serves. And for every soldier I bring to you as a result of this project, you will deed to me another square legua of land. Is that agreed?"

Portrait of "Dom Pedro, Duke of Braganza" (12 October, 1798—24 September, 1838) by John Simpson (1782-1847), from:
http://en.wikipedia.org/wiki/Emperor_Pedro_I.

Pedro looked at Jose. Jose told him, "This could mean a lot of land. And I think we should only give Jorge his land after a soldier's six-year term of service is completed."

Pedro nodded affirmatively and said, "We could give the soldiers' families land in the Rio Grande do Sul State in the south where there aren't many people. We have vast amounts of land there completely undeveloped and not bringing in any tax revenue anyway. Also, we need more people there who consider themselves my subjects because of the claims of Argentina."

George sensed that the discussion was going his way. "I will want the terms in writing," he said.

To this Pedro replied, "You write it up. Jose will read it and approve. And I'll sign it."

"I'll have it done tomorrow," said George.

The next day George brought a written description of his terms to Jose Bonifacio's office. Jose was less business-like now and cordial.

"Thank you for agreeing to help us in this, Jorge," he said. "Likely you know that the governments of Europe may not tolerate you taking away their citizens to Brazil, especially since Brazil will have a government Portugal will oppose them recognizing. I think you will have to weather some political storms in Europe."

"I hadn't really thought of that," admitted George. "I was thinking first of the storm I'll have to weather from my wife."

Sending an Army of Germans From Europe:

After he determined that he would be leaving Rio de Janeiro on September 1st for Le Havre on the French liner *Etienne* under Captain Edouard Drououz, George spent a week writing and rewriting a letter to Barbara. At last he decided to keep it brief:

"25 August, 1822

My Dearest Barbara,

I know that you will not be pleased to read that I have accepted a very important commission from their soon-to-be Imperial Majesties Pedro and Leopoldina to travel to Europe to recruit families of fellow Germans with men who will contract to join the army of an independent Brazil. But the benefits to us of this opportunity are many. We will be able to increase greatly Frankenthal's population by selecting from the families of settlers who are going, in the main, to Rio Grande do Sul. And I am to receive payment in land or gold for every soldier who completes his army service. Moreover, if Pedro is successful in establishing an independent Brazil with the help of the soldiers I recruit, I think he will reward me with the hereditary title of 'Baron of Frankenthal'...so that you, and later Inga, will be Baronesses. I promise that I will not stay away from you for any longer than is necessary. Trips back and forth to Europe only take a hundred twenty days now and I will try to keep my business there short so that I can return to you and Inga often. Trusting that you will be well there in our Eden of Frankenthal, I am—

Your loving husband, George."

Jose Bonifacio brought George an elaborately engraved document signed by "Emperor Dom Pedro I of Brazil" appointing him an "Ambassador-at-Large" and giving him plenipotentiary powers to represent Brazil in matters of state. The document, mentioning Pedro's title as Emperor, was being printed just for George, due to his eminent departure, even in advance of Pedro's official crowning.

"If you have any troubles with this Minister or that Mayor, Jorge," said Jose, "Just show this document. Hopefully it will help you. If it doesn't, you can write to us to see what else we might be able to do to help you."

"I'll be writing my letters to 'Dom Pedro'," George said, "Even though I know you'll likely be reading them."

"Yes, I will," said Jose. "Pedro is often occupied with other things and can't be bothered to read all his mail, so he has me do it and I advise him on what needs to be done."

"Have you given any thought, Brother Jose," asked George, "To what will happen to us all if Dom João, when he hears that Pedro has had himself crowned the Emperor of an independent Brazil, immediately orders his army to subdue his son's revolution?"

"I think about it all the time, Jorge," answered Jose. "But we're acting in many ways to see that it doesn't happen. Dom João had at times advised Pedro to become the Emperor of a separate Brazil. So, even though we fear his possible intervention, we will seek his recognition. But if he chooses to send force and removes Pedro as Emperor, I can conceive that Brazil, because of the constitution that will really determine its government, might function well even without an Emperor."

This comment caused George to startle and say, "Do you really put that amount of faith into your constitution, Jose?"

"Yes, I do," answered Jose. "And I have a copy of what I hope will be our constitution for you right here in the same envelope as your appointment document. I want you to read it carefully and use it to explain the governmental virtues of Brazil."

"All right, Jose," said George. "And I thank you for it."

Leopoldina gave George a letter she had written to her father, The Emperor Franz I, in Vienna.

"I'm asking you to include Vienna into your travel plans," she said. "The people of Austria are no different than those in Franconia or anywhere else as far as their desire to escape poverty and famine is concerned. We have land enough here for them too. I'm hoping that my father's government will be among the first to recognize Brazil as an independent state, and I tell him so in this letter. Also, I've mentioned to him in the letter, George, that he should give you every positive consideration...that you are a close confidant of mine and are acting in my behalf."

"Thank you, Your Highness," replied George. "I'm looking forward to seeing Vienna again, and I will tell your father how very well you are doing here. I'm sure he will be proud of you."

George told his friend Dr. Flach that he would not need his company in Europe, but would instead need him to meet the ships full of emigrant families that he anticipated sending to Rio de Janeiro from Germany.

"I want you to supervise the removal of the soldiers from each ship that I send here and record carefully their enrollment into Prince Pedro's army," explained George. "Then the soldiers' families on the ships will be traveling on to other locales that Minister de Andrada will specify for you. The most important thing is to keep an accurate count of the soldiers. I will pay you a commission on each one properly enrolled."

"You can count on me," said Dr. Flach.

On the eve of his departure, George was summoned to see Prince Pedro at the palace. To his surprise, Pedro presented him with a purple velvet box, in which was a beautiful silver cross with a diamond in the center of it. The cross was attached to a red ribbon, which Pedro draped around George's neck.

"With this cross I am giving you the rank of Knight in the Royal Ancient Order of Christ," he said. "Be sure to wear it at occasions where there is a Catholic ruler present. Several of the regents of Europe are also knights in this order."

George was speechless with gratitude at being given such an honor. He bowed low to Pedro and wiped tears from his eyes with his handkerchief.

The trip to Europe on the *Etienne* took almost twice the expected time of passage to Le Havre at 95 days due to storms blowing the ship off course and a long calm in the central Atlantic. George was irritated by the length of the trip, but he had plenty of time to draw up plans and to compile a written list of arguments for why a German should emigrate to Brazil. He spent a week in glorious Paris, and then traveled by coach to Amsterdam, where he looked up the shipping agent Conrad Meyer, who was most happy to see him.

"My goodness, George, you look fine," said Conrad. "You must have been working hard since I last saw you in Rio."

"Today is my 44th birthday," said George. "And I feel as if I were twenty years younger. Life at my colony in Brazil is very good...healthful and prosperous. But now I need your help in bringing more people to Brazil...many more people."

"Just tell me how many ships you will need, my friend," answered Conrad. "I can get them for you."

"Twenty ships might do it," said George.

Conrad was stunned. "Twenty ships?"

"Yes," said George. "Twenty ships. If I charter that many I am hoping to get quite a discount from the cargo rate."

"But you said you wanted to transport people," said Conrad. "And that would normally require a charter at the passenger rate like you chartered the *Argus*."

"That may be so, but I want you to find me ships I can charter at a discounted cargo rate," said George. "I'm sure you can do so in these hard times. And I will need them altered to my specifications. I will be transporting large numbers of people on them...families who will be contributing at least one male member each to serve in the new Brazilian army. These families will be allowed very little baggage so that we can fit as many as possible of them onto each ship. I've got some ideas about that...about how the ships might be altered to accommodate more people."

"For a ship the size of the *Argus*, how many people are you thinking of transporting?" asked Conrad.

"Indeed I was thinking of the *Argus* when I drew up my plan," answered George. "I think that with a few changes, the *Argus* could transport 300 people. The people would sleep in rows of hammocks strung one above the other in shifts. They would eat standing as they rotated through a mess line so that we can use the dining space for more hammocks. They would need more toilets aft, weekly freshwater showers, and..."

"That's half again the ship's design capacity for passengers," said Conrad, interrupting him. "It would be like a slave ship. The people would have to be stacked like cords of firewood. And they might just burst into flames."

George was incensed at this statement. "Not at all, Conrad," he protested. "Not at all. I have seen slave ships unloaded and I know that it wouldn't be the same at all. It would be more like a military troop ship...something appropriate, after all, for soldiers. So the families might endure some discomfort and inconvenience for the time of passage...two months or so...but with a military kind of discipline it can be done. They'll be well attended and fed by the crews as directed by charter agents I select and educate. And they will be so grateful for the opportunity given to them that they will not complain."

Conrad shrugged and said, "Well, I think I can get the ships, although perhaps not all at once. And you'll have to get the passengers to the ships in Bremen and Hamburg. That's where the ships will be. When do you want the first ship to depart?"

"Let's say July," said George.

"In that case, we'll get the *Argus* ready here in Amsterdam," said Conrad. "You can send the first group here. But then, after that...in early next year...you can send the groups to Hamburg."

"I'll advance you a deposit, Conrad," said George. "But I'll only pay in full upon each ship's return from Brazil. The ships will all go first to Rio de Janeiro to deliver the soldiers, but then they'll have to deliver the other family members to some other place in Brazil that the government agents there will specify. Most of these will be going to the southernmost State of Brazil called Rio Grande do Sul. Their disembarkation port will be through Rio Grande to Porto Alegre, where they'll be told where further to go. Whatever cargo the ships can find to return with will be up to them, and I make no claim upon it."

Later that month Conrad Meyer quoted to George a cargo charter rate that pleased him and George paid a deposit on the charter amount. Conrad said that he had sent a representative to Hamburg to engage the second of the twenty ships, the *Caroline* under Captain Jakob von der Wettern.

From Amsterdam George traveled to Frankfurt am Main, where he met Dr. August Kretzschmar, a fellow physician. He and Kretzschmar got along well. George had a Frankfurt printer create an elaborate document recognizing his appointment of the man as "Honorary Consul to Frankfurt of the Independent Republic of Brazil." Kretzschmar was a small man only a year or two younger than George, but he had a full head of bright silver-grey hair that gave him a distinguished older appearance. And he was always very well dressed.

"I hope your appointment as Brazilian Consul here will make your recruiting efforts easier, August," said George.

"That remains to be seen," said Dr. Kretzschmar. "The authorities here don't know what to think about my recruiting soldiers to go to Brazil. As you may know, the Congress of Vienna in 1815 set up a new government structure in all of Central Europe called the German Confederation, the Federal Diet of which is here in Frankfurt am Main. This Diet is largely controlled by Austria, with its Emperor Franz I's Minister of State, Prince Klemens von Metternich, exercising his will through it. He is clearly for prohibiting recruitment of citizens to emigrate, but the issue hasn't reached a decision of federal law. Our own Frankfurt Elector in the Diet, who largely acts in accord with our city Mayor, does not oppose my recruitment efforts. I have even rented a room from the city to give talks advocating emigration to Brazil, and the local police have left me alone...so far. Yet there is a likelihood that the law may turn against us. I don't know what effect on the matter Prince Pedro's claiming that Brazil is independent now from Portugal will have. The Diet likely doesn't know it yet, but will have to react to it in some way. Austrian Minister Metternich's opinion will probably prevail. And his opinion is hard to predict."

"But he serves the Emperor Franz I of Austria, the former Holy Roman Emperor," said George. "And the Emperor Franz's own daughter Maria Leopoldina is now Dom Pedro's wife and Empress of Brazil. Surely that fact will condition Minister Metternich's opinion of Brazil's independence, won't it?"

"We can't be sure whether it's the dog wagging the tail, or the tail wagging the dog," said Dr. Kretzschmar. "The Emperor professes the primary importance of family relations, but he leaves matters of diplomacy to Metternich."

"We will have to persuade every government official we encounter, Prince Metternich included, that independent Brazil should be recognized...and that it is a worthy place to send people," said George. "In certain cases, such persuasion may require the application of some financial 'encouragement,' if you know what I mean."

"Oh, I do know," said Dr. Kretzschmar. "My lack of your financial resources has required me to become quite inventive in just that way. For the most part, I've simply continued to recruit despite the difficulties, and I have a long list of eligibles for you, not only in Frankfurt, but in Hamburg and in Mecklenburg where I have valuable acquaintances. I have several Protestant pastors who want to find a new land for themselves and members of their congregations. I know that Brazil is a Catholic country, but hopefully the people there will welcome now these enterprising Protestants. I personally find the pastors to be quite honest and responsible. Also, among my acquaintances are a number of prison wardens whose prisons receive government funds based upon the number of men sentenced to serve their time there. Many of the incarcerated men are debtors or other people who are not really evil men, but are just 'victims of unfortunate circumstance'. These wardens of my acquaintance are quite amenable to letting these men go to be transported away without a trace...that is, to become Brazilian soldiers. Then they can use the government appropriations for these men in other ways...drawing the funds for indefinite periods until they declare the men dead and buried on the prison grounds. They are, in fact, even willing to pay me a slight fee for taking these men off their hands."

"Very clever," commented George. "I congratulate you on finding such a recruitment method. I am, as I've told you, committed to recruiting entire families, but I'll certainly cooperate with you in transporting these prisoners as recruits."

"I will write you letters of introduction to the appropriate people," said Dr. Kretzschmar. "And I think that some of these prisoners will have families

188

eager to accompany them. Only care must be taken that any record of these families'emigration doesn't mention the prisoners' names."

"I completely understand," said George.

George's offer to provide a family's transportation all the way from its current home to free land in Brazil evoked enthusiastic response everywhere he went. From Frankfurt and Stuttgart alone he was able to sign up 298 emigrants, including 150 pledged soldiers, and send them to Amsterdam to sail on the refitted *Argus* to Brazil. Conrad Meyer had taken responsibility for appointing charter agents and educating them as to the conditions of transport. Despite his propensity for seasickness he went again to Brazil as George's charter agent on this first shipment of emigrants, which turned out to be quite a trial. The *Argus* departed Amsterdam on 27 July, 1823. It lost a mast and had to return for repairs, and then storms forced Captain Bernhard Ehlers to find port in England, where they spent almost a month. In late October, only a day's sail from Santa Cruz, the capital city of Tenerife, the largest of the Canary Islands, a 36-gun pirate ship from the African coast overtook them from aft and its Captain shouted for them to drop sail. When Captain Ehlers ignored this demand, the pirate ship fired a salvo of grape shot and chain across the *Argus's* crowded deck. Fourteen passengers were killed, and another twenty injured. Pastor Frederico Sauerbronn, on behalf of the passengers, implored Captain Ehlers to obey the pirates' commands and drop sail. Within a half-hour after this was done, the pirate Captain and a colorfully dressed mate came aboard to inspect their prize. This Captain was a large bearded black man with a deep gravelly voice. He brusquely surveyed the carnage he had created on the *Argus's* deck, took out a pistol and, pointing it at Captain Ehlers, growled out some inquiry in a language no one on the deck understood. The passengers on deck all cowered in fear, anticipating that the pirate would shoot their Captain. But Captain Ehlers calmly shrugged his shoulders and held forth his hands, palms up in supplication. Then he slowly removed his own pistol from his belt and handed it butt-first to the pirate Captain. Then he handed over his leather purse, and asked everyone else on deck to do the same. In short order the pirate Captain's mate was tossing an appreciable number of the passengers' personal coin purses down into the pirate ship's rowboat. The pirate Captain then shouted loudly to his own ship, stationed about 500 yards to the windward. This shouting resulted in two more rowboats full of African pirates coming aboard the *Argus*. But this group had brought with them a dozen crates of fruit and vegetables, and three casks of wine, which they ceremoniously deposited in a pile around the *Argus's* mainmast. The pirate Captain smiled at Captain Ehlers and said something else unintelligible to him. Then the Captain and all his pirates got in their rowboats and rowed away. Then they sailed away in their ship, molesting the *Argus* no further. The *Argus's* entire company was stunned by this most curiously traumatic occurrence. But Pastor Sauerbronn led them in prayer, requesting heavenly reward for the departed, healing for the injured, and expressing their collective gratitude that most of them were whole and continuing their journey.

The navigator, Peter Zink, gave his opinion that the pirates had somehow been moved by their abject appearance in this circumstance. Obviously, he said, "we had no riches for them to take, no one who would ransom us from their captivity, and our captivity would only have been an obstacle to them." The next day in Santa Cruz, Captain Ehlers was told that this same pirate ship had only a few days before fired on, boarded, and robbed a Portuguese merchant ship within sight of the harbor. The *Argus* spent two weeks in Santa Cruz, during which time one of the women passengers gave birth to a baby who died the next day, casting yet a further pallor of gloom on the ship's company.

The ill-fated *Argus* arrived in Rio de Janeiro on 7 January 1824, discharging the 150 soldiers and sending the remaining 134 family members on to Nova Friburgo northeast of Rio in the mountains of the Rio de Janeiro State to join the community of German-speaking Swiss already established there. Conrad Meyer and Captain Bernhard Ehlers took on a cargo of valuable Brazilian hardwood for the *Argus's* return voyage, reaching Amsterdam on 20 May 1824. Conrad gave to George brief letters from Dr. Flach and from Jose Bonifacio, apprising him of diverse political developments in Brazil and telling him that his project was working well. "Send more soldiers," was the instruction transmitted from Dom Pedro. George made his first payment to Conrad Meyer.

In the second half of 1823, while the *Argus* was away, George traveled by coach and riverboat, recruiting as he went, diagonally across Germany from Frankfurt toward Vienna. He spent a week each in Würzburg and in his hometown of Münnerstadt, where he stayed not in an inn, but with the family of his brother Jacob, who was now quite infirm. With Jacob's assent, George enrolled his nephew Anton, Jacob's second son, into the Brazilian army and gave him the money to travel to Hamburg. He promised Jacob that he would look after Anton, and that Anton would be able, if he wanted, to come to live with him and Barbara at Frankenthal when his military service was completed.

After recruiting successes in Nürnburg where he had once observed a balloon ascent by the French Garnerins with Russian General Tormasov, and in Regensburg and Linz, George arrived in Vienna, the birthplace of his "Kaiserin Leopoldina." He was invigorated just by walking around the grand city as he and Barbara had fifteen years before. But he was intially unsuccessful at gaining an audience with Emperor Franz I, even when he appeared at the palace wearing his Order of Christ knight's cross and bearing a letter for the Emperor from his daughter. He was told that he would have to see the Emperor's Minister of State, Prince Klemens von Metternich.

George had heard much about Prince von Metternich since his time in Russia. He knew about the man's clever manipulation of international diplomacy on behalf of Austria. Metternich had accompanied Leopoldina's sister, Maria Louise, to Paris to marry Napoleon Bonaparte in 1810...a sign of subjugation in Austria's relations with Napoleon's France, after which it had participated as a French ally in the invasion of its former ally, Russia. But after the Russian invasion turned out to be a disaster for Napoleon, it was Metternich who managed to extract Austria from its alliance with France and rejoin its former allies of Great Britain, Russia, and Prussia in bringing about Napoleon's downfall and exile. Then it was he who hosted and managed the Congress of Vienna in 1814 and 1815 to restructure all of Europe. George was prepared to respect and admire the man, but when he met him at last, he was disappointed. Metternich seemed quite pompous and authoritarian.

Prince Klemans Wenzel von Metternich (15 May, 1773—11 June 1859) in a portrait, ca. 1825, by Thomas Lawrence (1769-1830), from: http://en.wikipedia.org/wiki/Klemens_von_Metternich.

"What do you wish to accomplish here in Vienna, Herr von Schaeffer," Metternich asked.

"I wish to speak with the Emperor to tell him about his daughter, with whom I am closely acquainted and from whom I've brought him a letter from Brazil," answered George.

Metternich gave George a patronizing smile. "But I am told that you have credentials as an ambassador of the new 'independent' Brazil, is that true?"

"I do have such credentials," said George. "Do you wish to see them?"

"No," said Metternich. "We don't recognize Brazil as an independent state, and our treaties with Portugal don't allow us to receive such an ambassador as these credentials purport you to be."

George's mind scrambled for how to respond. "But I have not presented these credentials to you, Minister Metternich," he said. "I'm not here as a diplomat. I'm here as a friend and confidant of the Emperor's daughter trying to give him news about her and deliver to him a letter she wrote and entrusted to me to transmit."

"Does the letter advocate that Emperor Franz have Austria recognize the rebel Pedro as the Emperor of an independent state of Brazil?" asked Metternich.

George was taken aback. "I don't know," he said, "I haven't opened the letter and don't know its contents."

"Well, you can give the letter to me and I will inform the Emperor of its contents," said Metternich.

"You will have to remove the letter from me by force, Your Highness," said George. "I promised the Emperor's daughter Leopoldina that I would deliver it personally to him, and that is what I am committed to doing."

Metternich stared at George with a scowl on his long, sharp face for a long time. Then he said, "You can speak with the Emperor and give him the letter at one of his 'office meetings' tomorrow. But I will be there with you. If you speak even one word apart from family news about Leopoldina, you will be arrested when you leave. You see, I know more about your true purposes here than you can imagine. Do you understand?"

"Yes, I understand," said George. "Where and when shall I appear?"

The next day Prince Metternich met George outside the entrance to the Emperor's palace where he maintained an office for regular meetings with the public. George was advanced ahead of numerous citizens who were there waiting for their scheduled audiences with the Emperor. He and Metternich walked into the Emperor's office together.

The Emperor was sitting behind what appeared to be an ordinary business desk. He was a man of fifty-five years, undistinguished by his appearance, with gray hair and a cleanly shaved face. He remained sitting when his Minister Prince Metternich entered with George, waiting to hear an introduction.

"Your Imperial Majesty, this man is here from your daughter Leopoldina in Brazil," Metternich announced. "He brings you a letter she has written to you."

Emperor Franz then stood up and walked out from behind his desk, approaching George, who bowed deeply and said, "I am Dr. George von

Schaeffer, Your Majesty...a Major in your daughter's personal guard...her friend and confidant."

"And I see that you are a Knight of the Order of Christ, as well," said Emperor Franz. "That commends you. So tell me, how is my daughter doing?"

"She is well, Your Majesty," said George. "But she has been continually pregnant and bearing children since she came to Brazil to be Prince Pedro's wife, and her doctors are concerned about her. She has the daughter Maria who gives her joy, but she has lost two sons and heirs, one at one day and one at a year of age. And only a month after the last son's death, she gave birth to daughter Januaria. And, when I left her in September of last year, she was expecting another child who was expected this past February."

Emperor Franz frowned, but said, "I'm happy to see that she is so positively engaged in the creation of a royal family. Family is the most important thing, don't you think?"

1832 portrait of the Emperor Franz II of Austria (2 February, 1768—2 March, 1835), by Friedrich von Amerling (1803-1887), from: http://en.wikipedia.org/wiki/Francis_II_Holy_Roman_Emperor.

"I can only agree, Your Majesty," said George. He noticed that Prince Metternich was eyeing him closely as he answered.

"And what kind of a husband for her is young Pedro?" asked Emperor Franz.

"He's a young man and is quite hot-blooded," said George cautiously. "But he respects your daughter and takes her advice in many matters. She is constantly trying to be charitable to the Brazilian people, for whom she cares a great deal. But Pedro does not allow her enough financial resources to accomplish all her purposes."

"I think he's a scoundrel. I have heard that he keeps mistresses, and that he flaunts one of them notoriously, having children with both her and her sister," said Emperor Franz. "If that is true, how does my daughter deal with that?"

"She ignores it," answered George.

"I see," said Emperor Franz, frowning even more deeply. Then pausing to think for a time, he asked, "Can you give me now the letter she wrote for me?"

"Certainly, Your Majesty," said George, taking the letter from his inside vest pocket and handing it to Emperor Franz.

Emperor Franz turned to his desk and took a letter opener off it to slice open the top of the wax-sealed envelope. He removed three pieces of fine paper, both sides of which were covered with ink in a fine handwriting. Holding an eyeglass in front of him, the Emperor took the time to read the entire letter. Near the end of his reading, he grunted and shook his head. Then he asked George, "What do you think of a constitution, Major von Schaeffer?"

George cast a quick glance at Prince Metternich, but Metternich's face revealed nothing but the continuation of a very serious attitude.

"I favor constitutions, Your Majesty," he said. "I think they make governance easier for a monarch."

"Have you read the planned Brazilian constitution?" the Emperor asked.

"Yes, I have, and think it a good one, Your Majesty," answered George.

"You don't think that such a constitution threatens a monarchy?" asked the Emperor Franz.

"No, I don't, Your Majesty," said George. "At least not necessarily. It depends on the monarchy. In Brazil I think that by far the majority of the people love their present monarchs, Dom Pedro and your daughter Leopoldina, and that the constitution does not threaten them."

The Emperor Franz looked significantly at Minister Metternich, then said, "I am not so sure. But we appreciate your assessment of the matter, Major von Schaeffer. Will you be returning to Brazil soon?"

"As soon as I can, Your Majesty," said George.

With that the Emperor turned and walked back behind his desk to sit down. Minister Metternich gestured to George that it was time to leave, and together they walked out of the palace.

"I trust that you will be leaving Vienna in a very short time," said Metternich. "And that you will thereafter desist in any recruitment of Brazilian soldiers on the territory of Austria proper. Do I make myself clear?"

"Indeed you do, Your Highness," said George, "Indeed you do."

George crossed out of Austria and into Bavaria within days of his meeting with Prince Metternich and Emperor Franz II in Vienna. In Munich he easily found his cousin Michael, who was the Head of the Accounting Department of King Maximilian's government. Michael looked quite well and healthy to George. He was tall and still red-haired, though the hair was thinning on top, and he had crooked teeth and acne-scarred cheeks. But his eartops had been pruned off as a result of the severe frostbite he had suffered during the Russian campaign in 1812, and he was missing three fingers on his left hand.

"George, how great it is to see you!" Michael exclaimed upon first seeing his cousin. "Do you remember how we used to sing that Latin drinking song together in the Biergarten? What fine days we then knew, eh?"

"Michael, do you know that we were within only a few kilometers of each other during the Battle for Moscow?" asked George.

Michael sighed and said, "That's what Wilhelm wrote to me...and he was there too. Mein Gott, what a miracle that we're all three still alive. I was the only one of all the Bavarian soldier-friends I had to survive the campaign. They all suffered cruel deaths, especially on the way out of Russia, what with the cold, the lice, the starvation and sickness, not to mention the Russian peasants and the raiding Cossacks. Bavaria suffered the loss of so many, many of its young men. And indeed I was more dead than alive when I got back here. It took me two years to recover. But what about you...you've done so very well for yourself, haven't you, George? Were you able to start a plantation in Brazil?"

George and Michael spent many hours reminiscing and reacquainting. George met Michael's wife Alicia, who was a lady-in-waiting in King Maximilian's court. She was a woman far more beautiful than George would have thought it within Michael's ability to attract, even taller than he and a decade younger. She was most pleasant in demeanor, and she actively engaged in conversation with Michael and George. When George suggested that he would like to meet King Maximilian to seek his permission, if not his sanction, to recruit Bavarian families to emigrate to Brazil, Alicia offered to help arrange the meeting.

Before meeting King Maximilian, George was worried about the fact that the King's daughter, Karoline Charlotte, was the fourth and current wife of Emperor Franz of Austria, whose domain he had just found so apparently inimical to an independent Brazil and even more so to his recruitment efforts. But this worry turned out to be unjustified. King Maximilian, a stern-appearing but seemingly jovial man, though quite old, was quite cordial.

Portrait ca. 1820 of Maximilian I Joseph, King of Bavaria (27 May, 1756—13 October, 1825) by Joseph Karl Stieler (1781-1858), from: http://en.wikipedia.org/wiki/Maximilian_I_Joseph_of_Bavaria.

"My good man," the King told George when he had been apprised of the reasons for George's audience with him, "I don't care who you might lure away from us and where you might take them. If they don't want to live here in Bavaria, let them take themselves where they might. God speed to them...and to you!"

In Hamburg on February 29, 1824, George was able to send off the ship *Caroline* under Captain Jakob von der Wettern. His charter agent, Johann von Kettler, was aboard with 231 family members, and 30 pledged soldiers, including George's nephew Anton Schaeffer. The 231 family members were sent to Nova Friburgo, as those from the *Argus* had been, after the *Caroline* reached Rio de Janeiro without difficulty in only two months time. It returned to Hamburg with another load of hardwood by August.

In what time he could find in Hamburg in early 1824, George wrote a book about the virtues of living in Brazil. He called it <u>Brazil as an Independent State in History, Commerce, and Politics</u>. The title page listed the author as "Dr./Major of Her Majesty the Empress's Personal Guard, and etc. etc. etc. George Anton Aloysius Ritter von Schaeffer." He dedicated the work to "Her Majesty Maria Leopoldina, Kaiserin of Brazil." And he began the work with a poem:

"Europe yearns for a Ruler

And for the place wherein he rules,

Where such a wondrous rare happiness

Reigns, of which I pray the power to tell.

As vanilla round the laurel's bark,

To such an Emperor all should cling,

A mighty one, whose state bequeaths

To all reward that's fair and just.

Listen, peoples, whom his arm will free,

Celebrate, serve him faithfully,

Because he gives a golden time.

How I long to accompany those,

Who dedicate themselves to his service.

Oh will what I write earn your approval.

v. Sch."

In the book, George described all of his journeys to Rio de Janeiro and his acquaintance with Dom João, Princes Pedro and Miguel, and the Princess Leopoldina, whom he praised in the most extravagant terms. He related a very detailed travelogue of his peregrinations through the diverse countrysides of Brazil, complete with descriptions of the geography, the flora and fauna, and the spectacular scenery, with characterizations of numerous notable people he encountered. He devoted chapters to a discussion of Brazil's history, opining on the motivations of the colonizers and the slavers and the state administrators as the country developed. He commented at length on the political ramifications of Brazil's independence, comparing it to the United States and other constitutional countries. He wrote on and on and on about the rich natural resources of Brazil and how they will assure Brazil and its residents the brightest imaginable future. And, at the end, he inserted a copy of the draft of a Brazilian constitution that Jose Bonifacio had given him.

George found a publisher, J. F. Hammerich, in the Hamburg suburb of Altona for his book. It came to 464 pages in length and was bound in both card stock and leather in an edition of 100 copies. George kept most of these copies himself, intending to distribute them without cost to individuals of importance who would use the information in the book to influence others to come to Brazil.

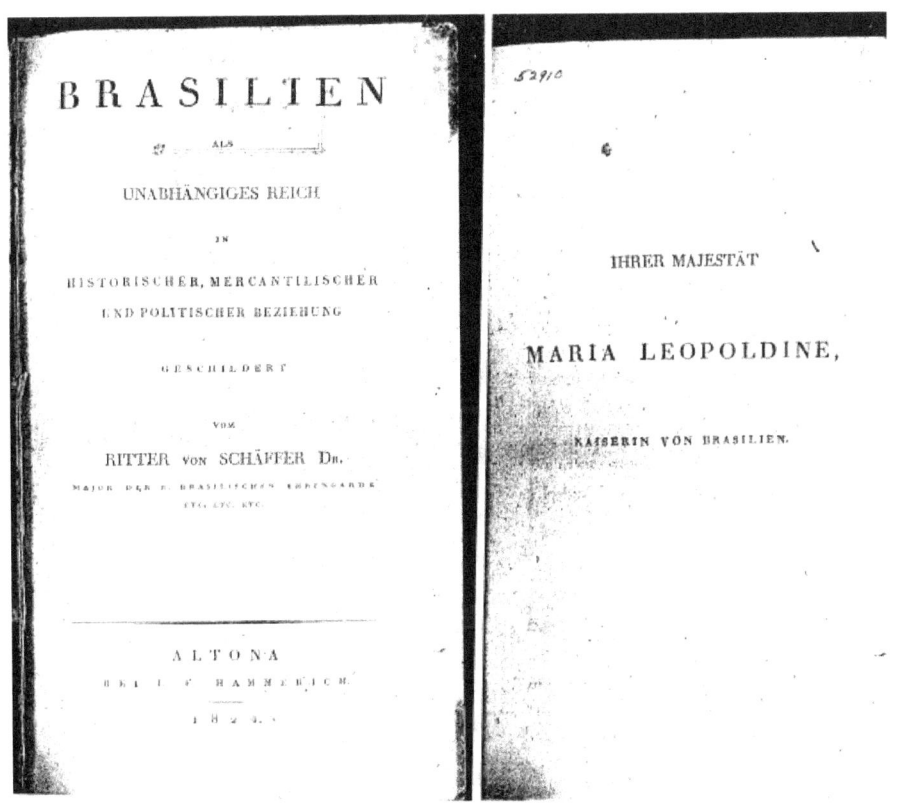

George's 1824 book on Brazil: The title page and dedication to "Her Majesty Maria Leopoldina, Empress ("Kaiserin") of Brazil." This illustration is from a copy of the book, acquisition numbered 52910, that had been on the shelf in the Vincent Archabbey Library of Latrobe, Pennsylvania, since 1846. How it got there is bound to be an interesting story. I accessed it through interlibrary loan in 1992. The book also exists in a Dutch translation…see notes under Schaeffer.

The *Anna Louise* left Hamburg under charter agent Matteus Sulz and Captain Johann Heinrich Knaack on March 24, 1824 with 200 soldiers, 27 of whom were released to George by the warden of the Hamburg prison upon Dr. August Kretzschmar's 'recommendation,' and 126 family members aboard. All reached Rio de Janeiro in good health on June 4 of that year, with the family members going on to Porto Alegre in the Rio Grande do Sul State to found a colony called São Leopoldo north of there. The *Anna Louise* waited months for a return cargo of dried meats and Brazilian leather, so that George was deprived of a timely word back from Rio as a result, but the ship arrived back in Hamburg in January of 1825.

The *Germania* Incident:

George Schaeffer's recruitment efforts kept him in Europe for six years...more than the length of time he was away from Barbara and Inga to circumnavigate the globe and have his adventures in Australia, Alaska, Hawai'i, China, Brazil, and Europe before returning to them in St. Petersburg in 1818. One important difference in his absence this time was that he had a regular and dependable avenue of ships to take a steady stream of his letters through Rio de Janeiro to Barbara and his company at Frankenthal. It may have been this that preserved his marriage. He received in turn more than fifty letters from Barbara that he kept in an engraved box in his Hamburg apartment so that he could read and reread them. He also wrote more than forty letters to Dom Pedro or to Leopoldina, and several to Jose Bonifacio de Andrada, that wound up in Brazilian governmental archives.

In the German Confederation George became notorious as the "Seelenverkaüfer"—the "Soul buyer," because of reports of severe hardships faced in Brazil by some of his soldiers and colonists filtering back by letter to German relatives, who came to call these far-off correspondents the "lost souls." George's taking whole families of colonists protected him from a law passed by the Frankfurt Diet banning the direct enrollment of soldiers by foreign agents. This law stopped the activity of Dr. Kretzschmar, who was arrested and fined. George was able to argue that his future soldiers were not directly enrolled, but only joined the Brazilian army when they had emigrated there. This was a fiction of convenience that enabled George to continue to supply both soldiers and colonists to Brazil, the narrow skirting of the law adding to his notoriety. But nothing caused him the notoriety that was caused by the event that transpired upon the ship *Germania* during the fourth of his transport voyages in 1824.

In the course of preparing for the voyage of the *Germania*, the largest ship to date under Captain Hans Voss, George engaged a charter agent named Ferdinand von Kiesewetter. He brought Ferdinand von Kiesewetter with him when he went to make arrangements with Hamburg Prison Warden Albrecht Richter to take 24 prisoners on board as future Brazilian soldiers. These 24 prisoners were to be part of a company of 401 passengers on the ship, the families on board including 277 colonists and 100 other prospective soldiers.

"Some of these men are real 'bad apples' this time George," said Warden Richter. "They're not all like the previous ones...debtors and malingerers and even the possibly innocent. Some of these men are dangerous, constantly causing trouble."

"What were they imprisoned for?" asked George.

"Mostly for criminal damage and assault, but some for rioting," answered Richter.

"Well, we are looking for soldiers," said George. "And soldiers need to know how to fight and cause damage to the enemy, isn't that so?"

Ferdinand, a tough combat veteran of the Prussian army, forthrightly said to George, "I don't think we should take any such people with us, Doctor von Schaeffer. We don't need any 'bad apples' on our voyage."

But George, thinking of the square legua of Brazilian land he planned to receive for their military service in Dom Pedro's foreign battalion, over-ruled Ferdinand, saying to Warden Richter, "We'll take all 24 of them. The discipline on the ship will keep them in line."

Among the passengers of the *Germania* were the families Bendixon, Berghan, Bischoff, Böhler, Bunte, Ehlers, Elbers, Fick, Gutzeit, Herzog, Hillebrand, Hockenmüller, Mentz, Petersen, Sänger, Sass, and Weinmann. The head of the Hillebrand family, whose son Daniel was pledged as a soldier, was Colonel Johann Daniel Hillebrand, a respected veteran of the Napoleonic wars and a municipal administrator. The Ehlers family was related to Captain Bernhard Ehlers of the *Argus* and was headed by the Rev. Johann Gregory Ehlers, a Lutheran Pastor whose twenty-year-old twin sons, Adam and Albert, were pledged as soldiers. Johann Liborious and Magdalena Ernestina Mentz from Thüringen were accompanied by their 21-year-old son George Ernest, a pledged soldier, and their 30-year-old spinster daughter Dorothea Elisabeth.

At the orientation meeting held two days before the May 15, 1824 departure, Dorothea Mentz caught the attention of 28-year-old Hannover-born Heinrich Hubertus Stock, one of the prisoners released from the Hamburg prison. Terming himself a "mercenary" and falsely claiming to be a hero of the Battle of Waterloo, he mercilessly wooed the shy Dorothea throughout the boarding process, telling her how she was "as beautiful as any rose." When he found out that she was thirty years old, he told her he was thirty-five. When she asked him if he had ever been married, he "forgot" two abandoned wives and answered that "his long career in the military" had prevented his marrying. In fact he had never been in the military at all, but had been known in Hamburg as a pimp who was arrested and sentenced for beating his whores. Gifted in seduction, he worked his wiles on Dorothea, proposing marriage to her and crudely initiating her into a sexual relationship in the alley behind the inn where she and her family were staying on the night before the *Germania* sailed.

The naive Dorothea was quite enraptured with her new lover and reported his marriage proposal to her parents. She told them she couldn't wait until they got to Brazil to be married...that she wished to be married on board. "Hubie" Stock did not demur from the wedding plans, and managed to convince Dorothea's parents, Johann and Magdalena, that he was a most desirable candidate for their beloved daughter's hand. He promised them that he would cherish her and that he welcomed becoming a member of their family. The only inkling they had that Stock was not what he claimed to be was their son George's negative intuition about the man, and the fact that he was clearly a member of a pretty rough-looking batch of passengers, headed by a loud and surly man named Gregor Rasch. Rasch, young George Mentz was later to say in deposition, gave off "evil humours." He was in fact a former Hamburg prison guard who had been so brutally abusive of the inmates that he was arrested and incarcerated himself.

It was Gregor Rasch's disconcerting opinion, expressed first during the orientation, that the *Germania* should sail not to Brazil, but to the United States, where a brother of his had easily "found his fortune" in New York City. "For one thing, it's closer," he said, "We won't have to endure such a crowded journey for as long. And no one will have to serve as a soldier." When he heard this expressed opinion, charter agent Ferdinand von Kiesewetter wanted to expel Rasch from the voyage right there, but again George over-ruled him, saying, "He'll be quieter when the ship is underway...from seasickness if nothing else." But Rasch was not quiet after the *Germania* sailed away from George's control, but kept spouting his opinions to the other passengers about how "we should just sail instead to New York City." Von Kiesewetter was irritated about how some of the other passengers seemed swayed by Rasch's expressed ideas...at least some of them were curious enough about the possibility that they asked him about it.

"Our way is being paid to Brazil...ultimately by the Emperor of that country, Dom Pedro I," said Ferdinand as often as he was asked about other possible destinations. "You have accepted his offer of free land and exemption from tax. So that is where we are sailing on the *Germania*."

The wedding was performed on the mid-deck on the 2nd of June, 1824, while the *Germania* was anchored at Glückstadt near the mouth of the Elbe River seaward of Hamburg. The ceremony, recorded in the ship's log by Captain Hans Voss, was performed by Pastor Ehlers since both Dorothea and Hubie professed Lutheran faith. After a brief celebration the couple retired to a second-deck area of sleeping hammocks that had been briefly screened off to provide them a "honeymoon." The honeymoon was exceptional treatment since there was generally no privacy for married couples on the *Germania*. Four passengers each shared a hammock for alternating designated shifts of six hours' possible sleep. Married couples, especially if they had young children, had adjacent hammocks during the same shift, but with row upon row of hammocks from floor to ceiling, conjugal consort was extremely impractical and therefore not practiced. And sleeping was difficult anyway, with so many bodies squeezed so closely together that moving among the swaying hammocks without touching and disturbing the people in them was not easy, and with the sound of snoring and the smell of unwashed body odor and, when they were at sea, the vomit from those who were seasick.

The *Germania* remained anchored off Glückstadt for two weeks due to a permit problem with the city officials. Also, it was hot in that month of June and the wind just wouldn't blow, so that Captain Voss could not have sailed away even if he had given the order. During that time Gregor Rasch and a cohort of seven other men, all of whom were former Hamburg prisoners, and including Hubie Stock, made an attempt to take over the ship by force. They jumped and overpowered the ship's mate and took his pistol. Then they forced Captain Voss at pistol point into his cabin, took his pistol also, and helped themselves to a bottle of rum the Captain had in a cabinet.

On the *Germania's* foredeck at noon, a drunken Gregor Rasch, flanked by Hubie Stock and six others, shouted at the top of his voice, "We're sailing to New York City! We'll get off this scow sooner and no one has to be a soldier!" Some people who heard him initially cheered this news, but then they began to ask, "Who will sail us to New York City?" "What about the Captain and crew?" "Isn't this a criminal mutiny?"

Rasch yelled at the gathered crowd on the mid-deck, "Shut up! The Captain and crew will sail us to wherever we say or we'll set fire to the ship. We can take the lifeboats to Glückstadt and get away. And you'll all damn well roast!"

That was when charter agent von Kiesewetter stepped forward with his own pistol pointed at the men on the foredeck and said, "Stand down, Herr Rasch." He walked closer to the stairs and noticed that Rasch's hand went to the Captain's pistol tucked in his belt. "If you remove that pistol from your belt, Herr Rasch, I will shoot you through," Ferdinand said. He started climbing the stairs, his manner calm, but resolute. Rasch, looking at him and the well-aimed pistol with a snarl, took his hand off his weapon. Ferdinand walked up to him and disarmed him, taking the pistol out of his belt with his left hand. Then he told the other mutineers, "Whoever has the mate's pistol better give it to me now." Hubie Stock stepped up to him and handed him the other pistol. The mutiny was over.

Ferdinand and Captain Voss decided to chain Gregor Rasch to a beam in a tightly packed lower storage compartment. There simply wasn't room on the ship to incarcerate the other mutineers as well. "Hopefully, they will consider their failure to take over the ship as a lesson and become peaceful shipmates for the duration of the voyage," Captain Voss said. "It was likely Rasch and the rum that lead them astray. But we'll keep our eyes on them now."

July of 1824 found the *Germania* in the Bay of Biscay headed for the central Atlantic in good wind at last. Captain Voss couldn't spare sailors to guard Gregor Rasch in the storage compartment, but left him chained there with a chamber pot and kept him fed. Everyone who took him food or came to change his chamber pot had to endure foul imprecations from the man. Several of his fellow mutineers came by to visit him also, but they were deterred from freeing him by the snugly padlocked iron cuffs above his ankles. Captain Voss kept the key in his cabin.

Hubie Stock quite quickly turned cruel toward his bride Dorothea. He began to send her to bring him things that he could more easily have gotten himself, berating her when she didn't get whatever it was for him quickly enough. She had been beautiful to him before, but now he openly called her "cow," or "sow," and made jokes about her physical appearance to his fellows. Once he deliberately humiliated her by telling three of the other mutineers that her legs were hairier than his and making Dorothea pull up her skirt and bloomers to show the other men her legs. After this these men began to call her "Hair-iette" and ask her to pull up her skirts even higher. Dorothea's younger brother George confronted Hubie about his treatment of his sister, threatening to punch him if he heard about any further such behavior. But Hubie scoffed at this threat, telling George, "Just you try it, young pup. I'll be ready for you."

Hubie was a chewer of tobacco. He and his cronies could often be seen standing near the ship's siderails along the aft row of toilets, spitting their brown saliva over the side into the wake. But Hubie's personal supply of tobacco ran out, and his cronies were reluctant to give him any, the tobacco being a commodity in limited supply...and he had no money to buy tobacco from anyone else. The crony with the most tobacco, a crude man called "Ash," firmly refused to part with any of his, even though Hubie cajoled and even begged him for some. For several days the mens' wrangling about their tobacco supply continued as Hubie's irritation increased. Finally a kind of bargain was agreed upon. Hubie would have Dorothea pleasure Ash by hand in his hammock in exchange for some chewing tobacco.

When Hubie told Dorothea to go to Ash during his sleeping shift and masturbate him, she was aghast and refused, saying, "That's horrible. How could you ask me to do such a thing? I won't do it."

"Don't come on delicate to me, you sow," said Hubie. "You're my wife and you'll do as I say. It'll only take a minute or two. Ash is waiting down there...hammock 10-center in the third row. Go down there as if you were going past him to another hammock yourself...take hold of him and do it. When he's satisfied he'll give you some chew for me."

When Dorothea said "No" again, Hubie slapped her hard in the face, put his hands around her neck and squeezed hard enough to make her gag.

"When I tell you to do something, you need to do it right off," said Hubie, still choking Dorothea. "Otherwise I'll squeeze the life right out of you. Now are you going down there and pleasure Ash for the chew, or not? Just nod your head...yes or no."

Dorothea nodded affirmatively and Hubie released his hold around her neck. "Remember, he's in hammock 10-center in the third row," he said. "Now go down there and bring me back the chew."

Dorothea went down into the sleeping deck crying. When she came back up in a few minutes, Hubie was standing among several of his cronies on the mid-deck. When they saw Dorothea they broke into laughter. Obviously Hubie had told them what he thought she was doing below. But in an instant more the men's expressions changed when they saw that Dorothea was being closely followed by her brother George, who was enraged. He ran across the mid-deck to Hubie and struck him in the face, knocking him down. Then he piled on top of Hubie, pummeling him wildly and shouting, "You bastard, I told you I'd teach you to treat my sister better. Take this...and this...and this..."

Hubie was taking a severe beating, but four of his cronies quickly stepped in and grabbed George, pulling him off Hubie. They held George horizontally at waist height, a man to each corner of him as George struggled to get himself free. Hubie got to his feet and nodded his head toward the ship's siderails. "Over the side with him!" he said, and the men scooted with George still in their grasp to the side and threw him over the rail into the ocean. Dorothea screamed at the top of her lungs, and kept screaming.

A great number of people who were also standing on the mid-deck at that time rushed to the same side to get a view of George, who had already come back up to the surface of the water and was in plain sight among the waves. But the ship was moving rapidly past and away from him. He was already treading water parallel with the stern. Cries of "Man overboard!" caused Captain Voss to come running out of his cabin and to order an emergency striking of all sail. The sailors sprang into action, climbing up into the yards to bring up the canvas. Captain Voss ordered the anchors to be lowered as a drag to help stop the ship's forward momentum. "Lower a boat right away!" he shouted, and several young men of the passengers helped the sailors accomplish this, even joining them in the boat and taking up oars.

It took two hours for the party in the rowboat to return to the now still *Germania* and bring young George Mentz back onto the deck. It was very fortunate for him, all agreed, that he was a good swimmer, and that his being thrown overboard had happened in broad daylight on a good-weather day...and that no shark had gotten to him before he could be found and hauled into the boat. But not everything was fortunate. During the hectic effort to stop the ship and lower the rescue boat, Hubie and Ash and the five other mutineers from the earlier attempt had gotten the key to Gregor Rasch's ankle cuffs and a pistol from the Captain's cabin, freed Rasch, and taken over the ship. Holding a pistol at Captain Voss's head, they disarmed the mate, and took charter agent von Kiesewetter by surprise during his sleeping shift. All three of these men were now at pistol point on the aft deck around the wheel, surrounded by eight men armed with three pistols and knives taken from the mess supplies. A crowd of over a hundred of the passengers jammed the mid-deck and listened to Gregor Rasch shout, "We are now in command of this ship. We are sailing it to New York City. If any of the crew doesn't do what we say, we'll pitch them over the side."

Ferdinand von Kiesewetter, even though one of the mutineers held a pistol to his back, shouted out to Rasch so that he could be heard by all, "So you know how to navigate to New York City, do you Herr Rasch? What is the heading?"

Rasch yelled out, "Captain Voss and his mate will navigate our way to where we want to go. If they don't we'll start shooting other people we don't like...like you." Then he called out to the passengers, "Who is with us in this? Who wants to see New York City? Who doesn't want to be a soldier? If you're with us, step up here aft and join us."

For almost a minute not one of the gathered passengers moved. But then a robust young pledged soldier named Aaron Bischoff stepped up toward the group of mutineers, saying "I'm with you." He was joined by several other young men, including Daniel Hillebrand and the Ehlers' twins Adam and Albert. In a moment more the mutineers were surrounded by an equal number of young men from the passengers.

"Is that all?" shouted Gregor Rasch. "There will be land in the United States for everyone too. The climate is more like that in Germany. We don't need to fight snakes and cannibals in Brazil."

At that instant Aaron Bischoff abruptly charged into Rasch, knocking his pistol arm aside and hitting him strongly in the jaw. The pistol discharged with a loud "BLAM" and a cloud of white smoke, but the ball was fired up into the air. Captain Voss wrapped his arms around Rasch's middle and wrestled him to the deck. Daniel Hillebrand had similarly attacked Hubie Stock who was holding a pistol to the side of the mate, and he had Hubie's pistol arm tucked under his own arm and was wheeling Hubie around to the side where Adam Ehlers was able to seize it and remove the pistol. Ferdinand von Kiesewetter swung around to swat at the pistol Ash had pointed into his back, but his hand only narrowly grazed the pistol's flash pan. For an instant he was looking into Ash's eyes as Ash pulled the trigger. But the pistol's hammer struck the pan with a hollow "click," and did not fire. Albert Ehlers helped him subdue Ash. In a few more moments the mutiny was, again as before at Glückstadt, over.

In the aftermath of the mutiny, Colonel Johann Daniel Hillebrand spoke to congratulate Aaron Bischoff for his ploy to get close enough to the mutineers to grapple physically with them...and to praise his own son and the others for joining the effort so effectively without overt communication. He asked Reverend Johann Gregory Ehlers to say a few words, and Reverend Ehlers said, "It is God Almighty who thwarted the evil here seen, my friends. Our sons were merely his instrument. We are indeed blessed."

Charter Agent von Kiesewetter asked Colonel Hillebrand to join him and Captain Voss in deciding what should be done with the now tightly bound mutineers. They retired to Captain Voss's cabin to discuss the matter.

"I think Reverend Ehlers is correct that we have seen real evil here," said Agent von Kiesewetter, "I knew it in my heart from the first time I heard about these men from their prison warden. 'Bad apples' he called them. I told Dr. Schaeffer that we shouldn't take them, but he wouldn't heed my advice. Now we have them subdued, but we can't guard them every second and they're still dangerous...a continuing threat to us. I think we have to execute them. Frankly, Brazil will be a better place without them."

"So these men were prisoners?" asked Colonel Hillebrand, who did not know this, "Do any of them have other members of their families with us?"

"No, all of these eight men are by themselves," answered von Kiesewetter. "And we have others aboard who were prisoners also, both with and without families. But they have not been a threat."

"I have no doubt they would have killed us," said Captain Voss. "Certainly they threw young George Mentz over the side without compunction. We are most fortunate that no one was killed. But if we have further trouble from them someone may be killed. What then would we say to the killed person's relatives...that we allowed these men to attack us THREE times?"

"In my military days," Colonel Hillebrand said, "The penalty for such acts as these men have committed was death. I saw executions carried out more than once, and I can tell you that they leave a lasting mark on those that see them. If we decide to execute them, how will we do it?"

Captain Voss spoke up at this point, saying, "Before we decide how...we should decide if. Are the three of us in firm agreement that the mutineers should be executed, and if we are in such agreement, is our judgment sufficient to satisfy any inquiring authority? Someone might say that all of us were personally threatened by the mutineers' actions...Ferdinand and me directly, Johann, and you through your son...so that in executing them we would be exacting personal retribution."

"I understand," said Colonel Hillebrand. "Perhaps we're not the ones to 'cast the first stone,' so to speak. We should ask the Reverend Ehlers what he thinks. He speaks often about how God's justice is not retribution."

When they consulted with Reverend Ehlers, he surprised them with the advice that they should let the entire ship's company, crew and passengers, decide the matter. He said: "Captain Voss can ask the question: 'Should these men be executed as double mutineers and a continued threat to our lives?' If all say aye, then execution is warranted. If any...even one say nay, then we continue to bind and watch them. Legally, this is a German ship and they are German citizens. Therefore, it would normally be a German court that decides the matter. Yet I can't imagine that we would transport these men back to Germany. In forsaking Germany we are forsaking German law. In Brazil we don't yet know what the law is, but we imagine that as colonists there we will have a voice in making the law. Perhaps God is giving us a chance to do so here in advance. Let's put it to a vote."

Captain Voss asked the ship's company to have a representative from every family, from the pledged soldiers who had no families, and from the crew on the mid-deck at noon the next day. Everyone on the ship was informed that a vote on the matter of the mutineers' execution was to take place...and that a unanimous vote without exception would be required for an execution to take place. That evening and night ardent discussions transpired in every quarter of the ship. Evaluations of the mutineers' character and behavior were the fare of every discussion.

On August 21, 1824, at noon, Captain Voss looked down onto the assembled representatives of all the company on the *Germania*. Certainly, he thought, there were a hundred or more present, representing all 401 passengers and 65 crew. To the side of the mid-deck were the mutineers, each tightly bound, hand and foot, with rope. They were in a guarded row facing the assembly.

In his loudest booming voice, Captain Voss said, "Now in the presence of the entire ship's company, I ask: Should these eight men be executed as double mutineers and a continued threat to our lives? If so, answer 'AYE'."

There was a loud low rumble of voices, saying "AYE."

Then Captain Voss continued. "Is there even one person who says that these men should not be executed as double mutineers and threats to our lives? If there is, will that person now say 'NAY'?"

Hubie Stock's eyes easily found Dorothea's eyes looking at him from the crowd of representatives. "Say NAY now, won't you love?" he shouted. But Dorothea was dead silent, as was everyone else.

Agent von Kiesewetter, Captain Voss, and Colonel Hillebrand then met to decide the method of execution. It was quickly decided that the eight mutineers should simply be thrown into the ocean like they had thrown George Mentz into the ocean and threatened to throw into the ocean any crew members who did not do their bidding. This method seemed appropriate to all three men. Captain Voss suggested that they be encased in weighted canvas sacks to make the task of throwing them overboard easier. These were the same canvas sacks held in reserve to commit the bodies of any deceased passengers or sailors to the sea. That also seemed appropriate.

At four bells that same afternoon, the execution was carried out. Each man, Gregor Rasch first and Hubie Stock second, then Ash and the others, was gagged and tied into a separate stout canvas sack weighted with bricks and thrown like logs into the ocean from the aft rail next to the toilet row. In a few minutes the task was completed. The canvas sacks and their contents immediately sank out of sight into the wake of the *Germania* on its way to Brazil.

In February of 1827, almost two years after the return of the *Germania* to Hamburg, George was visited in his Bremen apartment, from which he was then sending off more ships, by police officers who told him that he had been indicted in absentia by a federal board of inquiry in Frankfurt. The matter concerned the deaths of the eight prisoners on board the *Germania* in 1824. He had to post a large bond to stay out of jail until he could go to Frankfurt and testify at a required hearing. He took with him to Frankfurt all of the papers and several personal letters he had concerning the incident. There also to testify was his *Germania* charter agent Ferdinand von Kiesewetter and the ship's Captain Hans Voss.

The hearing turned out to be surprisingly informal, with a staff of lawyers and three federal judges in a room, all sitting around a large table. George took responsibility for taking the Hamburg prisoners as passengers on the ship, admitting to everyone there that "That was a sad mistake for which I am most sorry. I was motivated by greed. Emperor Dom Pedro of Brazil is paying me in land for every colonist I take there who enlists as a soldier. I thought that these men would be very likely to enlist."

One of the lawyers asked him, "Dr. von Schaeffer, did you know the incarceration status of the prisoners at the time you agreed to take them on the ship?"

"What do you mean by 'incarceration status'?" asked George.

"I mean...did you know if these men were being released to you because their terms of penal servitude had expired or were you taking them prematurely because of some financial advantage to the warden?" said the lawyer.

George told the truth. "I paid the warden nothing, and I did not know the incarceration status of any of the prisoners. The Hamburg Warden, Herr Richter, only told me the reasons why some of them had been imprisoned. He never informed me of when their prison terms were to expire."

That was all that was required of George. Agent von Kiesewetter and Captain Voss were questioned at considerably more length. One of the lawyers read aloud a letter from Brazilian soldier George Mentz telling his version of the events and entered the letter into the file of evidence. Another letter was from the Reverend Johann Ehlers from São Leopoldo in the Rio Grande do Sul State of Brazil where he had become the pastor of the community's major church. Yet a third letter, by Colonel Johann Hillebrand, now the council leader of the São Leopoldo colony of Germans, was also placed in the file.

As they waited sitting on chairs in the hallway outside the office for the Frankfurt panel of federal judges to decide if the evidence merited court prosecution of any of them, George, Captain Voss, and Agent von Kiesewetter reminisced about their roles in the *Germania* incident.

"I'll always remember the look on the one fellow's face when even his new bride would not speak up to save him from execution," said Ferdinand. "His name was Stock...Heinrich, as I recall...they called him 'Hubie'."

"The wife Dorothea had the executed prisoner Stock's daughter in early 1825 and named her Ernestina," George said. "I got a letter about it from her father, Johann Liborious Mentz. It was among those I submitted to the judges."

In a few minutes one of the lawyers appeared to announce that no charges would be pressed against any of the three men. The executions of the mutineers, he said, "was completely justified and appropriately done."

Achievements and Passages:

From July of 1823 to September of 1829 twenty-one ships chartered by Major/Dr./Ambassador-at-large George Anton von Schaeffer made twenty-seven voyages to Brazil from the ports of Amsterdam, Hamburg, or Bremen. George kept quite meticulous records of these ships, his agents on the ships, the ships' captains, and the numbers of passengers each ship carried, listing the family names of the colonists, and recording the number of pledged soldiers. The twenty-seven voyages in order were: 1) *Argus* (Amsterdam, 134 colonists, 150 soldiers, total 284 passengers delivered (fourteen killed by pirates, one infant death)); 2) *Caroline* (Hamburg, 231, 30, total 261); 3) *Anna Louise* (H, 126, 200, 326); 4) *Germania* (H, 124, 277, 401 delivered (8 didn't make it to Brazil, because of their execution)); 5) *George Friedrich* (H, 145, 330, 475); 6) *Peter und Marie* (H (Glückstadt), 64, 201, 270); 7) *Kranich* (H, 282, 77, 359); 8) *Caroline* (H, 192, 90, 282); 9) *Triton* (H, 101, 99, 200); 10) *Wilhelmine* (H, 140, 244, 384); 11) *Friedrich Heinrich* (H, 81, 283, 364); 12) *George Friedrich* (H, 88, 354, 462); 13) *Creole* (H (Altona), approx. 50, 70, 120); 14) *Fortuna* (H, 52, 200, 252); 15) *Kranich* (H, 216, 85, 301); 16) *Company Patie* (A, 81, 200, 281); 17) *Anna Louise* (H, 50, 350, 400); 18) *Caroline* (H, 80, 200, 280); 19) *Friedrich* (Bremen, 80, 158, 238); 20) *Fliegender Adler* (B, 220, 290, 510); 21) *Brödtoe* (B, 122, 155, 277); 22) *Creole* (H (Altona), approx. 130, 170, 300); 23) *Fortuna* (B, 65, 200, 265); 24) *Betzy & Marianne* (B, 6, 32, 38); 25) *Harmonie* (B, 140, 150, 290); 26) *Cecilie* (B, 80, 50, 130); and 27) *Olbers* (B, 456, 418, 874). George bragged that, other than the fourteen deaths on the *Argus* caused by the African pirates, a single infant death on Tenerife, and the *execution* of the eight mutineers on the *Germania*, he had transported by his program 27 shiploads of emigrants to Brazil, and that no one transported had lodged any complaint about the conditions of their passage. This means that George paid the way to Brazil for (approximately) 8,574 German people, including 3,536 family members as colonists...most to the Rio Grande do Sul State, and 5,038 pledged soldiers. This cost him a colossal sum of money...so much that he began to borrow from Hamburg and Bremen bankers in 1827. But he had documentary assurance that Emperor Dom Pedro I of Brazil was going to be paying him a square legua of land or its assessed value in gold for every soldier he sent who completed a six-year term in Brazil's army. He anticipated that this would result in a tremendous profit for him, making him an extremely wealthy, and royally titled, Baron of a vast estate in Brazil.

Early on in his European efforts, George received a letter from Dr. Flach informing him that Jose Bonifacio de Andrada had "lost favor" with Dom Pedro and that Jose had taken exile in France. The effort to gain Dom Pedro's acceptance of the constitution that Jose Bonifacio had been working on was being carried on in the Brazilian popular assembly by Jose's brothers Antonio and Martim and others. Dom Pedro accepted the constitution in 1824, and soon after gained diplomatic recognition from the United States. In a short time after this Dom João's government of Portugal recognized its former colony of Brazil as an independent country also. George was concerned that this would mean that his recruitment of Germans as soldiers to defend Brazil against Dom João's Portugal would no longer be needed. But he kept receiving the same word from Dom Pedro...both directly and indirectly...and this word was: "Send more soldiers." Dr. Flach's letters said that this was because of a conflict with Argentina that was not going well. Also, Pedro feared his brother Miguel's ambitions."

The death of Dom João VI of Portugal on March 10, 1826 caused a succession crisis between the brothers Pedro and Miguel. Dom Pedro, the older, initially sailed to Portugal to be recognized as Dom Pedro IV of Portugal, the Algarve and Brazil, but he knew that his brother Miguel, who was already well installed in Portugal, regarded himself as rightful heir since Pedro had chosen to become the Emperor of an independent Brazil. So Pedro decided to abdicate his Portuguese throne in favor of his and Leopoldina's now seven-year-old daughter Maria da Gloria, with his sister Isabel Maria as regent, on the condition that Maria marry her uncle Miguel when she came of age at 14 years. Then she and Miguel would rule together. Dom Pedro thought that this kind of marital regency would satisfy Miguel's desire to rule Portugal, but he also stipulated that Miguel and Maria should rule Portugal under the terms of a liberalized version of its 1822 constitution, similar to the one he had accepted for Brazil. Miguel initially accepted these conditions, allowing the Portuguese constitution to be liberalized, and taking an oath of loyalty to Pedro, who appointed Miguel a General before returning to Brazil. When George learned of this situation, he worried mostly about Leopoldina. "How could she allow Pedro to propose the marriage of the underage Princess Maria to her Uncle Miguel?" he asked himself, concluding, "She must not be well."

George took delight in whatever he could find out about his "Kaiserin" Leopoldina. He treasured the few notes she sent him, especially those on the royal stationery. From Dr. Flach's letters he kept track of her efforts to give Pedro an heir. She gave birth to a daughter Paula on February 17, 1823 and to another daughter Francisca on August 2, 1824. Dr. Flach wrote that she was weak from the trials of birth and from the lack of proper waiting periods between pregnancies. "But Pedro must have an heir," Dr. Flach reported her as saying.   On December 2, 1826 Leopoldina died giving birth to a son...the heir Pedro.   When George was informed of this he wept for hours.   He wrote to Barbara that "my patroness and inspiration is gone."

One of the virtues of life in Hamburg for George was that he could read newspapers.   But in a newspaper in late June of 1826 his eye caught the headline: "Karamzin, Prominent Russian Author and Historian, Dies."   The obituary article mentioned Nikolai Mikhailovich's long life of achievement in literature, in editorship, and as the author of the definitive multi-volume History of the Russian State, but focused attention on the fact that Nikolai had spent time in Germany in his youth and spoke German well.   He had died on the 22nd of May, which was June 3 on the European calendar, but no cause of death was mentioned.   George was very saddened by this news, and wrote to Barbara that he had thought of Nikolai not only as a senior "brother Mason," but as an actual brother.   "It's hard to lose an older brother," he wrote.   Then, in early 1827, he remembered writing this about Nikolai Karamzin when he received word in his new Bremen apartment that his older brother Jacob Schaeffer had died in Münnerstadt at age 63.   The news came too late for him to travel there to attend the funeral and he was very busy, so he stayed in Bremen, sending only a letter of condolence to Jacob's wife and family.   He also wrote a letter to Wilhelm and Julia in Frankenthal to give them the news.

One of the first letters from Barbara to reach George in Bremen, still one forwarded from his Hamburg address, read as follows:

"27 January, 1827

From Frankenthal

Dear George,

Inga and I and everyone here wish you the very happiest birthday.   It's hard to believe that you could be forty-eight years old.   We haven't seen you now for four and a half years.   We trust God that you are doing well without my care for you, and that you will soon decide that you have done enough and return to us.

The families Gerhard and Lahm you selected to send here to Frankenthal from the passengers on the ship Kranich's second voyage are very good people and are already a help to us.   Our population is now more than fifty and all those living here are doing well.

But I must report to you that our colony has now endured its first death.   My mother, God bless her, died peacefully in her sleep the night after New Year's day.   Even at seventy-five years of age, she was working until the end.   Her death has been hardest of all on Inga.   She has taken over the care of mother's cat Tommie.   Johann Henning was wonderful in speaking about mother at the funeral.   We buried her here in a cemetery we have made.

A letter reached me very belatedly from Vasilii Shelikhov in St. Petersburg. It is dated from 1823 well before Nikolai Karamzin's death and comes to me via Dr. von Langsdorff who returned to Brazil some time ago to go on his expedition. In it is the news that your young cadet friend Antipatr Baranov died there. He caught a cold after being saddened to learn that that Hawaiian Governor's daughter Hannah he dreamed of marrying had married a Yankee Captain named Davis and he simply lost the will to live. He never got to command a ship himself. I regret sending you such sad news, knowing what affection you had for him.

George, we love you and we hug you on your birthday and wish you many many more. Please return to us as soon as you can. Inga is growing into a young lady now without you. You won't believe how beautiful she is.

Your loving wife, Barbara."

George realized that Barbara had written this letter after the death of Empress Leopoldina but before being informed of it. It also had no mention of Jacob's death, about which he had sent news to Wilhelm and Julia, but it did mention the death of Nikolai Karamzin he had written to Barbara earlier. He wasn't as saddened about the death of Barbara's mother, Ingrid Hindernacht, as he was about the death of Antipatr Baranov. Antipatr, he thought, was just beginning the adult course of his life and had such potential to do great things. He was a dreamer, and a very endearing one. His death seemed more tragic to George than that of Ingrid Hindernacht who had lived long enough to realize many of her dreams. For one thing, he thought, she had lived to see her granddaughter, named after her, reach young womanhood at the age of almost fifteen. The thought of Inga being fifteen years old caused him to shake his head in consternation, realizing that he had been away from her for ten of those years.

George had already known from his correspondence with Dr. Flach that Georg Heinrich von Langsdorff had obtained the necessary funding from Tsar Aleksandr and begun his grand expedition north into the Amazon basin. That had happened in 1822 or 1823, as George recalled. And he knew from the newspapers that the Russian Tsar Aleksandr I had died far from the capital in mysterious circumstances in late November of 1825, followed within a very short time into death by his consort Elizabeth, after whom George had once named a fort on the island of Kaua'i. The Russian people apparently thought that the Tsar's next-in-age brother, the Grand Duke Konstantin, who had once given George a commendation, would succeed him. But Konstantin had, unbeknownst to the public, voluntarily surrendered his right to rule to their much younger brother Nicholas, whom Barbara had once met. In the period of public confusion about the succession, a group of army officers and government officials, including the man named Kondratii Ryleev who worked at the Russian-American Company office in St. Petersburg with Vasilii Shelikhov, tried to overthrow the government. But they were shortly overpowered by

212

troops on Nicholas' orders and the leaders of the revolt, including Ryleev, were hanged. Many of St. Petersburg's leading intellectuals, who had sympathies with the "Decembrists," as the rebels were called after the month of their activity, were exiled to Siberia. George was happy then that he had left Russia. Almost all the people of his acquaintance and concern there were now gone.

The next time George wrote a letter to Barbara he mused to her that he had personally met several of the world's prominent leaders: a Tsar (Aleksandr I), three Emperors and an Empress (Dom João VI, Dom Pedro I, Franz I, and Leopoldina), and three Kings (Kamehameha, Kaumuali'i, and Maximilian I). But she, he wrote, had become acquainted on her own with two prominent leaders he had not met: United States President John Quincy Adams and Tsar Nicholas I of Russia. "Together," he wrote, "We've stood in the presence of the high and mighty in our lives."

On a cold day in February of 1828, George answered a knock on his Bremen apartment door to find his Hawai'i and China friend John Marshall standing outside on the landing.

"Mein Gott, it's John Marshall!" exclaimed George. "It's John Marshall knocking on my door! What in Heaven are you doing here in Bremen?"

John Marshall hugged George warmly and said, "You may remember that I was born in Germany...in the same Baden-Baden area where my Uncle John Jacob Astor was born. It's south of Heidelberg and Karlsruhe. I inherited a house there after the death of my aunt, and so I came from New York City to settle my affairs there and sell it. I sailed into Bremen and am now about to sail out of Bremen, but when I first came through the city nine months ago I had no idea you were here. But in my hometown I heard about a "Soul Buyer" named Dr. George von Schaeffer who was paying people's way to Brazil through Bremen. So of course I knew it had to be you and decided to find you on my way back through."

"Well, I'm so very glad you did, John," said George. "I have such memories of the times we shared—climbing that Hawaiian volcano together with young Antipatr Baranov, and being together on Maui, for example, not to mention your helping rescue me at Honolulu and our sailing together to China. But, say, do you know that Antipatr has died?'

"A young man like that? The Russian-American Governor's son? What happened to him?"

"He came to St. Petersburg to become a naval officer and studied well," George answered, "But he lost heart when he found out the girl who taught him to swim at Waikīkī had married Captain William Davis...whom you may know. Antipatr dreamed of returning to Hawai'i as a Captain himself and marrying her. We're talking about Hannah Holmes, the daughter of O'ahu Governor Oliver Holmes...called 'Homa'."

213

"Homa is no longer the O'ahu Governor. William Heath Davis I did know," said John Marshall, "But he died in 1823. I was there in Hawai'i when it happened."

"Really? Then his marriage to Hannah Holmes must have been a short one. Antipatr died in 1821 or 1822, I think," said George.

"Was it just the news of the marriage that killed him?" asked John, "It seems like it had to be something else as well."

"Yes," said George. "He had caught a strong cold."

"Too bad," commented John.

George invited John to come with him to his favorite restaurant nearby. "We'll have the best food you ever tasted," he told his friend. "And they have the best beer in all the world."

At the restaurant, George and John Marshall talked until midnight as they ate and drank. George told John all about his work in Brazil to found the colony of Frankenthal, and about his relationship with Dom Pedro and his now deceased wife Leopoldina. He related his hopes of gaining a fortune to rival that of John Jacob Astor and obtaining the title of "Baron." John had been working for only the past year in his uncle's shipping business in New York City. Before that he had continued to work on the ships in Hawai'i, to which he had returned from China with Captain Isaiah Lewis.

"So tell me about what has happened in Hawai'i, John," requested George. "I know that Kamehameha died in May of 1819 and that his successor Liholiho was having trouble with the people. The Russian-American Company asked a man named Peter Dobell to go there too, sometime in 1820, I think. Do you know him? He became quite close to my wife while he was in St. Petersburg."

"Yes, I did meet Peter Dobell," said John. "He's quite a decent fellow...has a ship called *Sylph*. He told me that he is a native of Philadelphia and once worked for the shipping magnate there, Stephen Girard. In Hawai'i he advised Liholiho about how to handle Billy Pitt...Kalanimoku...after the death of Kamehameha. Kalanimoku may have been thinking about ruling in his own right, but shortly he came around to help Liholiho and Ka'ahumanu, who is the real ruler. They went to battle with some of their own chiefs when they tried to forsake the kapus. And they won the battle...the kapus are no more. And making sure they don't come back are the missionaries. From 1820 on Hawai'i has had Christian missionary after missionary changing things. You'd find it hard to believe. Ka'ahumanu became a Christian, Keōpuōlani became a christian...quite devout, and even Kalanimoku became a christian."

"You don't say," said George, surprised. "What about the new King Liholiho? Did he also become a Christian? I recall that you were teaching him to read English when he was young. Were you able to stay in his favor?"

"He's dead already and replaced by his half-brother Kauikeaouli as 'Kamehameha III,'" said John. "Liholiho and his favorite queen Kamamalu

214

traveled to England in late 1823 to see how the King there, George IV, rules his land. They made quite a sensation there, but then they both caught the measles and died in the same month of July 1824 before they could meet the King."

"My goodness. That's sad," said George. "But tell me now about Kaumuali'i. How is he?"

"He's dead...died in May of 1824. I watched his funeral march on O'ahu. It was most impressive."

"Why was his funeral march on O'ahu instead of Kaua'i?" asked George, who was immediately saddened to hear of King Kaumuali'i's death, no matter the conditions under which they had once parted their association.

"After Kamehameha died, Queen Ka'ahumanu took power as Kuhina nui on behalf of Liholiho," related John. "She and Liholiho got to worrying about whether King Kaumuali'i would continue to abide by his agreement with Kamehameha to cede to his heirs, meaning first Liholiho, the rule of Kaua'i and Ni'ihau. So Liholiho sailed to Kaua'i on the ship *Pride of Hawai'i* that was a gift of the British and took Kaumuali'i aboard for a feast on Hanalei Bay. He gave Kaumuali'i enough rum to pickle him, and when Kaumuali'i woke up he was on his way to O'ahu. There, in captivity she had arranged, Ka'ahumanu married him."

"She married him?" asked George, incredulous.

"Yes, she did," insisted John. "The native marriage ceremony where they lie on a mat together was actually observed by missionaries in October of 1821. But it was really a captive's life for him. And he didn't try to get away either, because he fell so in love with the Sacred Queen Keōpuōlani, who stayed with Ka'ahumanu on O'ahu. And then Ka'ahumanu also married Kaumuali'i's tall tall son Keali'iahonui by his wife Kapua'ahmohu...married Keali'iahonui after he had replaced his father in consort with Kaua'i Queen Kekaiha'akulou, who had become known as 'Deborah Kapule'."

"Of course I remember Kekaiha'akulou well," said George. "But Ka'ahumanu married both father and son?"

"Yes, and she kept them both under watch on O'ahu. But then in September of 1823, Keōpuōlani died and Kaumuali'i lost his spirit. He died the next May after saying that he wished to be buried with Keōpuōlani...and I think he is, on Mau'i at Moku'ula. After he died, his son George Humehume, who had returned to Hawai'i with the missionaries after living away in New England most of his life, tried to become the ruler of Kaua'i and led a rebellion from the very fort you built there. But Kalanimoku went to Kaua'i and quelled the rebellion in short order, becoming the governor there. Humehume was also then sent to be watched in O'ahu and died there a couple years ago. He had married that daughter Betty of Isaac Davis's that John Young adopted. But he drank too much."

"Do you know anything about Timofei Osipovich Tarakanov?" asked George. "When I had to leave Honolulu harbor with you on the *Panther* in July of 1817, I left him in charge of the others. I know that he and the rest were rescued by Governor Baranov and made it back to Novo-Arkhangelsk, but I wonder what he might be doing now?"

"I don't know, George," said John Marshall. "I've never heard anything more about him."

"Well you've done a wonderful job relating all the rest of it to me," said George. "It really is an astonishing history. Someone ought to write it all down."

When their time together in the restaurant was over, George asked John to accompany him back to his apartment so that he could give John a copy of his 1824 book on Brazil. He told John that he had had an associate, Conrad Meyer, have an abbreviated version of the book translated into Dutch and published in Amsterdam in 1825. "But I'm giving you a copy of the original German version, of course," he told John.

George took a copy of the book out of a large trunk he had in his apartment, took up a quill and, dipping it into an inkwell on his desk, wrote an inscription on the title page saying "To my good friend, John Marshall, who saved me in Hawai'i and took me to China. Best wishes for a long and prosperous life," and signed it "George Schaeffer—'Kepa'." He dated it also, "12 February, 1828. Bremen."

When John Marshall was departing from George's apartment, he asked George, "When do you think you'll go back to Brazil?'

"I'm planning to go back this coming summer," answered George. "I have three more voyages arranged...but after them, no more. As my recruitment efforts progressed, I gave myself the goal of sending 5,000 soldiers to Dom Pedro's army. I've done that now. Kaiserin Leopoldina has been dead a year and a half, and I don't want Pedro to forget me. And, it's time for me to get back to my wife and daughter."

Dealing with Dom Pedro:

After settling all accounts with Conrad Meyer, George sailed back to Rio de Janeiro, functioning as the charter agent himself, on the Bremen ship *Harmonie* under Captain Josef Cornelius with 265 passengers on board, reaching Guanabara Bay on July 2, 1828. Two more voyages, those of the *Cecilie* and the largest ship by far, the *Olbers*, sailed from Bremen after George had left.

George went first to the office of his financial advisors Wolf and Kelsey, where he dealt only with the two namesakes of the firm, who requested that he call them by their first names, "Tim," and "Ray." They told him that despite all his orders of withdrawal and transmittal during the past six years, the *Banco do*

Brasil accounts in his name still held a quarter million réis. But they advised him that Dom Pedro had mismanaged the domestic financial affairs so seriously that the *Banco do Brasil* was no longer a secure place for him to have most of his money. The national debt had risen, inflation was out of control, the exchange rate for the real had dropped precipitously. The paper money, issued by the bale, was not accepted in all quarters any longer. And the *Banco do Brasil* had been forced to prohibit withdrawals of amounts over ten milréis per month. Dom Pedro, they said, blamed all this economic woe on the Portuguese, saying that extortionate Portuguese merchants still controlled the retail markets on most commodities. But Tim and Ray said that the real problem was Dom Pedro's massive expenditures to cope with the disastrous war against Argentina, after which the Brazilian Cisplatine State seceded to become Uruguay, and the frequent revolts, as in Pernambuco and different parts of the country. They also said that Dom Pedro was excessively preoccupied with the politics of Portugal, acting against his absolutist brother Miguel by funding liberal-oppositionist groups in both London and Lisbon. Rumors were that the child-Princess Maria da Gloria and her chaperones, on a British ship to Portugal, had been rerouted from the Azores to London because Miguel planned to seize power in Portugal on his own and declare himself Dom Miguel I any day. This would likely cause Dom Pedro to initiate armed conflict on behalf of his daughter's claim to Portugal's throne. And this would be very expensive and cause further economic debilitation.

Most upsetting to George in his interaction with Tim and Ray was their telling him that pamphlets had been widely circulated after the death of the popular Empress Leopoldina saying that Dom Pedro had physically beaten her during her last pregnancy while flaunting to her his relationship with Domitilla, the Marqueza de Santos. He told Tim and Ray, "If that's true, his time as Emperor will be short. God will see to it."

George also conferred right away with his Swiss-Brazilian friend, Dr. João Martinho Flach, who told him that he, Dr. Flach, who had been one of Leopoldina's physicians and German-speaking confidants, was no longer allowed unscheduled access to the palace, and he was quite sure that George would also have to apply for an audience with Dom Pedro through the palace office administrator.

"But am I not still a palace chamberlain?" asked George.

"Everything has changed since Leopoldina's death, George," said Dr. Flach. "There are new chamberlains now and you're not one of them."

"So I'll go schedule an audience then," said George. "It shouldn't take too long. As you know, I've written to Dom Pedro quite often in the course of my recruiting efforts and I think he appreciates what I've done."

"Don't be too sure, George," said Dr. Flach. "Others have reported difficulties in seeing Pedro these days, and that he often cancels scheduled audiences."

"Martin, what count do you have to date for the number of soldiers who have enlisted in Dom Pedro's foreign battalion?" asked George.

"Including those from the *Harmonie*, I have 4,570," answered Dr. Flach.

"And there are another 468 coming on the *Cecilie* and the *Olbers*," said George. "By my reckoning, the first of the soldiers that I sent, who arrived here to enlist in 1824, should be completing their six-year terms of service two years from now in July of 1830. Is that the way you figure it?"

"Yes, it is," answered Dr. Flach. "And that's when you can expect to start becoming tremendously wealthy. A square legua of land for even 4000 of the soldiers who might complete their terms would equal such an amount of territory that private citizens rarely, if ever, own. I've calculated that it would be in total a square plot of land 158 kilometers on a side. That's a land area equal to many principalities in Europe."

"That's also the way I figure it, Martin," said George. "But I doubt that Dom Pedro thought when he made the agreement with me that I would be sending him so many soldiers. I think he may have envisioned several hundred at most. So, knowing him and hearing about some of his problems, he will find some way to underpay me...or not to pay me at all...and I won't be able to do anything about it. For that reason I plan to approach him and propose a change in our agreement."

"What kind of change?" asked Dr. Flach.

"I will ask him for less than the projected amount if he pays me immediately," said George. "I'll still make a great profit, and he will be able to tell his accountants and the State Assembly that he's saving the government the payment of a huge future debt."

"I assume you still plan to pay me a commission per soldier, don't you George?" asked Dr. Flach.

"Absolutely," George assured him. "Your work has been most valuable to me. If I am paid, you will be paid."

It took George more than a month to gain an audience with Dom Pedro. Two scheduled meetings in that time were cancelled. But at last, in early September, the meeting took place. George appeared before Dom Pedro wearing the Order of Christ cross that Dom Pedro had given him. He presented to Dom Pedro a copy of his German book on Brazil, pointing out the introductory poem about him that he had written, and translating for him the part saying, "To such an Emperor all should cling, A mighty one, whose state bequeaths, To all reward that's fair and just."

"I didn't know you were a poet, Major von Schaeffer," said a smiling Dom Pedro. "I thank you for the book. And I thank you for your fine service to me in raising an army and in bringing so many colonists here to Brazil. Certainly no one else has matched your record of bringing Germans here. But please tell me why you have come before me today."

"First, Your Majesty, I want to offer you my sincere condolences on the loss of the Empress Leopoldina," George said. "Do you know that I met her father, the Emperor Franz, in Vienna? She was such a fine person, so caring and kind...and a wonderful wife and mother. It must be difficult to raise the children she gave you on your own. It's hard for me to imagine."

"Leopoldina was indeed a good wife, and I've only now begun looking for another one," said Dom Pedro, deliberately ignoring George's mention of the Emperor Franz. "And with the children I have help. But what business brings you to me?"

"I want to propose to you that you pay me now in full for my recruiting services so that you can save a great deal of time and money from the projected terms of our agreement," said George. "This will enable you to eliminate in advance a huge state debt."

"Indeed I have given some thought to how much land the terms of our agreement will be deeding to you," said Dom Pedro. "And the State Assembly's assessment of the value of that much land...even if completely undeveloped...will no doubt cause me further woe in these troubled times. But this is a problem still two years and more away. No soldier has yet completed his term of service."

"But I'm proposing a substantial reduction in the expected amount," said George. Then he repeated, "...a substantial reduction."

"How large a reduction?" asked Dom Pedro.

"Instead of an expected 4,000-to-5,000 leguas of land being deeded to me from 1830 to 1836, I would take 1,000 leguas of land as payment in full right now," said George. "And I would need some money too...say, a half million réis in gold at the current exchange. Also, I want you to give me the title of 'Baron of Frankenthal' with privileges of direct access to you."

Dom Pedro said nothing for a minute or two as he thought about George's proposal. Then he said, "I will grant you the title. You deserve it now for your service to us, as I remember my father once explained to you. But I will send you a counter-proposal on the amount of land and the money. If you sign it, we are quits. If you don't, you will have to petition the State Assembly for satisfaction of your contract, because I'll not be paying you anything at all."

"I understand, Your Majesty," said George. "When will I have the counter-proposal?"

"You will have it within three days," answered Dom Pedro.

Five days later George was summoned from his hotel room down to the hotel lobby to meet a delegation of officials from Dom Pedro. The delegation consisted of five men, including an Imperial Guards Colonel, a palace chamberlain in charge of royal appointments, a court lawyer, and two accountants. The Colonel led George to a table and laid before him a set of papers. The first was a document attesting that "Major Doctor Jorge Antonio

Ritter von Schaeffer, member of the Brazilian Order of Christ" was now given the title of "His Majesty Dom Pedro I's 'Baron of Frankenthal' in the Brazilian State of Bahia." This document, the Colonel explained, was George's to keep without condition. But the others were for him to consider...and to sign if he agreed to the terms specified in them.

"How long do I have to consider them?" asked George, looking at a formidable stack of papers.

"We are to bring them back with us within the hour," was the Colonel's answer.

George started going through the papers looking for the key figures. Shortly he discerned that he was being offered 500 square leguas of land contiguous with his current square legua around Frankenthal and a quarter million réis-- half in gold, but half in a credit at the *Banco do Brasil*. To make sure, he asked the accountants, "500 square leguas of land and a quarter million réis—half in gold and half in credit?" The accountants nodded affirmatively and added the information that the current tax rate on undeveloped land was 10 réis per legua per year. George walked over to the hotel registration desk and took its quill and inkwell over to the table. He signed the documents, keeping a signed set for his own records. He and Dom Pedro were, as Pedro had said, "quits."

Home for Good:

George gave his friend Dr. Flach 50 milréis worth of gold as his commission for assuring the enlistment of the pledged soldiers that George had recruited and sent to Rio de Janeiro. Dr. Flach was very happy with this payment and promised George that he would continue in his former capacity to enlist the soldiers coming on the remaining two ships.

Sailing from Rio de Janeiro on the regular mail ship north, George reached Vila Viçosa on October 10, 1828. There he found that Arthur Mason was still the government agent and mayor. He registered his new acquisition of land with Arthur the next day, and, on the morning of the next, took a horse and a cargo carriage large enough to hold his three trunks to travel the remaining way to Frankenthal. There was now a two-rut road instead of a single rut path, so that, even with a brief stop at Colônia Leopoldina, he was able to reach Frankenthal by evening.

When George drove up to the Frankenthal gate, he was greeted by the barking of the dog Fitzli. Putzli was nowhere to be seen. The first person he saw was his brother Wilhelm, who looked the same to him except that he had cut his hair short.

"George, you're back at last," Wilhelm said. "Barbara and Inga will be so happy to see you. They're in the new house now."

The "new house" was what the colonists called the former military post's administrative center after Johann Henning had completely transformed it into a large two-story house with a surrounding first-floor porch. Wilhelm led George to it and pulled a bell cord to signal the occupants inside that they had a visitor.

Inga came to the door and saw her uncle and father standing on the porch. She took a deep breath and rushed out to hug her father. George was stunned by her womanly appearance. She was the very image of her mother in the days he had courted her in Würzburg. He was struck dumb and said nothing as Inga shouted into the house, "Mama, Mama...Papa's back. It's Papa."

Barbara came quickly into view, stepping out the door and onto the porch. She looked thinner to George, and her hair had more grey in it, but she was still beautiful. She came closer, entering George's embrace. They held each other close for more than a minute, not saying anything. Inga burst into tears.

Wilhelm broke the silence, saying to his brother, "George, you'll be impressed with some of the changes here. Johann has built several houses on outlying plots of land so that the barracks here are only used for storage now. The crops have done well. We're shipping cotton, coffee, and fruit out of here now on rafts of hardwood...and even the rafts are sold to bring us some income."

George didn't respond to this, but at last said something to Barbara, "Barbara, I won't leave you again. I'm home for good."

And George did not leave Barbara again. In 1829, despite the damaging collapse and close of the *Banco do Brasil*, George and Barbara were able to travel together to Rio de Janeiro to place Inga into an expensive young women's finishing school. There they heard that Dom Pedro was to marry there in Rio the Princess Amélie de Beauharnais von Leuchtenberg, daughter of Eugène de Beauharnais, son of Napoleon Bonaparte's first wife Josephine. They went there again in June of 1831 after the April abdication of Dom Pedro I in favor of his and Leopoldina's son Pedro. The former Emperor Dom Pedro, taking the title "Duke of Braganza" then sailed off to Portugal to war with his brother Miguel, eventually winning the struggle and placing his daughter on the throne of Portugal and the Algarve as Empress Maria II. And in 1834, after Dom Pedro's death of tuberculosis in Lisbon's Queluz Palace, they attended Inga's graduation ceremony in Rio de Janeiro and met her fiancé, Carlos Almodovar, a cousin of Jose Bonifacio de Andrada e Silva, who had returned to Brazil in 1829 and functioned as underaged Dom Pedro II's tutor and advisor until 1833 when his activities attempting to restore Dom Pedro I caused his removal from government influence.

In 1830 Johann Phillipp and Sylvia Henning decided to move to São Paulo where Johann thought he could direct larger-scale construction projects in the booming city. George agreed to send Johann his share of the Frankenthal colony's profits in perpetuity, parting with the man amicably, but, after the Hennings' departure, the profits began to slide. Wilhelm died in 1834 and his leadership of the agricultural side of Frankenthal's production was sorely missed. Gradually the logging operation of Slava Petrov and Misha Arbuzov became the colony's economic mainstay. This effort relied heavily upon Pataxó labor, but the Pataxó population around Frankenthal was devastated by a contagious respiratory disease that George was unable to cure. So many of the Pataxó died that the logging operation had to be cut back to less than a half of what it had been, and the colony's profits slid yet further. When George paid the taxes on his land to Arthur Mason for the 1835 year, he told Arthur that the money was coming from his savings and that Frankenthal had not been a profitable enterprise that year.

Barbara did not live to see Inga marry, though she knew that the marriage was to take place in Rio de Janeiro. She took ill with a painful ailment in her lower abdomen. It kept getting worse no matter what remedies George tried. She was unable to keep food down, and then completely lost her appetite. George put her to bed and gave her laudanum to quell the pain. After a few days of drifting in and out of consciousness, Barbara managed to sit up suddenly in their bed and grab George's arm. "I'm dying, George," she said. "It's been a wonderful life with you and with Inga. Tell her that I wish her the happiness that we've had. I love you." Then she died in George's arms.

George had Barbara buried in the Frankenthal cemetery where her mother's grave was. He had placed on the grave a headstone carved to read in German: "Sacred to the Memory of the Baroness Barbara Hindernacht von Schaeffer. August 25, 1785-September 19, 1835. Rest in Peace." For weeks he couldn't stop crying.

George decided not to write to Inga about her mother's death. He took his sister Julia with him to Rio de Janeiro in late November to help him console Inga, who was to marry Carlos Almodovar in the Catholic Church there the next month. Inga was residing temporarily then in the large house of Dr. Flach and his wife Gloria, who had become like an uncle and an aunt to her. George and Julia stayed with them also.

Inga, as expected, took the news of her mother's death very hard. She shrieked and shouted "No!" over and over again, and then lapsed into inconsolable crying for the longest time. Julia calmly told her that her mother's time of illness and pain had been short and that her last words were about her."

"What did she say?" sobbed Inga.

"She told me she wishes for you the same happiness in life that she and I have had," George told his daughter. "Her only regret was that she couldn't be here to see you married. She so wanted to be a grandmother to your children."

"But what if I don't have any children?" said Inga.

"You will have children, Inga," George assured her. "It's meant to be. Your mother and I have known it since before we had you, and even before we were married. You will have children, and their children will have children. And some day in the far far future one of your progeny will find a way to come back to you and become helpful in your life. You may not be aware of it, but it will happen."

Julia was surprised to hear George say this to Inga, who was puzzled by her father's assurance and did not respond directly to it. Later, no longer in Inga's presence, Julia asked George, "Do you really believe that someone from Inga's future offspring will come back to help her in life?"

George said, "Yes I do. I've come to think that that's who angels are...our own offspring who have come back to us from the future to help us."

"Why didn't one of them help Barbara then, George?" Julia asked.

"God knows," said George, shaking his head. Then he repeated, "God knows."

A likeness of George Anton Schaeffer at age 55.

After Inga's wedding in December, George had an attorney at Wolf and Kelsey write a will for him. In his will he bequeathed all his worldly wealth...the land and gold and money... to his daughter, "Baroness Ingrid Margarita von Schaeffer Almodovar," with the stipulation that she care for his sister Julia, for the wife and children of his brother Wilhelm, and for her cousin

Anton, Jacob's brother who was serving in the Brazilian army. He gave copies of this will to Inga, to Dr. Flach, to Julia, and to Arthur Mason when he and Julia went back through Vila Viçosa to Frankenthal.

In July of 1836 George received a letter from Inga, who now lived with her husband Carlos in a Rio de Janeiro villa, saying that she was pregnant. "Carlos says he doesn't care if it's a boy or a girl," she wrote. "But I can tell that he really wants a son. The baby is due in October and I'm expecting you to be here."

But George did not live to see his grandson Jorge. While at Barbara's grave "speaking with her" about her coming birthday on a sunny morning at Frankenthal, his chest was suddenly seized by a sharp pain that radiated into his neck, back, and down his left arm. He tried to catch his breath, but could not. He fell just to the side of the grave and curled onto his side. Looking up, he was surprised to see his father Nicholas and mother Margarita standing there, and Barbara was with them. They were smiling at him and motioning him toward them. With a sudden sense of ease he got to his feet and followed them away.

Julia found George's body at Barbara's grave. "How appropriate that death should strike him here," she thought. After the most elaborate of funerals she and the company of Frankenthal could manage, she had George buried just where he had fallen...at Barbara's side. The inscription on George's headstone, similar to Barbara's, was: "Sacred to the Memory of Baron George Anton Aloysius, Ritter von Schaeffer, Founder of Frankenthal, January 27, 1779- August 21, 1836."

EPILOGUE OF THE TRILOGY:

    After the narration, the twenty-second-century woman had the thought that all of her predecessor's life had been resurrected by the technology available to her and filed into her own brain as valuable knowledge and vicarious experience. She felt enriched by her understanding of it. But she wondered what remained of the colony her predecessor had founded. She directed her infowall display to show her an enhanced-resolution video view of the Peruípe River upstream from the place called Nova Viçosa on the Atlantic coast of the Bahia State of Brazil, the place known to her predecessor in the nineteenth century as "Vila Viçosa." She guided the video eye inland along the Peruípe, passing on its way upstream through the community of Helvecia, that was known in the nineteenth century as "Colônia Leopoldina," until the view showed her the north bank of the river where it was joined by the Jackarander Creek. She had thought virtually to view the remnants of Frankenthal and to visit from her distance in time and space the graves of her progenitors, George and Barbara Schaeffer. But the site had been completely reclaimed by the earth and the jungle and there was not a trace of it in evidence.

BIBLIOGRAPHY

First, you should know that this bibliography is a list of the sources for the entire GEORGE ANTON SCHAEFFER trilogy…all three parts. It is given in each of the other two parts as well. This bibliography is meant primarily as a resource for those who wish to delve more deeply into any of the topics touched in this trilogy. I have tried to make it convenient and informative to use. That is why I include commentary on how the work cited relates to George Anton Schaeffer and various aspects of his peripatetic life. I realize that this bibliography may stray from canonical citation format in some places and I do not apologize for that. I include internet sites as well as printed texts, since this is the way of modern information exchange. I caution the reader about the dynamic nature of the internet. Sites that I accessed for information from 2000 to 2009 may have been taken down or altered. The reader may be able to retrieve them from the search-engine archives. Despite this seeming lack of permanence, however, the internet keeps adding more sources than it loses and remains in its dynamic state a most valuable resource. Indeed I have been impressed over and over again as I wrote this book with how much easier the internet, when used judiciously, of course, makes the search for needed facts. I began my scholarly career as a virtually perennial resident of libraries, typing my doctoral dissertation on a broken-down typewriter, hitting the keys with almost destructive force to make six copies through layers of carbon paper…no desktop computer, no word processor or printer, not even photocopy, which was too expensive for a poor graduate student per slick-paper sheet as late as 1972. Yet as easy as it might now be to find, you still have to help others find it too. So here it is:

Adam, Albrecht. Napoleon's Army in Russia: The Illustrated Memoirs of Albrecht Adam-1812. See North, Jonathan (below). Also see my review of this work at www.Amazon.com.

Adams, Alexander. "Extracts from an Ancient Log: Selections from the Logbook of Captain Alexander Adams in Connection with the Early History of Hawaii—Occurrences on Board the Brig *Forester*, of London, from Conception Towards the Hawaiian Islands." Hawaiian Almanac and Journal. 1906. pp. 66-74. Adams was Kamehameha's Captain of the *Forester* after it became the *Ka'ahumanu* in April 1816. These are selections from his logbook from January 16, 1816 to December 26, 1818.

Adams, John Quincy (1767-1848), sixth President of the United States (1825-1829) and, previously, Ambassador (1809-1815) to Russia. See primarily Claffey and Sikes below.

Aleksandrovskaia, O. "The Writings of Decembrist K. P. Torson, a Member of the First Russian Antarctic Expedition (1819-21)." This is about Konstantin

Petrovich Torson (1793-1851), exiled as a "Decembrist" in 1826, who participated as a watch officer on Captain Faddei Bellingshausen's flagship *Vostok*. This is published by the Museum of the World Ocean website on a 2002 Conference at http://vitiaz.ru/congress/en/thesis/72.html.

Alexander, W. D. "The Funeral Rites of Prince Kealiiahonui" in The 14th Annual Report of the Hawaiian Historical Society for the Year Ending December 31, 1906. Honolulu, Hawaiian Gazette Co, Ltd. Pp. 26-28. Accessed in 2009 also at http://www.horrormasters.com/Text/a0910.pdf. This concerns the tall son of Kaumuali'i, last King of Kaua'i who also was once married to Ka'ahumanu...mentions possible funereal sacrifices of humans as late as 1849.

Ancient Hawaiian Civilization: A Series of Lectures Delivered at the (Introduction by Glen Grant). Mutual Publishing. Honolulu, Hawaii. 1999. This is a reprint of a classic collection of studies of ancient Hawaiian life.

Antonson, Joan M. "Sitka." In Russian America: The Forgotten Frontier. Barbara Sweetland Smith and Redmond J. Barnett, eds. Tacoma: The Washington State Historical Press. 1990. pp. 165-175.

Arago, Jacques Etienne. Narrative of a Voyage Around the World, in the *Uranie* and Physicienne corvettes, commanded by Captain Freycinet, during the years 1817, 1818, 1819, and 1820. Treuttel & Wurtz, Treuttel, jun. & Richter. 1823. This is one of the primary artists depicting Hawaiian life in the early contact era. His life is a most fascinating one and his Wikipedia site at http://en.wikipedia.org/wiki/Jacques_Arago provides a link to a French work about curiosities in his travels he wrote while blind in 1853 without once using the French alphabet letter "a." Curious indeed.

Armitage, John (1807-1865). The History of Brazil from the Period of the Arrival of the Braganza Family in 1808, to the Abdication of Don Pedro the First in 1831. Compiled from State Documents and Other Original Sources. Forming a Continuation to Southey's History of That Country. Smith, Elder. London. 1836. (University Microfilms, Ann Arbor, Michigan, 1970). Appendix 1 by pre-1779 Portuguese Viceroy of Brazil the Marquis de Lavradio, mentions the situation of African Slaves.

Armstrong, Scott. Russian Snows: Coming of Age in Napoleon's Army. RedBarn Publications, Douglassville, PA. 2011. ISBN 978-1466331549. See http://www.RussianSnows.com and http://napoleon1812.wordpress.com. Also see my reviews of this book on www.Amazon.com and www.Shvoong.com.

Aroutunova, Bayara. Lives in Letters: Princess Zinaida Volkonskaya and her Correspondence. Slavica Publishers, Inc. Bloomington, IN. 1994. Includes letters from Tsar Alexander I (nothing about the balloon project at all) dating from 1812, and much cultural detail from Russian elite circles, 1812-50...includes salon activities in St. P. and Moscow prior to the 1825 Decembrist Revolt. The source here was most useful in informing activities of Barbara Schaeffer in St. Petersburg while her husband was away.

ASTOR, JOHN JACOB (1763-1848). "America's First Multimillionaire," Astor came to control the United States' fur trade in the first quarter of the 19th century. His ancestors have also been interesting characters in American history. See primarily the work by Axel Madsen (below).

Atherton, Gertrude. Rezanov. (With Introduction by William Marion Reedy). A Gutenberg Project e-publication, available at http://www.totse.com/en/ego/literary_genius/reznv10.html.

Austin, Paul Britten. 1812: Napoleon in Moscow. Greenhill Books. London (and Stackpole Books, Pennsylvania). 1995. There is a fine description of Rostopchin's estate at Voronovo and the hosting there of Mdme Germaine de Stael on pp. 124-30...also mention of how Rostopchin's daughter later marries "Phillipe de Segur" (nephew of Napoleon's aide and later historian, cf. the note by J. David Townsend on pp. 93 of Phillipe-Paul de Segur's Napoleon's Russian Campaign).

BARANOV, ALEXANDER ANDREEVICH (1746 or 1747-1819), Russian-American Company Manager and first Governor of Russian America (1791-1818). A modern comprehensive biography awaits (see Chevigny below, however, and Khlebnikov), but the National Endowment for the Humanities has given in 2003 a $75,000 grant to UC-Sacramento Prof. Kenneth Owens, with the collaboration of Russian scholar Alex Petrov, to complete one based on archival materials from both America and Russia. The project title is "Alexander Baranov and Russia's Multi-cultural Borderlands Empire in North America." See the online work through http://alexander-baranov.biography.ms/ or at www.bookrags.com (the biography on Baranov costs $6.99) and also through sites related to the history of Sitka, Alaska (see below). Baranov is treated peripherally but well by the site of the Congress of Russian Americans at www.russian-americans.org/CRA_History.htm. See also the citations below for Sitka, Fort Ross, Veniaminov. For a more negative portrayal of Baranov and his activities see the sources for Herman below. See the Rezanov citations for periphereal information.

Barratt, Glynn. The Russians at Port Jackson, 1814-1822. Australian Institute of Aboriginal Studies. Canberra, Australia. 1981. This work includes the memoirs of Russian sailors who visited Port Jackson (Sydney). Very thoroughly researched it includes a complete bibliography of archival sources.

Barratt, Glynn. Russia in Pacific Waters, 1725-1825: A Survey of the Origins of Russia's Naval Presence in the North and South Pacific. University of British

228

Columbia Press. Vancouver and London. 1981. The chapter of most interest here is entitled "The Company Under Attack" about the latter days of the Russian-American Company's operations. There is a fine illustrations section with the only known likeness of M.P. Lazarev and contemporary artists' views of the RAK settlement at Novo-Arkhangel'sk (Sitka, Alaska) in the early years of the nineteenth century.

Barratt, Glynn. The Russian Discovery of Hawai'i: The Ethnographic and Historic Record. Editions Limited. Honolulu, HI. 1987. Note: dedication to Pat Polansky (conferred with at U-Hawaii Hamilton Library, June 10, 2001). Translated documents of Hawaiian observers from the 1803-6 voyage of the Nadezhda (Ivan F.Kruzenshtern) and Neva (Iurii F. Lisianskii). Nikolai Rezanoff and Georg Heinrich Langsdorff were aboard. Mention of Hawaiian Kaneohe/Kenokhoia/adoption by Vasilii Fedorovich Moller...pp. 96 footnote, 102.

Barratt, Glynn. The Russian View of Honolulu: 1809-26. Carlton University Press. Toronto. 1988. A detailed scholarly work with a fine bibliography.

Barratt, Glynn. The Russians and Australia (Volume I of Russia and the South Pacific, 1696-1840). University of British Columbia Press. Vancouver. 1988. This is the most detailed treatment in English of the circumnavigation of the Suvorov and its consequences to Russian Pacific policy. Chapter 3, "The First Russian Visits to Port Jackson, 1807-14," explains the conflicts on the Suvorov between the "navy" men, including Captain Lazarev, and the "company" men, including Dr. George Anton Schaeffer and RAK supercargo Germann Molvo.

Bartholomew, Gail. (Photo research by Bren Bailey). Maui Remembers: A Local History. Mutual Publishing. Honolulu, Hawaii. 1994. Interesting is the brief treatment of "Kamehameha and Kahekili: Clash of Warriors" in chapter 3 and "Metcalfe and the Olawalu Massacre" in chapter 5.

Bass, Robert D. Gamecock: The Life and Campaigns of General Thomas Sumter. Holt, Rhinehart, and Winston. New York. 1961. See also www.virtualology.com/virtualwarmuseum.com/revolutionarywarhall/ThomasSumter.com. At the end of his active career in politics (U.S. Rep. and Senator), the U.S. Revolutionary War hero, General Thomas Sumter (1734-1832), was U.S. Minister to Brazil (1809-1811...notice that the title is not "Ambassador" really since Brazil at the time was still officially a Portuguese Colony). The story of how he, at the age of 76, pulled pistols on the guard-escorts of Brazil's eccentric Regent Consort Dona Carlota in Rio de Janeiro to prevent their forcing him to kneel in obeisance, is representative of his character. Fort Sumter in Charleston, South Carolina-the site of the first shots fired in the U.S. Civil War, is named after him. There is a city and a county in South Carolina that were given his name in 1800, even before he served as Minister to Brazil. Sumter (SC) High School and the University of South Carolina have given his nickname, the

"Gamecock," to their sports team, and he is one of the revolutionary war figures informing actor Mel Gibson's character, Benjamin Martin, in the popular movie, *The Patriot* (2002). When General Sumter died at the age of 98 in Statesburg, South Carolina, he was the last surviving general officer of the U.S. Revolutionary War.

Becher, Hans.   Georg Heinrich Freiherr Von Langsdorff in Brasilien: Forschungen eines deutschen Gelehrten im 19 Jahrhundert.   Dietrich Reimer Verlag. Berlin. 1987. See the mention of "Major" "Ritter Von Schaffer" on pp. 16-7 and the citation of Sheffer's book, pp. 89.

Beckwith, Martha Warren, ed. Kepelino's Traditions of Hawai'i.   Bernice P. Bishop Museum Bulletin 95, Bishop Museum Press, Honolulu, HI, 2007 from a 1932 original publication.

Beeche, Arturo.   "The Amazon Throne: The Orleans-Braganza of Brazil." Accessed in January, 2005 at http://www.eurohistory.com/braganza.html.   This is a concise relation of the history of Brazil's royal family after the move from Portugal in 1807.

Bell, Susan N.   Unforgettable True Stories of the Kingdom of Hawaii.   Press Pacifica. Pacific Trade Group, P.O. Box 668, Pearl City, Hawaii 96782.   This work has information about early Hawaiians who visited Europe soon after western contact and stories based on less well-known observers of post-contact cultural matters.

Berdnikov, Lev.   "The Loud American," in Russian Life, Vol. 49, No. 5, (Sept./Oct. 2006), pp. 34-43 illustrated.   This is a fine relation about the character of Fyodor Ivanovich Tolstoi, the "American."   See also O. Vozdvizhenskaia and S. L. Tolstoi.

Berthels, D. E., Komissarov, B. N., Lysenko, T.I. (eds.)   Materialien Der Brasilien-Expedition 1821-1829 Des Akademiemitgliedes Georg Heinrich Freiherr Von Langsdorff (Grigorij Ivanovich Langsdorff).   Völkerkundliche Abhandlungen, Band VII: Publikationsreihe Der Volkerkunde-Abteilung Des Niedersächsischen Landesmuseums under Ethnologischen Gesellschaft Hannover E. V.   VERLAG DIETRICH REIMER. Berlin, 1979. The English "Foreword" to this work describes it: "Vol. VII of the "Völkerkundliche Abhandlungen" presents, for the first time in German, the complete, immeasurably rich research material collected during the first Russian expedition to Brazil, 1821-1829, led by the German scholar Georg Heinrich Freiherr von Langsdorff."   And, later in explanation: "During the above mentioned Brazil expedition, which had been beautifully organized, von Langsdorff unfortunately developed a severe psychological disorder as a result of malaria and other tropical diseases. Thus it was not possible for him to publish his scientific results."

Bezotosnyi, V. M. et. al. Otechestvennaia voina 1812 goda: Entsiklopediia. (The Great Patriotic War of 1812: and Encyclopedia). ROSSPEN. Moscow. 2004. 878 pp. ISBN 582430324X. This is a comprehensive reference work on the war between Russia and Napoleon's France in 1812. See the entry on "Leppich's Balloon" ("Vozdushnyi shar Leppikha," str. 141 and on "Tormasov," str. 707). I had no access to it while I was writing the chapter on Moscow and the war with Napoleon, but I fortunately found no substantive contradictions in the wok here and certainly recommend this outstanding work. See the review by Dominic Lieven in Kritika: Explorations in Russian and Eurasian History. 7, 1 (Winter 2006), pp. 133-35. Lieven terms it "the most valuable work on the history of the Napoleonic wars published in any language in recent years."

Binyon, T. J. Pushkin: A Biography. Vintage edition. Random House. New York. 2004 (reprint from London copyright, 2002). The most recent and detailed life of the great Russian Poet, Aleksandr Sergeevich Pushkin (1799-1837), this work includes a comprehensive depiction of life in Russia, particularly St. Petersburg, from 1812 to 1837. It includes many personal relationships in Pushkin's life…for example, Prince Repnin-Volkonskii, Prince Viazemskii, Nikolai and Ekaterina Karamzin and their children, and Fedor Ivanovich Tolstoi "the American," all of whom are characters in this book. It has a fine illustration section and is adorned throughout with Pushkin's own sketches of his acquaintances (e.g. Fedor Tolstoi). See also the review of this and three other recent biographical works on Pushkin by Caryl Emerson (below).

Birkett, Mary Ellen. "Hawai'i in 1819: An Account by Camille de Roquefeuil" in The Hawaiian Journal of History (A Publication of the Hawaiian Historical Society), Vol. XXXIV (2000), pp. 69-92. This account mentions Don Francisco de Paula Marin and precedes the better-known account of Freycinet (below) after the death, May 8, 1819, of Kamehameha.

Black, Lydia T. Russians in Alaska, 1732-1867. University of Alaska Press (PO Box 756240). Fairbanks, AK 99775-6240. ISBN 1-889963-05-4. 2004. This work has a most complete bibliography.

Black, Lydia T. "Native Artists of Russian America." In Russian America: The Forgotten Frontier. Barbara Sweetland Smith and Redmond J. Barnett, eds. Tacoma: The Washington State Historical Press. 1990. pp. 197-205.

Blinov, S. G., Voronin, S. D., Gorokhov, A. A., Mel'nikov, V. M., and Filii, M. D. et. al. 1812-1814: Reljatsii. Pis'ma. Dnevniki. Terra. Moskva. 1992. This is a compilation of letters and entries from journals and diaries taken from the collection of the Russian State Historical Museum, and copiously annotated. Here are secret correspondences of General Bagration, General Raevsky,

General Vorontsov, and other officers of the Russian army during the years 1812-4. One whole section is devoted to the correspondence between General Bagration and General Tormasov. Also prominent are the letters of Governor-General Rostopchin and Nikolai Karamzin. Letter 172 (pp. 173-5) from General Barclay-de-Tolly to General Bagration includes the ruminations of a scholar from Derpst University, Wilhelm Friederich Getsel', on the cabbalistic numerology of Napoleon's title and age (L'Empereur Napoleon and quarante deux=42), revealing Napoleon to be the beast, signified by the number 666 in St. John's vision of the Apocalypse in Revelations, 13.

Blond, Charles. La Grande Armée. (Translated by Marshall May). Arms and Armour Press. London. 1995. Mention is made of Napoleon's horse "Moscow" that he rode in the city during the Moscow fire (pp. 333).

Bobrova, Helene. "Russian Diplomats in Paris, 1791-1815." cf. www.museum.ru/artel of the project "1812 year," 1999-2000.

Boitsov, M. (red.). K chesti Rossii: iz chastnoi perepiski 1812 goda. Sovremennik. Moskva. 1988. This is a compilation of personal letters written by people who witnessed the events of Napoleon's invasion of Russia in 1812. It includes letters by Rostopchin, Batiushkov, Viazemskii, Konovnitsyn, Kutuzov, Karamzin, and others.

Bolkhovitinov, Nikolai N. The Beginnings of Russian-American Relations 1775-1815. Translated by Elena Levin. Harvard University Press, Cambridge, Massachusetts and London, England. 1975. This work has detailed information about the activities of Alexander Baranov on behalf of the Russian-American Company in Novo-Arkhangelsk (Sitka), Alaska.

Bolkhovitinov, N. N. "The Adventure of Doctor Schaeffer on Hawai'i, 1815-1819," in Hawaiian Journal of History, Vol. 7 (1973), pp. 55-70.

Bolkhovitinov, N.N. and Narochnitskii, A. L. red. Issledovaniia russkikh na Tikhom okeane v XVIII-pervoi polovine XIX v: Rossiisko-Amerikanskaia Kompaniia i izuchenie tikhookeanskogo severa 1799-1815: sbornik dokumentov. Nauka. Moskva. 1994. See document 167 by Lt. Unkovskii about the trip of the Suvorov from 11 November 1814 to 5 August 1815…and also note 115 (str. 256) which indicates that the Suvorov's route from Kronshtadt to Alaska went around the Cape of Good Hope (not Cape Horn), after provisioning in Rio de Janeiro, and spent time in August of 1814 in the Australian Port Jackson (Sydney). Documents 155 and 156 describe the staff and cargo of the ship, including "Doctor Collegiate Assessor Egor Anton Sheffer."

Bolkhovitinov, N. N. "Vydvizhenie i proval proektov Dobella," ("The Advancement and Failure of Dobell's Projects") in Amerikanskii ezhegodnik, Nauka, Moskva, 1976, str. 264-282.

Bolkhovitinov, N.N. Istoriia Russkoi Ameriki, 1732-1867 v trekh tomakh. Mezhdunarodnye otnosheniia. Moskva. 1997-9. Especially see volume 2, Deiatel'nost' Rossiisko-amerikanskoi kompanii, 1799-1825. This work is reviewed by Basil Dmytryshyn in Slavic and East European Journal, Vol. 61, No. 2 (Summer 2002), pp. 407-8.

Bondarenko, Viacheslav Vasilievich. Kniaz Viazemskii: Zhizneopisanie. ("Prince Vyazemsky: A Life Description"). Izdatelnyi tsentr "Ekonompress." Minsk. 2000. Prince Pyotr Andreevich Viazemskii (12/VI/1792-10/XI/1878) was the younger step-brother and ward of Nikolai Karamzin's second wife, Ekaterina. He inherited the Ostafievo estate near Moscow of the Vyazemskii family. Prince Pyotr, himself a significant poet, was a close friend of Aleksandr Sergeevich Pushkin and writes into the memoirs of his long life descriptions and characterizations of many contemporaries. In 1818 he wrote a poem entitled "To Tolstoy" portraying the character of Fedor Ivanovich Tolstoi, "the American." This work by Bondarenko includes a chronology of events in Vyazemskii's life, including his activities and political sympathies being reported to Tsar Nicholas' I's Third Section (Secret Police) by Faddei Bulgarin (see below under A. I. Reitblat, ed). See Viazemskii citations below.

Book, Martin. Opium: A History. Simon and Schuster. New York. 1996. This work mentions the importation of Turkish opium into European countries and China. In 1800 the British Levant Company purchased nearly one-half of all opium coming out of Smyrna, Turkey, for importation into Great Britain and the United States. In 1816 John Jacob Astor joined the opium smuggling trade when his American Fur Company purchased ten tons of opium in Smyrna, Turkey, and shipped the contraband (i.e. outlawed by the Chinese) narcotic to Canton, China on the ship Macedonian.

BORODINO, Battle of. (August 26/September 7, 1812). See Armstrong, Austin, Bezotosnyi, Blinov, Blonde, Bobrova, Boitsov, Brett-James, Cate, Chandler, Chuquet, DeCaulaincourt, Duffy, Duhem, Ezerskaya, Griess, Kulagin, Mikerabidze (2), Monakhov, Museum.ru, North (2), Olivier, Palmer, Porter (Robert), Putnam, Riehn, Rostopchin, de Segur, Smith, Tarle (2), Tolstoy, Uffindell, Zamoyski, and Zhilin. Note the "Virtual Battle of Borodino" by Brett Nolan, Shawn Murphy, and Natasha Sopevia for Prof. Frank Sciaca of Hamilton College's Russian Studies Dept. at http://hamilton.edu/academics/Russian/warandpeace/vb/. Also, a more recent and well-illustrated relation can be found at http://napoleonistyka.atspace.com/Borodino_battle.htm.

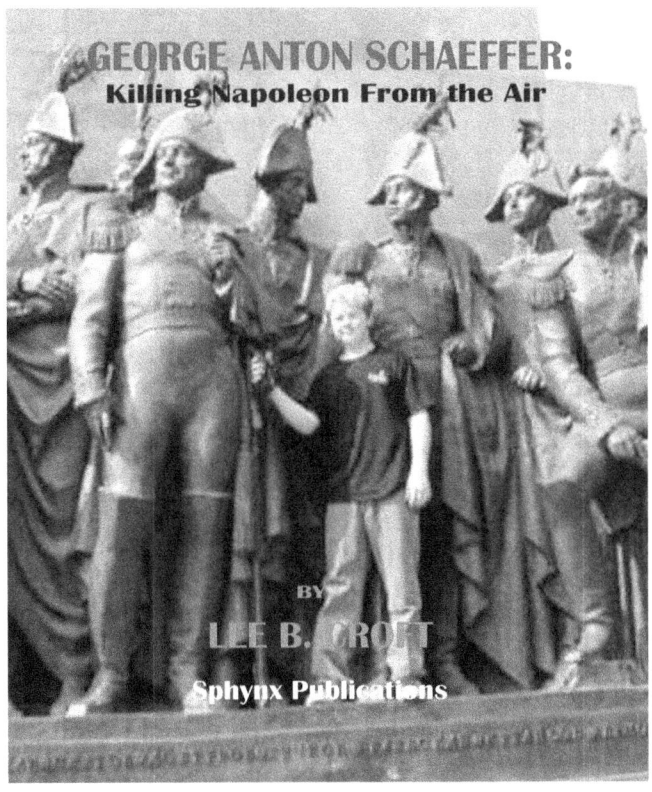

An unused draft of the First Book in the Trilogy's cover, showing the Author's son, Hayden L. Croft, among the statues of the Russian Generals at Moscow's Battle of Borodino Museum.   Photo by Lesley Hoyt Croft, April 2002.

BRAZILIAN CURRENCY (MONEY). Useful websites here are http://www.v-brazil.com/information/ and http://en.wikipedia.org/wiki/Brazilian_real and http://www.gwu.edu/~ibi/statistics%20files/Brazilian%20currencies. Notice that the Brazilian Portuguese plural of "real" is "réis," so that "mil réis" is a thousand réis.

Brett-James, Anthony (Compiler, Editor, Translator).   1812: Eyewitness Accounts of Napoleon's Defeat in Russia. St. Martin's Press. New York. 1966. These memoirs are arranged chronologically as to the events of Napoleon's campaign in Russia. The index is one of the few that lists the first names of the figures involved wherever possible…much appreciated exactitude.

Buck, Sir Peter H. Arts and Crafts of Hawaii. See Hiroa, Te Rangi.

Burns, E. Bradford. A History of Brazil. Third Edition. Columbia University Press. New York. 1993.   See chapters 2 and 3 on "The Colonial Experience" and "Nation Building," pp. 37-149.

Bushnell, O.A. (ed.) (Illustrations by Joseph Feher). The Illustrated Atlas of Hawaii, Including a Brief History of Hawaii by Gavan Daws. First Edition, Thirty-second Printing, 2003, from the 1970 copyright. An Island Heritage Book. Madden Corporation, 94-411 Ko'aki Street, Waipahu, Hawaii 96797. A fine simple resource.

Cahill, Emmett. The Life and Times of John Young: Confidant and Advisor to Kamehameha the Great. Island Heritage Publishing. Aiea, HI 96701. 1999. This recent work, with illustrations and art by Herb Kawainui Kane, has a chapter (14:pp. 111-7) entitled "The Russians are Coming" which treats Young's advice to Kamehameha concerning Schaeffer.

CALENDAR. For matching day with date in a "10,000 year Calendar" a very handy site is http://calendarhome.com. The site also has more information than needed about other calendars, rendering conversions between the old style (Julian) and new style (Gregorian) Russian dates. Also, to find out which day of the week any date of either Gregorian or Julian calendar is, see the Danish Perpetual Calendar schemes at www.Norbyhus.dk/calendar.html. Generally the Russians' calendar, the Julian, was 11 days behind the European/American Gregorian calendar in the eighteenth century, 12 days behind in the nineteenth century, and 13 days behind in the twentieth century until the Soviets changed to the Gregorian calendar Feb. 28/March 14, 1918. A complication is that, because there was no established dateline in a circumnavigation of the globe, the Russian-Americans in Alaska were, in Schaeffer's time, not 12 days behind as was Russia itself, but 13 days behind. Dates from personal logs or notes are sometimes confusing on this and one must be careful.

CARMINA BURANA. The translations here of the Carmina Burana are from http://www.classical.net/music/comp.1st/works/orff-cb/carbur1.html (carmlyr.html) (accessed 4 August 2003). See below the work by Frederic M. Wheelock.

Carrell, Jennifer Lee. The Speckled Monster: A Historical Tale of Battling Smallpox. Dutton: Penguin Group. New York. 2003. ISBN 0-525-94736-1. This is a historical novel, but with research and notes, detailing Lady Mary Wortley Montagu's life of struggle with smallpox, including early (late 17th and early 18th century) inoculations based on knowledge gained from Africa and Turkey.

Casey, Susan. "The Devil's Teeth." In Sports Illustrated. Vol. 102, No. 18 (May 2, 2005). Pp. 54-62. This article, with photography by Peter Pyle and illustrations of sharks by Ivy Rutzki, presages publication of Susan Casey's book (by Henry Holt and Company in June 2005) on the subject of the Farallon Islands off the California coast (the "Devil's Teeth"…10 very stark islets comprising 211 acres, now a wildlife refuge) and the studies done there of great white sharks. Timofei Tarakanov had seal hunted there with crews of Aleuts in baidarkas poaching on Spanish territory, which Casey now describes as "27 miles west of the Golden Gate Bridge."

Cassidy, Ed. (compiler). Hawaii Trivia. Rutledge Hill Press. Nashville, Tennessee. 1996. Diverse facts about Hawaii. "Scheffer" is mentioned twice on pp. 82.

Cate, Curtis. The War of the Two Emperors: The Duel Between Napoleon and Alexander: Russia, 1812. Random House. New York. 1985. See pp. 259-60 for the balloon episode.

Chamisso, Adelbert von. A Voyage Around the World with the Romanzov (sic) Exploring Expedition, 1815-1818. Edited and Translated by Henry Katz. University of Hawaii Press. Honolulu. 1986. Chamisso, a noted poet and prose writer in Germany, served as ship's scientist on the *Riurik* and was in Hawai'i in 1816. See Kotsebue and Choris and Schweizer (below).

Chandler, David G. The Campaigns of Napoleon: The Mind and Method of History's Greatest Soldier. Scribner. New York. 1966. This is a comprehensive and thorough description of Napoleon's military campaigns in chronological order by a distinguished military historian. It is 1172 pages in length but only mentions "balloons" in one illustration caption concerning the unrealized proposal to invade England by air. The indexing, however, is not completely thorough (cf. at least two mentions of the indexed Bavarian General Wrede are missed). The Moscow balloon project is not mentioned. Moscow Governor General Rostopchin is only mentioned once. But there are appendices listing the command structure of Napoleon's armies in 1808, 1809, 1812, and 1815...very useful.

CHANTS. "Church Singing." Russian Orthodox Church, Moscow. 1982. pp. 246-252. Translated into English from the Russian by Doris Bradbury. See www.hello-online.ru/content.php?contid=1590. This is a brief history of church singing in the Russian Orthodox Church tradition...choral chants of male voices without musical instruments (znamennye chants, domestvennye chants, putevye chants and the introduction, in the sixteenth century, of polyphonic singing). Hawai'ians were also masters of chanting, though for other purposes.

Chapman, Don with William Kaihe'ekai Mai'oho. Mauna 'Ala: Hawai'i's Royal Mausoleum—Last Remnant of a Lost Kingdom. Foreword by Palani Vaughan. Mutual Publishing LLC, 1215 Center Street, Suite 210, Honolulu, HI 96816, 2004 (ISBN 1-56647-700-X). This 70-pp. book relates the history and lore associated with the burial place of Hawai'i's leading Ali'i and their relatives at Mauna 'Ala on Nu'uanu Street in Honolulu. It shows deep respect for these Ali'is' "mana," and the role of the Mauna 'Ala guardians. Interesting is the "Final Mystery" (Chapter 8) surrounding the fates of the Ka'ai covered Iwi of early big-island kings Liloa and Lonoikamakahiki. See also Klieger (below) on the Mau'i burial site, Moku'ula.

Charlot, Jean. Choris and Kamehameha. Bishop Museum Press. Honolulu. 1958. Charlot is a modern artist who created a mural in a Honolulu bank showing Ludwig Choris at work making a portrait of Kamehameha with Adelbert Chamisso looking on. Choris and Chamisso were on the Russian navy ship *Riurik* under Captain Otto von Kotzebue (Kotsebue) when it visited Hawai'i in late 1816. See Chamisso, Choris, Kotzebue, and Schweizer.

Chevigny, Hector. Lost Empire: The Life and Adventures of Nikolai Rezanov. Binfords and Mort. Portland, Oregon. 1937. This is a fictionalization (and romanticization) of Rezanov's life and his adventure in California.

Chevigny, Hector. Lord of Alaska: Baranov and the Russian Adventure. The Viking Press, New York. 1943. A popularized biography of Alexander Baranov, wonderfully written (especially the "Foreword") and without general sacrifice of historical accuracy…though Owens (see below) demonstrates how some of the relations therein are derived from stories fabricated by 1970's researcher and translator Ivan Petrov (Petroff).

Chevigny, Hector. Russian America: The Great Alaskan Adventure, 1741-1867. The Viking Press, New York. 1965. This is the story of Alaska, developed by the Russians and sold to the Americans, including tales of the major personalities involved. This is the work in which the assertion is made that Ivan Kuskov had a "peg-leg" (cf. pp. 88, 122). This assertion is not evidenced by any contemporary account I can find.

Choris, Louis (Ludwig or Liudovik). Voyage pittoresque autour du monde. Iles Sandwich. Paris. 1822. This work can be found in antiquarian shops on-line (expensive). Choris was the artist on Captain Kotsebue's ship *Riurik* and made likenesses of Kamehameha in 1816, which are our primary sources on Kamehameha's appearance late in his life. Choris was an adventurous young man and was shot and killed in 1828 by armed robbers in Mexico. See Kotsebue and Chamisso, Schweizer and Charlot.

Chuquet, Arthur. Human Voices from the Russian Campaign of 1812. Translated from "Etudes d'Histoire" by M. Harriet M. Capes. Andrew Melrose Publishers. London. 1913.

Claffey, Mary and Sara Sikes. "The First Ambassador: John Quincy Adams in St. Petersburg, 1809-1815," in Russian Life, Vol. 51, No. 5 (Number 526) (Sept./Oct. 2008), pp. 48-58. Authors Claffey and Sikes edit the Adams Papers for the Massachusetts Historical Society, and here they have produced a masterpiece of fascinating detail from John Quincy Adams' diaries about his service as U.S. Ambassador to Russia in St. Petersburg. Here can be found information about his salary, what he paid his servants, what gifts he purchased, his meetings, official and unofficial, with Tsar Alexander I, poignant relation of his family life, of the people he met, of his efforts to learn Russian, and, in fact, EVERYTHING he did EVERY DAY of his five-plus years of consequential service there.   This is because John Quincy Adams meticulously kept a handwritten diary of his daily activities for **68 years**, from age 12 to his death at 81. The **fifty volumes** of this monumental work have been scanned and made available online at www.masshist.org/jqadiaries. There, for instance, I had little trouble finding in Diary number 29 John Quincy Adams' diary entries from February through April 1814 about meeting on more than one occasion with "an Irishman who spent time in Philadelphia" named Peter Dobell, including mention of Dobell's story about "being completely plundered" by Chinese pirates under the command of a woman. This conversation between Peter Dobell and John Quincy Adams I had earlier conjectured and included in the text, then, after the publication of the Claffey/Sikes article, I found the diary entry from John Quincy Adams that it had really happened...only did I have to change the venue.

Clark, Manning.   A Short History of Australia. (Fourth revised edition). Penguin Books Australia, Ltd., 487 Maroondah Highway, P.O. Box 257, Ringwood, Victoria 3134, Australia. 1995. This is a classic work on Australian history, the focus here being on the status of things in Port Jackson and Sydney at the time Schaeffer passed through in 1814.

Cleeland, Hokulani.   Olelo Oiwi Ke Kahua: He Puke A'o Olelo Hawai'i. Distributed by 'Aha Punana Leo, 1744 Kino'ole Street, Hilo, Hawai'i 96720. 1994. This is a modern pedagogical text for learning the Hawaiian language.

Connolly, James B. Master Mariner: The Life and Voyages of Amasa Delano. 1943. This is available at www.delanoye.org/Primary/AmasaXV.html.   See also Delano, Amasa (below).

Cook, Chris (Editor and Contributor). A Kauai Reader: The Exotic Heritage of the Garden Island. Mutual Publishing, 1215 Center Street, Suite 210, Honolulu, HI 96816 (808-732-1709, fax 808-734-4094), ISBN 1-56647-006-8.   This collection, typographically flawed for some reason (cf. pp. 47,8,9), includes useful mythology on Kauai's earlier Alii by King David Kalakaua (cf. pp. 40 for Mo'ikeha's contest recitation of his genealogical "kuauhau"), Chris Cook's article on "Kaumualii—Kauai's Last King," and Sheldon Dibble's 1838 version of "The Russian Incident."

Conrad, Agnes C. (ed.) The Letters and Journal of Francisco de Paula Marin. See entry under "Gast, Ross H."

Cordy, Ross H. A Study of Prehistoric Social Change: The Development of Complex Societies in the Hawaiian Islands. Academic Press (A Subsidiary of

Harcourt Brace Jovanovich Publishers. New York and elsewhere. 1981. In Chapter 7 (Epilogue) there is a section entitled "Hawaiian Oral Traditions and the Hypotheses" which lists the successions of Hawaiian rulers on the individual islands going back, by oral accounts, to the 13th century...see pp.200-15.

Cordy, Ross. Exalted Sits the Chief: The Ancient History of Hawai'i Island. Mutual Publishing. Honolulu, Hawaii. 2000. This is a wonderfully researched and detailed history of pre-contact Hawai'i Island...geneologies, family relationships, battles, heiaus, photos, site explanations...just amazing, and complete with copious sources and index.

Cordy, Ross. The Rise and Fall of the O'ahu Kingdom: A Brief Overview of O'ahu's History. Mutual Publishing, 1215 Center Street, Suite 210, Honolulu, HI 96816. 2002 (ISBN 1-56647-562-7). The detail of historical geographic description (e.g. moku and ahupua'a) here is valuable as is the table of rulers of O'ahu and the history itself.

Correa da Costa, Sergio. Every Inch a King: A Biography of Dom Pedro I, the First Emperor of Brazil. Translated from the Portuguese by Samuel Putnam. Robert Hale and Company. London. 1972 edition (reprinted from the original 1950 edition). This biography (230 pp.) is conventional in form in that it is chronological in narrative order, includes much valuable detail, and is equipped with a bibliography and an index. The author is a former Brazilian Ambassador to the Court of St. James (England) and, in November 1976, inscribed the copy I have to Zbigniew Brzezinski, U.S. Secretary of State during the tenure of President Jimmy Carter. Interesting is the contrast between this biography of Dom Pedro I and Gloria Kaiser's very different biography of Dom Pedro's wife, Dona Leopoldina (see below). It isn't so much a difference of fact...both biographies agree, for the most part, on the facts...but a difference of perspective and tone. Reading Kaiser's later work, I could not, in the absence of a bibliography, decide whether she had consulted the work by Correa da Costa. Correa da Costa mentions "Schaeffer" as a "devoted friend" of Leopoldina only twice, and the bibliography has no work specific to him or his activities in bringing Germans to Brazil. I also note that Correa da Costa's work is not included in the "bibliografia" of the 1973 work by Carlos H. Oberacker, Jr. on Schaeffer's bringing Germans to Brazil (see below). Only Oberacker cites Schaeffer's book, published in German in Altona (Hamburg) in 1824, on Brazil.

Craig, Robert. Captain Cook in the Pacific. Pamphlets Polynesia Series of the Institute for Polynesian Studies, Brigham Young University—Hawai'i Campus, Laie, HI 96762-1294. 1978. ISBN 0-939154-00-5. A 33-pp. overview, but accurate. Lacks a treatment of the disposition of the parts of Cook's body after his death.

Croft, Lee B. See my reviews on www.shvoong.com of: Daniel Harrington's www.hawaiianencyclopedia.com and Hanalei: A Kaua'i River Town; Bill Fernandez's Rainbows over Kapa'a; Donald Donohugh's The Story of Koloa: A Kaua'i Plantation Town; S. N. Hale'ole, et. al.'s La'eikawai; Neil Bernard Dukas' (below cited separately) A Pocket Guide to the Battle of Nu'uanu, 1795; Peter R. Mills' (cited below separately) Hawai'i's Russian Adventure: A New Look at Old History; Chuck Blay and Robert Siemers' Kaua'i's Geologic History: A Simplified Guide; and Raymond Massey's (cited separately below) Discovery of Hawai'i & Honolulu. Search shvoong under contiguous "LeeBCroft." Also reviews there, and on www.Amazon.com of North (2), and Armstrong.

Croft, Lee B. "A Chronology of George Anton Schaeffer's Life as Related by Lee B. Croft, Ph.D." A 10 pp. illustrated brochure, with recommended sources in English, Russian, and Portuguese, accompanying a lecture given at the Ship Store Gallery, 4-1379 Kuhio Hwy, Kapa'a, HI, on October 25th, 2011. See: http//www.shipstoregalleries.net.

Croft, Lee B. "George Anton Schaeffer: The Builder of Kaua'i's Russian Forts…And His Hawai'ian Fluency." Accepted in late 2010 for publication as a 4 pp. illustrated article in Pacific Journal (Tammi Andersland and John Lydgate, Editors), forthcoming.

Crosby, Alfred W., Jr. America, Russia, Hemp and Napoleon. Ohio State University Press. Columbus, Ohio. 1965. In Napoleon's time Russia produced most of the world's sailcloth fiber from its crops in Ukraine and elsewhere of hemp. The very word "canvas" is a contraction of "cannabis" from "Cannabis sativa," the Linnaeus designation for hemp. The Russian cognate is "kanoplia." The purpose here is to evidence Napoleon's desire to hamstring the British navy of its sail canvas by embargoing Russia's trade in hemp. See also the work of contemporary pot advocate Jack Herer, who calls Chapter 11 of his "The Emperor Wears No Clothes" "The Hemp War of 1812/Napoleon Invades Russia" at www.jackherer.com.

Cross, A.G. N.M.Karamzin: A Study of his Literary Career, 1783-1803. Southern Illinois University Press, Carbondale and Edwardsville/Feffer and Simons, Inc., London and Amsterdam. 1971. This study treats well Karamzin's involvement with freemasonry, but ceases its focus before the period of Napoleon's invasion.

Crouch, Tom D. The Eagle Aloft: Two Centuries of the Balloon in America. Smithsonian Institution Press. Washington, D.C. 1983. On pp. 120 is an illustration "The process of inflating a hydrogen balloon" ca. 1800.

Crowe, Ellie and William. Exploring Hawaii: Places of Power, History, Mystery, and Magic. Island Heritage Publishing. 94-411 Ko'aki Street,

Waipahu, Hawai'i 96797. First edition, second printing 2002. ISBN 0-89610-383-8. This work shows photographs of selected heiaus and other places on six of the Hawaiian islands with explanations of their historical significance and anecdotes about their spiritual power or "mana." A parenthesis in the introduction states, contrary to numerous other historical accounts, that "(Kamehameha I was over seven feet in height)," thus early establishing its primacy of mythology over a relation of objective reality...yet this is a work of value in its depiction of early Hawaiian life which was so dominated by concern for "mana" and mythology.

Currier, Dean P. "Adventures in Cybersound: Johann Wilhelm Ritter: 1776-1810." At http://www.acmi.net.au/AIC/RITTER_BIO.html, accessed May 16, 2002.

Damon, Ethel M. "George Prince Kaumualii," Fifty-fifth Annual Report of the Hawaiian Historical Society For the Year 1946. Honolulu Star Bulletin, Honolulu, 1948, pp. 10.

DauBach, Daniel Carl. Peter Dobell, 1775-1852: An American Opportunist in Russian Service in Early Nineteenth Century Siberia. University of Kansas Ph.D. dissertation, 1993. Available through University Microfilms International, 300 Zeeb Rd., Ann Arbor, MI 48106-1346 as order number 9425901. The internet presence of this work rephrases the title, replacing the word "opportunist" with "huckster." Dobell was from Philadelphia, but disavowed America and claimed to be an Irishman, being named Russian minister to the Philippines after trade activity in Canton. Dobell and Schaeffer never met, although their trails crossed several times...in Canton (Macao, Whampoa) and in St. Petersburg. Dobell's advice to the Russian government coincided with Schaeffer's as far as Hawai'i was concerned. He advocated a Russian annexation of the islands for trade purposes. See also Dobell (below).

Dauenhauer, Richard L. "Education in Russian America." In Russian America: The Forgotten Frontier. Barbara Sweetland Smith and Redmond J. Barnett, eds. Tacoma: The Washington State Historical Press. 1990. pp. 155-165.

Daws, Gavan. Shoal of Time: A History of the Hawaiian Islands. University of Hawaii Press. Honolulu, Hawaii. 1968 copyright, first printing in 1974. A most readable account, treating "Schaffer of Schafferthal" pages 49-53, foregrounding the sandalwood trade.

Day, A. Grove. "Georg Anton Scheffer: Russian Flags Over Hawaii" in Rogues of the South Seas. Foreword by James Michener. Mutual Publishing. Honolulu. 1986. An anecdotal treatment in a popular paperback, but accurate.

Day, A. Grove. Pacific Islands Literature: One Hundred Basic Books. University Press of Hawaii. Honolulu. 1971. In this collection of book synopses author A. Grove Day shares his vast knowledge of the literature of the Pacific Islands. Of particular interest to me here are the entries on William E. Giles "A Cruise in a Queensland Labour Vessel to the South Seas," describing an enterprise (called "blackbirding") which once involved my own Great Great Grandfather John Croft, who resided at his estate called "Mount Adelaide" on Darling Point in Sydney with wife Mary Stead Croft (died 7 March, 1857, interred with four children, who died in infancy, at Newtown's (Sydney) Camperdown Cemetery of Australian Pioneers) until returning to England with three surviving children in 1858, and Robert Dean Frisbie's "The Book of Puka-Puka" about life in the Cook Islands.

DEBRECEN. For city history, see http://www.debrecen.com/debrecen/angol/auth.html, accessed August 9, 2003. This is an outstanding city website, created by Editor-Systemorganiser Dr. Tamás Várhelyi and Web Constructor Dr. Laszló Szabó. The multipage site features streaming video of city and regional events. The text was written by Pál S. Varga and Pál Tóth, and is available in English. Copyright is held by OPTONET Co of Hadházi 38, Debrecen, Hungary 4028.

De Caulaincourt, General (Marquis) Armand, Duke of Vicenza. With Napoleon in Russia. The Universal Library. Grosset and Dunlap. New York. 1935 copyright by William Morrow and Company. These are the memoirs of an aide and confidant of Napoleon and a former French ambassador to the St. Petersburg court of Tsar Alexander I. It does not mention the balloon.

Delano, Amasa (1763-1823). A Narrative of Voyages and Travels in the Northern and Southern Hemispheres: Comprising Three Voyages Round the World; Together with a Voyage of Survey and Discovery in the Pacific Ocean and Oriental Islands. E. G. House. Boston. 1817. This work is the memoirs of American Revolutionary War hero and Boston "Master Mariner," Amasa Delano, who, after a visit to Hawai'i at Kealakekua Bay in 1801 on the *Perseverance,* carried away a son of Kamehameha's, calling himself Alexander Stewart (see text), together with four other Hawai'ian kanakas, to be trained as sailors and educated in the United States. Delano records innoculating the five kanakas with "kinepox" serum as they approached Canton, China, later that year. Thus a son of Kamehameha's was one of the first Hawai'ians vaccinated against smallpox. In Canton, this son transferred himself to a British Indiaman (trade ship) and was last heard of in London. See also the biography by James Connolly at www.delanoye.org/Primary/AmasaXV.html. Delano's adventures at sea inspired a short story by Herman Melville from 1855 entitled "Benito Cereno."

DERZHAVIN, GAVRIL ROMANOVICH. (1743-1816) Russian poet. See Glinka, and entries on Rezanov and especially Shelikhov, G.

Desha, Stephen L. Kamehameha and His Warrior Kekūhaupi'o. Translated by Frances N. Frazier. Kamehameha Schools Press. Honolulu, HI. 2000.

Dinklage, Karl Führer von. Münnerstadt mittelalterliches Kleinod. Würzburg. ca 1985. A history of Münnerstadt's position as the center of the Franconian catholic diocese.

Dobell, Peter. Travels in Kamchatka and Siberia: With a Narrative of a Residence in China. Arno Press Reprint. New York. 1970. Dobell wrote the original in 1828-30 based on articles he wrote in St. Petersburg's journal Syn Otechestva (Son of the Fatherland) in 1815-6 (cf. 1815, part 22, No. 25-6, str. 205; 1815, part 25, No. 45, str. 249; and 1815, part 26, No. 47, str.55) under the title "Otryvki iz zapisok puteshestvennika po Kamchatke i Sibiri" ("Excerpts from the Notes of a Traveler Through Kamchatka and Siberia"). As an advisor to the Russian-American Company, it is likely that he met Barbara Schaeffer while he was in St. Petersburg for the first time from 1814-1818 (he was there again later from 1827-1835, and yet again in 1852 where he died, after serving as Russian Consul to Helsingfors, Denmark, for 16 years) and that she likely read his notes. Peter Dobell traveled to Hawai'i not long after Schaeffer had left the islands, and later claimed to have acted to preserve Hawai'ian unity after the death of Kamehameha in 1819 by advising the successor Liholiho on how to deal with his father's leading chief, Kalanimoku. He is also the author of a pamphlet published in English in London in 1833 entitled "Russia as it is and not as it has been represented." Dobell is a character as colorful as Schaeffer...an American who disavowed his country, got involved in the opium trade in Canton, became a Consul for the Russian government...he was the uncle of Captain James Bennett of the wrecked *Bering* who accompanied Schaeffer to Hawai'i in 1815. Bennett, the son of Dobell's sister Ruth and her husband, Dobell's early partner, Samuel Bennett of Philadelphia, also had an adventurous life. In 1820 while with Dobell in Manila during a smallpox outbreak, he was captured and tortured by natives, but escaped. Dobell converted to Russian Orthodoxy and married a Russian woman, Dariia Andreevna, in Tobolsk in 1818, with whom he had children...but their fate is unknown. Peter and Dariia lived out their lives together, dying in the same year, 1852, in St. Petersburg...he at age 76, she at age 52. They were buried side-by-side in a catacomb beneath the floors of the Church of the Smolensk Mother of God in St. Petersburg. Part of their sepulcher was destroyed during the Soviet Civil War, ca. 1920, and reconstruction efforts in the 1990's did not include the preservation of their graves. See Bolkhovitinov and DauBach (above). Mention of Peter Dobell can be found as well in the diaries of John Quincy Adams (see Claffey and Sikes, above).

Dorrance, William H. O'ahu's Hidden History. Mutual Publishing, 1215 Center Street, Suite 210, Honolulu, HI 96816. Copyright 1998. Third Printing, March 2001 (ISBN 1-56647-211-3).

Dmytryshyn, Basil and E.A.P. Crownhart-Vaughan (translators and editors, with introduction and notes). Colonial Russian America: Kyrill Khlebnikov's Reports, 1817-1832. Oregon Historical Society, Portland. 1976. This is a great source of detail on the fur-trade values (appendix 1 has all furs taken by ship and captain from 1746-1797, and appendix 3 has all furs taken on Kodiak Island from 1803-1817 e.g.), the ships and their cargo and diverse other data defining life in Russia Alaska in this period...a very useful work by a personal acquaintance.

Duffy, Christopher. Borodino and the War of 1812. Charles Scribner's Sons. New York. 1973. Mention is made of Napoleon's horse, L'Embelli, ridden during the battle. Later, in other sources, two other horses are mentioned...L'Emir, on which he entered Moscow, and another (?) in addition to Blond's (passim) mention of the horse "Moscow." There is a chapter on "Borodino in History and Fiction," including synopses of the noted film treatments...e.g. the U.S. and USSR versions of War and Peace. For other works, including the "Virtual Battle of Borodino," see Ezerskaya, Kulagin, Mikherabidze and Monakhov below.

Duhem, Jules. "Le Ballon incendiaire de Moscou en 1812" in Revue de l'Institute Napoleon. Vol. 2, 2nd Quarter (1938), pp. 81-91. This article, a synopsis of the balloon project from French primary observers, confuses the parties but mentions a Würzburg physician 'nomme obscurement Sch...' (Schaeffer). There is also a sketch of the aerostat done by French officer de Segur, who investigated the Vorontsovo site after the balloon project's evacuation and interviewed local witnesses to it (see Napoleon, below, for a later 1876 German likeness from Tsar Alexander's archives).

Dukas, Neil Bernard. A Military History of Sovereign Hawai'i. Mutual Publishing. 1215 Center Street, Suite 210, Honolulu, HI 96816. First printing May 2004 (ISBN 1-56647-636-4). This is a fresh perspective on the Hawai'ian culture, characterizing the mana motivations for a warrior culture and its following military in the royal period of the 19th century.

Dukas, Neil Bernard. A Pocket Guide to the Battle of Nu'uanu Pali: An Illustrated Guide to the O'ahu Battlefield. Mutual Publishing, 1215 Center Street, Suite 210, Honolulu, HI 96816, First Printing May, 2010. ISBN 978-1-56647-922-6.   I   review   this   very   fine   work   at http://www.shvoong.com/books/dictionary/2226308-pocket-guide-battle-nu-uanu/. It blazes new trails in the understanding of this important battle and features maps and site descriptions "then and now" with modern addresses given. Illustrators include Herb Kawainui Kane and Brook Kapukuniahi Parker.

Dwight, Edwin Welles, et. al. Memoirs of Henry Obookiah, a Native of Owhyhee, and a Member of the Foreign Mission School, Who Died in Cornwall, Conn. Feb. 17, 1818, age 26 years. Nathan Whiting, New Haven,

Conn., 1819. This book of memoirs is in the University of Hawai'i-Manoa's Hamilton Library's rare book collection at BV 3680.H4 O33 1819. Dwight is NOT directly related to the Rev. Timothy Dwight, President of Yale College. The collection includes an Inaugural Address (1817 formal opening of the Foreign Mission school where Obookiah and three other Hawai'ian youths (including Kaumuali'i's son Humehume or "George Prince Tomaree (see Warne below) were being 'christianized' and trained) by Governor John Treadwell of Connecticut, who is himself the author of A Narrative of Five Youths from the Sandwich Islands, J. Seymour, NY, 1816 (cited in Warne, below...I have not seen). The Obookiah memoirs are also published (and cited by Warne) as Memoirs of Henry Obookiah by the Kingsport Press of Kingsport, TN, 1968.

D'Wolf, John. A Voyage to the North Pacific. Ye Galleon Press. Fairfield, Washington. 1968. D'Wolf was an American trader who was the first to sell his ship to Aleksandr Baranov and the Russian-American Company. He then crossed Siberia to St. Petersburg on his way back to America, the first American to do so. The original version of this travelogue was published in Cambridge, Massachusetts in 1861.

EASTER ISLAND. For a description of Easter Island and its mysteries, see www.netaxs.com/trance/rapanui.html. The best starting place on the rapanui "hieroglyphics" is www.rongorongo.org. On the first page of this extremely rich website is mention of a link to the website by current Russian cryptanalyst Sergei Rjabchikov: www.openweb.ru/rongo, but, as is mentioned there, the link is very unreliable and the site almost never comes up. Instead, try it in the Google search field and then see it as stored in the Google cache...most of the links there also work.

Ebbets, John (New York Captain, 1775-1835, m. Sarah Woodward). See Steele, Edward E. below for a genealogical sketch of the Ebbets family.

Ellis, William. A Narrative of an 1823 Tour Through Hawai'i: With Remarks on the History, Traditions, Manners, Customs, and Language of the Inhabitants of the Sandwich Islands. Mutual Publishing, 1215 Center Street, Suite 210, Honolulu, HI 96816, 2004 edition (ISBN 1-56647-605-4). This is the journal, first published in 1825, of English-born missionary William Ellis (1794-1872) concerning his early days in Hawai'i. It is very interesting.

Emerson, Caryl. "Our Everything." In Slavic and East European Journal. Vol. 48, No. 1 (Spring 2004), pp. 79-98. This is a most comprehensive and detailed review of four recent biographies of Aleksandr Sergeevich Pushkin (1799-1837). Many of Pushkin's contemporaries and their relationships to him and to each other are discussed in this review. It gives its own picture of life in Russia after the expulsion of Napoleon and his army.

Engstrom, Elton and Allan Engstrom. <u>Alexander Baranov and a Pacific Empire</u>. Elton and Allan Engstrom, Box 723, Juneau, AK 99802. ISBN 0964570130.

Evatt, Herbert Vere (Justice of the High Court of Australia). <u>Rum Rebellion: A Study of the Overthrow of Governor Bligh by John Macarthur and the New South Wales Corps</u>. Includes the John Murtagh Macrossan Memorial lectures delivered at the University of Queensland, June 1937. Angus and Robertson Ltd. 89 Castelreigh Street. Sydney. 1938. This is a detailed and colorful treatment of the "Rum Rebellion" in the New South Wales Colony in 1808 against Governor William Bligh.

Ezerskaya, Irina. <u>Frants Rubo I ego panorama 'Borodinskaja Bitva'</u>. Izdatel'stvo gumanitarnoj literatury. Moskva. 2001. (ISBN 5-87121-011-2) The address of the Panorama Museum of the Battle of Borodino is 38 Kutuzovsky Prospect, 121170 Moscow, Russia. (telephone is 148-19-67, fax 148-94-89, e-mail <u>b1812@online.ru</u>). See "Borodino" above.

Faber du Faur (von), Christian Wilhelm. <u>With Napoleon in Russia: The Illustrated Memoirs of Major Faber du Faur, 1812</u>. See North, Jonathan (below). Also see my review of this work at www.Amazon.com.

Fenn, Elizabeth A. <u>Pox Americana: The Great Smallpox Epidemic of 1775-82</u>. Hill and Wang (Farrar, Straus and Giroux). New York. 2001. ISBN 0-8090-7821-X. This is a fine "personalized" historical treatment of the impact of smallpox.

FERDINAND III, GRAND DUKE OF TUSCANY and Archduke of Austria (Son of Holy Roman Emperor Leopold II and Princess Maria Luisa, infanta of Spain). For immediate family circumstances see <u>http://www.wikipedia.org/w/wiki.phtml?title=Ferdinand_III%2C_Grand_Duke_ Tuscany</u>. Also very interesting, and including a fine color portrait of Ferdinand III is the genealogical work by Ingeborg Brigitte Gastel (1944-) at <u>www.worldroots.com/brigitte/royal/habs-f.htm</u>. This source is also definitive on the 13 children (by the first two wives, including the 12 with Elizabeth Wilhelmine Loise, Grand Duchess of Wurttemburg) of Franz Joseph II (Franz I), (1768-1835...Holy Roman Emperor Franz II until 1806, then Emperor Franz I of Austria until his death). See also mention of Ferdinand's role in Napoleon's marriage to Austrian Grand Duchess Marie Louise (Ferdinand's niece) at Fernwood, I. "Napoleon's Coronation as Emperor of the French," a 7-pp "E-article accessed January 15, 2002 at <u>http://www.geocities.com/ifernwood/coronation/coronation.html</u>.

FORT ROSS, CALIFORNIA. This was the southernmost outpost of the Russian-American Company, headed by Ivan Kuskov, a colorful character sent south from Sitka in 1811 by RAC Manager Alexander Baranov. See "History of the Russian Settlement at Fort Ross, California" at

http://parks.sonoma.net/rosshist.html.   See   also
www.basecamp.cnchost.com/fortross.htm. This latter site includes information
from the Congress of Russian Americans that is also available at www.russian-
americans.org/CRA_History.htm. This source is very good on both Alexander
Baranov and Father Ioann Veniaminov (later Metropolitan and Saint Innokentii).
On the character of Ivan Kuskov, I have tried to pin down the factuality from
original sources of the occasionally published mention that Kuskov had a "peg-
leg," and have been so far unable to do so. On this I note the museum in
Tot'ma, Russia, Kuskov's home town to which he returned late in life with his
wife, a native American. Sarah Gould of the guide staff at Fort Ross, who
consulted with the producers of a recent television program on the Russian
colonization of America (and which portrayed Kuskov with a peg-leg) has also
been trying to identify the source of this allegation. I communicated and
commiserated with her on it after finding her inquiry where I placed mine, at
www.vologda-oblast.ru/chat.asp?Page=Object&Code=37&LNG=ENG.
So far (May 2005), there is no definitive original source. No contemporary of
Kuskov's mentions any peg-leg (cf. e.g. Khlebnikov below). See also source by
Watrous (below) and related "Role Play: Founding of Settlement Ross" at
http://www.mcn.org/1/rrparks/fortross/Curriculum/roleplay.htm (accessed May
2005). This work includes much useful information about Fort Ross from Ivan
Kuskov's 1821 census and reference to other works treating daily life in the
settlement after its founding.

Fortuine, Robert, M.D. "Health and Medical Care in Russian America." In
Russian America: The Forgotten Frontier. Barbara Sweetland Smith and
Redmond J. Barnett, eds. Tacoma: The Washington State Historical Press.
1990. pp. 121-131.

Franchere, Gabriel. Narrative of a Voyage to Northwest Coast of America in
the Years 1811, 1812, 1813, and 1814 of the First American Settlement on the
Pacific. Translated and Edited by J. V. Huntington. Redfield. 110 and 112
Nassau Street. New York. 1854. The author, a Canadian working for John
Jacob Astor's Pacific Fur Company, sailed on the *Tonquin* (Jonathan Thorn,
Captain) from New York around Cape Horn to Hawaii and then the settlement
called Astoria near the mouth of the Columbia River. His memoirs, which he
wrote in 1819 and prepared for publication in the 1840's, provide historical
accuracy to the related fiction of Washington Irving's novel Astoria (authored
with Pierre Irving in 1836), which deals with some of the same dramatic events.
The text here is a wonderful period piece with great detail concerning
Kamehameha's Hawaii and western (coastal and inland) America during the
time of the War of 1812 with England. It also gives a fine picture of life on a
sailing ship at that time. The work is available completely online at
http://roxen.xmission.com/~drudy/mrman/html/franchere/franchere.html. The
story of how the *Tonquin*'s boatswain, John Anderson, a friend of character John
Marshall in my relation, left the ship in Hawai'i, before its destruction, is in
Chapter III, page 59.

FRANKENTHAL. The location in Brazil of George Schaeffer's initial plantation estate on that first square "legua" (2.5 km) of land was long a problem to me. I was mislead by the fact that modern maps show a "Leopoldina" and a reasonably nearby "Vila Vicosa" in the Minas Gerais State about 100 km north of Rio de Janeiro. I recall that Dr. Enrico Schaeffer, who, in 1959-60 described himself as a "collateral relative" of George Anton Schaeffer, wrote that he had tried to find the original estate of Frankenthal...and ostensibly George's grave... in the environs of Vila Vicosa and could not find any trace of it. The estate, he wrote, had "returned to the jungle." This may be true, but near which "Vila Vicosa" was he searching? My reading carefully through George Schaeffer's German book on Brazil and my search with internet advantage and Google Earth indicates to me that the site of the Frankenthal estate is inland along the Peruipe River from the modern extreme southern Bahia State city of Nova Vicosa...which in 1824 was named, as George writes, "Vila Vicosa." The site of Georg Wilhelm Freyreiss's colony, that George Schaeffer describes as being "downstream" from his Frankenthal estate, is to be found in the municipality of Helvecia...which in 1824 was named "Colonia Leopoldina." George's description includes the –18 degrees latitude, the River Peruipe's north bank overlooking the confluence of the tributary stream he calls "Jackarander," the downstream location of Freyreiss's colony, and the largest nearby city being "Vila Vicosa" that has needed things in abundance and from where agricultural products of his estate might easily be shipped to more populous markets. Thus, I am convinced that FRANKENTHAL is on this north bluff above the confluence of the Peruipe River and the Jackarander Stream about 25 KM upstream from the municipality of Helvecia (Colonia Leopoldina in George's time)which is 20 KM inland on the Peruipe from the substantial city of Nova Vicosa (Vila Vicosa in George's time) which is 750 km (i.e. five to seven weeks of overland mule travel in George's time, crossing a succession of rivers by ferry and ford, or a week's travel by ship if the wind is right) to Rio de Janeiro. The Minas Gerais sites called Leopoldina and Vila Vicosa are "red herrings" and do NOT meet George's detailed description of the location of his estate.

Freyreiss, G. Wilhelm. Reisen in Brasilien. The Ethnological Museum of Sweden Monograph Series, Publication number 13, Stockholm, 1968. Freyreiss (1789-1825) followed George Heinrich von Langsdorff to Brazil and led an exploratory expedition to the Minas Gerais area of Brazil in 1814-1815, previous to Langsdorff's own first expedition of 1816-17 mentioned in this book. Freyreiss was the leader of the "Leopoldina Colony" of Germans in the Vila Vicosa area, and is mentioned in Schaeffer's 1824 book. Freyreiss was a participant of Langsdorff's later expedition in the early 1820's and, like Schaeffer, wrote a book about Brazil in 1824 that was published in Germany the year before his death in 1825.

Frisbie, Robert Dean ("Ropati" in his works). The Island of Desire. Doubleday/Doran. New York. 1944. This work and others by Pacific island writer Frisbie inspired the residence of Tom Neale on Suvarov island…which was described to Neale by Frisbie as the most beautiful atoll in the Pacific. As Frisbie inspired Neale, so Frisbie was himself inspired by the writer James Norman Hall (1887-1951), co-author with Charles Nordhoff (1887-1947) of Mutiny on the Bounty. On these prolific authors on South Seas life, A. Grove Day recommends the biographical work by Paul L. Briand, Jr., In Search of Paradise: The Nordhoff-Hall Story (Duell, Sloan and Pearce, New York, 1966).

Gast, Ross H. Don Francisco de Paula Marin: A Biography; The Letters and Journal of Francisco de Paula Marin. Edited by Agnes C. Conrad. University of Hawai'i Press (2840 Kolowalu Street, Honolulu, HI 96822, www.uhpress.hawaii.edu) for the Hawaiian Historical Society, Honolulu, 1973, ISBN 0-945048-09-2. See Lee, Blanche (below) for a varying view about Marin's introduction of the pineapple to Hawai'i. Also Ten Bruggencate (below).

Gately, Iain. Tobacco: A Cultural History of How an Exotic Plant Seduced Civilization. Grove Press. New York. 2001. ISBN0-8021-3960-4. This interesting work informs the stance of Schaeffer and his wife towards tobacco.

Gibson, James R. Imperial Russia in Frontier America: The Changing Geography of Supply of Russian America, 1784-1867. With cartographer Miklos Pinther. Oxford University Press. New York. 1976. Table 7, pp. 78, has a log of supply ships' journeys, including the Suvorov under "Lt. M. P. Lazarev, 1813-6, value of cargo 246,476 rubles."

GIRARD, STEPHEN (1750-1831, Philadelphia magnate, philanthropist and early mentor of Peter Dobell…see above under Dobell, DauBach). Girard was wealthy enough by 1812 to bankroll the United States during its war with England and prevent its bankruptcy. He is a very eccentric character in American history and had an interesting personal life, involving a wife who was committed to a lunatic asylum, two long-term mistresses, and African-american slave named Hannah. See: www.ushistory.org/Girard or www.famousamericans.net/stephengirard. There is a feminist play by Laine Robertson entitled The Insanity of Mary Girard loosely based on Girard's relationship with his wife, Mary Lum Girard, and her life in the asylum. See http://students.washcoll.edu/Club-Pages/rsp/01_MaryGirard.html. There is even a man named Allen Hampton, an employee of the Pennsylvania Hospital in Philadelphia (endowed by Stephen Girard) who reports a 1999 dream about a "Sally (Bickham) Girard" at www.wirenot.net/X/Stories/Ghost/Ghost%20C-D/DreamofMaryandMistress.sthml.

Glinka, Natal'ia Ivanovna. Derzhavin v Peterburge. ("Derzhavin in Petersburg"). Leninizdat. Leningrad. 1985. This work describes the great poet Gavriil Romanovich Derzhavin's (1743-1816) activities in St. Petersburg and gives a list of his places of residence in the city and their more modern addresses. There is a floor plan and an illustration of his residence and garden on the fontanka near the Obukhov bridge. Derzhavin was once Nikolai Rezanov's superior. He wrote a poem characterizing M. S. Golikov and another memorializing Gregorii Ivanovich Shelikhov (see Shelikhov, below).

Glusing, Jean. "Brasilien Reproduktive Bauche" in Der Spiegel, Vol. 25 (2001), pp. 148. This article describes the selective breeding of African slaves in Brazil, particularly one "Santa Clara" estate of a Francisco Thereziano de Bustamente 250 kilometers west of Rio de Janeiro which masked its notorious slave breeding with coffee operations. The Bustamente operation began in 1824 and continued until his death in 1860. Glusing cites a "classic work" called "Herrenhaus und Sklavenhutte" by "Sociologist and Historian Gilberto Feyre Schildert" (undated) who describes how the slaves were considered "only reproductive vessels" and how the slave buyers were instructed to pay strict attention to the Negroes' sexual organs and reject any slaves who had undersized or misshapen organs. Despite several descriptions to the contrary (e.g. the early Brazilian Viceroy Lavradio or Wilhelm Humboldt), Schaeffer, in his 1824 work, describes the conditions of slave transport to be better than that for the transport of soldiers of the time.

Golovnin, Vasilii M. Around the World on the Kamchatka, 1817-1819. (Translated with introduction and notes by Ella Lury Wiswell (who once taught Russian to the parents of President Barack Obama, who met in her class)). University of Hawaii Press. Manoa. 1979. ISBN is 0-8248-0640-9.

Gomes, Dival da Costa. "Independence of Brazil: Expertise and Personalities of Maçonaria," at www.triplov.com/carbonaria/dival_gomes_costa/independencia_brasil/masonry. htm. This treats Schaeffer's contributions to founding the German Emigration to Brazil, listing the families' names of those brought to Brazil by ships Schaeffer chartered (see also Weissheimer below) and lamenting that this brother mason is not mentioned on any memorials thereby...no streets or plazas or cities named after him, etc. See also Weissheimer (below).

Govor, Elena. "Russian Ships in Australia During the First Half of the XIX Century," "Russian Convicts in Australia," "The Russian Odyssey of the Governor Macquarie," "The 'Otkrytie i Blagonamerennyi' in Australia," and (with Alexander Massov) "'Neva'—the First Russian Naval Ship in Australia." These wonderfully detailed articles, complete with tables and illustrations, are accessible at www.argo.net.au/andre/... adding final strings for each: russhipsbeforeCWENFIN.htm; RussianconvictsENFIN.htm; MacquarieENFIN.htm; OTKRYTIEenfin.htm; and nevaENFIN.htm. Since the Neva (under Lieutenant Leontii Andrianovich Gagemeister, 1807), the Otkrytie (Capt.-Lieutenant Mikhail Nikolaevich Vasiliev, 1820) and the Blagonamerennyi (Lieutenant Gleb Semyonovich Shishmarev, 1820) were Russian navy ships, the ships' logs and officers diaries became widely known public records, whereas the 1814 visit of the *Suvorov* was officially a venture of the Russian-American Company. The ship's log and the diaries of the parties involved were not public records and are therefore not as available to historians' examination. One specific memoir, that of "podshturman" Aleksei Ivanovich Rossiyskiy, and excerpts from Lieutenants Lazarev and Unkovskiy are included in the work, Russkie flotovodtsy: M.P.Lazarev: Dokumenty ("Russian Fleet Commanders: M.P. Lazarev: Documents") by Andrei A. Samarov (cf. below).

Grant, Glen. Waikiki Yesteryear. Mutual Publishing, 1215 Center Street, Suite 210, Honolulu, HI 96816. Copyright 1996. Third Printing, June 2002. (ISBN 1-56647-107-9). This work has many historical photographs of the Waikiki area and includes good topographical description of early Waikiki.

Grantham, Fred W. Did America Overthrow the Kingdom of Hawai'i & Steal the Hawaiian Islands? (For Those Who Want to Know!). Royal Designs, 44-106 BayView Haven Place, Kaneohe, HI 96744, copyright 2005 to F.W. Grantham. On page 14 of this work, author Grantham mentions the Russian presence in Honolulu during the reign of Kamehameha I. One particular detail of his narration caught my eye...a parenthesis saying "a memento of this action, we believe, is the Russian ship's cannon that is on display in Walker Park off Nimitz Hwy, right across from Honolulu Harbor and the Hawaiian Electric plant right on our waterfront." It took me awhile to find Walker Park mauka across Nimitz/Ala Moana from the Ewa side of the Aloha Tower Center...dedicated to the Mr. Walker who headed Amfac and was prominent in Hawaiian and Honolulu development...nice. There IS an old, looks to have been once submerged, cannon there on a wooden carriage that may have been added for purposes of land display later. It is a VERY heavy cast-iron cannon with no markings to be seen by the naked eye...it is a bit more than 10 feet in length, tapering from about 20" in diameter at the butt to 10" at the muzzle. The caliber is just a hair shy of 6". If author Grantham is correct (and I think he may well be), then *this is yet another physical memento that I have touched with my hands* that George Anton Schaeffer likely once touched (like the rocks of his Kaua'i forts, a copy of his 1824 book, the door of the Juliusspital in Würzburg...). He was in command of the Russian-American Company ship *Kadiak* when it came to Honolulu in the first days of July 1817 after he had been forcibly expelled

Author Lee B. Croft with the cannon alleged to be from the RAK ship *Kadiak* (sunk at Honolulu Harbor shoreline July 5-6, 1817). Photo by Lesley Hoyt Croft, September 2011.

from Kaua'i. It was leaking terribly...the men pumping twenty feet or more of water out of it daily. On 4 July 1817 George was rescued off it by Captain Isaiah Lewis of the *Panther* as George and his men were about to attack another ship and sail away on it in escape, since Kamehameha's advisor John Young and the British and American advisors wanted to kill George. After George was sailed away, the *Kadiak* sank on 5 and 6 July to the bottom of Honolulu harbor, very likely very close to the display position its cannon (if it IS a cannon from the *Kadiak*) now occupies, since the shoreline in 1817 was surprisingly inland of the current shoreline, as shown by an extent 1810 map. It was reportedly found during the excavation of the basement of the Amfac Building at a considerable depth of 15 feet below ground level. Grantham is correct that the rest of the Russians and Aleuts on the *Kadiak* were allowed to stay peacefully in their previous Waikiki settlement until Russian America Governor Alexander Baranov could send a ship to bring them back to Novo-Arkhangelsk (Sitka) in Alaska.

Gräter, Dr. Carlheinz (text), Elmar Hahn (photography) and Tina Neil (English Transl.). Würzburg: Tourist Guide. Elmar Hahn Verlag. Veitshöchheim. 4th revised ed. 2002. This guide book includes a table of "Important Dates in Würzburg's History."

Gray, Robert. Captain Robert Gray (1755-1806) is the namesake of Gray's Harbor on the northwest coast and the discoverer and namer of the Columbia River after his ship *Columbia* on which he, together with Captain John Kendrick (1745-1794, of the *Lady Washington*) explored and traded in the north Pacific in the 1780's and 1790's. See www.oregonpioneers.com/gray.htm. See also the entries on Kendrick, John and by Scofield, John (below). Also Ridley, Scott (below).

Greer, Richard A. "Memoirs of Thomas Hopo'o" in Hawaiian Journal of History (A Publication of the Hawaiian Historical Society), Vol. II (1968), pp. 42-54.

Greer, Richard A. "Along the Old Honolulu Waterfront" in Hawaiian Journal of History (A Publication of the Hawaiian Historical Society), Vol. XXXII (1998), pp. 25-66. Good detailed history, with included maps from 1810 and others, of Honolulu and environs, with relation of related events and historical developments.

GRIEB, BALTHASAR. The Brazilian family of descendents of this "Balthasar Grieb," whose last name has now changed to "Gripp," is responsible for relating online the tale of the "ill-fated journey of the ship *Argus*." See this at http://www.gripp.com.br/Historicofam.htm. I suggest "googling" "George Anton Schaeffer" and then, on page 3 of listed sites, clicking on the "translate this page" instruction. See also related genealogy at Weissheimer (below).

Griess, Thomas E. (Series Editor). West Point Atlas for the Wars of Napoleon. Square One Publishers. Garden City Park, New York, 11040. (telephone 516-535-2010...cf. www.squareonepublishers.com). 2003. This is a large-format compendium of military-style maps of troop movements, etc. There are six maps describing the stages of Napoleon's "Russian Campaign" (pp. 46-52).

Grimsted, Patricia K. The Foreign Ministers of Alexander I: Political Attitudes and the Conduct of Russian Diplomacy, 1801-1825. Berkeley, Ca. University of California Press. 1969.

Gusliarov, Evgenii. Vse dueli Pushkina. ("All the Duels of Pushkin"). Iantarnyi skaz. Kaliningrad. 2001. This work lists the circumstances of 21 conflicts the poet Aleksandr Sergeevich Pushkin (1799-1837) had over "points of honor" in which duels were mentioned, avoided, or took place. One of these (#14, pp. 72-75) concerns Pushkin's conflict with Count Fyodor Tolstoi, the American, and lists several memoirists' impressions of Tolstoi, including those of M. I. Semenovskii from conversation with Aleksei Vul'f, F. N. Luginin, Tolstoi's niece M. F. Kamenskaia, and Faddei Bulgarin. The artist A. Il'in provides a drawing of Tolstoi in his room, adorned as described by Kamenskaia with artifacts of Aleutian tribes and with the backs of his hands tattooed (pp. 75).

Gutmanis, June. Hawaiian Herbal Medicine. Translations by Theodore Kelsey. Illustrations by Susan G. Monden. Island Heritage Publishing.
94-411 Kō'aki Street, Waipahu, HI 96797. First edition, copyright 1976, fifteenth printing in 2004 (ISBN 0-89610-330-7). This work includes also a glossary of medical terms in Hawaiian.

Gutmanis, June. Na Pule Kahiko: Ancient Hawaiian Prayers. Drawings by Susanne Indich. An Editions Limited Book, P.O. Box 10150, Honolulu, HI 96816, 1983 (fourth printing, ISBN 0-9607938-6-0). Explanations and translations of native Hawai'ian prayers for a host of purposes. No mention, however, of Kaumuali'i's "Ane'ekapuahi" prayer, though "praying a person to death" is treated with a specific example of the prayer and the ritual (p. 27-8).

Handy, Willowdean Chatterson. Tattooing in the Marquesas. 2008 Dover Publications edition, Mineola, New York (ISBN 978-0-486-46612—5) from the original Bernice P. Bishop Museum Publication of 1922. Mentions Langsdorff's and Krusenstern's descriptions of tattoos from Nuku Hiva and elsewhere. See also Krutak and Kwiatkowski on tattoos.

Hartley, Janet M. Alexander I. Profiles in Power Series. Longman Group. London and New York. 1994. Here are the roles of Lord Castelreagh and George Canning as British Foreign Ministers in relations with Prince Clement Metternich in the chapter "Master of Europe: 1815-1825."

Haughton, Christine. Herb Profiles. Revised September 23, 2001. http://www.purplesage.org.uk/profiles. accessed April 11, 2002.

HAWAI"I...history of: For foreign ship contact see the list of "Ships to Hawaii Before 1819" at www.Hawaiian-roots.com/shipsB1880.htm. This is a very useful work, though not complete. See Howay (below). And, see these labors of love on Hawai'ian history: Daniel Harrington's http://www.hawaiianencyclopedia.com; and the new blogs: Peter T. Young's exciting and vital http://totakeresponsibility.blogspot.com/2012 and the related http://hookuleana.com; and the still unknown-to-me "Island Expat's" http://hawaiiantimemachine.blogspot.com/2011/.

Haycox, Stephen W. "Merchants and Diplomats: Russian America and the United States." In Russian America: The Forgotten Frontier. Barbara Sweetland Smith and Redmond J. Barnett, eds. Tacoma: The Washington State Historical Press. 1990. pp. 55-73.

Hellberg, Harry. Anders Ljungstedt och breven från Kina. Stalgarden Publishing House. Sweden. (undated...87 pp. 150 SEK, ISBN 91-87262-23-6). Hellberg, formerly Dean of Anders Ljungstedt College in Linköping, Sweden, is the author of this Swedish biography of Anders Ljungstedt. See Ljungstedt (below).

Helminger, Berhard. Mozart: His Life in Salzburg. Colorama. Salzburg. 2nd English edition of March 2002. An illustrated version of Mozart's life in Salzburg. Cf. portrait of Prince-bishop Hieronymus Graf von Colloredo, pp. 25 and entry under "1781."

Henry, Alexander (the Younger). (ca. 1765-1814) New Light on the Early History of the Greater Northwest: The Manuscript Journals of Alexander Henry and of David Thompson, 1799-1814. Elliot Coues, Ed. Ross and Haines. Minneapolis, MN. 1965, a republication of that by Francis P. Harper, New York, 1897. Three volumes, with three maps, 1027 pp. This is a treatment of interesting figures in the early fur trade. Also see: The Journal of Alexander Henry the Younger, 1799-1814. Barry Gough, Ed. Published by the Champlain Society and the University of Toronto Press. Toronto. 1988, and, about the interesting women (Jane Barnes, Isobell Gunn, and Anna Petrovna Bulygin) encountered by Henry, see the article by Alan Twigg for the BC Bookworld Author Bank at www.abcbookworld.com/?state=view_author&author_id=8484.

HERMAN, (Father or Elder, and later Saint, Herman of Alaska…1756-1837). The hermitic Father Herman (Elder Germann in the text), ministering on Kodiak Island and later at New Valaam on Spruce Island from 1794 on, opposed Manager Baranov and his policies because of perceived cruelty and exploitation of the Aleut population. On this see www.conciliarpress.com/again/content/view/55/31/9/9/ and also the explanation of an icon depicting Herman's activities at www.sspeterpaul.org/stherman.htm.

Hibberd, Isaac Norris. Sixteen Times Round Cape Horn: The Reminiscences of Captain Isaac Norris Hibberd. Foreword by Frederick H. Hibberd. Mystic Seaport Museum, Incorporated. Mystic, Connecticut. 1980. This is a valuable reminiscence of day to day details of life on a sailing ship going 'round the horn' in the later nineteenth century.

Hiroa, Te Rangi (Sir Peter H. Buck). Arts and Crafts of Hawaii. Bernice P. Bishop Museum Special Publication 45. Bishop Museum Press. Honolulu, HI. Copyright 1957. This is a classic treatment of Hawaiian arts and crafts with copious drawings and related historical anecdotes by a former (1936-1951) Director of the Bishop Museum. When it comes to pre-contact Hawaiian life and how things were done, what it doesn't have in it, you don't need. It's just amazingly comprehensive and detailed.

Hobbs, Christopher, L.Ac., A.H.G. Valerian and Other Anti-Hysterics in European and American Medicine (1733-1936). http://www.healthy.net/asp/templates/article.asp?PageType=Article&ID=961.

Ho'omāka'ika'i: Explorations! Compiled by the staff of the Kamehameha Schools Explorations Program (1968—summers). Fourth Edition. Kamehameha Publishing, 567 South King Street, Honolulu, HI 96813, 2007 (ISBN 978-0-87336-074-6). A wonderful illustrated textbook on the "foundations" of Hawai'ian culture.

Hopkins, Alberta Pualani. Ka Lei Ha'aheo: Beginning Hawaiian. University of Hawaii Press. Honolulu, Hawaii. 1992. This is a beginning Hawaiian language text.

Horwitz, Tony. Blue Latitudes: Boldly going Where Captain Cook Has Gone Before. Henry Holt and company. New York. 2002. This work provides most detailed descriptions of what it was like to sail long distances by sailing ship in the late 18th century. Horwitz describes a voyage on a replica of Captain James Cook's *Resolution.*

Howay, Frederic William, editor. The Voyage of the New Hazard, 1810-1813 (by Stephen Reynolds). Peabody Museum Publication, Salem, Mass., No. 49, pp. 148-9.

Howay, Frederic William. "The Last Days of the Atahualpa, Alias Bering," in The Forty-first Annual Report of the Hawaiian Historical Society for the Year 1932. Printshop Co., Honolulu, 1933, pp. 70-80.

Howay, Frederic William (Judge F.W. Howay, F.R.S.C., 1867-1943). "An Outline Sketch of the Maritime Fur Trade." Annual Meeting Presidential Address (see the entry below for information on the possible scholarly organizations to which Howay might have given a "presidential address"). Available at http://cha-shc.ca/bilingue/addresses/1932.htm.

Howay, Judge F. W., F.R.S.C. "A List of Trading Vessels in the Maritime Fur Trade, 1785-1794." Available at http://web.uvic.ca/~jlutz/courses/hist469/howay1.html. This work is also published posthumously with Richard Pierce as "A List of Trading Vessels in the Maritime Fur Trade, 1785-1794," Materials for the Study of Alaskan History, Limestone Press, Kingston, Ontario, 1973. Elsewhere online one can find Howay's expansion of the listing of ships to the year 1804, though this is not as complete. When you think you've done some historical digging and that the digging has gotten impressively comprehensive, then you encounter such work as this…the fruit of Howay's avocation for many years…and realize that you've only just begun. It is from this work, for example, that I discovered that "Alexander Stewart," the namesake of one of Kamehameha's sons, the one taken away by Captain Amasa Delano in 1801, was the master of the *Jackal* that had visited Hawai'i ten years before, when Kamehameha's son was ten years old. See also the essay on Howay entitled "Judge Howay—A Collector, the Student" at http://www.library.ubc.ca/spcoll/how_reid/howay.html. Another site for finding the whereabout of various ships in particular segments of time is www.Hawaiian-roots.com/shipsB1880.htm.

Hunsaker, Joyce Badgley. Sacagawea Speaks: Beyond the Shining Mountains with Lewis and Clark. A TwoDot Book of the Globe Pequot Press. P.O. Box 480 Guilford, Connecticut 06437. ISBN 1-58592-079-7. First edition/First printing. Copyright 2001. This is an edifying and valuable work on the "Corps of Discovery," treating Sacagewea's role from a first-person point of view. Much of the travel technology of the day is included, with specific illustrations…tea in cakes, sugar in cones, tobacco in braids and twists, the fire starter kit, the writing kit, the artist kit, the medical kit and its medicines, the muskets, including the calibers and the espontoon as a firing brace, the swivel-mounted blunderbuss and cannon. All of these things were part of George Schaeffer's life of travel also…as was the relationship between the Native and European American cultures.

Hunsche, Karl-Heinrich. Früheste Berichte über Schicksale deutscher Auswanderer nach Brasilien. Acht Todesurteile auf hoher see. Major von Schäffers "Seelenverkäuferey." Em: "Kalender fuer die Deutschen in Brasilien" (Rotermund-Kalender), 1937, p. 37 ss.

Hunsche, Karl-Heinrich. Major von Schäffers "Seelenverkäuferey." Eine "Unterthänigste Bittschrift" aus dem Jahre 1825. Em: "Kalender fuer die Deutschen in Brasilien" (Rotermund-Kalender), 1938, p. 38 ss.

Ii, John Papa. Fragments of Hawaiian History. Bishop Museum Press, 1525 Bernice Street, Honolulu, Hawaii. Copyright 1959. Sixth printing revised 1995. John Papa Ii was a personal witness to Hawaiian affairs since the time of Kamehameha I, having been attached to the Hawaiian royal household as a youth.

Iversen, Eve. The Romance of Nikolai Rezanov and Concepcion Arguello: A Literary Legend and its Effect of California History. Edited and with historical notes by Richard A. Pierce (see Pierce below). Alaska History No. 48. The Limestone Press. Kingston, Ontario and Fairbanks, Alaska. 1998.

James, Van. Ancient Sites of Kaua'i, Moloka'i and Lana'i. Mutual Publishing, 1215 Center Street, Suite 210, Honolulu, HI 96816. 2001. (ISBN 1-56647-529-5). A very concise work, with illustrations, photos, and sketched maps with the Hawaiian names.

James, Van. Ancient Sites of Hawai'i: Archaelogical Places of Interest on the Big Island. Mutual Publishing, 1215 Center Street, Suite 210, Honolulu, HI 96816. 1995. (ISBN 1-56647-200-8). An earlier volume in the series above...also one by James on O'ahu.

Joesting, Edward. Hawaii: An Uncommon History. W.W. Norton and Company, inc. New York. 1972. "Scheffer" is treated pages 60-64.

Joesting, Edward. Kauai: The Separate Kingdom. University of Hawaii Press and Kauai Museum Association, Ltd. Honolulu and Lihue, HI. 1984. A scholarly treatment, especially on King Kaumualii, with a fine bibliography.

Juliusspital. For information on the Juliusspital in Würzburg, Germany, consult: http://www.juliusspital.de. See below for "Würzburg" as well.

Kaeppler, Adrienne L. "Feather Cloaks, Ship Captains, and Lords." Occasional Papers of Bernice P. Bishop Museum. Vol. XXIV, No. 6 (July 8, 1970). Honolulu, HI. This is a treatment of the histories of notable particular feather cloaks, the 'ahu'ula of the Hawai'ian Ali'i, including the Kintore Cloak and the Elgin Cloak which wound up for a time in the hands of British lords. In this well illustrated monograph author Kaeppler states that "of the approximately 50 cloaks known today, 20 are still (1970, ostensibly) in the British isles."

Kaiser, Gloria. Dona Leopoldina: The Habsburg Empress of Brazil. Translated from the German by Lowell A. Bangerter with an Afterword by Ernestine Schlant. Ariadne Press. Riverside, California. 1998. The German work was published by Verlag Styria in Austria and Germany in 1994. The narrative is not chronological and incorporates dreams and hallucinations attributed to Dona Leopoldina as she is dying in 1826. The work is feminist in tone and elevates the role of Dona Leopoldina in establishing an independent Brazil over that of her husband, Dom Pedro I, who is portrayed quite negatively, especially as regards the issue of slavery. "Schäffer" is mentioned several times, but the description of him and his role in Leopoldina's life is seriously flawed (age, physical description, official position(s), apparent marital status and fidelity, personal wealth...all in error). Nevertheless, despite the lack of scholarly apparatus (e.g. no index), there is a great deal of useful detail about the lives of Dona Leopoldina and Dom Pedro I...and about European politics of the time...that can be gleaned from the "innovative" text here.

Kamakau, Samuel M. Ruling Chiefs of Hawaii (Revised edition). Kamehameha Schools Press. Honolulu, Hawaii. 1992 revision of the 1961 printing of this seminal history of the Hawaiian chiefs "from the time of 'Umi, eighteen generations before Kamehameha the Great, until the time of Kamehameha III in the 1840s" (when Kamakau wrote his original work).

Kamakau, Samuel Manaiakalani. Ka Po'e Kahiko: The People of Old. Translated from the Newspaper Ke Au 'Oko'a by Mary Kawena Pukui. Arranged and Edited by Dorothy B. Barrére. Illustrated by Joseph Feher. Bernice P. Bishop Museum Special Publication 51. Bishop Museum Press. Honolulu, HI. 1991. Tales of old Hawai'i by seminal historian Kamakau have good treatments of the family 'aumāku'a, medical practices and sorcery...e.g. "praying a person to death" and its consequences (cf. pp. 36-37 under "Kuni rituals").

Kame'eleihiwa, Lilikalā. Native Land and Foreign Desires: Pehea Lā E Pono Ai? (A History of Land Tenure Change in Hawai'i from Traditional Times until the 1848 Māhele, including an Analysis of Hawai'ian Ali'i Nui and American

Calvinists). Bishop Museum Press, Honolulu, HI. 2003 edition of 1992 copyright work (ISBN 0-930897-59-5). This is a very thoroughly researched and acute work on the concept of land ownership and its attribution in pre and post-contact times. Especially useful is the explanation of the Ali'i Nui's motivations, based on their endeavor to increase the "mana" of their place in the genealogy of rulers. The genealogies and the relationships of the Ali'i to the missionaries and their teaching are very detailed and insightful. This is a key work to understanding many philosophical and religious aspects of the European/Hawai'ian contact era.

KAMEHAMEHA I (The Great, (1758?-1819)), Sources here that touch on Kamehameha are many, but see: Adams, Barratt (3,4), Bartholomew, Birkett, Bolkhovitinob (1,2,3), Bushnell, Cahill, Charlot, Choris, Cordy (2,3), Crowe, Daws, Delano, Desha, Dorrance, Dukas (1,2), HAWAI'I, Ii, Joesting (1.2), Kamakau (1,2), Kane (2), Kotsebue, Kuykendahl, Levathes, Lundberg, Mahr, Malo, Mazour, Mehnert, Mills (2), Pierce (1,6), Pratt, Soboleski (1,2), Tregaskis, Warne (1,2), Wichman (2), Williams, Wisniewski, Withington.

Kane, Charlotte N. "Descendents of Kaumuali'i (1776-1824)" accessed in 2009 at http://familytreemaker.genealogy.com/users/k/a/n/Charlotte-Kane-HI/PDFGENE02.pdf.

Kane, Herb Kawainui. Voyagers: A Collection of Words and Images. WhaleSong, inc. (1-800-Whale-89). Bellevue, Washington. 1991. Kane, who has been elected a "Living Treasure of Hawaii," has read everything there is in print about Hawaiian-European contact history and gives his version of diverse aspects of it in this wonderful book. Prominent in this work is the treatment of the native Pacific sailing vessels and canoes. Schaeffer is not mentioned.

Kane, Herb Kawainui. Ancient Hawaii. The Kawainui Press. Captain Cook, Hawaii. 1997. A wonderfully illustrated, by Kane's art, relation of Hawaiian history and especially pre-contact customs. Kane is a resident of South Kona.

Kane, Herb Kawainui. Pele: Goddess of Hawaii's Volcanoes. The Kawainui Press. Captain Cook, Hawaii. Expanded edition, ninth printing, 2000. Here are stories and mythology associated with Pele. Kane includes some interesting personal experiences of a supernatural nature.

Karskens, Grace. The Rocks: Life in Early Sydney. Melbourne University Press. Carlton, Victoria. 1997. This is the definitive scholarly history of the "Rocks" area of Sydney. Author Karskens generally tries to refute or to explain away the stereotypic view of the Rocks as an uncivilized, wild and wooly place that preyed on visiting seamen. Nevertheless, the area's colorful history shines through, augmented by Karsken's very thorough scholarship. See also Messent's work below.

KAUA'I MUSEUM. There is an exhibit on "Russians on Kauai" at this museum, 4428 Rice Street, Lihue, HI 96766…see www.kauaimuseum.org (808-245-6931). Included is "Georg Anton Scheffer" with a concise but accurate recent rewriting of the information about him, including mention of the Russian balloon episode and the Brazilian emigration work. The only likeness of Schaeffer is represented by the oil painting there by Ardis Hertford, done in 1845, nine years after Schaeffer's death—meaning that it was done either from memory of a personal encounter (likely in his Brazil period) or by the description of others. It shows Schaeffer from the right side with bushy gray sideburns, beard and moustache. He is wearing a brown coat with medals and awards.

This is the Ardis Hertford portrait of Dr. "Georg Anton Schaffer" from 1845 that hangs in the Kaua'i Museum in Lihue, Hawaii. From: http://en.wikipedia.org/wiki/Georg_Anton_Schaffer.

The exhibit in the Kauai Museum discusses the lava rock "Russian Fort Elisabeth" at Waimea and shows pictures of it from 1890 after its cannon had been removed and with no surrounding vegetation but with a "pili" grass house atop its west battlement, and an aerial photo from the sea side done in 1924 showing encroaching trees and bushes on the Waimea River side. I have visited the "Russian Fort" many times in the past two decades. It is a pleasant spot, but is not maintained in accord with its historical significance, in my opinion. The place where Kaumuali'i, the last king of Kauai, last resided on the island, just outside the walls to the east of the fort, is now covered with bushes and cast-off rusted cars and appliances. There is no mention on the signage that this was the site where the 1824 rebellion against the Oahu Ali'i placed in control of Kauai by Kamehameha's successors…a rebellion of Kaua'ians led by Kaumualii's son,

George Kaumuali'i, was put down and George Kaumuali'i captured (see Warne below). The earthen Fort Alexander, now featured at the entrance to the Princeville resort above Hanalei, is mentioned, but the other earthen Fort built by Schaeffer and his men, Fort Barclay, once examined by archeologists in the 1950s, is now gone. My wife and son and I found the hump that was left of it in 2001 just across from the parking lot at the Hanalei Pier. It was on private land. We crossed a wire fence to walk around it and photograph it. The circular earthen hump, fifty yards across, had been filled in with mature trees and bushes. But by 2003 the site had been bulldozed flat and a house constructed at 4911 Weke Road where it had been since 1816. There has been too much of this kind of destruction of historical sites in Hawaii. The golf course cutting across the sacred "Holua" slide and the burial ground of those who died in the conflict to eliminate the ancient kapus in the Kailua-Kona area of the big island of Hawaii is an egregious example. Another is in Lahaina, Maui, where a baseball field now surmounts the sacred "Moku'ula" burial ground of the ruling Ali'i's remains. Kaumuali'i's remains were interred there until the later years of the 19th century when Moku'ula was trammeled. His remains were transported (by the order of Bernice Pauahi Bishop) to the Waiola Congregational Church cemetery on Wainee Street and Shaw Street in Lahaina, Maui (he has never been returned to Kauai, apparently because of his stated desire to be buried "at the feet of Keōpūolani"). He is there with Keōpūolani, Nahi'ena'ena and Liliha. The white obelisk tombstone records his death in "1825," though he died May 26, 1824, and the epitaph after his name reads only "Kaahumanu was his wife, 1822." See Joesting, Soboleski, Warne, and Zambucka...also Pierce.

KAUMUALI'I, last King of Kaua'I (c. 1780-26 May, 1824). See Kane (Charlotte), Joesting, Lydgate, Mills, Pierce, Soboleski, Warne, Zambucka, and others. Also: http://en.wikipedia.org/wiki/Kaumualii, which is well done.

My thought here is to interpose a mini-article on aspects of Kaumuali'i's genealogy and family. I should start with his mother, Kamakahelei. The website http://en.wikipedia.org/wiki/Kamakahelei states Kamakahelei was "the 22nd ruling chiefess (Ali'i Aimoku) of Kaua'i, reigning from 1770-1794 and that her powerful mana derived primarily from her being the daughter of Peleioholani, 22nd Ali'i Aimoku of O'ahu and 21st Ali'i Aimoku of Kaua'i. These facts are repeated in the site http://www.guide2womenleaders.com/USA_Sub_States.htm (a very significant historical site, in my opinion), which adds the statement that "her daughter Kawalu married her half-brother George Kaumualii, King of Kauai (1794-1810)." This essentially adds a daughter to the conventional list of Kamakahelei's children, an addition my own research agrees with.

This daughter Kawalu is not the only recent scholarly addition to Kamakahelei's family. The consensus of current sources is that Kamakahelei was born about 1755 and that she had, in her life, two marriages, first to O'ahu Prince Kaneoneo in approximately 1770, and then, circa 1777, to Mau'i Federation King Kahekili's half-brother

Ka'eokulani (Ka'eo). But I was present at the November 12, 2011 lecture by former Kauai'i Mayor Maryanne Kusaka (see, of course, http://www.kauaihistoricalsociety.org and also http://www.remaxkauai.com/bio_maryanne-kusaka.htm) entitled "Kamakahelei as a 'Woman of Achievement'. In this lecture, Maryanne Kusaka added a husband to Kamakahelei's conventional list, this being Ni'ihau Prince "Kina" (or "Kuina"), with whom Kamakahelei ostensibly had her first children. This explains to me some of the temporal discordances my own research has found in the ages of her listed children, and the paternity of son Keawe when all is sorted out. The data in the splendid and useful site http://www.royalark.net/Hawaii/Kauai.htm adheres to the conventional two husbands consensus, but has resultant flaws in its accounts of Kaumuali'i's siblings, wives, and children.

Heeding all my sources, including George Anton Schaeffer's relation, and agreeing with both the www.guide2womenleaders.com website and with Maryanne Kusaka (and disagreeing some with www.royalark.net), I would move Kamakahelei's birth year back to ca. 1750 and list her children (Kaumuali'i's siblings, half and whole) as:

1. Daughter Lelemahoalani (with Kina...ca. 1765)
2. Daughter Kapua'amohu (with Kina...ca. 1773)
3. Daughter Kawalu (with Kaneoneo...ca. 1776)
4. Son Keawe (with Kaneoneo...ca. 1777)
5. Son Kaumuali'i (with Ka'eo...ca. 1780)
6. Daughter Kapiolani (with Ka'eo...ca. 1783)
7. Daughter Kaininoa (Naoa) (with Ka'eo...ca. 1785).

This order allows for the temporal plausibility of Kamakahelei's assenting to the offer (see Kamakau on this) of Lelemahoalani as a sexual partner for Captain Cook in 1778 (though barely), and of the regency of Inamo'o. Also, we must note that Kaumuali'i's wives include three of his sisters: Kawalu, Kapua'amohu, and Kaininoa (Naoa). Several of these wives are in George Anton Schaeffer's relation of events, but not all. Nevertheless, compiling from all sources, I get these (in approximate order of marriage):

1. Kapua'amohu (K's half-sister, m. ca. 1796)
2. Namahana (m. ca. 1798)
3. Kawalu (K's half-sister) (m. 1799)
4. Kaininoa (Naoa) (K's full-sister) (m. 1801)
5. Monalau (m. ca. 1802)
6. Naluahi (m. ca. 1803)
7. Makua (m. ca. 1806)
8. Kekaiha'akulou (later Deborah Kapule) (m. 1809)
9. Ka'ahumanu (by abduction), (m. 1821)

The list of Kaumuali'i's children includes, but is likely not limited to:

1. Son Humehume (Prince George Humehume, b. 1798, died 3 May, 1825 (see Warne below), mother listed as an unknown 'commoner')
2. Daughter Kekaulike Kinoiki (b. 1799 to Kapua'amohu)
3. Son Kelia'iahonui (b. 17 August, 1800 to Kapua'amohu, died 23 June, 1849)
4. Daughter Kapiolani (from Naoa, b. ca. 1802)
5. Son Kahekili (from Namahana, b. ca. 1808)

From these children of Kaumuali'i are drawn several of the current succession claims (see, of course, http://en.wikipedia.org/wiki/Kaumualii). Hawai'i and Kaua'i icon, Prince Jonah Kuhio Kalanianole (26 March, 1871-7 January, 1922) was Kaumuali'i's great grandson through daughter Kinoiki's marriage to a Prince Kalanianole. Kaumuali'i's line also figures into the Kawananakoa claims of succession. On these claims see: http://www.royalark.net/Hawaii/hawaii10.htm   and http://en.wikipedia.org/wiki/Line_of_succession_to_the_former_Hawaiian_throne, and http://www.hawaiian-roots.com/chiefgen.htm. In addition, see the claim of Aleka Dayne Aipoalani, a "direct descendent of Kaumuali'i," to be the "Ali'i Nui of Modern Day Polynesia" at http://www.smokesignalsclothing.com/dayne-aipoalani.php.

This concludes my "mini-article" on Kaumuali'i's genealogy and family. ---Lee B. Croft.

Kendrick, John. Captain John Kendrick (1745-1794), together with Captain Robert Gray (1755-1806), were early traders on the northwest coast of America. Their ships, *Columbia* and its tender *Lady Washington*, later converted to a brig, made important journeys in the history of Pacific exploration and commerce. Gray in the *Columbia*, for example, discovered the river which now bears his ship's name. Kendrick was killed as a result of accidentally loaded salute fire from British ships at Pearl Harbor near Honolulu on December 7th, 1794 after involving himself in the battles between O'ahu's Chief Kalanikūpule and Kaumuali'i's   father,   Ka'eokulani.   See www.Ladywashington.net/historyhawaii.php which also cites Scofield, John (below). See also the entry on Robert Gray. See also Scott Ridley (below).

Keneally, Thomas. A Commonwealth of Thieves: The Improbable Birth of Australia. Nan A. Talese: Doubleday. New York, London, Toronto, Sydney, and Auckland. 2006. ISBN 978-0-385-51459-0.

Khlebnikov, K. T. Baranov: Chief Manager of the Russian Colonies in America. (Translated by Colin Bearne and edited by Richard A. Pierce). The

Limestone Press. Kingston, Ontario, Canada. 1973. Kiril Timofeevich Khlebnikov (1776-1838) was a long-time employee of the RAK who, after 1817, helped assess Baranov's role in the development of Russian America. His relation of Baranov's life and career is the real key to all further work (e.g. Chevigny's biography and others), and the annotations and other scholarly work by Richard Pierce (see also below) make this a most valuable work. Kiril Khlebnikov's reports (1817-1832) on "Colonial Russian America" are included here also under Dmytryshyn, Basil and E.A.P. Crownhart-Vaughan...see above.

Klieger, P. Christiaan. Moku'ula: Maui's Sacred Island. Bishop Museum Press. Honolulu, Hawaii. 1998. This is a treatment of the island of Moku'ula in the fishpond of Loko o Mokuhinia—currently a Lahaina, Maui, public baseball field—which was a Hawaiian sacred site from which Kamehameha III ruled Hawaii in the first days of its royalty period. Several prominent Ali'i were interred, either originally or subsequently, in Moku'ula, including Keopuolani, Nahienaena, and Kaumualii, before their remains were transferred in the 1880s to the Wainee (now Waiola) churchyard in Lahaina by the Bishop estate. See also Chapman (above) on Ala Mauna...sacred burial place in Honolulu on O'ahu.

Kochetkova, Natalya. Nikolay Karamzin. Twayne Publishers World Authors Series (G.K. Hall and Co.). Boston. 1975. This is a concise biography of Karamzin...the best one in English for details of his family life. Best on this, however, is Lotman (below).

Komissarov, Boris Nikolaevich (B. N.) Grigorii Ivanovich Langsdorf, 1774-1852. Izdatel'stvo "Nauka," Leningradskoe otdelenie, Leningrad, 1975, 124 pp. with portrait frontispiece. This is the biography of Dr. Georg Heinrich von Langsdorff (see Langsdorff below). It has a useful chronology of Langsdorff's interesting life, and mentions family detail in text.

Kootz, Wolfgang (text) with photography by Willi Sauer, Ulrich Strauch and others. Frankfurt: An Illustrated Guide to the Metropolis on the Main. Kraichgau Verlag. Ubstadt-Weiher, Germany. 2001. This guidebook to Frankfurt has a table of dates on the history of Frankfurt and its surrounding area.

Kopp, Sebastian. Die Augustinerkirche in Münnerstadt. Karl Robert Langewiesche Verlag. Königstein. Undated. A pictorial treatment of the Augustine Church in Münnerstadt, site of one of the city's church schools founded before Schaeffer's time.

Kotzebue (Kotsebue), Otto von (Russian Sea Captain, born Dec. 30, 1787 in Revel (Tallin), Estonia, died also there Feb. 15, 1846). A Voyage of Discovery, 1815-1818, on the ship Rurick. Longman, Hurst, Rees, Orme and Brown. London. 1821 (also published by Da Capo Publishers, New York, 1967).

Kotzebue captained the Russian navy brig *Riurik* on world explorations from 1815-1818, including Hawai'i. He and his father, author, anti-Napoleon journalist (e.g. Die Biene and Die Grille) and diplomat August Friedrich Ferdinand von Kotzebue (5/3/1761-3/23/1819, stabbed to death in Mannheim by Karl Ludwig Sand who was executed, becoming a martyr for the cause of German nationalism). See the biographic entries on both father and son at www.en.wikipedia.org. See also entries on the *Rurik's* artist, Ludwig Choris (1795-1828), famous for his likeness of Kamehameha, and its noted author of Peter Schlemihl (1813) and scientist, Adelbert von Chamisso (1/30-1781-8/21/1838). On Chamisso see Niklaus R. Schweizer (below).

Krauss, Michael E. "Alaska Native Languages in Russian America." In Russian America: The Forgotten Frontier. Barbara Sweetland Smith and Redmond J. Barnett, eds. Tacoma: The Washington State Historical Press. 1990. pp. 205-215.

Krusenstern, Adam J. von (in Russian this is Ivan Fedorovich Kruzenshtern). Voyage Round the World in the years 1803, 1804, 1805, and 1806. Volumes 1 and 2. A republication of the English version of the original travel log of Captain Kruzenshtern of the *Nadezhda* originally published for John Murray in London in 1813. Now by The Gregg Press. Ridgewood, New Jersey. 1968. The scholarship available on this, the first Russian circumnavigation by the *Nadezhda* and the *Neva*, is unusually complete and offers diverse views, useful since the crews were badly factionalized by authority dispute and this colored the versions available. See Kruzenshtern, Lisianskii, Langsdorff and Löwenstern's contemporary views and the scholarship of Barratt, Becher, Chevigny, Iversen, and Pierce which include also parts of letters from Shemelin and Rezanov.

Krutak, Lars. "St. Lawrence Island Joint-Tattooing: Spiritual/Medicinal Functions and Intercontinental Possibilities." In Etudes/Inuit/Studies. 23 (1-2), 1999, pp.229-252. Krutak is a well published authority on native tattooing among the tribes with which Alexander Baranov had to deal: Yupiget, Aleut, Eskimo, Inuit, Kenaitze, Tlingit, and others. Baranov was given a captive Inuit girl as a gift by an Eskimo chief in the 1790's, and his wife, Anna Grigorievna, was from the woman-tattooing Kenaitze tribe.

Krutak, Lars. "Chapter 19: The Arctic." In A Source Book: Tattoo History. Edited and Introduced by Steve Gilbert with the collaboration of Cheralea Gilbert. Juno Books. New York. 2000. The methods and manners of native tattoo patterns are detailed in this work by a leading anthropological scholar of tattooing. See also Handy and Kwiatkowski on tattoos.

Krutak, Lars. "Many Stitches for Life: Traditional Tattooing on St. Lawrence Island (Sivuqaq), Alaska." In Skin and Ink, July 2001, pp. 37-43.

Kulagin, R. A. <u>Borodino v vospominaniiakh sovremennikov.</u> Izdatel'stvo "Skarabei." Sankt Peterburg. 2001. This work has appendices detailing the composition of both French and Russian armies at Borodino. The memoirs clarify many details of the battle. If one types "Battle of Borodino" into the Google search field, the first site seen will be the "Virtual Battle of Borodino" by Brett Nolan, Shawn Murphy, and Natasha Sopevia, done in 1996 for a Hamilton College Computer Sciences Seminar project for Prof. Frank Sciaca of the Hamilton College Russian Studies Department. This site is a marvel, with associated music, art, Tolstoy's text from <u>War and Peace</u>, and streaming video from the 1968 Russian version (Directed by and starring Sergei Bondarchuk) of the film, <u>War and Peace.</u> The site lets one follow either Napoleon or Kutuzov through the battle. See also Duffy and Ezerskaya above.

Kuykendall, Ralph S. <u>The Hawaiian Kingdom: 1778-1854.</u> 3 Vol., University of Hawaii Press. Honolulu, HI. 1938 but since reprinted at least five times. 462 pp. This is a fine work that is wonderful to read because it cites original logs and memoirs in the language as originally written.

Kwiatkowski, P. F. <u>The Hawaiian Tattoo.</u> Illustrated by Tom O'o Mehau. Halona, Inc. of Kohala, HI, 1996. (ISBN 0-9655756-0-8). This work is a bit rough (spelling and inclusion of a "Forward" (sic)), but is a good treatment of the unique aspects of Hawai'ian tattoos, both ancient and modern.

Langsdorff, George H. von. <u>Voyages and Travels in Various Parts of the World During the Years 1803, 1804, 1805, 1806, and 1807.</u> Volumes 1 and 2. (A facsimile of the English version printed for Henry Colburn in London in 1813) The Gregg Press. Ridgewood, New Jersey. 1968. This is a memoir truly wonderful to read. Langsdorff even includes musical notation to describe native songs from Nuku Hiva in the Marquesas. He makes no mention of the pranks of Count F. I. Tolstoi nor of his monkey (see Lowenstern and Rezanov below), but includes the amazing story of Frenchman Jean Baptiste Cabri (see the plate, pp. 96 of Volume 1, showing Cabri with his tattooing). Both Langsdorff and Lisiansii, in their memoirs describing the Marquesans and Hawaiians, marveled at their swimming ability and Lisianskii records timing one native's underwater dive at four minutes. Langsdorff lists the physical measurements of a Marquesan native, also an impressive swimmer and diver, named "Mufau" who, at "6 feet 2 inches high, Paris measure" caused Dr. Tilesius to remark that he had "never seen anyone so perfectly proportioned." Later a comparison of the measurements was made to the Apollo of Belvedere, one of the foremost masterpieces of Grecian art…and the measurements exactly coincided (pp. 109 of Vol. 1). Langsdorff writes that they were told of a neighboring island chieftain named Upoa who was of the same proportions as Mufau, but "a head taller…nearly seven Paris feet high."

Langsdorff, Georg Heinrich von. <u>Remarks and Observations on a Voyage Around the World From 1803 to 1807.</u> Vol. 1 "The Voyage From Copenhagen to Brazil, the South Sea, Kamtschatka and Japan; and Vol. 2 "The Voyage From Kamtschatka to the Island of St. Paul, Unalaska, Kodiak, Sitcha, New Albion, Kamtschatka, Ochotsk and Through Siberia to St. Petersburg." Translated and annotated by Victoria Joan Moessner. Edited by Richard A. Pierce. The Limestone Press. Kingston, Ontario and Fairbanks, Alaska. (Alaska History No. 41) 1993. This is a "new" and more accurate translation of the original text from the German with detailed notes and appendices, including one listing the original subscribers to Dr. Langsdorff's 1813 edition (see below for English facsimile edition in two volumes).

Langsdorff, Georg Heinrich von (Georg Heinrich/Grigorii Ivanovich Langsdorf (1774-1852). Materialen der Brasilien-Expedition 1821-1829 des Akademiemitgliedes Georg Heinrich Freiherr von Langsdorff: Vollständige Wissenschaftliche Bescchreibung. D. E. Berthels, B. N. Komissarov, and T. I. Lysenko, editors and compilers. Verlag Dietrich Reimer. Berlin. 1979. This work, also published by "Nauka" ("Science") Publishers in Leningrad in 1973, is a compilation of Langsdorff's reports to Russian Foreign Minister Karl Vasilievich Nesselrode concerning the findings of his Russian-government-funded (40,000 rubles plus 10,000 per year) naturalists' expedition to the Brazilian Amazon. For a biography of Langsdorff, see Komissarov above.

Langsdorff, Georg Heinrich von. Bemerkungen über Brasilien. Mit gewissenhafter Belehrung für auswandernde Deutsche. Verlag Karl Groos, Heidelberg, 1821. This work, cited by Oberacker (see below) evidences already by 1821 an awareness by Langsdorff, designated Russian Consul to Rio de Janeiro, that Post-Napoleonic Germans wanted to leave Germany and might be considering coming to Brazil. Ostensibly he wrote this and published it in Heidelberg after seeing George Anton Schaeffer in Rio de Janeiro in January of 1821 arriving with his family group from Germany looking to establish a plantation "colony." Langsdorff was on his way to St. Petersburg to gain financial support from Tsar Alexander I through the St. Petersburg Academy of Sciences to fund a more comprehensive expedition of prominent scientists to the Amazon. As a consequence of his persisting in the planning of this expedition (after his earlier, 1816-17 expedition-related "insanity"), his wife Friederike left him and remained in Europe with his two children. (See Komissarov above). See http://en.wikipedia.org/wiki/Grigory_Langsdorff, where a 24 February, 2010, study by Francisco Albuquerque is cited to state that "Langsdorff has 1,500 descendants in Brazil, among them the most famous is Luma de Oliveira, a Brazilian carnival queen."

LAPEROUSE, Jean-Francoise de Galaup de (1741-1787). Laperouse was an early French voyager who visited Mau'i for one day (29-30 May, 1786) with two ships, the 500-600-ton *Boussole* and *L'Astrolabe* (Captain Paul-Antoine-Marie Fleuriot de Langle). A Bay on the south shore of Mau'i is named for him. Later he discovered and named Necker Island after a French Minister of Finance. He and his ships were lost in the Solomons in 1787, though his memoirs were mailed before this and survive. His ships crossed paths off Mau'i in the Hawai'ian islands with the two British ships, the *King George* and *Queen Charlotte* (at Kealakekua Bay on Hawai'i 24 May, and O'ahu 28 May, 1786), under the command of Captain Nathanial Portlock, but did not sight each other. See http://pages.quicksilver.net.nz/jcr/~lap3. Also, one of the possible explanations for the presence on Nuku Hiva of Jean Cabri (see Chapter Nine: Barbara in St. Petersburg) is that Cabri (who claimed to have known young Napoleon Bonaparte, who also applied (but unsuccessfully) to participate in the Laperouse expedition) was a sailor on the *Boussole* who left the ship in Nuku Hiva.

LAZAREV, MIKHAIL PETROVICH (Nov. 3, 1788-either April 11 or May 10, 1851, depending on source). M. P. Lazarev (also spelled Lazareff in non-Russian sources) was one of three brothers, all of whom became prominent in the Russian Navy. From 1804 to 1808, Lazarev served in the British Navy to enhance his career, learning English as he did so. He captained the *Suvorov* on its circumnavigation of the globe in 1813-6, clashing with Governor Aleksander Baranov and with Russian-American Company representatives on his ship, including George Anton Schaeffer. He faced a naval board of inquiry when he returned to St. Petersburg in July 1816 without Dr. Schaeffer and RAK supercargo Molvo, and had to answer the complaints of the latter as well as those of Governor Baranov. But the naval board acquitted him of the charges against him and he went on to other important captaincies in exploring the Pacific and in Russia's subsequent naval campaigns. His name has been given to many public places in Russia, including, for example, one of the Neva embankments in St. Petersburg. According to www.philately.com/philately/biolala.htm, three Russian postage stamps have been issued with his likeness on them. He is reported to have died of unknown causes in Vienna, but www.findagrave.com reports that he is buried in Baykova Cemetery in Kiev, Ukraine…even showing the grave stone and its damage from WWII. Other sources, including www.sailingnavies.com state that he is interred in the crypt of St. Vladimir's Cathedral in Sevastopol. Some of Lazarev's journal from the 1813-6 circumnavigation are published in Samarov (below). Online biographical information is at www.navy.ru/history/hrn7-e.htm and at www.explore-biography.com/biographies/M/Mikhail_Petrovich_Lazarev. For a likeness, see Barratt, Glynn...Russia in Pacific Waters (above).

Lee, Blanche Kaualua Lolokukalani. Don Francisco de Paula Marin: The Unforgettable Spaniard Who Gave Hawaii the First Pineapple. Illustrated by Joseph Feher. Copyright by Banche Kaualua L. Lee. 2002. ISBN 1-052-027. Printed by Best Printing. Honolulu. Purchased at the Bishop Museum store, Honolulu, June 2005. This work has good family information about Don Marin as well as information about his residence in Honololu's "Kapu'ukolo" or waterfront area known as "America." See Gast (above) for an earlier and more conventional biography wherein Gast maintains that Marin was not the first to grow pineapples in Hawai'i. See also Ten Bruggencate (below).

Leichter als Luft: Zur Geschichte der Ballonfahrt. (compilers Bernard Korzus and Burkhard Leismann) Westfalisches Landesmuseum fur Kunst und Kulturgeschichte Munster Landschaftsverband Westfalen-Lippe. 1978. An Anthology of long, heavily illustrated articles by diverse authors on the history of ballooning...most relevant is that of Walter Locher, "Militarische Verwendung des Ballons," pp. 237-251. This book is a goldmine of illustrations of early balloon ascents and even inflation process and includes the most comprehensive time-table of early ascents...cf. "Zeittafel" pp. 284-291 (1670-1978 prominent ascents)". For online illustrations of the early balloon ascents, including one showing the "Ascent at Moorfields of Vincent Lunardi," having prototype "rotary wings" like those in Franz Leppich's later design, see: http://marinni.livejournal.com/501633.html?thread=5614977. This site also has a bawdy illustration of "love in the air."

Levathes, Louise E. "Kamehameha: Hawaii's Warrior King." Photographs by Steve Raymer and paintings by Herb Kawainui Kane. In National Geographic. Vol. 164, No. 5 (November 1983), pp. 558-599. This is such a fine article, and so well illustrated and accompanied by the National Geographic's high quality annotated map of the Hawaiian Islands, that it is definitely a "must read" for anyone interested in Kamehameha or Hawaiian history.

Lieven, Dominic. Review of V. M. Bezotosnyi, et. al. Otechestvennaia voina 1812 goda: Entsiklopediia (The Great Patriotic War of 1812: An Encyclopedia) (see above) in Kritika: Explorations in Russian and Eurasian History. 7, 1 (Winter 2006), pp. 133-135.

Lili'uokalani. Hawaii's Story by Hawaii's Queen. (intro. by Glen Grant). Mutual Publishing. Honolulu, Hawaii. 1990. Interesting here is Lili'uokalani's early discussion of her adoptive family upbringing as a Hawaiian "Ali'i."

OGIZ: gosudarstvennoe isdatel'stvo geografischeskoi literatury. Moskva. 1947. This is the republication of Captain Yurii Fedorovich Lisiansky's travel log, originally published in St. Petersburg in 1812.

Lisiansky, Urey (Iurii or Yurii...same as above). Voyage Round the World in the years 1803, 1804, 1805, and 1806. This, #42 in the Bibliotheca Australiana series, is a republication of the English version of Captain Lisianskii's (see source above) travel log from the Neva, which was published for John Booth in London in 1814. Now by Da Capo Press (a Division of Plenum Publishing Corp.). 227 West 17th St. New York. 1968.

Littke, Peter. Russian-American Bibliography: An English Guide to Literature About the History of Russian-America (1741-1867) (with a special emphasis on Russian and other non-English publications. Littlestone, UK, copyright Peter Littke, 2003. (ISBN 3-8330-0705-2) This work, dedicated "in admiration of the lifetime work of Professor Dr. Richard A. Pierce, Kingston, Ontario, Canada" (see Pierce below) was shown to me by U-Hawaii-Manoa's Hamilton Librarian Patricia Polansky, a most able Slavic bibliographer. On the back cover of Littke's work is mention of:

Littke, Peter. <u>Vom Sarenadler sum Sternenbanner: Die Geschichte Russisch-Alaska"</u> ("From the Czar's Eagle to the Stars and Stripes—the History of Russian Alaska"). Magnus Verlag, Essen, Germany, 2003 (ISBN 3-88400-019-5). I have not seen this. Peter Littke is at Peter@irah.org.

Littke, Peter. "Benedict Cramer (Venedikt Kramer), Director of the Russian-American Company" posted on www.IRAH.org in May 2003, accessed August 2008.

Ljungstedt, Anders (Sir) (1759-1835). <u>An Historical Sketch of the Portuguese Settlements in China and of the Roman Catholic Church and Mission in China & Description of the City of Canton.</u> Viking Hong Kong Publications. Hong Kong. 1992 (xvi + 280 pp, 3 maps, 200 HKD, ISBN 962-7650-01-3). Preface by Father Manual Teixeira, leading Macau historian. This is the republication of Ljungstedt's historical work on Macau, Canton, and the East India Trade, originally published in Boston in 1836. The fact that Ljungstedt was writing such a "sketch" was mentioned by George Schaeffer in his own notes, which commend Ljungstedt's work. Schaeffer stayed with Ljungstedt in Macau in 1817, appointing him China representative of the Russian-American Company. See also Hellberg (above) and http://runeberg.org/authors/ljungand.html and www.HawaiiHistory.com to "Russians in Hawai'i" wherein Ljungstedt is mentioned, as well as Peter Dobell.

Lotman, Yurii M. <u>Karamzin.</u> "Issskustvo-SPB." Sankt-Peterburg. 1997. This is a wonderfully detailed and insightful biographic work on Nikolai M. Karamzin and his times. It is divided into three parts: Karamzin's biography, treatments of his articles and researches, and discussion of his observations and reviews. The citations on F.V. Rostopchin are interesting...on pp. 178-80 is mention of Karamzin's visit to England in 1790, and of his encounter there, in the group of Russian Ambassador to England S. R. Vorontsov, with Fyodor V. Rostopchin, later Governor-General of Moscow during Napoleon's invasion. Rostopchin got lessons in boxing from "renowned boxer 'Rein' (likely Benjamin Brain...cf. Roberts and Skutt, below)," discovering the hard way that "battle with the fists involves the same degree of science as battle with rapiers." Lotman, a seminal scholar of both literary and linguistic semiotics, has a similarly detailed biography of Pushkin, but I have used the Binyon biography, which credits Lotman, more.

Löwenstern, Hermann Ludwig von. <u>The First Russian Voyage Around the World: The Journal of Hermann Ludwig von Löwenstern (1803-1806).</u> Translated by Victoria Joan Moessner. University of Alaska Press. Fairbanks,

AK. 2003. This is the diary of a member of the crew of Captain Kruzenshtern's *Nadezhda*. The account is more personal than that of Kruzenshtern or of Dr. Langsdorff, revealing more about the dissension aboard. The episode of Count Fyodor Tolstoy's monkey is related on pp. 106-7...see also Rezanov below.

Lucas, Lois. Plants of Old Hawaii. With Illustrations by Joan Fleming and Poems by Julie Williams. Bess Press, 3565 Harding Avenue, Honolulu, HI 96816. See www.besspress.com. 1982, ISBN 0-935848-11-8. 112 pp. This is an elementary treatment (English and Hawaiian Name; Poem about; Habitat; Description; Native Uses; Labeled Drawing) on each of the twenty plants brought by the Polynesian emigrants to Hawaii circa 450 AD, providing a guide to the plants in Hawai'i at the time of European contact (Arrowroot, Awa, Bamboo, Banana, Breadfruit, Candlenut, Coconut, Bottle Gourd, Hau, Indian Mulberry, True Kou, Milo, Mountain Apple, Paper Mulberry, Sugar Cane, Sweet Potato, Taro, Ti, Turmeric, and Yam).

Luebke, Frederick C. Germans in Brazil: A Comparative History of Cultural Conflict During World War I. Louisiana State University Press. Baton Rouge, LA and London. 1987. Chapter one on "A Century of German Settlement I Brazil: A Survey, 1818-1918" (pp. 7-35) mentions the activities of "Major Georg Schaffer" on pp. 8 and cites Brazilian sources from Porto Alegre.

Lundberg, Murray. "The Russian-American Company in Hawaii." Available at www.explorenorth.com/library/yafeatures/bl-RussAmCo.htm.

Lundy, Derek. The Way of a Ship: A Square-Rigger Voyage in the Last Days of Sail. First published by Knopf Canada in 2002, but now by HarperCollins Publishers Inc., 10 East 53rd Street, New York, NY 10022 (ISBN 0-06-621012-7). 2004. The idea of reading this book was to familiarize myself with life aboard a square-rigged ship in the age of sail. But I found the "Prologue," explaining author Lundy's personal connection to his character, part real relative and part fictional persona, both moving and inspirational. As to method, Lundy quotes Robert Foulke to say: "Usually (in historical and literary voyage narratives like The Odyssey and its descendents in Foulke's The Sea Voyage Narrative) no clear demarcation exists between fact and fiction, experience and imagination." He continues to describe his own method (and mine) "So a different kind of book, then: take the fragments of what I know about Benjamin, and the great deal that's known about square-riggers and life aboard them in his time and create a voyage. It will be typical in its incidents, suffering and accomplishment. Its officers and crew will be representative seamen of that time and of those ships. The ship itself: an imaginary one, the *Beara Head*—a name of an Irish promontory—but an actual sister to the big iron Cape Horners in all other respects. I will imagine the tale of Benjamin's voyage; not the voyage itself—that's unrecoverable—but as it might have been and emphatically, could have been."

Lydgate, Rev. John M. "Kaumuali'i: the Last King of Kaua'i," in Hawaiian Historical Society 24th Annual Report for the Year 1915 (1916), pp. 21-43.

Lyons, Jeffrey K. "Memoirs of Henry Obookiah: A Rhetorical History," in The Hawaiian Journal of History (A Publication of the Hawaiian Historical Society), Vol. XXXVIII (2004), pp. 35-57.

MACQUARIE, LACHLAN (1761-1824, Governor of New South Wales, Australia, 1810-1821). Macquarie is a large figure in Australian history and there are many biographical treatments. A concise treatment may be found on the internet at www.lib.mq.edu.au/lmr/biography.html. Schaeffer met Macquarie in Sydney during the August-September 1814 visit of the *Suvorov*.

Madsen, Axel. John Jacob Astor: America's First Multimillionaire. John Wiley & Sons. New York. 2001 (vii + 312 pp, ISBN 0-471-38503-4). See also the e-review of this work by Ann Harper Fender at http://www.eh.net/bookreviews/library/0392.shtml. In her review, Ann Fender points out that author Madsen "joins a long list of John Jacob Astor biographers." She also mentions that Astor's friend, noted American author Washington Irving, together with his brother Pierre (see Franchere, Gabriel, above), penned a "chronicle of Astoria, the failed venture on the Pacific coast that was published in 1836 as Astoria: Adventure in the Pacific Northwest." Astor was a major figure in the fur trade involving Governor Baranov and others, but my major investigation here concerns the character of John Marshall, who told George Schaeffer he was Astor's "nephew who had come to America from Germany with him" and was shipwrecked in Hawai'i on Astor's trading ship *Lark*. It is known that Astor did not come directly from Germany to America, but resided for some time in England, where he made contacts later important to him. So I was surveying the biographies of Astor for some mention of the name Marshall in order to establish the credibility of John Marshall's claim. The first place that the name turned up was in the work of Fritz Springmeier (real name Victor Earl Schoof, born in Garden City, Kansas, on Sept. 24, 1955 and currently resident in an Oregon prison). When you think you have been exposed to every kookball aspect of our culture's psychopathology (most, including this, drug induced, in my opinion), check out: www.thewatcherfiles.com/astor.htm or www.theforbiddenknowledge.com/hardtruth/the_astor_bloodline.htm or www.whale.to/b/sp/blood.htm for Springmeier's rambling indictment of "The Astor Bloodline" as "illuminati" in control of our economic/political realities. See also the article "Fritz Springmeier—Another Human Tragedy" by John Torell at www.eaec.org for the section entitled "Who is Fritz Springmeier?" This includes input by one of Springmeier's wives. Also interesting is the related material at www.sleazereport.com. Some people think that research is boring…nay!

272

Mahr, August C. The Visit of the *Rurik* to San Francisco in 1816. Stanford University Publications, University Series on History, Economics and Political Science, No. II:2, Stanford, Ca., 1932. This work contains extracts from the works, originally in German, of poet and scientist Adelbert von Chamisso (1781-1838), the artist Ludwig Choris (1795-1828) who were with Captain Otto A. von Kotzebue (Kotsebue, 1787-1846) on the *Rurik* when it visited Hawai'i in 1816.

Malo, David. Hawaiian Antiquities (Moolelo Hawaii). Bernice P. Bishop Museum Special Publication 2, Second edition (translated from the Hawaiian in 1898 by Dr. Nathaniel B. Emerson). Copyright 1951 by Bishop Museum, 1525 Bernice Street, Honolulu, Hawaii 96817. 7th reprinting 1997. This is a relation of Hawaiian history and customs by native Hawaiian David Malo (ca. 1793-1853), a long-time Lahaina, Maui, school agent.

MARIN, Don Francisco de Paula (Manini). See Conrad, Agnes C. (Letters and Journal), Gast, Ross H. (Biography), Lee, Blanche Kaualua Lolokukalani (family biographical treatment), and Ten Bruggencate, Jan K. (Introduction of Pineapple to Hawai'i).

Marion, Fulgence. Wonderful Balloon Ascents: or, The Conquest of the Skies. This is an "E-book" at http://www.bookrags.com/books/wonba/PART16.htm accessed January 15, 2002.

Massey, Raymond (with Editors Jean McGarry and Zelda Feldman). Discovery of Hawaii and Honolulu Harbor. Copyright 2009 by Raymond Massey, ISBN 978-1-60725-967-1. This is a self-published work featuring the art of prominent maritime artist Raymond Massey, whose historical acumen is here strikingly revealed. See my review at www.shvoong.com/books/historical-novel/1975654-discovery-hawaii-honolulu-harbor/. Relative to events related in this book is a fine treatment of the native Battle of Punahawale for control of Oahu in 1794, involving Kae'o and Kalanikupule and mentioning Mare Amara (pp. 96). Well related also are the deaths of Captains (John) Kendrick and (William) Brown. The bibliography is one of the best and is highly recommended. Massey's book may be ordered through www.masseymarineart.com or through Kapa'a, Kauai's SHIPSTORE GALLERY at www.shipstoregalleries.net. See also the novel by Scott Ridley.

MAU'I Historical Walking Guide. Joan D'A McKelvey, Publisher. Anaka Productions, 537 Kai Hele Ku St., Lahaina, Maui, Hawaii 96761. This pamphlet features maps, photos, and stories of Lahaina and Ka'anapali. It is published three times per year and distributed to tourists in the Lahaina/Ka'anapali area by resorts, hotels, and the Lahaina Center of the Lahaina Restoration Foundation. Volume V, Issue 1 is in Spring/Summer of 2003.

Mazour, Anatole G. "Doctor Yegor Scheffer: Dreamer of a Russian Empire in the Pacific." in Pacific Historical Review. No. 6 (March 1937). pp. 15-20.

McBride, Likeke R. Petroglyphs of Hawai'i. Second Revised Edition of 2004. Copyright by Andrew S. McBride from original Petroglyph Press edition of 1969 by his father who died in 1993. Petroglyph Press, Ltd. 160 Kamehameha Avenue, Hilo, HI 96720 (ISBN 0-912180-60-9). This is an illustrated treatment of the Petroglyphs on the big island of Hawai'i.

McClellan, Edwin North. "John M. Gamble," in the Thirty-fifth Annual Report of the Hawaiian Historical Society for the Year 1926. Honolulu Advertiser Publishing Co., Honolulu, 1927, pp. 44-58.

McDougal, Walter A. Let the Sea Make a Noise: four Hundred Years of Cataclysm, Conquest, War and folly in the North Pacific. Avon Books. New York. 1994. McDougal conjectures a colloquy involving diverse North Pacific historical characters, including Kaahumanu, Hirosi Saito, William Seward, and Sergey Witte, concerning conflicting colonial aspirations.

McRae, Robert J. "Ritter, Johann Wilhelm." in Dictionary of Scientific Biography. Charles Coulston Gillespie, Editor-in-Chief. Charles Scribner's Sons. New York. 1975. Vol. XI (of XV volumes and two supplemental volumes). pp. 473-5.

Mehnert, Klaus. "The Russians in Hawaii, 1804-1819." University of Hawaii Occasional Paper No. 38. University of Hawaii Bulletin, Vol. 18, No 6 (April 1939), pp. 6-9.

Mellen, Kathleen Dickenson. The Magnificent Matriarch: Kaahumanu, Queen of Hawaii. Hastings House. New York. 1952.

Melville, Herman. Moby-Dick. Edited and with introduction by Charles Child Walcutt. Bantam Books. This is the 1967 version of the 1851 original with a sampling of contemporary reviews, six modern essays, and a bibliography. Melville's depiction of 19th century sailors informs this account...in particular his definition of "Gam" on pp. 227.

Messent, David. The Rocks. ("Sydney's Birthplace"). David Messent Photography. Sydney, Australia. (telephone Sydney 971 5970). National Library of Australia ISBN 0 64623025 5. An illustrated characterization of the "Rocks" district of Sydney, including the time when Schaeffer was there while on the Suvorov. This work is a picture book for tourists, though it depicts the area's colorful history well. A more scholarly work is that of Karskens (above).

274

Mikaberidze, Alexander. "Reader's Articles: Politics and Government: Franco-Turkish Relationship..." cf. www.NapoleonSeries.org, parts I and II from November, 2000.

Mikaberidze, Alexander. "The Mutiny of the Generals" (in 11 parts with bibliography). cf. www.napoleon-series.org/military/battles/c_mutiny3.html from September 2001. Mikaberidze, the "Chairman of the Napoleonic Society of Georgia," is certainly a great master of detail and provides the most recent historical treatment of military aspects of Napoleon's campaign in Russia in 1812, being in complete command of all earlier sources. Note the frequent citation on http://www.napoleonistyka.atspace.com/Borodino_battle.htm. Recent English-language books by Alexander Mikaberidze include: The Battle of Borodino: Napoleon Against Kutuzov, and The Battle of the Berezina: Napoleon's Great Escape.

Mills, Peter R. "A New View of Kaua'i as 'The Separate Kingdom' after 1810" in The Hawaiian Journal of History (A Publication of the Hawaiian Historical Society), Vol. XXX (1996), pp. 91-104. In this article Mills contends with points made in Edward Joesting's Kaua'i: The Separate Kingdom about Kaumuali'i and the building of the "Russian Fort" at Waimea. An important point argued therein is that Kaumuali'i had already evidenced non-compliance with his 1810 agreement to function as a tributary chief subordinate to Kamehameha before George Schaeffer's arrival in 1816.

Mills, Peter R. Hawai'i's Russian Adventure: A New Look at Old History. University of Hawai'i Press. Honolulu. 2002. ISBN 0-8248-2404-0. This work focuses attention on the building and use of the "Russian Fort" near Waimea on Kauai, but also has very good biographical treatment of Kaumuali'i. Mills' bibliography is one of the very best...very useful and highly recommended. See my review of this work on www.shvoong.com.

Mitchell, Donald D. Kilolani. Resource Units in HAWAIIAN CULTURE. Book design and illustrations by Nancy Middlesworth. Third printing in 2007 of the Fourth Revised Edition of 1992, expanded in 1982 from the first edition of 1969. Kamehameha Schools Press, Honolulu. ISBN 978-0-87336-016-6. This is a key resource to illustrated information about the pre-contact Hawaiian culture...just a treasure.

Monakhov, A. L. Muzej-Panorama: Borodinskaja Bitva: 1812 god. Sorek-poligrafija. Moskva. 1997. A history of the Battle of Borodino, profusely illustrated with art. There is also an associated fold-out miniature reprint of the battle panorama by Franz Alekseevich Roubeau entitled Muzej-Panorama Borodinskaja Bitva (Izdatel'stvo gumanitarnoj literatury, Moskva, 2002...cf. Ezerskaja source for address) with explanatory text in Russian, English, French, and German. See "Borodino" above.

275

Mo'okini, Esther T. "Keōpuōlani: Sacred Wife, Queen Mother, 1778-1823," in Hawaiian Journal of History (A Publication of the Hawaiian Historical Society), Vol. XXXII (1998), pp. 1-24. A fine biographical treatment of Keōpuōlani...the most comprehensive on her and her impact on Hawai'ian society.

MOROSI, GIUSEPPE. For information on this Florentine "mechanic," and fabricator of his chess "automaton" for Ferdinand III of Tuscany, see http://www.galileo.imss.firenze.it/pubblic/e1998.html, accessed August 9, 2003.

Moser, Peter. Würzburg: Geschichte einer Stadt. Babenberg Verlag. Bamberg. 1999. This is a chronological table of dates, spelling out the history of Würzburg, capital of Franconia and seat of the Franconian Prince Bishop until Georg Karl von Fechenbach signed his assent to the secularization of 1802.

MUSEUM.RU. At www.museum.ru there is an "1812 Project" which includes a richly illustrated treasure trove of detailed information, more in the Russian version than the English version, about the events and the personalities involved in Napoleon's invasion of Russia in 1812. In addition, there are tables of generals, ministers, and essays on selected topics...for example, Helen Bobrova's article on "Russian Diplomats in Paris, 1791-1815 (see above)." There is also a very comprehensive illustrated genealogy of Tsar Alexander I's family with links to biographical data. This is a most helpful site. See also the "Virtual Battle of Borodino" at Duffy above.

NAPOLEON BONAPARTE. The site at www.Napoleon-series.org is a very valuable resource with its articles on diverse aspects of Napoleon's life and campaigns. On Napoleon during the Battle of Borodino, see http://www.napoleonistyka.atspace.com/Borodino_battle.htm. The Napoleon-series.org site has a sketch from tsarist archives of the Leppich aerostat's design. This

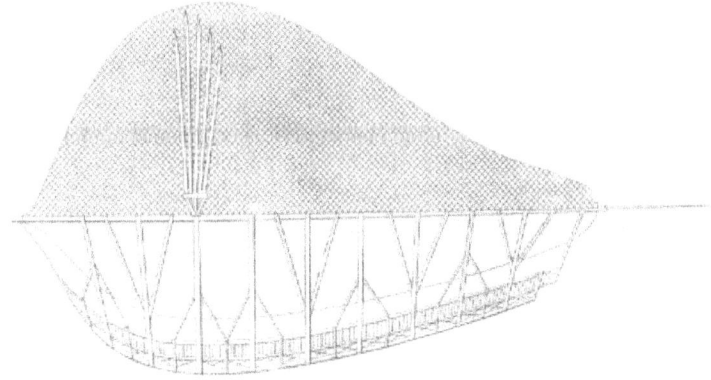

Kopie der Zeichnung des Luftballones von Franz Leppich, entnommen dem »Sammelband der historischen Unterlagen aus dem Archiv der Privatkanzlei Seiner Kaiserlichen Hoheit Alexanders I.«. St. Petersburg 1876.

sketch with its German caption ("A copy of a sketch of the airballoon of Franz Leppich, from historical notes in the private archive of his Imperial Majesty Alexander I—St. Petersburg, 1876") is very likely derived from a very similar one from French military archives drawn in 1812 by a French officer named de Segur (see Duhem, above, and de Segur, below) who inspected the Vorontsovo estate after the evacuation of the balloon project to Nizhnii Novgorod. The somewhat flawed explanation given on the napoleon-series site reads: "Franz Leppich (1776-1818) was a German inventor and musician. In 1811 he offered the idea of a hot air balloon to Napoleon, who turned it down, so Leppich went to Russia, where his offer was met with more success. Rastopchin (sic) hired him to build a military hot air balloon for the defence of Moscow. At this time ballooning was in its infancy. Leppich began work in a secret shipyard near Moscow, heavily defending the site against spies from France. But, during trials, the balloon failed to inflate, and Leppich left Russia in disgrace." These sketches only very roughly show the non-spherical "shark shape" of the aerostat's side view, and miss the rotary wings. Search also the site http://tywkiwdbi.blogspot.com under "killer-zeppelin-not-used-against-napoleon."

Neale, Tom. An Island to Myself. Introduction by Noel Barber. Holt Rinehart and Winston Co. New York. 1966. The first edition published in London by Collins the same year is entitled An Island to Oneself. This book is about Neale's solitary residence on Suvarov island from 1952 to 1954, then from 1960 to 1963. After the book was published he returned to the island and lived there from 1966 to 1972. He was originally inspired to go and live on the atoll by Robert Dean Frisbie (cf. above). The text of Neale's book is online at www.gutenberg.net.au/ebooks01/0100261.text. There is a very special "tribute" website to Tom Neale, with a remembrance article by Kenneth R. Vogel, a collection of photographs by Rhys Jones, photos of Tom Neale's gravesite in Rarotonga and his death certificate...contributions of photos by his daughter Stella and other information about his life and legacy at www.pacificislandsinfo.com.

Nebel, Henry M., Jr. N.M. Karamzin: A Russian Sentimentalist. Mouton and Co. The Hague and Paris. 1967. This is a literary treatment, but mentions the effects of freemasonry on Karamzin's thought and (cf. pp. 46) discusses political currents in the court of Tsar Alexander I.

Nickerson, Roy. Lahaina: Royal Capital of Hawaii. Hawaiian Service, P.O. Box 2835, Honolulu, Hawaii. 1978. A well illustrated treatment of Lahaina's history in its days "when kings and whalermen ruled the Sandwich isles."

Nicolson, Harold. The Congress of Vienna:A Study of Allied Unity: 1812-1822. A Harbinger Book. Harcourt, Brace, Jovanovich, Inc. New York. 1946. Here are the roles of Lord Castelreagh and Prince Klemens von Metternich in the post-Napoleonic situation in "the Italian and German Settlements" (pp. 182-199).

NINETEENTH CENTURY. The Illustrated History of the 19th Century: Month by Month, Year by Year. Text by Simon Adams, et. al. Hackberry Press on imprint of the Texas Bookman. Rebo International b.v., Lisse, Netherlands. ISBN 1-931104-001 X. An interesting illustrated compendium of prominent events in chronological order, as the title says, 'month by month, year by year.' Very useful to provide historical context for depicted events.

NEWSPAPERS, Hawaiian at www.nupepa.org, Ulukau Hawaiian Electronic Library. This source gives Hawaiian-language newspapers (e.g. Nupepa Kuokoa) published between 1834-1948 with word, title, and date searches possible.

North, Jonathan. With Napoleon In Russia: The Illustrated Memoirs of Major Faber du Faur, 1812. Greenhill Books, London, and Stackpole Books, Mechanicsburg, PA. 2001. ISBN 1-85367-454-0. North's presentation of Major Christian Wilhelm von Faber du Faur's (1780-1857) memoirs and sketches, with later prepared color plates is a real gem. See my review at the book's entry on www.Amazon.com.

North, Jonathan. Napoleon's Army in Russia: The illustrated Memoirs of Albrecht Adam-1812. Pen and Sword Books, South Yorkshire, UK. 2005. ISBN 1-84415-161-1. Another scholarly gem by prolific scholar of the Napoleonic Wars Jonathan North. See my review at www.Amazon.com.

Oberacker, Carlos H., Jr. Jorge Antonio Von Schaeffer: Criador Da Premeira Corrente Emigratoria Alema Para O Brasil. Editora Metropole. Instituto Estadual do Livro. Porto Alegre, Brasil. 1957 (reprinted in 1975). Includes much detail of Schaeffer's Brazilian emigration work in Europe, including a table of ships and the numbers of human cargo. See also http://www.brasilalemanhaonline.com.br/site/materias/1824_antesal.htm for a German article on the German emigration to Brazil mentioning the work of Jorge Antonio von Schaeffer, even giving the names of the first group of German émigrés to settle in the Rio Grande do Sul State. The terms of Schaeffer's offer to these émigrés is described in Portuguese at www.riogrande.com.br/historia/colonizacao4.htm. Both these latter two websites can be translated into rough English by accessing them through Google. For other sites on Schaeffer's role in the emigration of Germans to Brazil and yet more family detail, see http://www.es.beekeeping.wikia.com/wiki/Georg_Anton_von_Sch%C3%A4ffer and also Gomes (above), Sommer, Sawitzki, and Weissheimer (below) and the genealogical works on the families Grieb and Heuser.

Okun', Semen Bentsionovich. "Tsarskaia Rossia I Gavaiskie Ostrova" in Krasnyj arkhiv. Vol. 78 (1936): pp. 161-186. There are eight documents here of Sheffer's Russian correspondence, Russian-American Company Reports, and including King Kaumualii's (Sheffer's) signed proclamation of Kauai's Russian protectorateship. These are, specifically:

"1. A proclamation of May 21, 1816, signed by King Tomari (Kaumualii) of the two Sandwich Islands and acknowledging his willingness to accept a Russian Protectorate.
2. A report of a seven-man council of the Russian-American Company on the necessity for strengthening trade relations with the Sandwich Islands, March 26, 1818.
3. An extract from the journal of Dr. George Sheffer, representative of the Russian- American Company, describing his exploits in Hawaii in 1815-7.
4. A note from Sheffer to Alexander I on the political and commercial advantages of improving the Russian position in the Sandwich Islands, February 1819.
5. Comments on each of Sheffer's points by the Department of Manufacturing and Internal Trade, February 1819.
6. A supplement to Sheffer's note to Alexander I, March 2, 1819.
7. A note from the administrative officers of the Russian-American Company to the Department of Manufacturing and Internal Trade, March 18, 1819, concerning the Addition of the Sandwich Islands to the Russian possessions.
8. A letter from Count K. V. Nesselrode, Minister of Foreign Affairs, to O. P. Kozodavlev, Minister of Internal Affairs, June 24, 1819, revealing Alexander I's attitude toward the work of the Russian-American Company."

Okun', Semen Bentsionovich. The Russian-American Company. (Edited, with an introduction by B. D. Grekov, USSR Academy of Sciences, and with a preface by Robert J. Kerner, UC-Berkeley) (Translated by Carl Ginzburg, US Dept. of State). Harvard University Press, Cambridge, Mass. 1951.

Oleksa, Fr. Michael. "Intercessor and Defender of the Oppressed." This is an essay about the glorification of the Venerable Elder Herman of Alaska, presenting the reasons for his opposition to Alexander Baranov. See www.conciliarpress.com/again/index2. Undated.

Oleksa, Archpriest Michael J. "The Creoles and Their Contributions to the Development of Alaska." In Russian America: The Forgotten Frontier. Barbara Sweetland Smith and Redmond J. Barnett, eds. Tacoma: The Washington State Historical Press. 1990. pp. 185-197.

Olivier, Daria. The Burning of Moscow: 1812. (Translated by Michael Heron) Thomas Y. Crowell Company. New York. 1966. See pp. 29-30 for the balloon episode. There is also notice of French sources on pp. 216. This is a wonderful blend of detail and narrative on the topic…still unsurpassed.

O'Moore, Father Maurice M. The Concha Arguello Story: Memory Visits with Old Vinnie. Edited and with historical notes by Richard A. Pierce (see Pierce below). Published together in the Alaska History series No. 48 with the work by Eve Iversen (see Iversen above) by The Limestone Press. Kingston, Ontario and Fairbanks, Alaska. 1998.

Osetrov, Evgenii. Tri zhizni Karamzina: Roman-issledovanie. Izdatel'stvo "Moskovskii rabochii." Moskva. 1989. Here is considerable detail about Karamzin's life with illustrations and artwork on Russian history as related in Karamzin's History of the Russian State. Some of the pictures show various Moscow addresses and places as they were in the 1790s...as the Novikov typography site on pp. 43 and Prince Viazemskii's Ostafievo estate on pp. 204 and discussion of how Karamzin moved into Moscow Governor-General Rostopchin's Moscow home at the end of August 1812...before the fire destroyed his library.

Otto, Gerd (text) et. al. (English translation by Adrian Towersey). Munich. Schmid Verlag. Regensburg, Salzburg, Wien. Undated but recent. This is an English guidebook to Munich, profusely illustrated with an introductory history.

Owens, Kenneth N. (ed.) The Wreck of the Sv. Nikolai. Translated by Alton S. Donnelly. Lincoln and London: University of Nebraska Press (Bison Books). 2001. ISBN 0803286155. See the review by Dennis Reinhartz at the site of the Society for the History of Discoveries: http://www.sochistdisc.org/2002_book_reviews/owens.htm (accessed May 2005). This work is ostensibly a re-issue of Owens, Kenneth N. (ed./intro.) The Wreck of the Sv. Nikolai: Two Narratives of the First Russian Expedition to the Oregon Country 1808-1810. Translated by Alton S. Donnelly and outstandingly illustrated with drawings by Karen Beyers. Portland: Western Imprints. The Press of the Oregon Historical Society. 1985. In this work historian Owens thoroughly evidences the case that one too-often consulted source on the events in "Tarakanov's" life is that of Ivan Petrov (Petroff), assistant and translator for earlier historian Hubert Howe Bancroft, who, in the late 1870's, fabricated a "Statement of my Captivity among the Californians by a Russian Fur-Hunter" purported to be the work of a "Vasilli Pyotrovitch Tarakanoff," with whom the actual Timofei Tarakanov was subsequently confused. In his introduction and annotations, Owens demonstrates how later treatments fall into falsehoods (e.g. Chevigny's Lord of Alaska on Alexander Baranov who includes mention of Timofei Tarakanov's period of captivity by the California Spaniards and also includes a relation from the monk Juvenal's diary…a Petrov fabrication) because of this work.

Pahinui, Chelle. "The Hawaiian Instrument of Love: The Story of the Ka Ūkēkē." In Kaua'i Traveler magazine, May-August 2008, pp. 82-85. See www.myhawaiitraveler.com and also www.humumoolelo.com since the article is an excerpt from Humu Mo'olelo: Journal of the Hula Arts, a "quarterly dedicated to all things hula."

Palmer, Alan. Napoleon in Russia. Simon and Schuster. New York. 1967. A well-detailed account of balloon mastermind Leppich's activities, pp. 89-90. Palmer is another author with a penchant for complete accuracy, including the full names of involved figures in his index.

Palmer, Colin (with photographs by Maggie Steber and paintings by Jerry Pinkney). "African Slave Trade: The Cruelest Commerce." In National Geographic. Vol. 182, No. 3 (September 1992), pp. 62-91. National Geographic has had other features on the African slave trade, but this article is particularly useful here for its mention of the slave routes to Brazil and for its inclusion of a diagram (pp. 78-9) of the inhumane close arrangement of the slaves in a ship unloaded in Rio de Janeiro as witnessed by George Anton Schaeffer and others from the *Suvorov* in 1814.

Pierce, Richard A. Russia's Hawaiian Adventure, 1815-1817. University of California Press. Berkeley, CA. 1965. This is the seminal scholarly work in English on the Russian actitivities in Hawaii and it includes a very useful bibliography. Pierce, together with Nikolai Rokitiansky, designed a gold-plated medal, minted in 1988, to commemorate Sheffer's founding of Fort Elizabeth on Kauai in 1816. I have one of these medals, very kindly sent to me by Pierce.

Pierce, Richard A. (Translator and introduction). The Russian-American Company: Correspondence of the Governors' Communications Sent: 1818. The Limestone Press, Kingston, Ontario, Canada. 1984. Efforts of Baranov's successor Hagemeister to cope with Hawaiian "damage" of Sheffer. See index.

Pierce, Richard A., ed. Documents on the History of the Russian-American Company. (Translated by Marina Ramsay). The Limestone Press. Kingston, Ontario, Canada. 1976. The documents here describe RAC activities 1795-1808...before Sheffer's involvement, but it has a list of RAC ships...see index pp. 217-8.

Pierce, Richard A., ed., with historical notes. Alaska History No. 48: The Romance of Nikolai Rezanov and Concepcion Arguello: A Literary Legend and Its Effect on California History, by Eve Iversen, and The Concha Arguello Story: Memory Visits With Old Vinnie, by Father Maurice M. O'Moore, O.P. The Limestone Press. Kingston, Ontario, Canada. 1998. An account of Rezanov's betrothal to Concepcion Arguello and all the fascinating historical and cultural ramifications of the story...see Russian literary elaborations, pp. 30-7. See also Rezanov, Nikolai below.

Pierce, Richard A.   Russian America: A Biographical Dictionary.   The Limestone Press. Kingston, Ontario. 1990.

Pierce, Richard A. "Georg Anton Schaffer, Russia's Man in Hawaii, 1815-1817." in Pacific Historical Review. Vol. XXXII, No. 4 (November 1963), pp. 3-23. A concise view, illustrated, of Sheffer's hawaiian activities. A personal letter from Richard Pierce (30 May, 2001) relates that Schaeffer impressed Captain Lazarev in a trip into London in 1813 with his ability to sing Latin songs...likely the Carmina Burana (cf. Carl Orff's modern versions) in addition to the "Gaudeamus igitur..." graduation ditty.   These songs have an interesting history.

Pierce, Richard A. "Russian America and China" and "The Russian-American Company Currency." In Russian America: The Forgotten Frontier. Barbara Sweetland Smith and Redmond J. Barnett, eds. Tacoma: The Washington State Historical Press. 1990. pp. 73-81, pp. 145-155.

PITCAIRN ISLAND.   See http://en.wikipedia.org/wiki/Fletcher_Christian for the history of its population by the Bounty mutineers. For a description of its absence of anchorage and its topography, see Hibberd (above), pp. 8.

Porter, Robert Kerr, Sir. A Narrative of the Campaign in Russian During the Year 1812. With an essay on subsequent events by William Dunlap. Hartford, Andrus, and Starr. 1815. This work is in ASU Hayden Library's special collections…a leatherbound volume.

Porter, Roy. "Chapter 7: The Eighteenth Century." This 105-pp essay is part of the Stanford University Medical Sciences Organization's history of medicine, available   on-line   at http:www.stanford.edu/dept/HPS/SciMedOrg/portereighteenthcentury.pdf. (accessed 4 August, 2003).   Porter mentions (pp. 469) the Juliusspital in Würzburg for having a "well planned operating theater" after 1789, mentions (pp. 426) electric shock as becoming common to treat lunatics, and includes (pp.448) a description of German medical education and licensing. Johann Wilhelm Ritter is not mentioned, but Franz Anton Mesmer, Johann Christian Reil, and Johann Peter Frank (prominent contemporary physicians in the area) are.

Postnikov, A. "The First Russian Round-the-World Voyage and its Influence on Exploration and Development of Russian America." At the website publishing the proceedings of a scholarly conference at the Museum of the World Ocean in 2002: http://vitiaz.ru/congress/en/thesis/10.html.

Postnikov, A. "New Source on the History of the First Russian Round-the-World Expedition." This reports the author's finding, in France, of the travel diary of Lt. Makarii Borisovich Ratmanov, Capt. Kruzenshtern's mate on the *Nadezhda*. At the website publishing the proceedings of a scholarly conference in 2002 at the Museum of the World Ocean: http://vitiaz.ru/congress/en/thesis/11.html.

Pratt, High Chiefess Elizabeth Kekaaniau Laanui. Keoua: Father of Kings. Kealii Publishing, 2637 Kuilei Street, Honolulu, Hawaii 96826. Copyright by David Castro. 1999. This is a republication of personal recollections by Keoua's great-great-granddaughter, originally published in 1920, by her great-great-great nephew. Keoua is generally considered the father of Kamehameha I, although Maui King Kahekili late in his life claimed to be Kamehameha's biological father.

Pritchard, Diane Spencer. "Joint Tenants of the Frontier: Russian-Hispanic Relationships in Alta California." In Russian America: The Forgotten Frontier. Barbara Sweetland Smith and Redmond J. Barnett, eds. Tacoma: The Washington State Historical Press. 1990. pp. 81-95.

Pukui, Margaret Kawena, Haertig, E. W., M.D., and Lee, Catherine A. Nana I Ke Kumu (Look to the Source). Volume II. Hu Hanai: Queen Lili'uokalani Children's Center. Honolulu, Hawaii. 1972. An annotated personal relation of Hawaiian personal and social customs.

Putnam, John J. (with photographs by Gordon W. Gahan). "Napoleon." In National Geographic. Vol. 161, No. 2 (February 1982), pp. 142-189. This is a wonderfully illustrated concise treatment of Napoleon and his legacy. Full-page spreads depict the French army's disastrous crossing of the Berezina River in 1812 (pp. 176-7) and the Battle of Waterloo (pp. 182-3).

Raeff, Marc. Michael Speransky. Martinus Nijhoff. The Hague. 1957. This work discusses the influence of francophile advisor Speransky on the government of Tsar Alexander I.

Reitblat, A. I., ed. Vidok Figliarin: Pis'ma i agenturnye zapiski F. V. Bulgarin v III Otdelenie. ("Vidocq Figliarin: Letters and agent notes of F. V. Bulgarin to the Third Section"). Novoe Literaturnoe Obozrenie. Moskva. 1998. Faddei Bulgarin (1789-1859) has a most interesting personal history. He was a soldier in Napoleon's army during the invasion of 1812, but, resettling after the campaign in St. Petersburg, he became an influential publisher and an innovative author of historical novels and fanciful stories. He clashed with Aleksandr Pushkin, and, after the Decembrist Revolt in 1825 began writing notes on the activities of diverse people to Tsar Nicholas I's secret police, the "Third Section." In these notes, using sometimes his pseudonym of "Vidocq Figliarin," (a renowned fictional former-criminal detective) he gives written expression to all manner of candid rumors about the leading personalities of the time. Reitblat's very thorough scholarship, listing and describing all the people mentioned in the thirty-year course of these notes in the indices, is very useful and much appreciated. The conflict with Pushkin is well described in Binyon (above).

Rempel, Gerhard. "Alexander the Sphinx." cf. www.mars.acnet.wnec.edu/~grempel/courses/russia/lectures/17alexander.html.

REZANOV, NIKOLAI PETROVICH (1764-1807) was a Russian court chamberlain, a founder of the Russian-American Company (1799) and first Russian ambassador to Japan (1804-5 incarcerated during the Russians' first circumnavigation on the *Nadezhda* (Captain Ivan Fyodorovich Kruzenshtern) and the *Neva* (Lieutenant Yurii Fedorovich Lisianskii) in 1803-7). He visited Alexander Baranov in Sitka in 1806 and sailed on the *Juno* to San Francisco where his famous "romance" with the daughter of the Presidio's commander, Conchita Arguello, took place (see under Richard Pierce above…work by Eve Iversen…and also the work by Gertrude Atherton above). "Commander Rezanov" has an impressive website devoted to him at http://rezanov.krasu.ru/eng/commander. This is a website created by Krasnoiarsk University in the city where Rezanov died and is buried. It is a particularly rich website, including the possibility for questions and answers by email. In one entry, from http://rezanov.krasu.ru/eng/meeting/index.php?book=rezanov&size=10&page=2, a woman named "Irina" contends with the Krasnoiarsk University website staff over their rights to certain information about Aleksandr Andreevich Baranov. She writes that she is the "pra-pra-pra-pravnuchka" ("great-great-great-great granddaughter") of Baranov…although other sources (see, for example, Hector Chevigny) state that Baranov has no remaining modern issue genealogically. Of interest is the story "Taina komandora" ("Secret of the Commander") by Ol'ga Arzhanykh, describing the moving of Rezanov's remains from Krasnoiarsk's Voskresensky Church, which was destroyed, to the Troitskii Church cemetery, and about the monuments on the sites. For the conflict on the *Nadezhda* see the citation for Fedor Ivanovich Tolstoi (below) also the citations of Postnikov and Sverdlov, as well as the citations for Baranov and Shelikhov. Memoirs by Kruzenshtern, Lisiansky, Shemelin, Lowenstern (best here), Ratmanov (cf. Postnikov), and von Langsdorff all bear on Rezanov as well, showing both positive and negative sides to his character. Rezanov's 16 August 1804 "Report to Tsar Alexander I about the voyage on the vessel *Nadezhda* from Brazil to Kamchatka and activities there prior to the departure for Japan" is document number 51 in Bolkhovitinov and Narochnitskii (1994, above). Rezanov is very diplomatic, trying to minimize the conflict in his report and suggesting that Count Tolstoi's bad behavior was due to youthful "enthusiasm." He requests the Tsar's "most merciful forgiveness" for Tolstoy and suggests that his being removed from participation in the "great exploit" was sufficient punishment (pp. 88, 90). The fact that Rezanov and poet Gavriil Romanovich Derzhavin (1743-1816) were both members of Tsar Paul's "Order of St. John of Jerusalem" is established at the website of the Russian Grand Priory:

http://www2.prestel.co.uk/church/oosj/osj.htm. Of interest also is the website of the Joseph Brodsky Museum in St. Petersburg: http://brodsky.spb.ru/eng/muzuri4.htm. This site gives the history of the "Muzuri House" on Liteinyi Prospect and Pantaleimonovskaia Street (formerly Pestel), nos. 24-7, in which the Nobel Laureate poet spent his youth. The house was located at the address where Nikolai Rezanov had previously built his own wooden mansion. The complete history of the address is given in the chapters by authors A. Kobak and L. Lurie.

Richter, Klaus. Das Leben des Physikers Johann Wilhelm Ritter: Ein Schicksal in der Zeit der Romantik. H. Böhlaus Nachf. Weimar. 2003. ISBN 3740011912. This 265-pp work is available through Amazon.de for Euro 49.95. The blurb mentions that the author, science scholar Klaus Richter, died in 2001, so this is a posthumous publication. See the other biography of Ritter by W. Wetzels (below) for the citation of some anonymous (as opposed to the internet biography by Dean P. Currier (above)) biographies of Ritter. None of the internet sites include any personal details about Ritter, but only synopses of his scientific achievements.

Ridley, Jasper. The Freemasons: A History of the World's Most Powerful Secret Society. Arcade Publishing. New York. 1999. There is a chapter devoted to "Napoleon" and freemasonry.

Ridley, Scott. Morning of Fire: John Kendrick's Daring American Odyssey in the Pacific. William Morrow, an imprint of HarperCollins Publishers, 10 East 53rd St, New York City, NY, 10022, copyright Scott Ridley, 2010. ISBN 978-0-06-170012-5. This work has a useful bibliography. See my review on Amazon at http://www.amazon.com/Morning-Fire-Kendricks-American-Odyssey/product-reviews/B0057DCJMM/ref=cm_cr_pr_btm_link_3?ie=UTF8&showViewpoints=0&pageNumber=3. See also the work by Raymond Massey.

Riehn, Richard K. Napoleon's Russian Campaign. McGraw-Hill. New York. 1990. This is a thorough work of over 500 pp.

Ritchie, John. Lachlan Macquarie: A Biography. Melbourne University Press. Carlton, Victoria. 1986. This is a comprehensive scholarly biography of the "Father of Australia."

RITTER, JOHANN WILHELM. See Currier, Dean P.; Richter, Klaus; and Wetzels, Walter D.

Roberts, James B. and Skutt, Alexander G. The Boxing Register. McBooks Press, London, 3rd ed. 2002. Accessed by excerpts on internet, key words "Boxing Hall of Fame Enshrinees," January 2004.

Rolt, L.T.C. The Aeronauts: A History of Ballooning, 1783-1903. Walker and Company. New York. 1966. A comprehensive and readable account of the history of ballooning...includes all the major figures (e.g. English balloon pioneer James Sadler, whose grave in the churchyard of St. Peter-in-the-east at Oxford University I visited in 2002), but does not mention the 1812 attempt on Napoleon. Napoleon's "pathological...dislike of balloons" is explained (pp. 108-9, 164-5) and an 1804 St. Petersburg ascent by Etienne Robertson and "Prof. Sakharoff of the Russian Academy" (pp. 185-6). From this it emerges that Schaeffer had a place-and-time opportunity to have witnessed the Garnerins' tethered ascent in Nürnburg in 1799. He may have read of others, notably those of Zambeccari (1752-1812). On pp. 161 is given, in a footnote, the "British recipe for balloon varnish" (to prevent permeation loss of hydrogen through the silk...a key limitation to hydrogen ascents). Includes a good timetable and bibliography.

Rostopchin, Fedor Vasilievich. Okh, Frantsuzy! Russkaia kniga (Sovietskaia Rossiia). Moskva. 1992. Published here are the "literary" works of Moscow Governor-General Fyodor V. Rostopchin (1763-1826) as well as 20 of his flyers (afishi) including No. 10 from August 22, 1812 mentioning the balloon project, and from "Notes about the Year 1812" (pp. 242-315...cf. especially pp. 263-4 where is the first person narration of his balloon project involvement and also pp. 301 and 309 about his evacuation of "the charlatan Schmidt" from Moscow). There is no mention of Schaeffer or Schaeffer's role in the communication between Rostopchin and "Shmidt," but notice that Rostopchin does not use the name Leppich in this memoir, written in French in 1825, rendering curious Tolstoy's use of "Leppich" in War and Peace. Curious also is Rostopchin's discussion of the failing "springs," the description of the large balloon as "taffeta," and the specific mention of how "This Shmidt cost us 320 thousand rubles."

Safaralieva, Diliara. "M. T. Tikhonov (1769-1862), Artist-Traveler." In Russian America: The Forgotten Frontier. Barbara Sweetland Smith and Redmond J. Barnett, eds. Tacoma: The Washington State Historical Press. 1990. pp. 33-41.

Samarov, Andrei A. Russkie flotovodtsy: M.P Lazarev: dokumenty ("Russian Fleet Commanders: M. P. Lazarev: Documents"). Izdatel'stvo Istoriya. Moskva. 1952. Samarov's work, cited in the works of Glynn Barratt (cf. above), focuses on M. P. Lazarev, Captain of the Suvorov on its 1813-6 circumnavigation, but includes memoirs of second officer S. Ya Unkovskiy and assistant navigator Aleksei I. Rossiyskiy.

SAMBIR. For information on the city, see http://www.bohdanyurkiv.cityslide.com, accessed August 9, 2003.

Sawitzki, Sonja. "Die Erschiessung von acht 'Meuteren' an bord des Auswanderersleglers GERMANIA 1824: Bemerkungen zur offizielen Dokumentation." Deutsches Schiffahrtsarchiv (DSA), Bremerhaven, 28, 2005, pp. 267-281. See abstract at: http://www.dsm.museum/Pubs2/28_08.htm. Sawatzki examines documents on the "Germania incident" hearing and concludes that the execution of eight passengers was unjustified. See also Sommer and Weissheimer (below).

Schaeffer ("Ritter von Schäffer Dr./Major Der K. Brasilischen Khrengarde etc. etc. etc."), George Anton Aloysius. Brasilien als Unabhängiges Reich in Historischer, Mercantilischer und Politischer Beziehung. Altona (Hamburg, Germany) bei J. F. Hammerich. 1824. This is the 464-page book Schaeffer wrote and had printed in an edition of 100 copies. It is an important contemporary description of Brazil during the reign of Dom Pedro I. Schaeffer transported the copies himself around Germany and Austria in the late 1820's, giving copies to officials and to citizens in order to convince them of the virtues of emigrating to Brazil. He dedicates the work to "Ihrer Majestät Maria Leopoldine, Kaiserin von Brasilien." There is surprisingly little personal information about Schaeffer in it...no mention at all of his wife and daughter, for example. But there is interesting travelogue, social and political commentary, and laudatory descriptions of Brazil's natural resources and climate, and a copy of the Brazilian constitution. The copy I obtained by interlibrary loan from the St. Vincent Archabbey Library of Latrobe, Pennsylvania was apparently deposited there in 1846. As I first held the precariously aged paper-and-leather-bound book in my hands in 2001, I imagined that Schaeffer himself had also held it in his hands at some time as he distributed his copies in 1824, 177 years before. On Schaeffer, G. A. see: Barratt, Black, Bolkhovitinov, Gomes, Hunsche, the Kaua'i Museum, Oberacker, Mazour, Pierce, Schaeffer (Enrico), Sommer, Teilhet, Vasconcellos, Weissheimer, ...and others (above and below).

Schäffer, Georg Anton von. Brazilie, als onafhankelijk rijk, uit een geschied-koopandel-en staatkundig oogpunt: ook in betrekking tot Europa, beschouwd, in een historisch tafereel van deszelfs afscheiding van Portugal en verheffing tot zelfstandig keizzerijk: benevens een uitvoerig verslag der staatkundige gebeurtenissen in dit rijk, gedurende de jarn 1821, 1822, en 1823. C. L. Schleijer Editorial, Amsterdam, 1825. This is an abbreviated version of the above in Dutch translation.

Schaeffer, Enrico (Prof.). "De velhas Cronicas de Familias: O Cavalheiro George Antonio De Schaeffer (1779-1836) "Vendedor De Almas" e Confidante da Imperatriz D. Leopoldina." in Revista Genealogica Latina. No. 11 (1959). Pp. 157-161. This "Prof. Schaeffer" of Sao Paulo is described here as a "collateral relative" of "Cavalheiro George Antonio De Schaeffer." He had communicated with Richard Pierce in the 1970's, but I have been unable to find him (Richard Pierce sent me what contact information he had, but it was eventually to no avail, as Pierce advised me that he had also lost touch with the man). His photograph accompanying this article indicates, in 1959 or previous, a man of about fifty years of age, so that he is by now likely deceased. Since, according to this Prof. Schaeffer, George Anton Schaeffer left only a daughter behind (the "heiress of a considerable fortune"), the family connection of Prof. Enrico Schaeffer is not clear. Prof. Schaeffer mentions the above-described German book on Brazil by his relative and writes "this very rare book today is worth almost its weight in gold."

Schappelle, Benjamin, Ph.D. The German Element in Brazil: Colonies and Dialect. This 1917 book is available on Amazon.com, but was put online in 2005 by the Gutenberg project at http://www.gutenberg.org/17361/17361-8.txt. Schappelle lists the "founders of Frankenthal Colony" in Brazil's Bahia State as "Peter Weyll and Sauercrater." These were members of a group of Lutherans that George Anton Schaeffer invited into Frankenthal Colony in 1822, a year after its April 4, 1821 founding.

Schmitt, Robert C. (compiler) and Ronck, Ronn (ed.). Firsts and Almost Firsts in Hawaii. A Kolowalu Book. University of Hawaii Press. Honolulu, Hawaii. 1995. A listing of when all sorts of things first appeared or happened in Hawaii.

Schnell, Roland M. "A Short History about Alaska: Working Conditions in Sitka during the Baranov era (1791-1818)." This is a useful work, available at www.rollandinho.com/Rolland_the_artist/Essay_on_Alaska/essay_on_alaska.html.

Schom, Alan. Napoleon Bonaparte. HarperCollins Publishers. New York. 1997. A comprehensive biography of Napoleon, but no mention of balloons.

Schreiber, Peter (text) and Elmar Hahn (photography) and Tina Neil (English transl.). Würzburg: Scenes of a City. Elmar Hahn Verlag. Veitshöchheim. 3rd revised ed. 2001. This is an illustrated guide book to Würzburg, including a table of "historical dates." There are pictures of the apothecary in the Juliusspital, where Schaeffer studied medicine.

Schütz, Albert J. Things Hawaiian: A Pocket Guide to the Hawaiian Language. Island Heritage Publishing. 99-880 Iwaena Street, Aiea, Hawaii 96701-7299. ISBN 0-89610-307-2.

Schweizer, Niklaus R. A Poet Among Explorers: Chamisso in the South Seas. Herbert Lang Verlag. Bern und Frankfurt. 1973. Illustrations here include a surrealist depiction by Jean Charlot from his Honolulu bank mural of artist Ludwig Choris painting a portrait of Kamehameha, with the poet and scientist Adelbert von Chamisso looking on. Comparing Charlot's Kamehameha (pp.10 and 11) with the from-life likeness by Choris (plate V on pp. 22) makes a person wonder about Charlot's creation, especially since the likeness on his depiction of Choris' easel (pp. 10) clearly resembles Choris' work...? See Charlot (above).

Scofield, John. Hail Columbia. Oregon Historical Society Press. Oregon. 1993. This work, part of the Pacific History Series, deals with the careers of Captains Robert Gray (1755-1806, master of the *Columbia* after which the river is named) and also John Kendrick (1745-1794, master of the *Lady Washington* which participated in internecine battles of the Hawai'ian chiefs).

De Segur, Count Philippe-Paul. Napoleon's Russian Campaign. Translated by J. David Townsend. Houghton Mifflin Company. Boston. 1958. Count de Segur, a French participant in Napoleon's campaign who recorded his experiences in popular memoirs, mentions the balloon project as meant specifically to kill Napoleon. He wrote, that "several attempts to raise it had been made, the wings breaking off each time." De Segur is an uncle of the man who marries Fyodor Rostopchin's daughter Sophia in Paris. Sophie de Segur becomes a prominent author of children's books. Count Phillpe-Paul de Segur's sketch of the "machine diabolique" from witnessing remnants at Vorontsovo and interviewing Russians who had peeped through the fence at the aerostat is apparently the basis for a copy with German caption from 1876 cited by http://www.napoleon-series.org as being in Tsar Alexander's personal historical archives (see Napoleon (Bonaparte), above).

Seiden, Allan. Waikīkī: Magic Beside the Sea. Island Heritage Publishing, 94-411 Kō'aki Street, Waipahu, HI 96797. 2001. ISBN 0-89610-363-3. This large-format coffee-table book has an especially strong author's relation of Waikīkī's pre-history and early days...the description most used to describe it in the time when George Schaeffer leased his agricultural outpost there from Ka'ahumanu. See also the general Waikīkī entry.

Shelikhov, Grigorii Ivanovich. A Voyage to America. Translated by Marina Ramsay with an introduction by Richard A. Pierce. The Limestone Press. Kingston, Ontario. 1981. Evidence of "Inscriptions on the Monument Erected in Memory of Grigorii Shekikhov in Rylsk by (Gavriil Romanovich) Derzhavin with copies, 1795" are given at the website of the US Library of Congress' Meeting of Frontiers Digital Library Project-http://frontiers.loc.gov/intldl/mtfhtml/mfdigcol/lists/mtfyumTitles2.html. The original of the poem *in Derzhavin's actual handwriting*, in which he states "Kolumb zdes' Rosskii pogreben" ("The Russian Columbus is here interred"), is here along with other letters of Shelikhov's and Rezanov's as part of the "Gennadii V. Yudin Collection of Russian-American Company Papers."

Sherwood, Zelie Duvauchelle. Beginners Hawaiian. Ku Pa'a Publishing Incorporated and Press Palcifica, Ltd. PO Box 37460, Honolulu, Hawaii. Fifth Printing, copyright, 1996. ISBN 0-914916-56-4.

SHIPS—whereabouts when. See Govor, Howay, and Pierce.

Silverman, Jane L. <u>Kaahumanu: Molder of Change.</u> Friends of the Judiciary History Center of Hawaii. Honolulu, Hawaii. 1987. A biography of Ka'ahumanu...fresh perspectives on Kaumualii.

Simpson, Alexander. <u>The Sandwich Islands: Progress of Events Since their Discovery by Captain Cook.</u> Smith and Elder. London. 1843.

Sinclair, Marjorie. <u>Nahi'ena'ena: Sacred Daughter of Hawai'i: A Life Ensnared.</u> Mutual Publishing. Honolulu, Hawaii. 1995. A biography of Kamehameha's sacred daughter, stressing the clash of diverse cultural values in her life.

Sinyukov, V. "Short Information about the Marquis de Traverse's Life." This article, about the life of Jean Francoise de Traverse (1754-1831), head of the Russian Navy Ministry during and after the Napoleonic wars, is available at the website of the Museum of the World Ocean in Moscow where is published the proceedings of a 2002 scholarly conference: http://vitiaz.ru/congress/en/thesis/81.html.

SITKA, ALASKA (the modern name for the city where the Russian settlement of Novo-Arkhangelsk was situated). There are many scenic websites for Sitka, but www.untraveledroad.com/USA/Alaska/Sitka/Sitkamap.htm has a useful "photo tour" included in its map giving views of the various sites. Clicking to Sitka through www.basecamp.cnchost.com/fortross.com gets a concise modern synopsis with a brief history. See also the work by Roland Schnell above entitled "A Short History about Alaska: Working Conditions in Sitka during the Baranov era (1799-1818)." See Antonson (above).

Skornjakova, N. N. <u>Staraja Moskva glazami sovremennikov: Moskva pered Otechestvennoj vojnoj 1812 goda.</u> Izobrazitel'noe iskusstvo. Moskva. 1996. An album of art works and essays about Moscow before the 1812 fire.

Smith, Barbara Sweetland and Redmond J. Barnett (editors). <u>Russian America: The Forgotten Frontier.</u> Washington State Historical Society, Tacoma, Washington. 1990. This is a well illustrated anthology of articles on various aspects of Russian American life. Most useful to me were the articles by Richard Pierce on "Russian America and China" and "The Russian American Company Currency," by Richard L. Dauenhauer on "Education in Russian America," by Michael Krauss on "Alaska Native Languages in Russian America," by Stephen W. Haycox on "Merchants and Diplomats: Russian America and the United States," and by Diane Spencer Pritchard on "Joint Tenants of the Frontier: Russian-Hispanic Relationships in Alta California."

Smith, Digby. <u>Borodino.</u> Great Battles Series of the Windrush Press. Gloucestershire. UK. 1998. A very concise treatment of the battle with elaborated command charts and maps.

Soboleski, Hank. Thirty-Nine Biographical Stories: HISTORY MAKERS OF KAUAI. Copyright Hank Soboleski, 2003. Printed in Hawaii (Purchased in Borders Bookstore, Lihue, HI in June 2005). These 2-5-page stories include entries on Kaumuali'i, George Anton Schaeffer, and Deborah Kapule (Kekaiha'akulou). The stories were published between Sept. 2000 and May 2002 as a series entitled "History Makers of Kauai" in Kaua'i's The Garden Island newspaper and there are copies of photographs serving as illustrations for most of the entries, including a rare artist's likeness of Kaumuali'i.

Soboleski, Hank. Twenty Biographical Stories: HISTORY MAKERS OF KAUAI, VOLUME TWO. Copyright Hank Soboleski, undated. This is a clone of the above work, except that the entries, except for six published from Sept. 2003 to July 2004 in the Kauai News Journal, have not been published before. This collection has Soboleski's entry on "Kamehameha I," focusing on Kamehameha's relations with Kaua'i.

Sommer, Friedrich. Major Georg Anton Schäffer und das Schicksal der deutschen Truppenteile in Brasilien 1824-1830. Em "Kalender fuer die Deutschen in Brasilien." (Rotermund-Kalender). S. Leopoldo, 1926, pp. 38 ss.

Sommer, Friedrich. Major G. A. Schäffer un seine Tätigkeit als brasilianischer Werber. Em: "Deutsche Zeitung" (jornol), vol. 48, n. 30 (July 31, 1926), S. Paulo.

Sommer, Friedrich. Wilhelm Ludwig von Eschwege. Das Lebensbild eines Auslanddeutshen mit kulturgeschichtlichen Erinnerungen dan Deutschland, Portugal, und Brasilien, 1777-1855. Em: "Schriften des Deutschen Ausland-Instituts," Stuttgart. Ausland und Heimat Verlags-Aktiengeseltschaft, Stuttgart, 1928. Sommer's view is the least sympathetic of Schaeffer's biographers, depicting the conditions on Schaeffer's transport ships as abominable...justifying the Germania mutiny in 1824...and maintaining that Schaeffer's promises to the emigrants were unconscienably inaccurate and that they suffered terribly in the new land as a result. Prof. Enrico Schaeffer contends with Sommer's work in his genealogical treatment of his "collateral relative."

Speakman, Jr., Cummins E. (and update by Jill Engleedow). Mowee: A History of Maui, The Magic Isle. Originally published by Peabody Museum of Salem, Massachusetts, in 1978 with copyright reserved to Mrs. Cummins Speakman. But now it is published by Mutual Publishing, 1215 Center Street, Suite 210, Honolulu, HI 96816 (phone: 808-732-1709 or fax at 734-4094, email at mutual@lava.net). (ISBN 1-56647-489-2). 2001. Includes source notes and a comprehensive index.

Spoehr, Anne Harding. "Prince George Tamoree: Heir Apparent of Kaua'i and Ni'ihau." In The Hawai'ian Journal of History (A Publication of the Hawaiian Historical Society), Vol. XV (1981), pp. 31-49.

Stauder, Catherine. "George Prince of Hawai'i." In The Hawaiian Journal of History (A Publication of the Hawaiian Historical Society), Vol. VI (1972), pp. 28-44. This work includes the most published likeness of George Prince Kaumuali'i (Tamoree)...a portrait sketched by Samuel Finley Breese Morse, son of George's one-time caretaker Jedidiah Morse (a relative of Samuel F. B. Morse), and later painted, then made into an engraving in New Haven in 1822 by N. and S. S. Jocelyn...see Spoehr below for another derivative likeness and note pp. 43.

Steele, Edward E. Ebbets: The History and Genealogy of a New York Family. The internet site advertising this work includes an outline sketch of seven generations of the Ebbets family, from the seventeenth century through John (Sea Captain, 1775-1835, m. Sarah Woodward) and his younger brother Richard (Sea Captain, 1788-1824, m. Cornelia Wetmore) through Charles Ebbets, modern New York City sports magnate after whom Ebbets Field is named. See http://freepages.genealogy.rootsweb.com/Ebbets.

STORY OF LAHAINA. An excerpt from a report prepared for the County of Mau'i by Community Panning, inc. Published with the permission of the Mau'i Historic Commission by the Lahaina Restoration Foundation, Front Street at Dickenson, Lahaina, Mau'i. 1961. This booklet on Lahaina's history includes a chronological table of significant events in Mau'i's history from 1736 (Death of King Kekaulike) to 1959 (U.S. Statehood).

Strangford (Lord) (British Ambassador to Brazil, 1808-1815). Genealogical information on Percy Clinton Sydney Smythe (1780-1855) is to be found at www.stirnet.com/genealogy under "BE1883 'Smythe of Strangford and Penshurst." Lord Byron's mention of "Strangford" in his satiric poem "English Bards and Scotch Reviewers" can be found in the March 1809 Edinburgh Review. Lord Strangford's papers (e.g. correspondence with British Statesman George Canning (1770-1827)) are accessible at www.nra.nationalarchives.gov.uk/nra/searches/pidocs.asp?P=P26627. Lord Strangford, a "noted English lusophile" was the translator of Portuguese poet Luis de Camoes Poems, published in London in 1803 and in Philadelphia in 1805. A copy of the Philadelphia edition is currently (January 2005) for sale (for $585.00) at Philadelphia Rare Books and Manuscripts Company, Box 9536, Philadelphia, PA 19124 (cf. also www.prbm.com/interest/i.hrm?

Sumter, Thomas (Revolutionary War General and Minister to Brazil 1809-11). See above under Bass, R.D.

SUVOROV ISLAND…now most frequently spelled Suvarov (notice the "a" instead of the Russian stressed "o") or Suwarrow. This island has a colorful history. In the mid-19th century a salvage ship out of Tahiti unearthed a chest on one of Suvarov's islands containing $15,000 in coins dating from the 1740's, a period when the British navigator, George Anson, crossing the Pacific in a fleet led by the *HMS Centurion* lost five ships in a raid on Spanish shipping. In 1876 a New Zealander named Henry Mair discovered a cache of Spanish silver pieces-of-eight in a Suvarov island turtle nest, but reburied the treasure which remains unfound. See also the works by Robert Dean Frisbie (The Island of Desire) and Tom Neale (An Island to Myself) above. Online information is available with photographs and maps at: www.kiaorana.com/Suwarrow, www.janeresture.com/suvarov and at www.ck./suwarrow.htm. A Ukrainian "tall ship" called the *Batkivshchyna* visited Suvarov Island in October of 2003 and recorded that the atoll is now maintained as a preserve. A couple, "Papa" Ioane and Mareko Baker, are the wardens and only residents. They host ships in the inner harbor and entertain crews with tuna meals and shows of sharks for $50.00. See www.batkivshchyna.net/log2003.html.

Sverdlov, L. "Did Chamberlain Rezanov Have the Right to Consider Himself Chief of the Expedition?" At the website of the Museum of the World Ocean, Moscow, which in 2002 hosted a conference and published the proceedings at http://vitiaz.ru/congress/en/thesis/12.html.

Tabrah, Ruth M. Ni'ihau: The Last Hawaiian Island. Press Pacifica, P.O. Box 47, Kailua, Hawaii 96734. Copyright 1987. This is a history of Ni'ihau which includes mention of foreigners' contacts during Kaumualii's rule.

TAMBORA VOLCANO. The eruption of Tambora Volcano on Sumbawa Island in Indonesia in April of 1815 and its effect on worldwide weather is discussed at http://vulcan.wr.usgs.gov/Volcanoes/Indonesia/description_tambora_1815_eruption.htm.

TARAKANOV, TIMOFEI OSIPOVICH. "Calamity of the St. Nikolai: The Narrative of Timofei Tarakanov." Accessed May 2005 at http://www.corvalliscommunitypages.com/Europe/Russia_slavs/wreckofstnikolai.htm. See also Owens (above). The supposition that Tarakanov took a Hawai'ian wife on O'ahu derives from an entry of George Schaeffer's dated May 8, 1817 in his "Journal, January 1815-March 1818" (see Richard Pierce's Russia's Hawaiian Adventure, 1815-1817, University of California Press, Berkeley and Los Angeles, California, 1965, pp. 201 top) in which Schaeffer, expelled in a canoe to the *Kadiak* from Waimea, Kaua'i by Kaumuali'i's "thousand men," sent "our storekeeper Tarakanov" ashore to negotiate. Schaeffer writes that "At first they refused to let him ashore, but on his request to the King, that it was to get Company property, for which he was responsible, *and that he wanted to get his wife and children* (italics mine), they let him pass."

Since Tarakanov only arrived in the Hawai'ian Islands in May/June of 1816 on the *Ilmena* (on which he was most likely unaccompanied), having a "wife and children" to retrieve from Kaua'i by May of 1817 would imply his having taken a native wife who already had children. I believe there are Tarakanovs presently in Alaska who trace their genealogy to him. He could, of course, have had more than one wife.

Tarle, E. V. 1812 god. Izdatel'stvo akademii nauk SSSR. Moskva. 1961. This is the Russian version of the translation below...but is more complete. See str. 570-5 for the balloon episode and the episode of Rostopchin's ordering the execution of the merchant Vereshchagin (episode also depicted in Tolstoy's War and Peace).

Tarle, Eugene. Napoleon's Invasion of Russia, 1812. (Translated by "G.M.") Oxford University Press. New York. 1942. See pp. 217-19 for the balloon episode.

Teilhet, Darwin. Russian Flag Over Hawaii: The Mission of Jeffery Tolamy. Mutual Publishing. Honolulu, HI. 1986. This is an adventure novel about US President Jefferson's "secret agent" in Hawaii...and it includes a fictionalized "Dr. Scheffer" in command of a villainous band of Aleuts.

Ten Bruggencate, Jan K. Hawai'i's Pineapple Century: A History of the Crowned Fruit in the Hawaiian Islands. Mutual Publishing, 1215 Center Street, Suite 210, Honolulu, HI 96816. 2004 (ISBN 1-56647-667-4). This is a fine history of the Hawaiian pineapple industry, attributing the first cultivation of the pineapple in the islands to Don Francisco Marin. See Gast (above) and Lee (above).

Terras, Victor (ed.) Handbook of Russian Literature. Yale University Press. New Haven and London. 1985. This is a compendium of data on Russian literary figures, movements, and genres written by leading U.S. scholars.

Thompson, Scott. Russian Snows: Coming of Age in Napoleon's Army. 2010. See http://www.russiansnows.com. ISBN is 9781466331549. Thompson has a wonderfully educational blog on the 1812 campaign at http://napoleon1812.wordpress.com.

Tikhmenev, P. A. A History of the Russian-American Company. (Translated and edited by Richard A. Pierce and Alton S. Donnelly). University of Washington Press. Seattle and London. 1978. See pp. 120-5 for "Schaffer's" activities.

TOLSTOI, FYODOR IVANOVICH the "American" (1782-1846). On the Krasnoiarsk University website about Nikolai Petrovich Rezanov at http://rezanov.krasu.ru under "World Tour" is a brief article by Phillip Vigel entitled "They said about Count Tolstoy, F.I. that…" that includes an account of Tolstoi's unpleasant pranks on the *Nadezhda*. The "long-tailed macaque monkey" described by Lowenstern (see above) is described as an "orang-outang." Vigel points out that Alexander Pushkin later wrote one of his famous epigrams about Tolstoi, writing that he had "turned a new leaf in life," improving from abject dissipation to being a petty cheat. Pushkin tried to challenge Tolstoi to a duel at one point (ca. 1826-7), but later (1831) negotiated his marriage to Natalia Goncharova through him. Fyodor Ivanovich Tolstoi is mentioned in Aleksandr Griboedov's famous play, Woe From Wit, and described by his relative, Leo Nikolaevich Tolstoi, in his reminiscence, Childhood. The Wikipedia provides an essay on the Russian Tolstoy (Tolstoi) family, which mentions both Fyodor Ivanovich Tolstoi, the "American" and the famous author, Count Leo Nikolaevich Tolstoi (1828-1910) at www.answers.com/topic/tolstoy-1. A really comprehensive genealogy of the Tolstoi family, providing a decipherment of the exact relationship between Fyodor Ivanovich and Leo Nikolaevich (Leo's great grandfather and Fyodor's grandfather was Andrei Ivanovich Tolstoi (1721-1803) is made available by Alexandre Rozanov at http://gencircles.com/users/rozanov/1. See also L. Berdnikov, S. L. Tolstoi, and O. Vozdvizhenskaia. The Tolstoy family estate Kologriv has a website with a fine Russian relation of Count F. I. Tolstoi's life (http://Kologriv.com/index.php?option=com_content&task=views&id=20&item id=10).

Tolstoi, Sergei L'vovich. Fyodor Tolstoi-Amerikanets. Gosudarstvennaia Akademiia Khudozhestvennoi Nauki. Moskva. 1926. 96 str. with one frontispiece portrait. This is the seminal biography or memoir about Fyodor Ivanovich Tolstoi-the "American" by the son of the novelist Leo Tolstoy (see below), who was a first cousin, once removed, of Fyodor. See also Berdnikov and O. Vozdvizhenskaia.

Tolstoy, Leo Nikolaevich. War and Peace. (Translated by Louise and Aylmer Maude, edited by Henry Gifford). Oxford University Press. Oxford and New York. 1991 paperback edition. Tolstoy's great historical novel mentions the Russian balloon project in several places. Moscow Governor-General Fedor Vasilievich Rostopchin's "broadsheets" are best described on pp. 799-800. On pp. 805 protagonist Pierre Bezukhov drives, just prior to the battle of Borodino "to the village of Vorontsovo to see the great balloon Leppich was constructing" and records that the project was commissioned by Tsar Aleksandr I himself as evidenced by mentioned instructions in a letter to Rostopchin. In an explanatory note (pp. 1333), Tolstoy mentions facts about "Franz Leppich, a Dutchman," including Leppich's 1811 effort to sell the idea to Napoleon. He states that "Much time and government money were spent on this project," and that "At its trials in November 1812 (This date is curious, because it is after the battle at Borodino and after both Leppich and Schaeffer were in Nizhnii Novgorod and not yet in St. Petersburg) the balloon leaked gas and Leppich disappeared." On pp. 891-2 Tolstoy describes the September 1812 evacuation of Moscow,

295

including Rostopchin's use of "one hundred and thirty six (carts which) removed the balloon that was being constructed by Leppich." Tolstoy's very use of the name "Leppich" is curious since "Leppich's" Russian contemporaries only knew him by his secret nom-de-guerre of "Schmidt," given to him by Tsar Aleksandr's command staff, and Rostopchin's memoirs (ostensibly a Tolstoy source on this) mention only "Schmidt" (cf. Rostopchin's memoirs, above).

Travers, B.H.   The Captain-General: Being a Study of Lachlan Macquarie, Governor of New South Wales, 1809-1821. Shakespeare Head Press. Sydney. 1953. This biography of Macquarie focuses on his Governorship in Sydney. It is filled with details, charts, maps, and illustrations.

TRAVERSÉ, (Jean Francoise) (1754-1831)…French Marquis and Russian Admiral…see Sinyukov above.

Treadwell, John.   Narrative of Five Youths from the Sandwich Islands.   J. Seymour, NY, 1816. (see Dwight above and Warne below). This work is described by Anne Harding Spoehr as a "solid starting place" on the interesting character of George "Humehume" Prince Kaumuali'i (Tamoree). The Five youths are: Henry Obookiah ("Opuka'ia" see Dwight, Warne, Stauder), Thomas Hopoo (see Greer), William Tennooe (Keno'i...?), John Honooree (Honoli'i), and George Prince Tamoree. See Warne (below).

Tregaskis, Richard.   The Warrior King: Hawaii's Kamehameha the Great. MacMillan Publishing Co., inc. New York. 1973. See the family chart before the preface including an indirect assertion by Maui King Kahekili that he was Kamehameha's real father.

Trei, Peter. An essay on the Bavarian "Illuminati," freemasons, and modern mythology.   At   http://a-albionic.com/a-albionic/gopher/conspiracy/illuminati/illuminati.txt, accessed August 6, 2003.

Troyat, Henri. Alexander of Russia: Napoleon's Conqueror. (Translated by Joan Pinkham). E.P. Dutton, Inc. New York. 1982. This treatment has no mention of the balloon episode, but has a most useful "Chronology" (pp. 312-22).

Ullman, Dana, M.P.H... A Condensed History of Homeopathy. An excerpt from Discovering Homeopathy: Medicine for the 21st Century. At http://www.healthy.net/asp/templates/article.asp?PageType=Article&ID=860 accessed April 11, 2002.

Uffindell, Andrew. Great Generals of the Napoleonic Wars and Their Battles, 1805-1815. Spellmount Ltd. The Old Rectory, Staplehouse, Kent, TN12 0AZ, UK. 2003. This work gives a new look, including recent research, at the lives and military achievements of Napoleon himself and eleven other leading

Generals of his time: (French) de Beauharnais, Lasalle, (English) Moore, Wellington, Hill, (Austrian) Archduke Charles, (Prussian) Blücher, Gneisenau, and (Russian) Bagration, Barclay de Tolly, Kutusov.

Vasconcellos, Mario de e Andrä, Helmut. Weltumsegler, Naturforscher, Seelenverkäufer und Diplomat. Beitrage zum Lebensbild des Oberst-Leutnant Ritter Dr. G. Ant. Von Schäffer. Em: "Deutscher Morgen" (jornol), S. Paulo, 16 e 23. 2, 1940, 1.3. e 8.3.1940.

Vasconcellos, Mario de e Andrä. Schäffer e Mello Mattos nos Estados da Alemanha. Em: Archivo Diplomatico da Independencia, Vol. IV. Rio de Janeiro, 1922.

VENIAMINOV, FATHER IOANN ((1797-1879), born Ivan Popov in Siberia, later made Metropolitan and still later a Saint with the name of Innokentii). Fr. Veniaminov did not get to Alaska until 1823, but sources on him describe life in Alaska and in Sitka and deal with issues pertinent to the story here. See the Congress of Russian Americans' site at www.russian-americans.org/CRA_History.htm. For further elucidation of the relations between the Russian Orthodox priests and Russian-American Company Manager Alexander Baranov, see the citations on Elder Herman above.

Volkov, Genrikh. Mir Pushkina: Lichnost', Mirovozzrenie, Okruzhenie. ("The World of Pushkin: Personality, World View, Circle of Acquaintances"). Molodaia gvardiia. Moskva. 1989. This work treats Pushkin's personal relationships with several of the characters of this book…notably Fyodor Tolstoy (cf. pp. 77-80).

Von Faber du Faur, Christian Wilhelm. Napoleon's Army in Russia: The Illustrated Memoirs of Albrecht Adam-1812.

VORONTSOVO. Kratkii ekskurs v istoriiu Vorontsovo ("A Short Excursion into the History of Vorontsovo") Http://www.mmt.ru/vorontsovo.net/map/history.htm. This internet site, on the Moscow "microregion" of Vorontsovo, is very interesting and includes significant mention of the balloon project of 1812. It clarifies ownership of the estate before and after the conflict.

Vozdvizhenskaia, Ol'ga. "Tolstoi-Amerikanets," in Penthouse (The Russian version), Dekabr' 2007, str. 98-101 in the section entitled "Nravy" ("Morals"), illustrated feature.

Viazemskii, P. A. Stikhotvoreniia. ("Verse"). Vstupitel'naia stat'ia i premechaniia L. Ia. Ginzburg. (Introductory article and notes by L. Ia. Ginzburg). Biblioteka poeta. Sovietskii pisatel'. Leningrad. 1958. This is the volume on the poet and memoirist, Pyotr Andreevich Vyazemskii (1792-1878), of the renowned "Library of the Poet" series. It includes Vyazemskii's 1818 poem "To Tolstoy" about Fyodor Ivanovich Tolstoy, "the American."

Viazemskii, P. A. Zapisnye knizhki (1813-1848). ("Note books (1813-1848)"). V. S. Nechaeva, red. (ed.). Izdatel'stvo Akademii Nauk SSSR. Moskva. 1963. Here are Prince Vyazemskii's notebooks of all manner of personal, literary, and political observations. Editor Nechaeva's thorough listing and describing of the people mentioned in an index is very useful. When you want to know who is who when reading about events in early 19th century Russia (especially St. Petersburg around the time of the Decembrist Revolt in 1825), this is the place.

Waikīkī: Images of Yesteryear. A 48-pp. book of historical photographs by Mutual Publishing, 1215 Center Street, Suite 210, Honolulu, HI 96816. 2007. (ISBN 978-1-56647-824-3). See also White, Kai and Kraus, Jim, and Seiden, Allan.

Walker, Mack. Germany and the Emigration: 1816-1885. Harvard University Press. Cambridge, Massachusetts. 1964. PP. 38-41 lists the German recruitment activities of "Major Schaffer"...and "a certain Dr. Cretzshmar" from 1822-30, obtained from a US Library of Congress archive (LC PrAA 2-11...see pp. 253).

Wall, Bill. "The Chess Automatons by Bill Wall." An e-excerpt at http://www.geocities.com/siliconvalley/lab/7378/automat.htm, accessed August 9, 2003.

WAR OF 1812-4. US/Great Britain. See http://members.tripod.com/~war1812/intro or www.warof1812.ca/1812events.htm. Last accessed May 2005.

Warne, Douglas. "George Prince Kaumuali'i: The Forgotten Prince." In The Hawaiian Journal of History (A Publication of the Hawaiian Historical Society), Vol. XXXVI (2002), pp. 59-71.

Warne, Douglas. Humehume of Kaua'i: A Boy's Journey to America, an Ali'i's Return Home. Kamehameha Publishing, 567 South King Street, Honolulu, HI 96813, 2008 (ISBN 978-0-87336-151-4). A very positively impressive recent scholarly work on Kaumuali'i's son Humehume—his life in America and after his return to Kaua'i in 1820. It includes some great detail...for example part of Kaumuali'i's mele inoa chant, and the roster of the U.S. ship *Wasp* from 1813 showing "Geo. Prince" as a member of its Marine contingent. Good relation of events about Kaumuali'i, Kekaiha'akulou, Ka'ahumanu, Kalanimoku, Keali'iahonui and interisland politics after the 1819 death of Kamehameha and of Liholiho. 237 pp. with color ill. See also Dwight, Joesting, Lydgate, Mills, Soboleski, Treadwell, and Zambucka.

Watrous, Stephan. "The Cultural History of Fort Ross: Outpost of an Empire—Russian Expansion to America." Accessed May 2005 at http://www.mcn.org/1/rrparks/fortross/Russian%20American%20Company.htm.

Weissheimer, Egidio. "Imagração Alemã no RS." This work on the German Emigration of 1824- to the Rio Grande do Sul State of Brazil, expanding the information given by Oberacker *by listing the specific families brought to Brazil by George Schaeffer's expeditions*, was accessed in August of 2008 at www.marquardt.com.br/hist_imigr1.htm. See also Oberacker (above), Mack, Luebke, and http://heuser.pro.br/getperson.php?personID=O22239&tree=heusers. In this latter source (see also Gomez, Dival da Costa above, which has similar data in a relation from Hunsche and Oberacker) one can sleuth out of the genealogy of the Heuser family that a marriage took place (2 June, 1824) upon the later troubled ship *Germania* while it was waiting in the port of Glückstadt to depart for Brazil. This was the marriage, witnessed by ship's Captain Hans Voss and Schaeffer's Expedition Administrator Ferdinand von Kiesewetter and performed by later prominent pastor Johann Georg Ehlers, of Hanover-born 28-year-old mercenary Heinrich Hubertus Stock and Thüringen-born 30-year-old Dorothea Elisabeth Mentz, who was listed on board with her parents, Johann Liborious and Magdalena Ernestina (Lips) Mentz, as future settlers. From the Weissheimer source and others (e.g. Oberacker and the site http://www.es.beekeeping.wikia.com/wiki/Georg_Anton_von_Sch%C3%A4ffer) we can see the record that eight of the mercenaries mutinied against the ship's officers and the expedition's administration while in the Bay of Biscay in late August and early September of 1824. An initial quelling of the mutiny by force only led to another mutiny attempt in which the mutineers threatened to set the ship afire. By assent of the entire ship's company, according to the record of a subsequent investigation, these eight mutineers were then executed…most sources say shot, but one says hanged. Heinrich Stock was not listed among those who arrived in Brazil. His date of death in the family genealogy is listed as "Bef 6 Nov 1824" (the day of the *Germania's* arrival in Brazil)…ERGO, he must have been one of the eight executed mutineers. In the genealogy one notes also the interesting fact that Dorothea, who remarried in Brazil in 1848 and died in 1866, had a daughter named Ernestina who was 24 years old at the time of the second marriage, indicating that she was the mutineer Stock's biological daughter. My conclusion from these diverse facts is that Dorothea Mentz Stock (later Engelhaupt), then pregnant with Stock's child, and her parents gave assent to his execution. Another online source (July 2009 accessed) that has Weissheimer's excellent work is http://www.mluther.org.br/Imigracao/imigracao.ii.htm.
Also useful is the Wikipedia site: http://en.wikipedia.org/wiki/German_Brazilian See also the "contrary" 2005 article on this by Sonja Sawitzki (above) and also Sommers (above).

Wetzels, Walter D. Johann Wilhelm Ritter: Physik im Wirkungsfeld der deutschen Romanitk. Walter de Gruyter. Berlin and New York. 1973. This is a publication related to the topic of Prof. Wetzels' 1968 Princeton University doctoral dissertation. Wetzels is now, since 1996, a Professor Emeritus of German Studies at the University of Texas. Some English-language internet sites on Ritter's scientific achievements include: http://www.voltaicpower.com/Biographies/RitterBio.htm; http://www. hao.ucar.edu/public/education/images.jwritter.html; and http://www. geocities.com/bioelectrochemistry/ritter.html. All, accessed July 25, 2003, include likenesses of Ritter.

Wheeler, Mary Elizabeth. "Empires in Conflict and Cooperation: the 'Bostonians' and the Russian-American Company." Pacific Historical Review. No. 40, 4 (November, 1971), pp. 419-441.

Wheeler, Mary Elizabeth. The Origins and Formation of the Russian-American Company. University of North Carolina at Chapel Hill Ph.D. Dissertation, History, 1965. Published by University Microfilms, Inc., 66-4735, Ann Arbor, Michigan, 1980.

Wheelock, Frederic M. Latin Literature: A Book of Readings from Cicero, Livy, Ovid, Pliny, the Vulgate, Bede, Caedmon, Medieval Poetry. Waveland Press, Inc. Prospect Heights, Illinois. 1969. ISBN 0-88133-721-8. Notes here describe the history of the Carmina Burana and include the Latin lyrics with accompanying glossary and notes.

White, Kai and Kraus, Jim. Waikīkī: Images of America. Arcadia Publishing. Charleston, South Carolina and elsewhere. 2007 (ISBN 978-0-7385-4880-7). This work, published by the leading local history publishers (see www.arcadiapublishing.com), is essentially 128 pages of historical photographs with the captions providing the informational text. But it is very well done and is a fine resource on the history of Waikīkī.

Whitworth, Robert. Flights of Fancy: A Short History, or Overview, of Ballooning during the Georgian and Regency eras: Together with Interesting Eye-witness Accounts, to which are Added Numerous Woodcuts and Descriptions of the Various Balloons. This is a 35-page "E-book" at http://www.printsgeorge.com/ArtEccles_Aeronauts1.htm accessed January 15, 2002.

Wichman, Frederick B. Kauai: Ancient Place Names and Their Stories. A Latitude 20 Book. University of Hawaii Press. Honolulu. 1998. This work includes stories of Kaumualii's personal history and of his parents and accession to rule.

Wichman, Frederick B. Na Pua Ali'i O Kaua'i: Ruling Chiefs of Kaua'i. A Latitude 20 Book. University of Hawaii Press. Honolulu. 2003. This is a historical tracing of the geneology of the Kaua'i chiefs and associated legends taken from the chants, which constitute the oral history. Geneologies are given in table form at the end.

Williams, Julie Stewart. Kamehameha the Great. (revised ed., illustrations by Robin Yoko Burningham). Kamehameha Schools/Bernice Pauahi Bishop Estate. Honolulu. 1993. A reader for young people ("Intermediate Reading Program") about Kamehameha's life, stressing his Hawaiian native upbringing.

Williams, Julie Stewart. From the Mountains to the Sea: Early Hawaiian Life. (Illustrated by Robin Yoko Racoma). Kamehameha Schools/Bernice Pauahi Bishop Estate. Honolulu. 1997. An attempt to portray Hawaiian life as it was 500 years ago, with explanations of Hawaiian terms, maps and drawings of various aspects of life.

Willmann, Josef. Münnerstadt: wie es einst war. Verlag T. A. Schachenmayer. Bad Kissingen. 2000. This is a local historian's work on Münnerstadt, complete with names and business registries and 236 historical illustrations, maps, and photographs. Several "Schäfers" are mentioned and there is a "Schäfergasschen" street in the town.

Wisniewski, Richard A. The Rise and Fall of the Hawaiian Kingdom: A Pictorial History. Pacific Basin Enterprises, P.O. Box 8924, Honolulu, Hawaii 96830. 1979.

Withington, Antoinette. The Golden Cloak: The Romantic Story of Hawaii's Monarchs. Mutual Publishing, 1215 Center Street, Suite 210, Honolulu, HI 96816 (cf. Cook, Chris for telephone and fax numbers). 1986. (ISBN 0-935180-26-5). www.mutualpublishing.com and email at mutual@lava.net. This work includes a wonderfully detailed telling of the story of Kamehameha's life and of Hawaii in the post-contact days. The Russian episode is treated primarily, but also by Captain Otto von Kotzebue's relation of Kamehameha's telling him about his problems with his "Russian predecessor in the islands," George Schaeffer.

Würzburg (Germany). Scenes and descriptions of Würzburg may be found on the internet. A useful site (accessed 4 August, 2003) is http://www.romanticroad.com/wurzsigh.htm.

Zambucka, Kristin. Princess Ka'iulani of Hawai'i: The Monarchy's Last Hope. Mutual Publishing, LLC, 1215 Center Street, Suite 210, Honolulu, HI 96816, ISBN 1-56647-710-7, March 205 printing, based on Kristin Zambucka copyright from 1998, originally published by Green Glass Productions. Cf. www.mutualpublishing.com.

Zambucka, Kristin (compiler). <u>Kaumualii: King of Kauai: Excerpts from Early Writers (and a few later ones) on the Life and Times of Kaumualii, the King of Kauai</u>. Published by Kawananakoa. 1999. This isn't so much a biography as a compilation of recorded impressions of Kaumualii and the associated events of his life. Schaeffer is substantially included, with texts of his documents and his likeness. The work I have has no table of contents, no foreword or prologue or textual commentary, and no list of sources or index, but still it is useful to have so many recorded impressions in one place. See also Warne above, Soboleski and Joesting.

Zambucka, Kristin. <u>Kalakaua: Hawaii's Last King</u>. Mana Publishing Co., Box 22525, Honolulu, HI 96823-2525, ISBN 0-931897-04-1, March 2006 second printing edition, from Kristin Zambucka copyright 2002.

Zamoyski, Adam. <u>Moscow 1812: Napoleon's Fatal March</u>. HarperCollins Publishers. London. 2004. I didn't see this work until I had completed the writing of my book's section on Napoleon's invasion of Russia in 1812. There was not much new to me in it, but I note that the author, in his introductory note, explains that his principal aim is to tell again the extraordinary story, surmounting the political and nationalistic bias of previous narrations and focusing on the individual human aspects of the struggle. In general I think he does this well. I notice the lack, however, of internet sources in the bibliography of sources at the end. I can only wonder what he would think if he were to click his way through the "1812" project of <u>www.museum.ru</u> with its wellspring of detail and illustration, or go through the articles by Alexander Mikerabidze in the <u>www.Napoleon-series.org</u> pages. Yet I applaud the rigor shown in his index, where he gives the full names of characters, including the Russian patronymics whenever possible, and confines himself to the rank of his characters at the time of the conflict, instead of citing them as holding the highest rank achieved in their lives. He does mention "Leppich" and the "aerostat" as a failed project of Governor-General Rostopchin's in a single paragraph on page 243. Also, the book's illustrations, especially the ones from contemporary artists, are very fine and well captioned. The caption under Rostopchin's likeness by Orest Adamovich Kiprensky labels Rostopchin as "the destroyer of Moscow" and says that he was "possibly mad."

Zhilin, P. A. <u>Otechestvennaia Voina 1812 Goda.</u> Izdatel'stvo "Nauka." Moskva. 1988.

I hope the readers are moved to give some thought to the large number of real historical figures that my "resurrection" of George Anton Schaeffer has brought into their awareness: Napoleon Bonaparte and several of his marshals, Archduke Ferdinand III of Tuscany, Johann Wilhelm Ritter, several prominent aerostiers including the Garnerins, the Blanchards and Count Zambeccari, Tsar Aleksandr I, the Grand Duke Konstantin, Tsar Nicholas I, Nikolai Rumyantsev, John

Quincy Adams, Fyodor Rostopchin, Franz Leppich the balloon master, Russian Generals Platov, Tormasov, Bagration, Barclay de Tolley, Kutuzov, author and editor Nikolai Karamzin, the poet Gavril Derzhavin, Aleksandr Pushkin, Russian-American Company founder Grigorii Shelikhov, Nikolai Rezanoff, Georg Heinrich von Langsdorff, Count Fyodor Tolstoi the "American," Russian sea captains Krusenshtern, Kotsebue, Lazarev, Lisianskii and Hagemeister, Lachlan Macquarie, Aleksandr Baranov, Peter Dobell, John Jacob Astor, Stephen Girard, Kings Kamehameha and Kaumuali'i, Queens Ka'ahumanu, Keōpuōlani and Kekaiha'akulou (Deborah Kapule), Kalanimoku, Humehume, Governor Homa, Don Francisco de Paula Marin, John Elliot de Castro, Archibald Campbell, Isaac Davis, John Young, and a host of central pacific sea captains, Anders Ljungstedt, Apo-Tsy, Ching Shi the woman pirate, Dom João of Portugal and Brazil, Dom Pedro I, Dom Miguel I, Empress Leopoldina and her daughter who becomes Maria II of Portugal, Klemens von Metternich, Emperor Franz I, King Max I of Bavaria...the list goes on and on.

–Lee B. Croft

List of Illustrations